Jo W   son is an award-winning writer whose romantic comedies
were   iginally published on Wattpad. Her first novel *Burning Moon*
won   2014 Watty Award for being one of the site's most downloaded
titles   nd has now had over 7 million reads. Jo is an Adidas addict and
a De   e Mode devotee. She lives in South Africa with her family.

Foll   on Twitter @JoWatsonWrites and find her on Facebook
             at www.facebook.com/jowatsonwrites.

Praise for Jo Watson's hilarious romantic comedies:

'Witty, enjoyable and unique' *Harlequin Junkie*

'Fou   d myself frequently laughing out loud and grinning like a fool!'
BFF Book Blog

'I   rming, funny, sweet, romantic and just leaves you feeling
good inside' *Bridger Bitches Book Blog*

'   oi pure-joy romance, laugh-out-loud moments and tear-
jerkers' *Romantic Times*

By Jo Watson

Standalone
Love To Hate You

Destination Love Series
Burning Moon
Almost A Bride
Finding You
After The Rain

Love to Hate You

JO WATSON

HEADLINE
ETERNAL

First published in Great Britain in 2018
by HEADLINE ETERNAL
An imprint of HEADLINE PUBLISHING GROUP

1

Cataloguing in Publication Data is available from the British Library

ISBN 978 1 4722 5778 9

Typeset in 11.55/16.25 pt Granjon LT Std by Jouve (UK), Milton Keynes

Printed and bound in Great Britain by CPI Group (UK) Ltd, Croydon, CR0 4YY

Headline's policy is to use papers that are natural, renewable and recyclable
products and made from wood grown in well-managed forests and other
controlled sources. The logging and manufacturing processes are expected
to conform to the environmental regulations of the country of origin.

HEADLINE PUBLISHING GROUP
An Hachette UK Company
Carmelite House
50 Victoria Embankment
London EC4Y 0DZ

www.headlineeternal.com
www.headline.co.uk
www.hachette.co.uk

This one really does need to be dedicated to all my amazing Wattpad readers who loved this book from day one and made it so unbelievably popular! Also, to all the people at Wattpad HQ who've been so incredibly supportive of me and my career, especially Caitlin and Alysha! And my husband too, because he's awesome and some bits of this story are about us, but I won't tell you which ones . . . not yet anyway. Oh, and Depeche Mode. Because obviously!

Love
to
Hate
You

1

BAD TASTE IN WIGS

*D*on't ask me how the hell it happened . . .

I could blame it on the vodka.

Maybe I could blame it on JJ and Bruce. Maybe it was the strobing lights of the nightclub and the repetitive *doof doof* of the bass that triggered some kind of chemical reaction in my brain, causing me to go temporarily insane.

Maybe it was my outfit (NOTE: Never let a drag queen dress you for an evening out). I was wearing a sequined blue *thing* that could barely be described as a dress, and the famous "Marilyn wig" which they'd brought out especially for me, *God only knows why?* I looked like a crazed, transvestite prostitute with bad taste in wigs. Maybe that's why it happened?

But what are the chances?

To find a straight guy at a gay nightclub? Possibly the only one. And to find such a ridiculously hot one, who somehow knew my favorite drink and bought it for me all night long. Who kissed me like *that* on the dance floor and now had me pinned underneath him in the back seat of his car.

I *never* did this.

Someone else was half naked and sweating and moaning and grabbing at his tattooed shoulders. Someone else was licking Vodka Cranberry cocktails and sweat off his chest and having the best sex of her life—*deliciously dirty sex*—with possibly the hottest man that had ever walked the planet.

He'd made me feel like the sexiest woman alive, and that, coupled with the fact that I didn't know his name and would never see him again—*all that strong alcohol helped, too*—saw all my inhibitions fly right out the back window of his car. I did and said things I didn't even know I was capable of. With my face pressed into the seat, I told him how I wanted it. And he willingly gave it to me . . .

As well as several variations on the requested activity.

And when it was all over, he lay on top of me gasping for air and sweating beautiful glistening drops (God, even his sweat was sexy). It was easily the hottest experience of my entire life. But then he did something very odd, something that tipped me over the edge. He lifted his head and met my eyes with such intensity that everything around me went silent and blurry. He was looking at me like he knew me. Really, *really* knew me.

My mouth opened and an almost inaudible whisper came out, "Do I know you?"

He smiled at me. A naughty, skew, sexy smile. "Not yet." And then he kissed me. No one had kissed me like that before. It was the kind of kiss shared by long-lost lovers.

But when some nosey drag queens knocked on the car window

and made loud *oohing* noises and one of them mimed a comic blowjob gesture, I nearly died. I flung the door open and ran, leaving my Sex God shirtless and with his trousers still around his ankles. While I, the girl that never does stuff like this *(I reiterate)*, had to make an embarrassing run of shame across the now crowded parking lot. I could feel every single dramatically drawn, raised eyebrow watching me as I went.

Before I could get far, I was stopped by a distinctly masculine wolf whistle. Sex God clearly had NO inhibitions.

He was now leaning against his car, zipping up his jeans and doing it completely shirtless—*with a very appreciative audience, I might add*. He lit a cigarette, inhaled slowly and let the smoke curl out of his mouth.

He was like an advert for cool, in that *I-don't-give-a-flying-fuck-who-cares* kind of way. An advert for everything deplorable and lascivious, but downright filthy-sexy in a man. *Who the hell was he?*

I really had to go!

I climbed into my car and pulled out of the lot, allowing myself one last glance in his direction. The cigarette hung out of his mouth seductively; his wet hair clung to his face; he was leaning across the bonnet in such a way that he looked like a model from an X-rated Calvin Klein billboard. As I sped away, he blew me a kiss and shouted after me.

"I'm in love!"

2

I HEARD HE WAS RAISED
BY WOLVES . . .

In my head-pounding, hungover daze, I rolled, slipped, and fell out of bed, feeling like someone had poured sand into my eyes and pushed me down a steep cliff. I got up and pulled the now very itchy sequin dress off and got the fright of my life when I realized I wasn't wearing any underwear. I knew I'd left the house with panties on last night. *Hadn't I?*

I was already running late for work—I had accidentally pressed the snooze button on my phone way too many times— but I couldn't rush to work looking like I was.

I grabbed some cotton wool, dunked it in make-up remover and attempted to wipe the thick, chalky layers of black smoky eye make-up off my face. My red lipstick was smudged and one of the false lashes was clinging on like a dry spider. The make-up was coming off, but the glitter was more stubborn. "A highlighter, babe. Fab," JJ had said as he'd emptied the entire jar onto my face. The glitter was sticking to my face like glue and some bits had even lodged themselves into my hairline. The wig was even worse.

The clips holding it in place had twisted so badly that everything was completely stuck—*no doubt from rubbing my head back and forth in the back seat of a total stranger's car.* Instant nausea rose as I started to think about it again. *Crap, what the hell had I been thinking!*

But the wig was my top priority right now, and I was left with no choice but to painfully rip it off. I yelped in pain as tufts of brown hair came out in chunks, then I cursed the wig and tossed it onto the floor. I couldn't believe I'd actually worn the thing—it looked like a dead Maltese puppy.

I dissed my usual middle part, scraping my hair back into a ponytail. Contact lenses out—after inventing some new yoga poses to pry them from my dried-out eyes—and glasses on. Black pantsuit, white-collar shirt and a pair of semi-high heels. Then one last mirror check before running out.

On my way to grab my laptop bag and a handful of headache pills, I passed JJ and Bruce's room, but before I could give them a vengeful wake-up knock, my passive aggressive attempt at punishing them for their part in my early morning state, I saw the note.

Sera,

You naughty, naughty girl! We heard you caused quite the parking lot spectacle. Dinner tonight, we want all the juicy details.

XX

J&B

I sighed and, as I went out to my car, my face went red-hot at the thought of telling them what had happened.

My twenty-year-old Toyota had been acting up lately. Another thing to add to the growing to-buy list, along with socks without holes, black pumps with non-peeling soles and now some new undies. But I just couldn't afford a new car right now—*or ever*—not between paying back loans and secretly sending money home to my sister Katie.

"Please start, please start, please start," I pleaded with the hunk of metal junk.

My job was the most important thing in my life. Without it, I wouldn't be able to help Katie and she'd be at our dad's mercy. And there was no way I was going to let that happen. I simply couldn't afford to do anything that would jeopardize it especially since I was one of two interns vying for a permanent position at the company. Being late didn't exactly scream "hire me."

I also knew what being late meant. I would surely walk slap bang into an apocalyptic crisis lifted straight from the Book of Revelation. Working at an ad agency means going from one emergency to another. High stakes, lots of money on the line, demanding clients, demanding creatives and deadlines tighter than the skinny jeans they all wear.

My car finally started after a few smoky chugs and I threw a few thank-yous out into the universe. But as soon as I drove out of my apartment complex and turned onto the highway, I was assaulted by bumper-to-bumper Jo'burg traffic, made even worse by minibus taxis and their "creative" driving techniques. Currently I had one only centimeters from my bumper with a painted sign on his back window that read, *"What goes surround, Comes surround."* At least something about this morning was vaguely humorous. But the static traffic gave me too much time to think and reflect . . .

What the hell had happened last night? Most of it was a blur, but every now and then an image flashed through my mind.

Vodka. Lots.

"Is this seat taken?" That smooth move and that husky voice . . .

Slowly grinding himself into me on the dance floor of Club Six, running his hands up my thighs, creeping way, way too high for public decency laws, until his hands were . . .

"You're so fucking beautiful," he'd whispered in my ear, his hands coming up and cupping my face.

"I want you so badly, Sera." Hang on, how had he known my name?

"I need you." That was the moment I melted completely and decided to walk outside with him . . .

Fumbling for his car keys . . .

On him . . .

Under him . . .

Windows steaming up . . .

"Fuck, you're amazing." More words that made me lose my mind as I writhed on his lap and totally forgot myself in the moment . . .

His tattoos . . . those dark piercing eyes . . .

"I could do this forever," he'd whispered in my ear seductively.

"Sera." He rasped as he came on top of me, the weight of his body crushing me into the seat.

Oh. My. God.

Had I really fallen for every lame jackass line in the book? He probably said that to all the girls he had anonymous back-seat sex with. Was I really that stupid, or sex starved, or mad, or drunk, or all of those to have actually bought into his smooth-play-boy moves. *Mortified AF.* My only consolation was that I'd never see him again.

After a frustrating hour in traffic, I finally arrived at work, but the only parking space I could find was all the way on the other side of the office park, so I was forced to run with a pounding head and lurching stomach.

But when I finally got inside, I was downright shocked. Something was *very* wrong.

I was expecting to run straight into the usual office chaos: people screaming at each other, screaming into the phone, screaming at the coffee pot or the copy machine. But something bizarre was going on today. People were sitting around lazily . . . *chatting?*

It was as if someone had come in the night and tranquilized all my co-workers. Had someone put Xanor into the air conditioning system? That was surely the only explanation for this eerie calm. I inched my way to my desk feeling very uneasy—*was this the calm before the storm?*

Before I had a chance to pull out my chair, Becks slunk up to me and whispered conspiratorially into my ear.

"Have you heard?" she asked.

I half turned to her but she cut me off quickly before I could manage to respond.

"They hired a new Creative Director. Apparently he's a fucking rock star. Blake something I think—"

At the sound of that name, one of the junior copywriters who happened to be walking past quickly corrected her, "Isn't it Blade? I heard his name was Blade?"

Next thing I knew, an equally excitable art director joined the conversation, "Blaze? Isn't it Blaze? Or Slash?" She was practically squealing.

I looked from one glowing face to the other. Their eyes were lit up like firecrackers and their cheeks were flushed a bright shade of pink.

"I heard they offered him a huge financial package to come here," Becks said with a wild, wide-eye look. Becks, short for Rebecca, always seemed to know exactly what was going on in the office. I think she made it her business to know. She was also my toughest competition for the permanent job here.

The other creatives simultaneously nodded in agreement, declaring that he was probably worth every cent, maybe even more. *Yes*, he was definitely worth more, they concluded. Then they walked off—no doubt to spread more legends of this creative man-God.

In an ad agency, creativity is king. It's the currency and the Holy Grail. So when one of these so-called creative geniuses comes around, it whips everyone into a star-struck frenzy. He might as well have been an actual rock star because everyone here at JTS was whipped. I was too hungover to be vaguely interested, but the rest of the office buzzed like the static on a television.

"I heard he doesn't sleep . . . ever," the strange pale vampire girl from layout said dreamily.

"He's going to bring in a lot of new accounts . . . not to mention awards," two senior managers said as they passed.

"I heard he nailed all the chicks at his last job," two guys from IT said before a macho fist bump.

I sighed and started to roll my eyes, but they hurt too much.

I opened my email and there it was: "Meeting in the Canteen to introduce new CD" *(Creative Director).* The meeting was in ten minutes. I lay my head on my desk and waited for the headache pills to kick in.

I must have drifted off to sleep though because I thought I heard someone say, *"I heard he was raised by wolves."* I opened my eyes and looked around, but no one was there. I glanced at my watch—*Crap!*

I jumped up and ran to the canteen as fast as I could without tripping and landing on my face. When I finally got there, everyone was already inside and standing around a black-clad figure. I could only see the back of him from where I was. I glanced around looking for Becks and finally saw her standing in the front row with the other starry-eyed women. I carefully pushed my way forward trying not to be seen, but when I got there, he turned and suddenly I couldn't breathe—

3

A Big Load . . .

~

The storm had hit, and it was a fucking hurricane.

He was dressed head to toe in black—the uniform of a Creative Director—but there was nothing else typical about him. He wore dark sunglasses inside, and had a cigarette tucked behind one of his ears. His hair was strangely, unevenly cut and was slicked back and wet looking. He had a beard, obviously—it's practically a prerequisite in this world—but it wasn't one of those massive hipster beards that made ordinary men look like axe swinging lumberjacks. It was short and well-groomed and so damn sexy.

He would have been a sight under normal circumstances, but considering that only a few hours before he'd had me bent over his car seat, he was really, *really* quite a sight.

He wore a full suit, pants, jacket, waistcoat, tie—the works. He even had a black piece of fabric sticking out of his jacket pocket. *Who dresses like that? Does he think he's Don Draper from* Mad Men?

He was almost gentlemanly—*almost*. But the tattoo that popped out from under his cuff and ran the length of the back of his hand and the one peering out from his collar that went up his neck and stopped behind his ear were anything but gentlemanly. He loomed like a dark, mysterious creature. Fortunately, he still hadn't seen me.

"Oh my God, he's *soooo* fucking weird," Vampire girl said, rubbing her neck. Did she want him to bite her? "Weird" you must understand is a compliment in this world.

And then he looked directly at me and I nearly fainted. I inhaled sharply, so sharply that I started choking on a fleck of saliva. As Becks patted me on the back, his eyes lingered moment-arily and then they left me. He showed absolutely no recognition on his face and in that moment I was overcome by two very strong emotions. One, relief. Sleeping with your new boss is not the kind of thing that looks good on anyone's resume, not to mention the awkwardness it creates around the office. And two . . . I was pissed—*"I want you so badly, Sera. I need you, be mine, you're so hot"* . . . *and now he didn't recognize me?*

What an asshole! With his unnecessary indoor sunglasses, his oh-so-cool cigarette and his ridiculous black borderline-tuxedo.

I hated him.

* * *

Work was painfully slow that day. It seemed that the arrival of Ben—his name was Ben, just plain old Ben, not any of the afore-mentioned exotic names such as Blaze, Blade, Slade or Xenon . . . Ben—had caused people to forget they had jobs . . . and minds.

People were standing around, eagerly waiting for their names to be called. Ben said he was "very hands-on," a phrase that had caused me to both cringe with disgust and tremble with excitement all at the same time. He explained he was going to be speaking to all the members of his team "one-on-one"—another phrase that brought back images of back-seat bumping and grinding.

Ben had used several phrases that morning that had my panties in a twist—as JJ was so fond of saying. I couldn't figure out whether he was an innate pervert who tossed around sexual innuendos like salad croutons, or whether I was just being overly sensitive.

"I have a big load for you today," he'd said before he emphasized how he wanted to "get on top of things." All the innuendo caused strange feelings to pass through my body, but I almost passed out cold when he said he "wanted to really get his hands dirty and not be a back-seat driver." The mere mention of his back seat nearly put me in a coma.

But the worst thing was that my desk was directly across from his glass-walled office, so I had a front row seat and a clear view and—*Oh my God, he was sexy* . . .

He was calling people in for their one-on-ones, which caused a temporary traffic jam in the bathroom as women slicked on layers of fresh lip-gloss and fiddled with their hair and clothes.

Ben, however, seemed totally cool and calm as he sat at his desk looking devilish. He was the kind of man that your mother always warned you about. In fact, he was the kind of guy that should be made to wear a bright red, flashing warning sign around his neck. His casual, bordering on disinterested, way of leaning back in his chair and running his hands through his hair and—*oh God*—chewing on the end of his pencil was intoxicating. And not just for me. Every woman that left his office looked like they'd just had the best sex of their lives. They all had a sort of flustered, dazed look to them—even some of the guys. God only knew what he was saying to them.

As the day went on, I tried desperately to remain calm, but it was getting harder and harder as more co-workers came out with titillating stories of him—Vampire girl was especially vocal. He'd glanced over in my direction a few times when he'd called the names of people sitting nearby, but still he'd showed no recognition whatsoever.

The torturous hours dragged on until the day was almost over, and still my name hadn't been called. At five I got up and started packing, completely thrilled to have been overlooked, but then—"Sera De La Haye?"

4

THIS SMILE COULD BE DETRIMENTAL TO YOUR HEALTH . . .

~

*T*he sound of my name dripping from his lips caused a strange reaction inside. I froze, like a mime artist in mid movement. Then I sat back down in my chair, locked my eyes onto my computer screen and stared straight ahead, unblinking.

"Sera. Sera De La Haye?"

I didn't move. Out of the corner of my eye I saw his black figure striding towards me and within seconds, he was standing above me.

"Sera?"

I knew I couldn't keep pretending I hadn't heard him, so I nonchalantly held up my hand. "Just give me one moment please, I'm in the middle of something very important." As soon as the words were out of my mouth I imagined being fired on the spot. Not only had I slept with him, *my boss*, but now I was making him talk to the hand—*what a disaster*. I pretended to read a few more words on the screen, unnecessarily nodded several times, muttered to myself and wrote something down on a piece of paper for extra effect.

"Done," I said. Then I stood up and, totally misjudging how close he was, my body bumped into his. I took a quick step backwards but it was already too late, the damage had been done. And *OH*, how it had been done! His sudden close proximity and the brief feel of him set off an involuntary chain reaction inside my body and I found myself fantasizing about him bending me over the desk and showing me who was boss. I felt sweat beading on my forehead and I tried desperately to drag my eyes away from his mouth—*stop staring at his mouth. Stop staring at his mouth.*

I could still make out a few pieces of glitter stuck to the side of his face and caught in his beard. I guess I had marked my territory. Ben watched my eyes, and then his lips—*which I was still staring at*—curled up into a tiny, slight smile.

"Better things to do than meet the new boss?" he asked.

My heart crawled into the back of my throat and lodged itself there. "No . . . no," I said. I sounded panicked and tried to rein myself in a little. "There was just something very important from a client I had to look at. Very important, in fact, and it needed my immediate and undivided attention."

"Important?" he sounded amused.

"Yes! So very, very . . ." I paused, wondering how many times would technically be considered too many to utter the word 'important' in one sentence. His eyes drifted down to my lips as if he was waiting for me to say it again. "But of course my meeting with you is far more important than the client thing, it can wait and I'll—"

He held his hand up to stop my rambling, which I was grateful for, but all I could think about was how I'd sucked on his fingers the night before. I'd never sucked a finger before, but he'd obviously done some kind of black magic on me and unleashed my dormant inner porn star. I snapped out of it and willed myself to look up at his eyes, and, when I did, his smile grew.

"I like your dedication," he said casually, like he was speaking to any other employee. "It's good to know my staff are so hard working." There was still no recognition on his part, and a part of me still wanted to bitch slap him into tomorrow.

"Shall we?" he asked, gesturing with his arm toward his office.

When I stepped into his office, I immediately became aware of the smell lingering in the air—the same soapy, spicy, sandalwood smell as the night before—*minus the vodka and sweat, of course.*

Ben closed the door behind me and walked to his desk. "So . . . Sera?" he started, as he leaned back in his chair and looked me directly in the eye.

I felt an electric jolt reach across the table and shock all my senses to life. I sat up straight and crossed my arms over my body protectively. "Ben. Boss. I mean, Mr . . . um . . ." I stammered. I had no idea what this guy's surname was!

"White."

"Sorry, what's white?"

"My surname."

"*Oh.*" I felt the sudden hot flush of embarrassment sting my cheeks. "Of course. I knew that. Ben White."

He smiled at me curiously and I could see he knew that I had had no idea what his surname was. And I would never have guessed it either. White seemed like the most inappropriate surname for him. White conjured up images of sugar and spice and kittens in mittens. And he was none of these things. Ben *Black* would probably be more appropriate.

"So . . . Sera De La Haye," he said, breaking my train of thought.

"Yup. That's me." I tried to sound upbeat.

"That's a very interesting surname. Very . . ." he paused, looked me up and down and then smiled. "Exotic."

I swallowed hard at the sound of the word. Why did he have to say everything like he was in the middle of having sex with you?

His smile grew. That hot, sexy little devil smile—*his smile should come with a mandatory warning.*

WARNING: Females should be aware that this smile can be detrimental to your health. Side effects include rapid pulse, palpitation, sweaty palms and in severe cases sexual arousal leading to impromptu hot-as-hell back-seat sex.

"So you're my client service intern, I see." He bit down on the end of his pen. There it was again. Why did all his phrasing seem steeped in sexual innuendo? Accident? I think not. He was obviously some kind of modern-day sleazy Casanova, going around deliberately trying to make females amorous—*it was working.* I crossed my legs tightly . . . *just in case.*

"Mmmm, yes," I managed with a slight nod, trying to look as professional as possible.

"And are you finding you're on top of things?"

"On top of what?" My body stiffened as sudden images of me grinding away on his lap went careering through my mind.

"On top of your work?"

"Hahaha." I let out a small laugh. "Yes. Absolutely. Of course, I'm always on top." I flashed a smile that faltered quickly the second I heard the words that had just come out of my mouth.

"Good to know." Ben's eyes darkened and seemed to drift over me, or was it my imagination?

He suddenly looked away and cleared his throat. "Well, we're going to be working very closely on the next few campaigns."

"Mmmm, I'm very excited," I lied. I was terrified.

"I demand a lot from my staff, you know?" he leaned in looking serious, "but I'm guessing someone as dedicated to their job as you won't have a problem with pushing yourself and working under someone like me."

I swallowed. The previous images of me on top had just shifted to steamy images of Ben-on-top. I nodded and mumbled, the feelings surging through me were fast turning me into a blithering idiot. "Of course, I'm good on the bottom too . . ." *Shit!* "I mean, not on the bottom bottom per se." I frantically tried to correct myself. I was failing dismally, but continued anyway. "I'm good under you, though . . . *no*, I mean working under a boss, like you, I mean, um . . ." I stopped. If I opened my mouth again I was sure I was going to choke not just on my foot, but on my entire leg as well.

Ben smiled across at me and opened a file, "So I see you've only been here for six months. Straight out of college, enjoy long walks on the beach at sunset, badminton, puppies . . . hmm . . . Elton John?" he said.

"What? I beg your pardon. What the hell is that?"

"HR sent up files on everyone." He had that naughty smile on his face again.

"That's not in there . . . I don't like . . . why would that file say that?" I was totally confused and panicked now.

He chuckled. "Just joking, Sera De La Haye."

"Oh." I forced a nervous laugh. "Of course."

He closed the file, leaned in closer, put his elbows on the table and locked eyes with me. "Well Sera . . ." *He kept saying my name. No one had ever made it sound so wonderfully filthy before.* "I'm looking forward to working with you . . . *Sera*."

I stifled a gasp as my name dripped from his lips once more, "Th . . . thank you. Me too. Everyone is very, very excited . . ."

"Well," his voice suddenly went all husky, like it had been at the bar. "I can't tell you how excited I am to be here."

That was it!

His voice coupled with those smoldering eyes, his smile and smell, the seductive vibe that was oozing out of every one of his tattooed pores was driving me insane. I needed to put as much space between us as possible—*right now*. I stood up and stepped awkwardly away from the table. "I . . . I need to get home, so I better . . . leave now and . . . because it's the end of the day and that's what you do at the end of the day is . . . leave." My nonsensical words cascaded out like dropped marbles.

"Sure, I wouldn't want to keep you from going, because that's what you do at the end of the day, is go." He was smiling broadly now.

He was mocking me. "Okay. Thanks," I said flatly and headed out the door . . . until he stopped me.

"Oh Sera, I think you're forgetting something."

I turned and that's when I saw them. It took a few seconds to register because they were so out of place here, like seeing a polar bear take a leisurely stroll across the desert. But when I finally accepted what I was seeing, my brain felt like it was going to shatter into a billion fragments. *Because there they were.* Peeping out of an envelope he was pushing across the table.

Pink.

Lacey.

Panties.

My panties.

5

POSING FOR A
PLAYBOY SPREAD . . .

~

I gasped and then slapped my hands over my mouth in utter gut-wrenching shock. I closed my eyes tightly, hoping that when I opened them again, my underwear would not be laying on my boss's table.

I heard a small chuckle and opened my eyes again. He was wearing his back-seat look now. His eyes were doing that intense staring thing that had the power to make you feel completely naked. His lips were slightly parted and he was running his hand through his hair like he was posing for a *Playgirl* spread.

Then the words poured out . . .

"I . . . I . . . can explain. I mean . . . I . . . I've never done that before . . . seriously. It wasn't really me . . . *well, it was me*, but it wasn't in a way. Someone else dressed me, I don't even dress like that, so you can't blame me . . . the *real* me anyway. Shit. I didn't know who you were; I swear I had no idea that you were my boss. I'm not the kind of girl to sleep with my boss so I can get ahead or anything like that, if that's what you're thinking. If I had known, I would never have done it. Not that I *ever* do that! Ever. Please don't tell anyone. Please don't tell . . ." And then I caught myself and stuck my finger out at him accusingly, "Hey, it was sort of your fault too anyway; you plied me with vodka cocktails all night and—"

He cut me off with a laugh. "Well, I hope it wasn't *only* the cocktails that made you do it. I wouldn't want it to be like that next time."

"What!" I half shouted. "Next time? Seriously?" I couldn't believe the audacity of this man and it made me instantly angry. " Firstly—" I was fuming now. "Firstly, Mr. Pervert, there will be no next time and secondly, this is sexual harassment. I could report you for this, you know. Sexual harassment in the work place is a very serious crime. And don't think I won't . . . *Jesus*." I slapped my hand over my mouth again and bit down on my lip. "I'm threatening my boss. First I sleep with him and then I threaten him . . ." I sat back down in the chair. I needed to, it felt like my legs were going to give way under me. I slumped down and put my head in my hands.

"It's fine. You can fire me if you want. I'm okay with it. It's okay . . ." I placed my hand over the envelope and slowly slid it toward me, then quickly shoved it into my jacket pocket. I wanted the floor to swallow me up and never spit me out again. My head was still down when I heard him laugh again. "Fine. Fine," I said, "Laugh at me, too. Whatever. Ha, ha, ha."

His laughing stopped. "No one is getting fired," he said. He sounded calm. I looked up at him and noted that his demeanor changed to something that was completely businesslike. This waylaid my fears a bit.

"Really?" I asked, just to be sure.

"Sera, I'm not going to fire you."

"Thanks." I said faintly. "How did you even recognize me anyway?"

He leaned across the desk, coming in as close as possible. "I could never, ever, forget a face like yours."

I shivered. Goosebumps ran up and down my spine and my skin pebbled instantly. I had to get out of there, before some uncontrollable force threw me onto his large, *oh-so-large* and hard and perfectly shaped and . . . I shot out of my chair at the thought of it. Then I straightened myself and tried to look as dignified as possible.

"Well, it was nice meeting you, Ben Black, and I look forward to a good PROFESSIONAL working relationship where we can become great COLLEAGUES and CO-WORKERS." I shouted the words.

"Ben White." He stood up and walked around his desk toward me. "White."

"Doubtful," I half muttered under my breath.

"I can show you my ID book if you like?" He continued his approach.

"No, no. That won't be necessary." My breath quickened and I took a step back as he suddenly extended his hand. I looked at it in horror, as the various body parts that had come into contact with that hand began to tingle . . . especially my breasts. I quickly folded my arms across them.

"Can't we at least shake hands?" he asked, taking a step closer and looking at my folded arms.

"Sure. Okay." I reached out tentatively and took his hand, but as I did, something incredible happened—you know how psychics have those clairvoyant flashes and visions when they touch something significant? The necklace of a deceased person, or a missing child's toy? *Well, it was like that.*

Vivid, colorful visions of the two of us flashed through my mind. He was pulling off my panties with his teeth. He was running his tongue over my breasts. I was ripping the buttons off his shirt and unzipping his jeans with manic vigor. I pulled my hand away as quickly as possible and looked up at him. He had that look in his eye again, that look he'd had just before he'd kissed me for the first time in the club. He bit his lip and leaned in. Oh my God, was he going to kiss me? I couldn't let that happen.

"I . . . I . . . I'm going now." I leapt at the door and turned the handle, but it was locked. I jiggled it around a few times in a frenzied panic. *He locked me in his office!* The sick twisted pervert had deliberately called my name out last so he could get me alone in his office after everyone had gone home. My heart started beating fast and that primal fight-or-flight instinct took over.

"Let me out! Let me out, *now*. What were you hoping for? To have me on your desk?! Let me out—"

He cut me off by reaching out and putting his hand over mine. He turned the handle in the opposite direction and the door popped open, much to my relief and surprise . . . and utter embarrassment.

"You were turning it the wrong way."

"Oh," I managed pathetically. I looked at the floor quickly and didn't say a word as I exited.

"Sera," he said. I didn't dare to look up. "Please close the door behind you on your way out," he continued. I nodded. "And Sera," he added, just as the door was almost shut. *"Now I know I'm in love . . ."*

6

ICBIJCIFOTHGOTPWAHT-BMNBWIAHSW!

~

My teenage sister sends me SMSs sometimes that I barely understand. Punchy terse messages with CAPS-a-plenty. This felt like one of those moments that required a whole string of them.

"Now I know I'm in love . . ." WTFH! OMG! AB bloody fucking C! Had he really said that?

My hands were shaking uncontrollably as I clutched the steering wheel. The road was long and straight, but we were creeping along slowly. All I wanted to do was speed up and away from the office as fast as possible.

My office had always been a happy place that I loved going to. But all that had changed in only a matter of hours. And I seriously doubted it would ever feel the same again. The implications of Ben working there were huge. It was only a matter of time before it came out and everyone in the office knew. I would no doubt be branded the office ho-ho. And it would only be a matter of time before he notched many more of my co-workers' names onto his bedpost. The thought revolted me.

I had to keep reminding myself to breathe. I wound down the window—my car was invented before such fancy things as electric windows and power steering—and stuck my face into the wind like an excited dog. I needed air. Air is good. Breathe.

The deep breathing did little to help, though. My pink panties were burning a hole in my pocket and a question was now burning a hole in my brain: Why the hell had he been carrying my panties around with him, in an envelope no less? *Does he have a panty-thieving fetish?*

I looked at the time on my cell phone, it had only been thirteen hours since I'd slept with him, and in that time it felt like my entire world had come crashing down around me. I needed to get home; at least I would be free of him there.

I drummed my steering wheel and turned on the radio in hopes it might distract me. My car had been built around the time dinosaurs walked the earth, so it only had a cassette player in it. But the music did little to distract. I just couldn't stop thinking about it. The thought of walking into work day after day scared the living shit out of me. I'd been mortified enough when I'd had to make the run of shame across the parking lot the night before, and now it would feel like I was making that same walk of shame every single morning as I marched past his office to my desk wondering if anyone in the office knew about it.

I felt sick. I needed chocolate.

I turned into the nearest gas station convenience store and raided the closest shelf of chocolates. Normally, it would be hard to choose, but at a time like this, less was definitely not more. I shoved several chocolates into my basket—dark, white, nuts, mint, M&Ms, you name it.

I had absolutely no shame at this point—*hey, half a gay club had seen me semi-nude and my boss had been walking around with my panties*—I started unwrapping the chocolates right there in the parking lot. I shoved a handful of M&Ms into my mouth and suddenly remembered that I needed milk, so I turned back toward the shop, but as I did . . .

"Sera." *It was him.*

I jumped as if I'd just seen a ghost.

"What the hell are you—"

But before I could finish the sentence, one of the M&Ms went down the wrong pipe and I started choking. *Real choking. Real gasping for air and going blue in the face choking.* I grabbed Ben's shoulders in a total panic and tried to communicate the seriousness to him. I couldn't breathe and for a moment there I actually thought I was going to die. But, just before it felt like I was going to black out from lack of oxygen, I felt two arms wrap around me tightly.

He was strong, and with every squeeze, my whole body lifted off the ground. He did this several times before a blue M&M shot out of my mouth and bounced off the pavement. He clearly hadn't seen it, though, because he kept on going.

"Stop!" I finally managed to say in between coughs and frantic gasps for air. "Stop."

"Are you okay?" His voice came out fast and urgent as he turned me around and looked at me with wide, frightened eyes.

I nodded, while grabbing hold of my throat and still coughing. *Crap. That hurt like hell.*

"Fuck, you gave me such a fright. Don't ever do that again," he said while putting both hands on my shoulders and trying to look me in the eye. "You sure you're okay?"

Was I sure I was okay? Okay you ask? . . . NO!

I was absolutely *not* okay. It was not okay that I'd slept with my new boss, that I'd left my underwear in his car, that I'd threatened to sue him for sexual harassment, called him a pervert and had now choked on an M&M in front of him. I was not okay at all. I was so embarrassed, I wanted to shrink down to the size of an ant and disappear.

"Sera? Are you okay?" he persisted, still trying to meet my gaze while I glanced anywhere but in his direction. He sounded genuinely concerned, more concerned than I thought he should be.

I nodded. "I'm fine. Sorry."

"Why are you saying sorry?" he asked as one of his hands came up and touched my cheek in such a strangely intimate gesture.

I shrugged him off and took a step back.

"Are you sure you're okay to drive? I could drive you if you want?"

I shook my head. The last thing I wanted right now was to be in his car again. And the absolute last thing I wanted was for him to know where I lived.

"Thank you. I'm fine." And then a thought struck me. "Hey, what are you doing here anyway?"

"Following you of course," he flashed me a cheeky, devilish grin.

"What!" I gasped, and then proceeded to cough a few more times; my throat was clearly not ready for dramatic gasping.

"Joking, Sera. In case you hadn't noticed, this is the closest gas station to our office."

I looked around. "Yeah, I suppose you're right."

"Well, I'm really glad I was here," Ben said. He smiled at me again, but not like before. Not with *that* smile. The one that made you lose your wits, your clothes, your sense and your virginity, if you still had it. It was a warm, friendly smile now, which was completely strange and made me even more uncomfortable than his *take-your-clothes-off-and-climb-under-me* smile. He was standing with his hands on his hips, and still looked totally ridiculous and utterly hot in that overly formal suit. He'd loosened the top button and tie now, so it had a slightly more casual look to it. The open button revealed a tiny bit of the chest tattoo that I'd run my tongue over thirteen hours before.

"Well, thanks then." I gave him a tiny appreciative smile and started walking back to my car before my whole face flushed red and I burst into tears from sheer humiliation.

ICBIJCIFOTHGOTPWAHTBMNBWIAHSW! (I can't believe I just choked in front of the hottest guy on the planet who also happens to be my new boss who I also had sex with.)

7

A PANTY SMUGGLER . . .

I've always loved collective nouns. A murder of crows, a business of ferrets, a mischief of mice. As I sat with JJ and Bruce, I wondered exactly what collective noun would apply:

A cackle of queens.

A gaggle of gays.

A hullabaloo of homosexuals.

To say they were screeching with laughter was an understatement. Bruce was currently bent over the couch squealing, broken up by fits of even higher pitched laughter. "He gave you the Heimlich maneuver?!"

And JJ . . . well, he was lying on the floor, tears running across his face, sobbing, "He's a panty smuggler."

It wasn't pretty.

"It's not funny, guys!" I said, slamming the dishwasher closed as if I was out to kill the thing. And just in case the dishwasher still wasn't aware that I was totally pissed off, I punched a few extra buttons for added effect. Still, their laughter continued.

They clung onto each other for support now, hooting and snorting like toddlers that had been given crack.

"It's a pity you didn't pass out cold so he could give you mouth-to-mouth," Bruce added in between his huge guffaws.

"He's a panty smuggler," JJ repeated. *At least Bruce had moved on somewhat.*

"It's not funny. This could seriously jeopardize my job," I said, as I stomped through the lounge and threw myself onto the couch. "What if it's really awkward working together, and then everyone finds out and he has to fire me?" A lump formed in my throat and I choked on the words slightly. Losing my job, especially now, would be the worst thing that could happen, especially for my sister. Her future would be over. I wouldn't let that happen, not over my dead body.

JJ and Bruce finally stopped with the hysterics and looked over at me. "Babe, he's not going to fire you," Bruce said, coming to sit next to me. "He said so." At least he was showing some compassion now.

JJ nodded. "No, he won't, besides . . ." He put on his drag queen Miss Ginny Tonic voice now. "He's in *lurve* with you!" Both JJ and Bruce *ooohed* with childish excitement.

"I hate you guys right now," I said, and shot them both a disapproving look. But of course I didn't hate them. On the contrary, JJ and Bruce had saved me when I was at my most vulnerable—and by extension, they'd saved my sister, too. There was a thirty-year age difference between me and them, so I looked at them like father figures—*my two weird adopted dads*. And they certainly treated me like that, apart from the totally inappropriate father/daughter conversations like this one.

"You're right, we're being totally insensitive," Bruce said.

JJ nodded. "We're just jealous. I would have paid good money to have him come up from behind and give me the Heimlich maneuver."

I laughed. "That's because you're a total ho!"

JJ cocked his head to the side and pouted his lips. "Um, look who's talking *Miss-take-me-in-the-back-seat-of-your-BMW.*"

At the mere mention of it, I felt my blood pressure rise and I wondered if my face looked as hot as it suddenly felt. The answer soon became obvious when JJ asked, "That good, huh?"

I bit my lip and nodded.

"You dirty bitch." Bruce nudged me playfully. "But seriously. I really think it will be okay. You made things clear and you're a professional. I'm sure he's reasonable and professional, too. Otherwise he wouldn't have the job he has. It's going to be okay." Bruce put his arm around me.

"Thanks, guys," I said, finally starting to feel better about this whole thing.

"We're off to the restaurant now," JJ said. "See you in the morning." They both blew air kisses and left.

I walked onto the balcony and had a seat on the huge daybed. The apartment building was on top of a hill in the suburb of Killarney. I'd have never been able to live in such a place if I had saved my entire salary for a whole decade. With their successful restaurant and its cabaret and comedy shows, they'd done really well for themselves, and their penthouse suite, with its incredible view of Jo'Burg, was a testament to that. I sat there watching the flickering city lights until I felt tired. I knew I would really benefit from an early night.

Another shower finally rid me of the pesky glitter. It was winter, so I bundled myself up in my big pink fluffy gown with heart-shaped print—a gift from my "dads" for Valentine's Day—and climbed into bed and closed my eyes. But, as soon as I did, the thoughts came pouring back. How was it possible to have such contradictory feelings about a guy? I was so physically attracted to him, yet repulsed at the same time. Well, repulsed might not be the right word, but downright pissed. He'd carried my panties around and then given them to me at work! *At work! In an envelope? Who does that?*

He'd been all sexy and seductive and pervy, something I decided I should dislike terribly about him—*even if it had driven me wild*. But he had saved me from possible death by choking. God, I hated him for turning me into such a pathetic puddle of hormones.

Vampira was right about him—she was seldom right about anything. She actually believed in real vampires and ran a Facebook fan page for them. But she was right about this.

He was so weird.

Which made him even more mysterious and sexy.

Aaaagggh! I was driving myself mental. I needed a good night's sleep. I was sure the hangover and lack of sleep were contributing to my usually rational brain being nowhere to be found. I really just needed to stop obsessing.

Everything would be clearer and better in the morning . . .

8

I WAS JUST THINKING ABOUT YOU . . .

The next evening after work, I walked into his office. No, I strode in. I felt confident and sexy and in charge. I locked the door behind me and drew the blinds.

"Take off your clothes," I said.

He looked up at me, his eyes going wide with shock.

"I said, take off your clothes."

He smiled—a sexy, dark, broody, naughty, beastly smile.

"Sure thing, ma'am," he said, peeling off his black suit. The jacket slipped to the floor, the tie was tossed to the other end of the room and he started unbuttoning his shirt, revealing the dark criss-crossing lines of his tattoos. His chest was now completely bare. He was muscular. Very. Not in a greasy body builder sort of way but in that defined *I-want-to-trace-all-those-lines-with-my-tongue* kind of way.

"Now your pants." I pointed at his trousers as he unbuttoned, unzipped, de-belted and dropped them to the floor. Then he stepped out of them and walked closer to me.

"These too?" he asked as he stuck his fingers under the elastic of his underwear and pulled them open to give me a little peep. I inhaled sharply.

"Yes."

He walked over to me.

"You take them off . . ." he said as he leaned towards me.

I swallowed hard. "Okay . . ."

My trembling fingers reached out and—"AAAHHHHHH!" I woke up with a jolt covered in sweat and breathing rapidly. What the hell? What the *hell*?

I jumped out of bed, ran for the kitchen and poured myself a glass of water. My mouth was horribly dry and I was actually shaking from the dream—*that's how real it felt*. The clock on the wall said 2:30 a.m.—*how ironic. That was the exact time last night that Ben and I had been at it.* I had a sudden fearful vision of waking up at this exact time for the rest of my life, as if the memory of the encounter had somehow seeped into my cells, rewritten my DNA and was now altering my internal clock.

I paced up and down the lounge a few times in a state of exhaustion, confusion and agitation. I needed a cold shower!

But as soon as I turned on the tap, I came to my senses—*it was the middle of winter for heaven's sake*. I didn't need to send myself into hypothermic shock, I just needed sleep—*Ben-free sleep*. So I climbed back into bed and closed my eyes, but a sudden noise made me sit up again.

The noise was coming from the apartment next door and the wall separating us was right behind my bed. I knew that someone had just moved in next door. I put my ear to the wall. The noise started up again and was even louder this time. It sounded like someone was dragging furniture across the wooden floors. I turned on the light and stared at the wall, as if I could send hate beams directly to the inconsiderate ass disturbing my sleep at this ungodly hour. But I clearly had no such power because another noise soon cut through the silence. This time it was a loud bang, like a chair being knocked over.

I put my ear to the wall again and was almost instantly rendered deaf as someone started drilling into the wall—"*Hey!*" I called out and banged on the wall with my fist, but there was no way they were going to hear me over the grind of metal boring into concrete. It seemed to go on for ages. As soon as there was a vague reprieve, it started up again.

I had to do something. I could either phone Raymond, the unpleasant and slightly mad eighty-nine-year-old caretaker, or I could deal with it myself.

When I heard a giant crash, as if a mirror had just been shattered, my mind was made up. Pissed off and tired, I stormed out the front door and marched down the hallway. This new neighbor wasn't off to a good start. What were they up to? *A home make-over in the a.m.?* I reached number six and knocked.

There were stacks of cardboard boxes outside and it was obvious that they were still in the process of moving in. Still, that was no excuse. I must have knocked about ten times, and with each knock my patience grew thinner. I finally gave up and tried the handle and the door opened. I took one small step inside . . .

"Hello!" I said. I figured I'd better call out before barging inside—unlike some people, I wasn't rude. But when after the fifth call I'd still had no reply, I felt well within my rights to investigate. I walked straight down a long corridor to the spare bedroom—the penthouses were all laid out the same—the drilling and banging were getting louder with each step. When I reached the room, the door was slightly ajar, and again I thought the polite thing to do would be to knock once more. So I did. And again. And again.

Fuck this. "I'm coming in," I said. And I did. Then I saw him standing on a ladder in his underwear—"YOU!" I pointed and stammered.

He turned and looked at me, shirtless, sweaty and wearing a smile. "Well, hello, Sera. What a coincidence. I was just thinking about you."

9

THAT PICTURE IS SKEW . . .

*S*everal extremely puzzling thoughts were running through my mind as I stood there staring at him—*okay, the lower half of him. I mean, he was wearing the exact same underwear from my dream, how was that even possible?*—I closed my eyes a few times and opened them again to make sure he was really there. I pinched my cheeks too, but he was still there. This wasn't a dream.

But why was he here? And why the hell was he doing home improvements in his underwear? And in the middle of the night? I didn't even know where to begin my line of questioning, so I said the first thing that came to mind.

"That picture is skew," I said, pointing at the framed picture on the wall behind him.

Ben climbed down the ladder slowly and walked right up to me. He turned to face the wall and looked. "I believe you're right. Thanks."

He climbed back up the ladder and readjusted the picture—*I'm not even going to even try and explain what Ben looks like when he climbs a ladder in his underwear.* There are just no words in any dictionary, in any modern or ancient or alien language that would do the spectacle justice. Trust me on this.

Once he'd straightened the picture, he turned, sat on the top step, crossed his legs and looked at me as if he was totally unperturbed. As if he was somehow completely separate from this reality and was on his own weird wavelength. It was as if nothing about the current situation was even vaguely bizarre to him. I opened my mouth a few times to try and say something, but I just ended up staring at him as he pulled a cigarette out from behind his ear, lit it, took a drag and let the smoke tumble seductively out his mouth. I suddenly pictured this moment being captured by a photographer in black and white and hung in some French gallery for a whole bunch of pretentious, vaping hipsters to admire and appreciate as modern art.

"You shouldn't smoke," I finally managed. "It's bad for you." I said this even though I was totally transfixed by it. It took the whole bad boy thing he had going on to an entirely different level.

"So they say," he said as he took the cigarette from his mouth and put it out on the top step of the ladder and stepped back down towards me.

"It's winter," I added. "You should put clothes on, you could get a cold"—*another fricking stupid thing to say.*

"Yes, Mom," he said as he took another step closer to me, prowling like a wild animal about to pounce. I had a momentary lapse in sanity when my eyes met his, my mouth opened and a little breathy sound came out.

Snap out of it!

"Okay. Stop. Stop right there. Stop that walking or whatever it is that you're doing immediately." I pointed at him.

He stopped and smiled. "Yes, ma'am."

"Ahhhhh," I gasped out loud and slapped my hands over my mouth in total shock—*he'd said that in my dream too.* Did he possess some kind of sexual, supernatural superpower that made him able to manipulate women's dreams?

"Stay back," I said, fully aware that I looked like a crazed woman backing away from a criminal, but if I didn't keep him at bay, I was almost certain he would have me bent over that ladder—and I probably wouldn't object.

Ben burst out laughing and held his arms in the air like he was under arrest—*images of handcuffs flashed through my mind.*

"So how long did it take you to find me?" he asked.

"I beg your pardon?"

"To find me? Have you been running around the city knocking on doors looking for me all night?" He flashed me an iceberg-melting smile.

"What! NO! You think I've been looking for you?" Ben was definitely the most arrogant, cocky and self-assured person I'd ever met—*God, it was hot.* And so fucking annoying too. "I can assure you I haven't."

"Joking again, Sera."

Thanks to all the distracting hot nakedness, I'd almost forgotten why I'd come here in the first place. "Well, forgive me if I don't have a sense of humor at two in the morning after being woken up by a drill in my ear," I said with as much venom as possible.

He watched me for a few seconds while some cogs turned in

his head, "You live there?" He pointed to the wall looking genuinely shocked. "Seriously? You live *there* ?"

"Yes, on the other side of the wall you've been drilling into for
the past half hour."

Ben blinked a few times before bursting out laughing, a big
hearty laugh. "Well, it's official," he said. "I'm never going to be
able to sleep again knowing that only a few inches separate us."

I swallowed hard, and my breath caught in my throat as I too
pondered the implications.

"Some people at the office think you don't sleep anyway," I
said, trying to steer the conversation in another direction.

"Really? What else do people think?" he asked with a knowing smile, as if he was used to such rumors and stories following
him around.

I debated whether to say it or not but decided I would so he
would know that I knew what kind of man he was. "I heard you
'nailed,'" I gestured air commas, directly quoting the IT guys,
"all the women in your last office." I immediately felt silly for
using that ridiculous word.

"Nailed?" A tiny smile tugged at the corners of his mouth.

"Well, you know what I mean," I said.

"No, I actually don't." He took a step forward. "What is this
'nailed'?" He copied my air commas in a decidedly mocking way.

I shook my head. "You're incorrigible! You know exactly what
I mean, you're just trying to get me to say it."

"Incorrigible?" A tiny chuckle escaped his lips. "I don't think
anyone has ever called me that before."

"Well, they should have," I folded my arms belligerently.

"So let's get back to this supposed 'nailing,' I'm meant to have done." He was mocking me now, and not even trying to hide it.

I shook my head. "Okay, fucked. Screwed. Banged. How's that? Better?"

He smiled. "Do you think I fucked, screwed and banged all the women in my last office?" He ended the question with a slow, mischievous smile, and a deadly glint flashed in his eyes; it stole my breath.

"I wouldn't know." I swallowed, my mouth was so damn dry. "People have been saying a lot of different things about you."

"Well, what do you think?" he asked as he met my eyes.

"About what?"

"What do you think about me?"

"Um . . . What do you mean?"

He'd started walking forward again, and I continued my backwards shuffle.

"Be careful of that box," he said, pointing behind me just as I was about to walk into it. But I kept on going, retreating while he continued moving forward.

"You walk backwards a lot," he finally said with another smile that could melt the entire polar ice cap.

"Well, you walk forwards a lot." *Great retort, Sera. Real genius one there!*

"So what do you think of me, Sera?"

I stopped walking, considering that this might actually be a great opportunity to redraw my line in the sand. I could make it quite clear to him that we would never have sex again—*although I'm sure I'd be tempted*—and make it clear that things should remain professional at all times—*despite the unprofessional images flashing through my mind right now.*

"Honestly?" I asked.

"One hundred percent."

"Okay. I think you're arrogant."

He nodded. "I've heard that before."

"And cocky."

He nodded again.

"And you're clearly a flirt. You've got all the women in the office whipped—"

He cut me off, "Do I have you whipped?"

I tisked loudly. "Absolutely not."

"Anything else?"

I collected myself. "You're obviously very good at what you do," I said. "And you seem very professional—like me—and I'm sure we will become very good colleagues."

"I'm sure we will," he said, folding his arms and leaning against the doorway in that cool, relaxed I-don't-give-a-crap way.

"Um . . . I have to go now. Early meeting, you know. Need my sleep."

His demeanor changed somewhat. "Right. I'm really sorry for waking you. The landlord—what a flaming weirdo that guy is, by the way," he said, suddenly seguing and I couldn't help but chuckle. "I thought he was going to strip search me when I came into the building."

"He's pretty mad, wait until you come to the next body corporate meeting . . ." I stopped myself mid-sentence. I didn't want to encourage more conversation.

"I bet!" Ben smiled again. Nothing melted this time but it did give me a very warm fuzzy feeling. "Anyway, he said the neighbors were a gay couple, so I assumed there'd be no children staying in the second bedroom."

"Nope," I said as I continued to walk towards the door, "I'm the child."

"Well, sorry again, Sera." *Stop saying my name. Stop saying my name.*

I gave him one last little nod as I walked into the corridor.

"Sera," he called after me. "Please close the door behind you."

"Sure," I called back without turning around.

"And Sera . . ." he called again. "Go out with me?"

I stopped dead in my tracks as his words stunned me into some strange silence. I paused for a moment before swiveling around and looking at him.

"What did you say?"

"Dinner? I'm a really good cook."

I shook my head involuntarily. "Sorry? What?"

"A date. Go out with me?" He smiled again—*more warm fuzzies*.

"I don't think so."

"Why not?" He started walking towards me again, but this time I didn't move—*couldn't move*—my feet felt like they'd frozen into the floor. He walked all the way up to me, stopped and then placed his body casually against the wall in another lethal lean.

"Why not?"

"Well, firstly, you're my boss, and secondly, I don't date."

"I don't believe that."

It was true actually. I didn't date. My life was way, way too complicated already that there was hardly any space for it. Certainly no time. And anyone who got involved with me would need to know about my family and all the craziness they brought, not to mention the tiresome responsibilities that came with them. My last boyfriend hadn't been able to handle all the very regular drama.

"I don't." I said firmly. "And certainly not my boss."

"Well . . ." The word came out slowly and deliberately. "I look forward to trying to change your mind then." Again, he seemed so unperturbed by everything, as if he existed in an alternate universe that obeyed a different set of physical laws. He spoke with an absolute confidence that was both sexy and slightly scary.

"Not going to happen."

"Wait and see."

I was almost about to exit when a sudden thought stopped me in my tracks.

Out of all the women he could choose? All the women that are a million times hotter and far, far cooler than me?

"Why me?" I turned and glared at him. "Why me?"

"I told you already. I'm totally in love."

I burst out laughing. "Does that line really work on women?" I felt all fired up now and stepped back inside. "Oh babe, you're the best," I said, imitating him now in my best arrogant man voice. "*Yeah, you're so sexy it's killing me, babe. You're so beautiful. I need you. I want you. I love you.* How many other women have you pulled those lines on?"

Ben suddenly swooped forward, looking more serious than I had ever, *ever* seen him. "None!" He was emphatic and it stopped my heart.

"Sorry?"

"I never say things I don't mean."

I looked at him, trying desperately to size him up. He sounded and looked completely serious—*But how could he be?* I had absolutely no idea what to make of him—*at all*.

10

MR. I'M TOO SEXY
FOR MY SHIRT . . .

*T*wo pairs of wide eyes looked up at me over coffee cups.

"Okay," one of the blinking eyes said. "Let's rewind a little more. Yesterday at the office, when you walked out, he said he was in love with you, too."

"He's not being serious, guys!" I said. "This is obviously some line that he thinks works on women."

Bruce nodded. "And rewinding some more to the night that you met—"

JJ smacked his hand down on the table. "Stop rewinding; I'm still on the part where you walk in and he's half-naked up a ladder. Can we go back to that part, please?"

I rolled my eyes. "JJ, you're such a cliché."

"I don't care . . . so he was up a ladder. With a hammer and a drill . . . ?"

I nodded at JJ—*I'd already been over this in great detail.*

"Was he holding the drill? Or did he have a big tool belt strapped to his sweaty body?"

Bruce and I burst out laughing.

"I'm just trying to get an accurate picture, if you don't mind."

Bruce slapped his partner of twenty years on the arm. "In your dreams he had a tool belt!" he said.

"Well, a guy can dream then."

"Can we get back to the important facts here?" I said while topping up my coffee—this was our morning ritual—"A pervy sex God, who also happens to be my boss and former one-night-stand, happens to be living next-door to me. *How the hell did that even happen by the way?* And not only that, but he's really strange and weird and playing some kind of mind trick on me by asking me out and telling me he loves me and I don't like it."

"And he does home renovations in his underwear," JJ added, "an important fact to consider when weighing up such things."

"What things?" I asked.

"Well, going out with him, silly."

"No." I shook my head. "I'm not going out with him. Besides, I don't date anymore, remember?" A while ago I'd decided that relationships required far too much work and I just didn't have the time for them, so had officially given up on them. And I certainly wasn't going to pursue a relationship with my boss that was just a bad idea.

"But he's in love with you," JJ repeated and I rolled my eyes at him.

"Please, he's clearly not being serious. It's all part of his clever *Mr.-I'm-too-sexy-for-my-shirt* act. He probably tells all the women that he loves them and then asks them all out."

A knock on the door interrupted us and we all turned. You

could almost hear the horror movie sound track swelling, as the tension built up and our eyes widened.

"It couldn't be?" JJ whispered.

I shook my head. *Please don't let it be, please don't*—"Hello? Sera?" His voice confirmed my worst nightmare.

Before I could stop him, JJ was already halfway across the room.

"I'm not here. I'm not here!" I hissed.

"It's six in the morning. Where else would you be?" Bruce asked getting up.

"Jogging," I said, moving to hide behind a pillar on the balcony.

"You don't jog."

"I do now," I whispered. Bruce rolled his eyes and walked away

"Oh. Hello, neighbor," JJ said, answering the door in all his glory. I could picture it quite clearly. JJ was probably fawning and drooling, and Bruce was probably not far behind.

"Hi, I'm Ben. I just moved in last night."

"Oh we know exactly who you are, sweetie," JJ said—*I almost died*.

I heard Ben chuckle slightly. "Yeah. I guess you do by now."

"So what brings you to our neck of the woods?"

"I came to apologize, I hope I didn't wake you up with the noise?"

"Nooo, nooooo, not at allll!" the chorus of JJ and Bruce rang out.

"Good. I would hate to make a bad impression on my first night here."

"Oh, too late for that. You've already made a *very* bad impression," I heard JJ say in a very loaded tone and I physically cringed.

"Is Sera here?" I heard him ask.

"Um . . ." JJ faltered, he was terrible at lying. "She's gone jogging."

"Really." Ben sounded unconvinced.

Bruce jumped in, "Oh she's a HUGE jogger. Loves it"—*oh God, he was hamming it up now.* "Very fit and athletic, our little Sera is. Such a jogger."

I heard a tiny chuckle from Ben, as if the perv was now thinking about my athleticism.

"What time does she leave? To jog?"

"Around five? Hey, JJ?"

"Mmm hmm," JJ helped. "Usually five-ish."

"Good to know. Well, nice meeting you guys." He must have started walking away because I heard the door start closing before JJ really pushed it too far.

"So what did you want with our Sera this morning?" he asked.

"I came to see if she wanted to drive to work together."

I heard the door close and within two seconds they were both next to me again.

"Oh God, he's gorgeous!" JJ exclaimed.

"That suit," Bruce added. "He looks like he's from the fifties or something—"

"Except for those tattoos," JJ corrected.

"And haircut," Bruce added again.

"WOW!" JJ and Bruce said together.

JJ sat down and fanned himself dramatically. "And he wanted to drive you to work."

"I have no idea why?" I was genuinely puzzled.

"It's because you're a hottie," Bruce said putting his arm around me. "And we are going to live vicariously through you."

"I'm *so* not his type, though," I said—and I meant it. His interest in me, even if it was all some kind of joke, was rather disconcerting. "I'm not some cool creative advertising chick. I'm just, normal."

"I don't know," JJ said. "He looked genuinely disappointed when we said you weren't here."

I shot JJ an incredulous look before I left to get ready for another awkward day at work.

11

RUN-OF-THE-MILL
MAN-WHORE . . .

～

*I*t took four tries that morning to start my car, and I had a sinking feeling that she was going to pack it in and call it a day pretty soon. The petrol tank was also dangerously low. And just to add a little extra worry to the morning—on top of the whole strange Ben thing—I got an SMS from my sister:

Katie: Dad broke into the house this morning and found the money you sent me!

That terrible plunging feeling formed in the pit of my stomach. It always formed at any mention of my father. In all my twenty-four years, the most shocking thing that had ever happened to me, the day my world fell apart, was the morning the bank and the police showed up at our house.

Apparently, we were being evicted.

My dad was out, as usual. We all knew where he was—that wasn't a secret. My mom looked shell-shocked, as usual. It was an expression she'd worn on her face for as long as I can remember.

I was fifteen at the time and my younger sister was only eight. I remember how terrified she was.

The bank was repossessing our house and my father had been aware of it for over six months. He hadn't bothered to mention to his family that he'd gambled the entire house away and spent the rest on prostitutes—we all knew he slept with them after a "big win."

They hauled us all out onto the pavement in front of all the neighbors while locks were changed and furniture was moved out. By the time they were all done, we were left with only our clothes, a few personal possessions, and an old rusty caravan that smelled of cheap perfume.

A ball of anxiety formed as I responded to my sister:

Sera: Bastard. Did you call the cops on him?

Katie: I tried. Mom stopped me.

Another ball of anxiety formed. My mother was a huge part of the problem, still supporting my dad even though he was constantly unfaithful and had ruined all of our lives. Worse, I knew the implications of his latest theft. I sighed again.

Sera: When do you need to buy your textbooks?

My mother didn't work, she suffered from paralyzing anxiety, depression and a pain pill addiction. Her small disability cheque barely covered food and basics around the house. So I was single-handedly putting my sister through school and supporting her. Katie was smart, and I was not going to let our father ruin her life. I wanted more than anything to give her a fair shot. She had such potential. She wanted to be a surgeon, and had the marks for it too. Med school was expensive though. But I was determined to see her do it. I had already started putting some money aside for it, not a lot though. But whenever I had a few spare cents, I quickly deposited them into my savings account for her.

Katie: End of the week. I'm so sorry. I feel so bad that you have to send me money again.

Sera: DON'T. We've spoken about this. You're my little sis. I'll pick up some extra shifts at the restaurant. It's going to be okay. Love you.

Katie: XXX. You're the best.

If I'd been harboring any doubts—however small—about whether I could go on a date with Ben, this had just reinforced the fact that I had absolutely no space for anything like that in my life. My sister was my top priority, and, therefore, so was my job. My last boyfriend hadn't understood that or been able to cope with my family's constant drama. Driving out in the middle of the night to console my sobbing, suicidal mother and pick her up off the floor when she'd "finally" kicked him out—*again*. The constant drama and embarrassment that came with having a father who was in and out of jail all the time for petty theft and fraud. Drunken scenes when he came out of prison, breaking and entering when he wanted money, begging and pleading when he needed a place to sleep . . . it was endless.

My ex had accused me of putting everyone else first, including my job—*well, of course I did! I had to.*

JJ and Bruce were probably the only two people in the world that knew how bad things really were. They knew the full, nasty unedited truth about my life and I wanted to keep it that way. If it hadn't been for their help, my mom and sister would probably still be living in that trailer, borrowing cups of sugar from the Meth cooks next door. But thanks to my rent-free living arrangement, and the flexibility of taking on shifts at their restaurant whenever I wanted, I'd managed to move my mom and sister into a small garden cottage. But the landlords were getting pissed off. Thanks to my father's constant, loud crap, they'd been threatening to kick them out. He wasn't actually living there at the moment, but between his late night arrivals, the drunken screaming he did when he was there and this latest breaking and entering, things weren't looking too good. *When it rains, it pours.*

I arrived at work after a thought-filled car ride and was shocked to find Ben already in the office. Usually, no one arrived before me, and I liked it that way. It gave me a chance to get on top of things before the usual chaos of the day descended in all its hellish glory. I also wouldn't have minded a moment to pull myself together before I had to engage with people. The SMS from my sister had thrown me.

He noticed me the second I walked in and smiled. I reciprocated with something that could barely be called a smile and sat at my desk. I lowered my head, opened my laptop, grabbed some files, and slapped them down loudly. I was hoping to convey a sense of very important *do-not-dare-disturb* busyness. Obviously it didn't work. Within seconds he was sitting at the desk next to me—*and smiling. DANGER!*

"How was your jog this morning?"

"My what—" I almost forgot my lie. "Oh. My jog. Yeah! Great. Great. Mmmmm, really great. Twenty miles clears the mind, you know" *What the hell am I saying? Do joggers really do twenty miles?*

"Twenty miles. Impressive. You must be a serious pro."

"Mmmmm." I nodded and picked up another do-not-dare-disturb prop which I used to staple some random papers together before slapping them down on my desk.

He sat and watched me as I opened my emails and answered a few, while I filed a few papers away—along with some more unnecessary stapling—and busied myself with my morning ritual, all the while trying to work out mathematically how much money I would need to make at the restaurant to buy my sister those books. But his stare was making me very uncomfortable and I wanted to turn and scream, "What?!" But he was the boss.

"Is something wrong?" he finally asked.

"What? . . . No . . . Nothing. I'm fine. Just tired."

"Is it an issue with your dads?" he asked.

"They're not really, officially, my dads, and nothing is wrong. I'm fine."

I looked up at him, feeling annoyed that he was trying to pull a Freud on me. Actually, I was irritated that he'd even picked up on it. Clearly he was perceptive—*most men weren't*. He leaned over the desk and looked at me, a mixture of sex and charm and concern all rolled into a very expensive-looking dark grey vintage suit. I didn't like this. Especially when he reached out and tried to take my hand in a commiserative fashion, as if he knew me and understood what I was going through. And then, that look again—*as if he did know me.* I pulled away quickly and cleared my throat.

I didn't want to do anything that would raise alarm bells and have him questioning me all day, and I certainly didn't want him to think I was the kind of employee that let her personal life inter-fere with work.

"It's something personal," I explained. "Nothing I can't deal with and nothing that will distract me from my job, I assure you."

He eyed me curiously. "That's not why I was asking you, Sera." Our eyes met, and once again something strange and intense and physically palpable passed between us. Thankfully, Becks arrived at that exact moment.

She and I usually had a chatty cup of coffee before starting work, but all her usual happy chattiness was gone the second she saw Ben. She transformed into a swoony someone I didn't recognize.

"Good morning, Ben," she said in a breathy whisper accom-panied by a playful hair flick. She looked at him, perhaps a little too long before finally turning to me, "Sera." I tried not to roll my eyes. Just another woman that had fallen victim to Ben's Voodoo charms.

"Morning, Rebecca."

"Becks," she corrected with a coy, girly smile that made me want to slap her into adulthood. I looked up at Ben and studied his interaction with her. He gave her a smile. Deadly. Iceberg melting. *What a flirtatious shit.*

"Good morning, Becks." His voice sounded super-friendly and enthused. Too enthused—*what a bastard.* I was right about him. He was like this with *all* the girls. He was just your average, run-of-the-mill man-whore.

I couldn't help it, but I actually felt a bolt of ugly jealously rush through me. Becks sat down and I took the opportunity to look across at Ben again. He was staring at me and then flashed me a smile—*a secondhand smile?* I glared at him in utter disapproval before looking away and unnecessarily flicking a pen to the other side of my desk—*not the most mature move, I'll admit.*

He looked at me as if he was slightly confused and then got up and walked away.

I looked after him feeling . . .

. . . *feeling what?*

12

I REMOVED ALL
THE BLUE ONES . . .

*D*espite the shaky start, the day wasn't as awkward as I'd expected. Perhaps it was because I hardly had any space in my brain for Ben. Since my sister's SMS, my father was all I could think about. Fume about. I was furious with him, and even more furious that he still had this effect on me, even though I was a grown woman.

He'd singlehandedly ruined our family and nothing good had ever come of him. Well, that wasn't entirely true. He was the reason that I'd met JJ and Bruce.

After the bank incident, I'd been forced to get a job. We'd been eating bread and jam for a month, so I was so proud and relieved when I got that first paycheck. I'd worked my butt off for that money, but, as it turned out, it was just to have him steal it after swearing blind he wouldn't gamble again.

But I knew exactly where I would find him, Caesars Palace. So that night I hitched a ride there, determined to get some of the money back before he gambled the whole lot away. When I got there, I could see my father only a few meters away from me, shoving money into a slot machine. I tried to get to him, but the security guard at the gate wouldn't let me in no matter how much I begged and pleaded. I was underage.

So I just stood there and watched my father flush all that money away. I finally broke down and started crying.

And it was at that exact moment that JJ and Bruce walked past. *The Rocky Horror Picture Show* was on at the casino and these two had taken the tradition of dressing up to a whole new level. Suddenly, I had two crazy-looking creatures in fishnet stockings and heels standing next to me.

JJ, always nosey as hell, asked what was going on. When I explained the whole sordid tale with tears streaming down my cheeks, JJ jumped into action. He stormed past the security gate and leapt on my father while Bruce cheered him on. It was one of the most shockingly funny things I'd ever seen. My dad made a run for it, zigzagging through the bright flashing rows of slot machines, but JJ was stealthy in those six-inch heels and was in hot pursuit. He finally caught up to my dad, just as the security guards caught up with him, and we were all escorted out of the casino—my dad kicking and screaming and punching, which got him banned permanently—*I was ever so grateful for this.*

They gave me a ride home that night, and were appalled to see where I was living. So they decided right there and then to make me their problem. They offered me a job at their restaurant and without asking, paid me upfront for the month. I hate accepting charity, and even now when they offer money, I don't accept it, but when my little sister ran out to the car crying, I knew that accepting help was the only way we could make it.

Meeting them was one of those strange life events, a fortuitous meeting that was meant to be. I owed them so much, but they did it all willingly. They told me once that they'd always wanted kids, but that was back in the days when the world wasn't keen on gay couples adopting. They say they have the best of both worlds now, a daughter and a friend.

I actually teared up at my desk at the thought of their kindness and love—such a stark contrast from my own parents. I reached for a tissue and surreptitiously dabbed my eye just as Ben happened to walk past.

He stopped and looked down at me and I immediately averted my eyes hoping that he hadn't seen the small tear. But he had.

"You sure you're okay?" He spoke softly and it sounded like genuine concern.

"Fine. Fine. Just allergies," I covered quickly and pretended to blow my nose into a tissue, although nothing came out. I then rubbed my eyes as if they were itchy, but all I'd managed to do was smudge my already moist mascara. I could see he wasn't convinced.

"I'm sure there're antihistamines in the first aid box," he offered.

"Great idea," I said, jumping up—*perhaps a little too enthusiastically*. I excused myself and started speed walking to the kitchen where the first aid box was. I lingered there for a second or two so he would think I'd taken a pill and then walked back to my desk looking sorted and confident and ready to do my work. When I got back, he wasn't there, which I was grateful for. I pulled out my phone and messaged JJ.

Sera: Can I pick up a shift tonight?

JJ: What did he do this time?

Sera: The usual.

JJ: Can I kill him?

Sera: Sure.

JJ: See you later then. XX

There was only one more meeting to get through before the end of the day, and then straight off to more work. Even though holding down two jobs was exhausting, I enjoyed working in the restaurant. The atmosphere there was always amazing and I'd gotten to know all the regular patrons there over the years.

When the meeting was over I ran back to my desk. When I got there I found a large envelope with my name written across it in a now-familiar handwriting. Sudden images of pink underwear flashed through my mind. I looked toward his office. Ben was doing a review with some creatives and not looking in my direction. I slipped my hand into the envelope and pulled out a packet of M&Ms. It had been opened and a small note had been inserted.

I removed all the blue ones, since they seem detrimental to your health.

I smiled to myself, and when I looked up, Ben caught my eye and smiled right back.

My heart actually skipped a beat as I read the note again.

13

LEANING MAY LEAD TO
HORIZONTAL ACTIVITIES . . .

I don't know what it is about me and sugar, but by the time I got to my car, I'd polished off the bag in two large mouthfuls and was already thinking about the next one—*if there was a group called Sugar Addicts Anonymous, I'd have to join it.* But I was also perturbed. And confused. I just didn't know what to make of Ben and it was driving me mad. He went from outrageous flirting to seeming sincerity in a matter of minutes. I still remembered how he'd been with Becks that morning—turning on the charm with that flirty, friendly voice of his.

Perhaps other women had also received snack packs with thoughtful little notes? Maybe it was part of his game plan, his modus operandi: ply all the woman in the office with chocolates, tell them all he loved them, and then get them in the back seat of his car and onto his lap? If his playboy reputation was anything to go by, that was definitely his plan. Well, whatever he was doing, it didn't matter, since I was *never* going to date him . . .

"Hey!" I turned. He whom I was thinking about was now running towards me, enthusiastically.

"I see you got through the bag without incident," he said, pointing to the finished packet in my hand. I felt a sudden stab of embarrassment at the fact he knew I'd just guzzled them down like a little hungry piggy.

"Yeah. Thanks. You didn't have to—"

"I wanted to."

I kept silent. He was leaning again, against my car— *DANGER: Leaning may lead to horizontal activities.*

"Do you want to go for a drink?" he asked.

"I don't drink anymore," I said, moving away from the dark mysterious man leaning against my dirty car. He was going to get one hell of a shock when he pulled away and realized one half of his suit was now tan.

"Since when?" His words were smothered in playful naughtiness.

I blushed. "Since it drives me to make terrible impulsive mistakes."

"Like what?" His voice was deep and husky again. He shot me a playful wink, which, despite all my self-control, made my knees weak. I mentally berated myself for being such a weak-willed woman and then stood up straight again, ready to battle this sexual force of nature.

He was smiling and I could tell he was trying to lure me into some kind of flirtatious game. Well, I wasn't going to fall for those sotto tones and dreamy, chocolaty bedroom eyes. I folded my arms and shot him a pointed look. "Like ending up in the back seat of a car with a stranger."

"Really!" He feigned shock. "And here I thought you were a good girl with those librarian glasses."

For some reason, at the mention of my glasses, I fiddled with them, which seemed to make him smile even more.

"I've got to go." I turned and slipped my keys into the car door—*invented before such modern things as battery controlled locking mechanisms—probably batteries too.*

"Coffee then?" he asked. His hand slid over mine and I slapped it away.

"I've already had far too many cups today." I jiggled my keys around; there was a certain trick to opening the lock—especially since my father tried to pick it one night in a rather lame attempt to steal it.

"Decaf?"

I sighed loudly. A long, loud exasperated sigh. "Why? Why do you keep asking me out?"

He slid his shoulder closer to me, "I told you—"

"Yeah, yeah, you're in love." I said it sarcastically and mockingly.

He opened his mouth and was just about to say something when Angie walked past.

Perhaps it's important to pause here and take this opportunity to talk about Angie. Before Ben, she was the one everyone drooled over. The one that everyone whispered about. Her creative genius was legendary. Her amazing fashion sense was envied by all. The uber-cool fact that she was also a deejay and played in trendy exclusive clubs at night made her just that much more desirable. In short, she was the kind of girl I imagined Ben with.

"Bye, Ben, see you tomorrow. Can't wait to start work on the shoot," she said as she ran her hand through her ridiculously trendy mint-green hair and pranced across the car park like a ballerina.

Ben held up his hand and flashed her one of those killer smiles. "Not as much as I'm looking forward to it."

I scoffed so loudly that I actually think she heard. I went back to jiggling the key.

"What?" he asked innocently, as if he didn't know what he was doing—*please!*

"In love with her too?" I asked, as I finally managed to get the door open.

"No. Just you."

I climbed into my car feeling a whole array of emotions I wasn't sure I understood, or liked. I barely knew this guy, so why the hell was I acting like this? I was just about to close the door when Ben stuck his leg out and stopped it with his foot.

"Okay, we don't have to drink any liquids if you would prefer?"

He was still going on about it, after blatantly flirting with blondie-greenie across the parking lot. After looking at the steering wheel for a moment, I finally looked up at him.

"You really confuse me. I don't think I get you—at all."

"Well, why don't you go out with me and I'll try to explain myself?" He flashed me another secondhand million-dollar smile. There had to be an antidote to counteract the effects of it, if not, I sincerely hoped that scientists somewhere were working on one.

"I have to work tonight."

"Work?"

"Yes, I work at JJ and Bruce's restaurant. I'm going to be late for my shift if I don't go now."

Ben's demeanor changed somewhat as he looked at me like he was trying to figure something out. "You have two jobs?"

I hated this part.

This, right here, was why I didn't want to get involved with people, because I would soon have to be explaining my sad, poor, pathetic life to them—*Yes, I was also embarrassed. Of course I was, we went from living in a modest house in the middle class suburbs, to a rusty, sticky-walled trailer.*

"Yes, I have two jobs, Ben."

"You must be exhausted."

"Don't worry. It doesn't affect my work during the day if that's what you're concerned about."

"That's not why I mentioned it."

He put his hand on my door and held it open, looking like he had all the time in the world to have a full-blown conversation with me.

"I really have to go. My shift starts in half an hour."

"Okay," he said, finally letting go of the car door and closing it. "Some other time then," I heard him say as he started walking away.

I quickly reversed out of the parking place and, as I drove off, I looked in the rear view mirror—*God, this was bringing back memories of our first night.* He waved a tiny wave as he disappeared from sight, and I was struck by a feeling—no, not a feeling, *a knowing*—this wasn't going to be the last of him, I wasn't going to get rid of him that easily.

14

WIMBLEDON 1967 . . .

⤳

$\mathscr{T}$he early morning knock on the door sent me flying out of my bed. The first few knocks had somehow incorporated themselves into my dreams, but the fourth and fifth had me jumping. It was freezing, still dark, and I had no idea who the hell was at the door. I was exhausted from my night at the restaurant and JJ and Bruce were probably unconscious. I opened the door and peered out.

"Morning." It was Ben. It was a perky, enthusiastic version of him dressed in . . .

What the hell was he wearing?

He was dressed head-to-toe in a sporty purple, polyester Adidas tracksuit—*of all things decent in this world.* The whole outfit seemed totally incongruous to what I was used to. He was also jogging up and down on the spot looking wide-eyed and bushy-tailed. I wondered if I was still sleeping.

"What the hell?" I said in a sleepy voice, yawning in between words. I was too tired and shocked to care that he was seeing me in my pajamas with my sleepy, puffy no make-up face on.

He looked at his watch. "It's five; aren't you going jogging this morning?"

"Huh? Jog—" I knew this was going to come back to bite me. "Oh. Jogging. Um . . ."

"Great morning for it!" He sounded fired up and enthusiastic, with his brand-new bright orange sneakers and matching headband—*who wears a headband? That is so Wimbledon 1967!* The sight of him in those clothes was almost more shocking than the fact he was at my house at five in the morning.

"Ben, seriously, what are you doing here?"

He feigned a look of shock. "Look, I know you don't want to go out with me, but there's no rule against being friends, right? And you jog, and I need to do some exercise. You'd be doing me a favor, actually."

"Um . . ." I was still semi-conscious and had no idea what to say to him. I opened the door further and he came jogging straight in with a spring in his step as if he was some kind of gazelle buck.

Mister Overly Enthused then started jogging in circles around my living room. All he needed were some pom-poms, blonde pigtails and a cheesy war cry to complete the look. This was a far, far cry from the guy with a cigarette behind his ear and his perfect vintage suits. And then he did something disturbing; he actually gave the air a fist pump.

"Whoa!" he whooped. "I am fired up!" He continued to jog in circles. Surely he wasn't serious? It was hard to know what to do. I had to find a way out of this.

"Look. I lied. I'm not going jogging this morning, or any morning."

"You're just saying that because you don't want me to come with you."

"I'm not."

"Are you scared I'll hold you back, keep you from cracking those twenty miles?" He said it with a smile on his face.

"Ben. I'm not going jogging with you."

He suddenly swung himself up and put his arms in the air, moving his hands in large circles—he was clearly making this shit up as he went. "But I went out and bought the whole outfit," he complained. "I even downloaded a running app and it's hooked up to this watch. Look." He stuck his arm out in front of my nose. "It counts steps, calories, miles, everything."

I sighed. Ben was just about the most persistent person I'd ever met and he was now bending his knees and doing what I assume was meant to be a hamstring stretch.

"I'm serious. I lied to you. I don't jog. Ever."

He stopped stretching and looked up at me. "You lied? To me? Your boss?"

I swallowed hard and felt a little panicked. I wasn't sure how to read Ben. I wasn't sure if he was seriously angry or not? "No. Of course I wouldn't lie to you. My boss."

He smiled. "I didn't think so. An employee such as yourself knows the value of trust in the work place." And then he winked at me as if he was teasing.

"Fine. Wait here." I conceded and walked off to my room. How hard could it be to jog? It was just a fast variation of walking. I opened my cupboard and pulled out an old tracksuit and slipped on an equally old pair of sneakers. I passed the mirror and caught sight of myself. I had serious bed head, so I ran a brush through my hair and scraped it into a messy bun. I couldn't believe I was actually about to go jogging, with Ben, at five in the morning, in winter. Clearly I'd lost my mind.

"Okay, let's go, I guess." I exited the room and found him mid-stretch. Despite myself, I couldn't help a small laugh. He looked utterly absurd.

"What? They say stretching is as important as working out!" he said, standing up again with a rather pleased look on his face.

"Mmmm." I nodded.

We walked downstairs towards the foyer, but when I got there and looked outside, I knew I needed someone to have me committed. It was still dark and it looked freezing.

"Okay," I cringed as I pushed the doors open and walked into Antarctica. My nose felt like it had just been flash frozen and I could barely see through the steam of my hot breath. Ben, however . . . .

"Refreshing," he said with an unnatural amount of vigor. "Which way?" He was still jogging on the spot, bobbing up and down enthusiastically.

"Whichever."

"Well, don't you have a route? A twenty-mile one?" *Fuck! This was getting way out of hand.*

"Follow me." I started jogging in a random direction—which sadly happened to be up a steep hill. It didn't take long until I was doubled-over and completely out of breath.

"STOP! Oh my God . . . Crap, shit . . ." (gasp, gasp, gasp) "Holy . . . Stop." I was gasping for air and clutching my knees.

My lungs felt like they were on fire, my muscles stung, my lips felt like they were going to be ripped off by the cold wind, and my nose was running far better than I was.

"Okay, I give up. I lied. I don't flippin' jog, okay, I lied to my boss!"

Ben gasped dramatically. "You didn't?!"

"I did. I'm a liar, a lying untrustworthy employee or whatever you want to think, but I . . ." (pant, pant, pant) " . . . *Oh my God I think I taste blood.* Is it supposed to hurt like this? I need to sit down . . ." (gasp, gasp, gasp)

I flopped down dramatically onto the cold hard pavement. Ben had stopped jogging too and was now leaning against a low wall.

"So I guess twenty miles is out of the question then?" he said with a mocking smile plastered across that stupidly good-looking face of his.

"Shut up," I spat back at him. "Is your heart supposed to beat like this?" I clutched my chest tightly in case my heart decided to burst out of it.

A few seconds later Ben was kneeling next to me and had a hand on my back, rubbing it in slow, soothing circles. I was too exhausted to resist and soon the feel of it brought back bad thoughts—*me on his lap riding him, him kissing my neck, running his hands over my ba . . . a . . . aaa . . . c . . .*

Stop!

I jumped up quickly but something caught my eye. "Aaahhh. Crappin' hell. What's that?" A giant rat looked at me before diving back into the drain. "See? It's not natural for people to be out on the streets at this time."

"I couldn't agree more," Ben said, smirking. "So pancakes and coffee at my place then? I make these amazing berry pancakes. I've been told they're unforgettable."

"Really?" I flashed him a look even though my face felt like it was going to crack. "By whom?" I imagined all the droves of women that had crawled out of his bed or back seat in the morning being made pancakes as they picked their panties up off the floor—*if he didn't steal them and put them in his pocket first.*

A gust of wind blew and it felt like a million icy pins piercing my entire body.

"It's freezing out here, let's get inside and then we can debate how good my pancakes are." Ben was off running in the direction of our building. "Last one there's a rotten egg," he called over his shoulder. I hadn't heard that phrase since my sister and I'd played catch in the garden.

I shook my head. This was disastrous. All my attempts at avoidance weren't working—*pancakes? At his place?*

15

THERE'S NOTHING SINISTER
ABOUT BATTER . . .

~

I stood outside his door as if crossing the threshold would be like taking a step into a great, unchartered black abyss. This wasn't as dramatic as it sounded, because it was an abyss of sorts. If I stepped into his apartment, I would be plunging into something that took our relationship from *awkward-boss-with-ex-benefits*, to *awkward-boss-with-ex-benefits-and-pancakes-together-in-the-morning*. There was a very clear difference between the two, eating breakfast together was intimate.

"I think I'm going to go back to my place," I eventually said.

He unlocked the door and held it open for me like a gentlemen. "Pancakes, Sera. Innocent pancakes. There's nothing sinister about batter being flung into a pan."

"Um, I don't know. It's all just a bit strange."

"What is?"

"You and I. Pancakes at your place. In the morning. Before work. After everything that's happened. It's just a bit inappropriate."

"I don't see anything inappropriate about this, it's not like I'm inviting you in for sex."

"What?" All my blood immediately rushed in a southerly direction. "You can't say stuff like that, Ben!"

"I'm just trying to prove a point. Sex would be inappropriate, pancakes are not." He smiled, he was clearly amused and enjoying the fact that he had worked me up. "Breakfast, Sera? Breakfast is not even a date meal. People don't go out on dates to breakfast, it's just . . ."

"Innocent pancakes?"

"Exactly."

I rubbed my forehead and I swear I felt an actual sweat-bead icicle.

"Please," he said softly, almost under his breath.

"Why are you doing this? Taking such an . . ." I could barely say the word out loud. " . . . an interest in me? Is it a joke? I mean, are you being serious?"

Ben walked up to me. Close. Too close. "Why you? Are you being serious?"

I nodded.

"Okay . . ." he said moving even closer. Way, *way* too close. He deliberately, and very inappropriately, pressed his body into mine now and I tried to hold down a breathy gasp, but couldn't manage it. "It may have something to do with the fact that I met the funniest, craziest, sexiest, most beautiful girl at a club the other night. We had such fun dancing together and then we had the best, *the best*, sex of my life and something about it just felt so different. And then, when I was about to go looking for her, she landed up right in front of me, at work and then next door. And now I can't help wondering if it's fate?"

My face flushed red-hot at the out-loud acknowledgement of the sex we'd had. Yes, it had pretty much taken the cake for the best sex I'd ever had, too, and, yes, it had definitely felt different in some way. In a way I wasn't sure I understood yet. I was rendered speechless by his confession. My tongue tied itself into knots and then the cat stole it.

"I think this conversation has crossed over the inappropriate line," I managed in a small voice.

"Maybe just a little bit."

"I don't date, Ben. And certainly not my boss."

"Why not?"

"You don't want to date me. Believe me."

"Why?"

"If you knew the kind of complications I come with, you'd keep away."

"Why don't you let me be the judge of that?"

I sighed loudly and shook my head; determined to stand my ground. "No. It's not going to happen."

He looked deflated for a moment and then smiled again. "Does that mean we can't be friends either?"

"I don't know."

"I promise I'll be the perfect gentleman."

"Really?" I gave him a deliberately suspicious look. "You weren't very gentlemanly the other night."

"Now who's being inappropriate?" He paused and our eyes locked. It was the kind of eye lock that I felt like I never wanted to look away from.

"You don't even have to eat the pancakes." His eyes crinkled into a smile.

"Fine!" I let out a resigned sigh. Clearly he wasn't going to give up. "Sure. Pancakes and coffee. Why not?" I followed the sentence with a shrug and followed him inside.

His place looked amazing, not something I would have pictured. It didn't have that cool bachelor pad thing going on; in fact it looked rather homey.

"I like what you've done with the place."

"Thanks. I still have a few boxes to unpack, but getting there." He rushed into the lounge and turned the big gas heater on.

"Oh yes!" I rushed over to the heater, I was still freezing. I stood as close as I could to the thing without catching fire. Ben did the same and we both stood together huddling by the fire.

"I'm glad you don't go jogging in winter," he said. "I would never consider going out with anyone who was clearly mad."

"You knew I didn't jog?" I asked, knowing the answer to this already.

"From the second JJ and Bruce told me, besides, I could see your little foot sticking out from behind the wall."

I smiled up at him, he was less than a foot away from me. "So you just decided it would be fun to what . . . come around, wake me and see how long it took for me to crack?"

Ben's eyes lit up and he leaned towards me. "No, I just thought it would be a good excuse to get you over for breakfast."

My heart jumped into my throat. *This was so not friendly.* "Really, so this whole thing was premeditated?"

"Right down to the ingredients being ready and waiting for us." He walked off towards the kitchen and I couldn't help it, but I was flattered. More than flattered.

"You really cook?" I asked trying to wipe the smile from my voice.

"Only desserts."

"Interesting," I said watching him expertly crack the eggs with one hand.

"If you got to know me you would find I'm an interesting person."

"And arrogant."

"Some people find it charming."

"Yeah, tell me about it, like the entire female population of our office." With my legs sufficiently warm I moved over to the kitchen and sat on a bar stool at the counter.

"Tsk-tsk, Sera, do I sense a hint of jealousy in your voice?"

"What? No. Absolutely not."

He turned and smiled at me slowly. That slightly skew heart-stopping smile that friends should not give each other.

"You know, you're such a . . . a . . ." I was searching for the right words. "A man-whore flirt. You go around flirting with everyone."

"I don't."

"Oh please. Don't act all innocent. The way you spoke to Becks and Angie yesterday, or can't you help the fact that everything you say is laced with sexual innuendo, and don't tell me you're not in control of that husky sexy voice you do. Even your 'hello' speech was dripping with it."

Ben started to laugh. "I admit the speech I gave was." His eyes twinkled. "But that was solely for your benefit."

"What?"

"Didn't you like my whole, *I don't want to be a back-seat driver* thing?" He laughed again as he whisked the batter.

"You did that on purpose?"

"Yup." He turned and winked at me before spooning the batter into the hot pan.

"So you recognized me straight away?"

"The second I saw you." He flipped the pancake over expertly.

"How's that even possible with what I was wearing? The wig?"

"I've spent a long time wa—" He cut that sentence off so fast I almost didn't hear it. "I'm good with faces," he quickly corrected. For the first time since I'd known him, he sounded caught off guard. I got the distinct impression he wasn't telling me something.

"What do you mean, you spent—?"

"Especially such a beautiful face," he interrupted with a charming smile and husky tone.

Stupidly, I forgot myself momentarily and felt my pulse start to race at the sudden compliment.

"So what were you doing at a gay club anyway?" I asked. I'd been wondering this for a few days now.

"My brother was performing." He was putting the pancakes on a plate now, gluing them into a tower with generous dollops of chocolate sauce and berries and topping the whole thing with way too much syrup.

"Who's your brother?"

"Miss Behave."

"NO!" I gasped "You're kidding?"

He shook his head.

I burst out laughing. The guys were going to have a shit-fit when they found out—*Miss Behave was JJ's nemesis*. Not that she knew that.

"Have you seen her perform?" he asked, sliding the plate in front of me and leaning across the counter.

"Oh indeed I have," I said, looking down at the pile of sugar-coated calories in front of me.

"You say it like there's a juicy story behind it."

I smiled up at him. "Oh believe me. There is."

The truth was that over the past two months we'd all gone in disguise to a couple of different clubs to watch Miss Behave perform so JJ could scope out the competition. She was new on the drag club scene and JJ's natural competitive streak was flaring.

Ben looked at me curiously. "Now I am dying to know." He pulled out a fork and passed it to me, it was a clear indication that we'd be sharing off the same plate. I suppose friends share, so why did it feel so damn intimate? The two of us sitting across the counter, after our early morning "run" sharing breakfast. I calmed myself by changing the subject.

"Are you and your brother close?" I asked.

"Very!"

"So he might come and visit you here sometimes?"

Ben looked slightly confused by the question. "I'm sure he'll come."

"Well, then I'm pretty sure you'll know the story behind it *very* soon."

I winked at him this time, but immediately wished I hadn't, because his face lit up. I returned to the pancakes . . .

"Mmmm. Oh my God these are . . ." I said, closing my eyes and taking in the flavors—*Oh sweet sugar. Sugary-sugar fest*—this was my kind of breakfast—*I confess I eat chocolate for breakfast sometimes*—I opened my eyes and looked at Ben, he was staring at me.

"Has anyone ever told you how adorable you are when you eat?"

"Um . . . you know that sounds mildly creepy and fetish-y, right?"

"Am I creepy, Sera?"

"Mmm, it's borderline sometimes." I looked at him closely. "The only reason you get away with it, is that you're just so weird, people don't know what to make of you."

Ben laughed, reached out and tucked a strand of hair behind my ear. My stomach flipped and I wanted to quickly change the subject again.

"So how are you finding the new job?" I asked.

"It's going okay, we have that massive calendar shoot coming up soon and none of the creatives are really cracking the idea yet."

"Aaaah, the calendar shoot," I said. It was infamous. One of the clients, a luxury car brand, did a once-a-year calendar shoot usually in amazing exotic locations and everyone wanted to be a part of the team that went. They only took a small group of people, and it was usually based on good work. It was almost a competition each year to see who would go.

"It's the only piece of work the CEO cares about. He never even looks at the other work we do. This is a bit of an ego trip for him, I think. He likes to hand out pretty, glossy calendars to people and watch them being shot with gorgeous models. And they always want to work with some pretentious, overpriced photographer flown in from Milan or something. As if they think our local photographers aren't good enough."

"High stakes?" I asked.

"Very, and not to be offensive, but you guys have been coming up with pretty lame ideas for the last few years. I really want to do something interesting this year, but no one is thinking outside the box."

"Lucky they have you to force them out of the box then." I smiled at him, it felt so comfortable and natural talking to him about work like this. As if we had been colleagues for years.

"I think Angie is probably the only one who'll make it out the box."

At the mere sound of her name I stiffened up. I jumped up quickly. "I have to go."

"But you haven't finished."

"I know, but I don't want to be late for work."

"Really, afraid your boss might have to discipline you? And yes, that was a purposeful sexual innuendo, in case you were confused about it."

"Friends," I corrected him. "Remember."

"Okay. Friends." But his smile said something else entirely.

"I'm going now," I said and started walking towards the door but then turned around, went back to the kitchen and stole the plate of pancakes.

"Friends share," I said playfully and let myself out.

16

WORD AT THE WATER COOLER . . .

~

*C*offee on the balcony was very eventful that morning.

"NOOOOO!" JJ said as he paced. "Miss Behave. That bitch."

"Maybe you guys could become friends." Bruce burst out laughing and I quickly followed. "Maybe you could do a duet together," Bruce added in between more laughter.

"It's not funny."

"It's hysterical," I clarified.

"No, this won't do. This won't do at all," JJ said and walked off to his room.

Bruce and I were left alone to imagine the antics that would ensue when Ben's brother came to visit.

"He'll probably pull a *Mission: Impossible* and climb the walls to try get a look inside that apartment," Bruce said.

"I would pay good money to see that."

"So you and Ben, huh? Jogging? Pancakes?"

"Just friends," I said firmly.

"Yeah right." Bruce studied my face, probably looking for a sign of something telling. "Why don't you just go out with him?"

I shook my head. "I can't. Not with all the shit in my life. Remember what happened with the last guy."

Bruce looked unconvinced. "You know, some people don't care where you came from. Some of us don't care that you lived in a trailer park and that you're 'trailer trash.' Some of us think that makes you a better person than ninety-nine point nine percent of the people out there in the world who don't know what it's like to struggle to rise above your circumstances."

I hung my head. "I don't know."

"You should give it a go."

"Do you know what all my colleagues think of people like me?" I asked. "Whenever we make a TV or radio ad one of the first things everyone says is, who is the target market? What LSM are they? How much money do they have?"

LSM meant Living Standard Measurement, and, every time the ad was for anything lower than LSM 5, everyone started joking about having to "dumb it down." Little did they know, they had an LSM lower than 5 sitting at the same table as them.

"You of all people should know how judgmental and cruel people can be," I said to Bruce.

He nodded. "Perhaps. But if you don't give it a try, you'll never know."

"Maybe."

"It doesn't even have to be a formal date. Start by knocking on his door. Take some pizza around or something, whatever. Or just pop in to say hi," Bruce said.

"I'll think about it."

Bruce gave me a smile, patted me on the leg and got up. "Time to console JJ." He started walking away and then stopped, "You should wear red lipstick to work today, just in case."

"In case what?" I asked, amused at the mere suggestion.

He shrugged and gave me a small smile.

* * *

I didn't see Ben the entire day at work. He was out at meetings. I was actually grateful for this because it gave me the whole day to think about what Bruce had said, and I allowed my mind to wonder, to imagine what it would be like to actually go on a proper date with him.

But not seeing Ben in the office didn't mean he was absent. Every few moments I would hear his name being whispered. At one stage I saw two of the creatives rushing past looking frightened as they spoke about the calendar shoot. Clearly he still wasn't winning with it. But the whispers of him weren't just confined to work-related matters.

"So I think Angie is going after him," Becks said, sidling up to me conspiratorially.

"Who?"

"Ben. You should have seen her today, practically throwing herself at him. She was basically dry humping his desk."

"Gross." *Becks had such a way with words.*

"I know. She might as well have taken her clothes off right there and then and let him do her on the boardroom table."

"Okay. I think I've heard enough." I shuffled in my seat. God, this conversation was making me feel all sorts of things I *seriously* shouldn't be feeling!

She continued. "Word at the water cooler—"

"We don't have a water cooler."

"Word at the metaphorical cooler," she corrected, "Is she's planning on fucking Ben at the calendar shoot."

Like I said, such a way with words.

Vampira had obviously tuned her hearing for the word "Ben" because she was at the desk in seconds—*had she flown here?*

"Slut."

Becks and I both turned and stared at her. She was wearing an unusual amount of black eyeliner that day and her lips were stained a very dark mauve. That was all she said before she slunk off again back to her seat in the shadows from whence the intriguing creature came.

Becks turned to me. "She's obviously talking about Angie, right?"

"I hope so," I replied.

"I'm sure Angie can't wait to be away with him on this shoot. And you know what they say, *what happens on shoot, stays on shoot.*"

"Really, they say that?" I'd never heard this before.

Becks nodded. "Last year she and Andrew hooked up." She gave me a conspiratorial smile. Andrew was the previous Creative Director. "Apparently, everyone heard them going for it all night."

"Seriously?"

"Yup. And she likes to have her hair pulled and let's guys come all over her face."

"Stop! Okay! Enough." I put my hand up. I didn't need that

image in my head, especially when the image of Andrew morphed into Ben.

"Or maybe I'll hook up with him." She pouted playfully. "Since
I'll be there too."

"You will?"

"Well, I am client service on the job and I've become a very
indispensable member of his team." She winked and went back to
her desk and suddenly I was so damn jealous. Here I was stuck
with trying to get the creatives and clients to agree on whether the
new print ad for their toothpaste should show actual teeth in it,
since apparently market research shows that exposed teeth can
come across as aggressive.

"Don't worry, Sera. If we hook up, I'll give you all the details,"
she chuckled next to me. She was joking, but still, the conversation disturbed me. I know I had no claim over him. Eating
pancakes together and sharing one night in his car didn't mean I
should feel anything about who was coming on to him, or who's
face he was coming on . . . *God, I wish she hadn't told me that*. It
was an image I was really struggling to get out of my head.

But I was bothered. A lot. Angie was gorgeous. She was tal-
ented, creative and men flocked to her. Becks had the biggest
boobs you'd ever seen and men were rarely able to look her in the
eyes when they talked to her.

There was no way she, or Angie for that matter, wouldn't be
able to charm the pants off Ben—*they came down pretty quickly as
far as I remember*. Maybe even both of them. At the same time.
The fact that all the women in the office wanted him, and would
probably continue to throw themselves at him for all eternity, just
complicated things even more.

Just then, Ben came striding past my desk and without looking at me, not even a tiny eye glance in my direction, said "Rebecca, uh, Becks, can I see you in my office."

Becks flew out of her chair and ran after him. I sat there trying not to stare at them and not be offended by the fact that he hadn't looked at me once—despite the fact I *had* put on the red lipstick. I tried to busy myself, but the toothpaste client wasn't exactly captivating. A movement caught my attention and I looked up to see Angie stride past and go straight into Ben's office too. My stomach dropped when she entered and gave him a way too friendly looking pat on the shoulder followed by an ever so slight squeeze. And then they all started talking for what seemed like forever and all I could think about was their upcoming *ménage à trois*.

I really wanted this day to end. I wasn't enjoying it. At all.

17

REAL PRINCESS CLOTHES

~

$\mathcal{M}$y apartment has a huge, beautiful garden attached to it and at the very bottom of it, there's a bench under an enormous oak tree. I sometimes go there to sit and think when I need alone time. And right now, after the day I'd just had at work, I had a lot to think about.

But when I got there I quickly discovered I wasn't alone. A young girl, not more than five years old, dressed in a pink tutu and tiara was sitting under the tree holding a tea party with her teddy bear.

I'd never seen her before. She looked up at me and smiled and I was quite taken aback by how pretty she was. She was Asian with pretty eyes and silky black hair. Her face was perfectly round and I could see she had attempted to put pink lipstick on, but had painted outside of the lines. I smiled back at her.

"Looks like a lovely tea party," I finally said, sitting down on the bench next to her.

"Here," she said and poured me an imaginary cup of tea, which I took and drank.

"Mmm . . . delicious . . . thanks, and I like your outfit."

"My daddy bought it for me. He said a princess should have real princess clothes."

I smiled at her. "He sounds like a smart man."

"He is. The smartest."

Then she leaned in and whispered to me. "They say I'm allowed to play in the garden all by myself without my nanny now that I am nearly six," she said before looking around quickly. "But she thinks I don't see her, but I do. She's hiding over there," she said, gesturing to the far side of the garden where, sure enough, a nanny was hovering in the distance trying not to look in our direction.

"Wow, you're very smart," I said.

She nodded proudly. "I'm turning six very soon. But I'm not really meant to talk to strangers, my dad says, and you're a stranger, even though you're a pretty one. I probably shouldn't really be talking to you."

"Your dad's right. You mustn't talk to strangers, so I'll leave you here to have your tea."

I stood up and started walking away. She called after me.

"My name is Li-Hau," she said.

"That's a very pretty name."

"It was my granny's name. Daddy says she's resting in a faraway beautiful, magical land where she is very happy and not sick anymore. He says I can still talk to her if I want because she is always listening and still loves me."

"Your dad sounds like a wise man."

"My name means pearl blossom," she said enthusiastically.

"Lovely." *I couldn't imagine a better name for her.*

"What's your name?" she asked. I was about to tell her when she stopped me. "You have red lips and black hair. Your name should be Snow White."

"Snow White it is then." I reached up and touched my lips, at least someone had noticed them.

"Now we're not strangers," the little girl said triumphantly.

I smiled at her. "You're very clever."

"Daddy says so too, but he says being a nice person is more important."

I actually sighed out loud. Who was this child's father? Dad of the year? He sounded like he should have an Olympic gold medal in parenting.

"He's right again!"

She suddenly jumped up. "I better go inside so I can be responsible."

"Do you live here?" I asked. I hadn't seen her before, but people were constantly moving in and out of the building.

"No, I'm just visiting." And with that she picked up her things and skipped off.

Oh to be a child again without a care and a worry in the world.

I watched her as she disappeared and was left feeling a little empty inside, thinking about my own "father of the year." Li-Hau reminded me of all the things that my sister and I hadn't had in life. She seemed to have happiness and confidence. We'd had betrayal and lies and instability. A knot started to form in my stomach as I realized how this still had such an effect on me, even today. How it stopped me from getting close to, or trusting people. If I was truly honest with myself, I didn't really have any friends, other than the guys. I went through life avoiding connections with people, rather than seeking them out and I found it very hard to trust, especially men.

* * *

Later that evening I told JJ and Bruce about my encounter with the Princess in the garden—they are always game for anyone who wears tutus. They both *ooohhhed* and *aaaahhed* at all the appropriate parts.

"Forget Ben, where can I get me a dad like hers?" JJ said.

"JJ, the guy is married with a daughter."

"How old is the kid?" he asked.

"Nearly six."

"Then he's definitely divorced. All straight people get divorced."

I laughed. "That is such a generalization."

"And all Asian men are hot," he added.

"Another generalization," I quipped.

"Besides, you can't go out with Ben now that we know who his brother is!"

Bruce rolled his eyes. "He's been talking about this all day."

I stood up and started walking towards the door.

"Hey," JJ called out, "Where you going?"

"To work!"

"Oh, good. Don't let me catch you knocking on that next-door neighbor's door." He waved a threatening finger at me.

Bruce slapped him on the arm. "Don't listen to him. Go and knock."

"Bye, guys. See you later."

"Traitor!" JJ called out after me.

18

ITALIAN STALLION . . .

~

*W*ork on a Friday night at the restaurant is always hectic. Big John's—*or BJ's for short*—is a small restaurant, and all the tables are set out around a stage that hosts drag shows and comedy nights. The stage also doubles as a dance floor for those special themed evenings when everyone is invited to bust a move, and does. The place is pretty crowded and JJ and Bruce have been trying to buy the shop next door to make the club bigger, but the nice thing about its size is that, when it's full, it buzzes. The atmosphere is alive, and there's usually something exciting going on every evening. The interior is bright pink and a massive sign hangs from the ceiling: "Eat, drink and be Mary".

The menu is another thing entirely. The food is simple but good: gourmet burgers, hotdogs and interesting pizzas, with names like Long John (a hotdog), Big beef daddy (a large hamburger) and Italian Stallion (a pizza)—JJ named the dishes, so you get the picture.

All the waiters wear shirts that say, "Is it gay in here, or is it just me?" Most of them are of the gorgeous, muscular, tanned variety—JJ does the hiring, too. And then there's me, who practically grew up here and knows just about everyone that comes in. Big John's attracts a very loyal crowd who come week after week for the shows and parties but more for the good food and friends. And because it's been around for so long, it's become a kind of sanctuary for many. A place of total acceptance, no matter who you are.

Tonight was just a normal non-themed, non-show night, but still it was packed and the usual crowd was there, except for one. Even though his back was to me, I knew it was him the second I walked up to the table with a menu under my arm—*no one else oozed such sexiness.*

"Sera, what a surprise," he said as he turned and looked at me. "I didn't know this was where you worked. And yet, here we are, face-to-face."

Shit! The awful image was back. *Stop thinking about him coming on people's faces!*

"What's wrong?" he asked.

"Nothing." I shook my head hard, hoping the image might dislodge itself.

"Looked like you were thinking about something there?"

"Nope. No thinking."

"That's not what it looked like." He smiled at me, and leaned forward. "So, what were you thinking about? Me?"

I bit my lip. This conversation was doing nothing to help remove the image. "So what will it be?" I said quickly, half-slamming the big purple menu down on his table.

He opened it and looked down momentarily before looking back up at me again with a deadly smile. "I like your shirt."

"Thanks. So what are you doing here?"

"What, a guy can't come out for dinner on a Friday night?"

"Sure he can. I was just wondering why the guy would come *here* specifically?"

He looked up and winked at me and I think I felt my ovaries tingle—*if that's even possible.* "Because I knew you were going to be here, obviously."

"I see," I said flatly.

"I hardly had a chance to see you at work today so I thought I'd come say hi." He smiled at me and I felt my insides melt. This man was trouble.

"No red lipstick?" he asked, his eyes sliding down to my lips. I felt them burn.

"I didn't think you noticed," I said.

"Oh," he leaned forward in his chair, coming closer to me, "I noticed. Believe me."

And just like that, I felt myself being sucked back under his spell. Our eyes locked, and I tried to will myself to look away, but couldn't.

"Move that sexy ass," one of the waiters, Ryan, suddenly said as he came mincing past, giving me a butt slap. This was pretty much the standard way of communicating here.

"Hey, babe," I said and shifted out of his way before we blew each other a few air kisses.

"Wow," Ben said, eying my bum. "What I wouldn't give to be a gay man right now."

"Hey, have you forgotten that we're friends?" I said before moving around the table so my posterior was pointing away from him. "Friends don't talk about each other's . . . um—"

"Sexy asses?" Ben offered.

"Exactly."

He tilted his head to the side and his eyes narrowed. "I knew I was going to regret agreeing to be friends with you." He opened his menu and looked at it for a few seconds before raising his eyes to mine again. "So . . . to be clear, just so I don't overstep the mark again, what body parts of yours am I allowed to compliment . . . as a friend?"

I laughed. I couldn't help it and he smiled back at me in response.

"Would it be okay, *for example*, if I said you had a nice smile?" he asked with a twinkle in his eye that told me he was up to trouble. "I mean, is that appropriate for one friend to say to another?"

"I think that would be okay." I was trying not to blush but I could feel the heat rising.

"Good," he said and looked back down at the menu quickly before looking up again. "So if I said you have nice eyes, would that be okay?"

"Mmmm, I think that's bordering on the wrong side of the friend zone."

"Okay. I think I'm starting to get the hang of it."

"Glad I could clarify," I said and bit the end of my pen because I wasn't quite sure what to do with my mouth.

"Hang on . . ." he said and sat up straight. "Just so I understand this one hundred percent." His eyes scanned me up and down. "If I had to say, *for example again*, that you are the sexiest woman I've ever seen, would that *not* be allowed?"

At the sound of those words my body stiffened instantly and I bit the pen a little too hard. "No. That would not be appropriate at all."

He nodded, looking contemplative. "Okay, so I shouldn't say something like, how good you look naked and on top of me, *for example*."

"Oh my God!" I was stunned. "I can't believe you just said that."

"I didn't. I only asked if it was okay to say something like that."

"No, it is not okay to say that! At all. At all." I felt flustered.

He looked at me with those large chocolate-brown eyes. "Great! Then I won't say how perfect you look when you're naked and on top of me."

But it was too late. He'd said it again and all I could think about was climbing right back onto his lap. I shuffled from side to side and then away from him. "Did you come here to eat or to discuss the parameters of our friendship?"

He was looking way too pleased with himself right now, but he finally looked down at the menu on his table. "What do you recommend, Sera?"

"I recommend you stop saying my name so often and order something."

"Whoa," he said and slapped the menu down on the table. "Feisty."

"Well, I do have other customers," I said, flashing him a stern look. "As difficult as that might be to accept, my world doesn't revolve around you."

"Fine. Bring me whatever you want."

"Fine." I took the menu. "And would you like anything to drink with that?"

"Sparkling water."

"Sparkling water? Not Tequila? Not beer—"

"I'm not drinking tonight," he said, leaning back in his chair and crossing his legs. He wasn't wearing a suit, but he still looked way too formal in his black jeans and long-sleeved black and white checked shirt.

"I'll be right back."

"Hurry," I heard him say as I walked away.

I had about three other tables to deal with, but the place was laid out so that, everywhere I went, I could see Ben. Ben from behind, Ben from the side, Ben from the other side. His eyes followed me from table to table, even when I walked behind him he would swivel his head around to look at me. His stare was intense and I was acutely aware of the way it made me feel, how it made me want to peel my clothes off and throw myself at him. I wasn't sure how it was actually possible, but tonight he looked hotter than I'd ever seen him. Maybe it was because he'd reminded me that he'd seen me naked. I was feeling both excitement and utter dread at the prospect of going over to his table again.

"Here you go." I put the burger down. "A Big Johnson with everything."

"A Big Johnson?" He looked amused. "I must bring my brother here."

"Mmm." I nodded, although I knew that would probably be a terrible idea.

"Enjoy your meal," I said and started walking away, but as I did I felt a hand clamp around my wrist. I turned. Ben was leaning all the way out of his chair now clutching my wrist tightly.

"Go out with me?" He looked at me with such intensity that my face flushed instantly.

"Are you being serious?"

"Yes."

"So why am I not sure whether to believe you, then?"

"I told you, I don't say things I don't mean." He pulled me closer, let go of my wrist, and brought his hands up to straighten my shirt which had bunched up a bit at my jeans—*inappropriate*. He slowly straightened it and pulled it back down, his hands dangerously close to an area that should have been totally off-limits. I stepped back, but he hooked his finger in my belt loop.

"One date."

He kept his finger hooked in my belt loop and we looked at each other. But the more he looked, the more the sexual tension that I feared threatened to overwhelm me built up.

"I'll think about it," I said quickly, but more so he would leave me alone and I could free myself from his sexual clutches.

He looked genuinely taken aback, as if he hadn't been expecting that answer at all. "Really? You'll think about it?"

"Maybe. I'll maybe think about it," I quickly corrected.

He smiled that smile—*it should be illegal*.

"You'll think about it," he repeated, looking very pleased with himself and then bit into his burger.

I walked away from him feeling a whole bunch of feelings I hadn't felt in ages.

19

X, Y, Z . . .

~

*B*y the time I left work that night, it was well after midnight and I was exhausted. My neck and shoulders were sore and my feet probably smelt as bad as they felt. But I'd made enough money to buy the textbooks my sister needed, so that made it all worth it.

I was going to go with my sister personally the next day to buy them and, while I was there, try and talk some sense into my mother—*not that she could be reasoned with*. My dad was all my mother knew, and she claimed, even after everything he'd put her through, that she still loved him. I'd read enough books on the subject to know that was just her codependence talking. What my mother needed to do was go to counseling, find the inner strength to kick him out once and for all, and never allow him back into her life.

My dad was another story. A few years back I'd tried to get him to go to a Gamblers Anonymous meeting, but he'd refused. He didn't see it as a problem. He said the problem was not his gambling; the problem was his "unlucky streak." But he was always on an unlucky streak.

My dad had gotten fired shortly after we'd been evicted. He'd worked in the City Council accounts department. "Suspected fraud," they'd said. That little tit-bit even managed to make the local papers, so, not only did we have nothing, but everyone knew about it too. It's amazing how people look at you differently when they learn your father is a criminal. It's amazing how friends suddenly disappear. And it's amazing how quickly you get taunted and teased in the schoolyard by all the cool girls who start looking at you as if you're nothing.

But my mother stuck by him, and, with the little savings she had, she threw all of it into lawyers for my dad when it was blatantly obvious to everyone he was guilty. At the time I hoped he would go to jail, so that we could get on with our lives without him, but he got off on some kind of technicality that I'm yet to understand.

I'd also naively hoped that my mother would finally leave him, especially when the court case started and she'd caught him gambling again and sleeping with another hooker. But she hadn't. When we were kicked out of our house, the few relatives we did have offered us a place to stay. On one condition, though: that my father didn't stay with us—he'd stolen things and "borrowed" money from just about everyone we knew. But she'd turned down all the offers because she wanted to "stick by her man." That's how we'd landed in that trailer park.

A part of me hated my mother for that, even though JJ kept reminding me that she was just as sick as him, but I still couldn't help it. If I had a child, they would come first. I wouldn't choose some drunken, stealing, lying, cheating, gambling addict, criminal over the safety and welfare of my own children. My children would always come first. I bet Li-Hau's father put her first, and I bet that was the reason she was such a smart, savvy little girl without a care in the world. I bet she wouldn't have to grow up ashamed and embarrassed by her family—let down by the parents who were supposed to protect her from hurt.

When I arrived home, I immediately saw an envelope with my name on it stuck to my front door. I smiled because I knew exactly who it was from. Ben had a very distinctive handwriting: it was big, bold and curly. I looked in the direction of his door. The light outside was off and I wondered if he was still awake. If the rumors were true, maybe he didn't sleep. I opened the envelope and a strange card fell out.

"Tap Code," it read. I glanced over the chart of numbers and letters quickly.

What the hell was that? I was still trying to figure out what it meant when I got to my bedroom and turned on the shower. All I wanted to do was climb into bed and sleep, but, when I did, I heard a tap on the wall.

I jumped, suddenly realizing what "Tap Code" meant. I smiled to myself—*Ben, Ben, Ben*—he had to be the most unique person I'd ever met. I studied the card and counted the taps.

"Hi," he had tapped.

"Hi," I tapped back. It was a slow, laborious process.

"How U?" I heard the tap come back.

"Tired," I responded.

There was a pause before I heard the next one.

"Sweet dreams, beautiful."

I swooned, a proper melting swoon that made all my limbs and face feel like jelly.

"X," he tapped again. The swooning increased to critical levels. I was contemplating sending him an X back, but it seemed like a big deal. So I didn't.

"Y." I tapped.

There was a pause, and I knew Ben well enough by then to know he was probably amused by this.

"Z," he tapped back, before the tapping went silent.

I stared at the dark ceiling with a smile plastered across my face. He was good at this. He was a pro-flirter. If flirting and wooing were an Olympic sport, he would win the gold. I just hoped he was being serious; that this wasn't some kind of sport for him—*because I was seriously starting to feel a little giddy and intoxicated by it all.*

20

SNOW WHITE . . .

I woke up early the next day and contemplated tapping on the wall again, but thought better of it. At nine on a Saturday morning, most normal people were still asleep. So I took my coffee, bundled myself up in a knitted hat and scarf and went to the tree. I was secretly hoping to bump into Li-Hau again, and I wasn't disappointed. She was picking flowers this time and she turned and flashed me a big grin. She wasn't alone this time, though.

"Hi," I said as I moved to sit on the bench. I turned to the woman that was with her and greeted her, but Li-Hau jumped in.

"This is my nanny Lerato, her name means love."

"Hi, Lerato," I said.

"And you're the Snow White I've heard about?" Lerato asked with a smile on her face.

"I believe so."

"Lerato came to help me cut flowers, my dad says that an adult should always help you with scissors and that you should never run with them."

Dad of the year strikes again. She was dressed head to toe in pink. A bright pink tracksuit, pink Adidas sneakers and a large pink scarf. She also had her tutu over her pants.

"I like your outfit." *JJ would kill for a tracksuit like that.*

"Here," she said as she stepped forward to give me a white daisy. I felt a tiny lump develop in my throat. This little girl had such an effect on me.

"Thanks, it's beautiful."

"My dad says I'm not allowed to cut too many flowers because I must be environmental to the earth."

And at that, I actually burst out laughing. Who was this man? Did he also rescue stray puppies in his spare time? Feed the homeless, read to the blind?

"Your dad's right!"

"I know. He's always right," she said holding up a mixture of white and yellow daisies in her hand.

"You should come to my birthday party," she said.

"Oh, that's very sweet of you. But I could only come if your mom and dad invited me."

"Okay. I will give you an official invitation then." She flashed me another grin. "I need to put these in water," she said again before skipping off. I smiled and looked up at Lerato.

"Bundle of energy!" she said with a smile.

"I can see,"—*time for some intelligence gathering*—"So are you just visiting?" I asked.

She nodded. "We live in Rosebank."

"Okay." I said, slightly disappointed that I wouldn't be bumping into hot Super-Dad. She was obviously visiting relatives, or family friends.

Lerato got up and followed after Li-Hau.

"See you around," I said and waved at them as they went.

I sat sipping my coffee and looking at the flowers. Strange, I'd never noticed them before. Kids always have that effect on you. They make you see the world slightly differently. I finished my coffee and went over and picked an orange one.

Of course when I went upstairs I had to regale JJ with the latest pink princess story.

"We need to find out more about this father," JJ said. "I think I'm in love."

"Stop it. You're incorrigible," Bruce snapped and shot him a look.

I laughed. "I must say I'm curious myself. If I get an invite to her party, I'll definitely go, even if it's just to lay eyes on this legend. I wonder what her mom is like? She hardly mentions her."

"Maybe she's just a daddy's girl. Like me," JJ cooed.

It was true, JJ was a full-blown "daddy's girl." His father was the one who'd encouraged him to come leaping out of the closet. Apparently he'd known his son was gay since the age of twelve. His father, at the age of sixty-seven, had even come to Gay Pride last year wearing a shirt that said, "Gay sons are fun!" It had garnered so much attention that a photographer had taken a photo of them that ended up in the *Gay Times*. The article was framed and hanging on the wall. Bruce's deeply religious dad had not been so accepting though, and they barely spoke. *Parents! They really have the power to shape you. Make you, or break you.*

21

LOVE TO HATE IT . . .

I was grateful my day had started with Li-Hau and the guys because it was the crappiest Saturday I'd had in a while. My mother was not to be reasoned with, at all. Dad had promised not to gamble again and—*surprise fucking surprise*—she was giving him the benefit of the doubt.

Fortunately I got to spend some time with my sister.

Katie had one year left at school before she went off to University—Medical School being the goal. After shopping for her books, we stopped to grab a cup of coffee.

"So, I printed out the bursary forms for Med school," she said, sliding them across the table. "I want to apply as soon as possible. They only award fifty scholarships a year. Competition is tough."

I read over the papers knowing that if anyone was going to get her through Med School, that responsibility lay solely on my shoulders. The papers indicated that they didn't pay the full amount. They contributed one third of the fee, meaning you had to fork out the other two thirds. Not to mention all the additional costs too. I felt a stab of panic in my chest, but tried hard not to show it. Katie already felt awful enough about taking money from me.

"Obviously I'll get a job too," she offered.

"No. You must focus on your studies. Med school will be too hectic for you to work on the side. Don't worry, I'll figure something out."

I had no idea how the hell that was going to happen. To rustle up that kind of money was going to be hard—*near impossible*. There was only so much work I could do at the restaurant. When the reality of this set in, it made me realize just how dangerous something like dating the boss could be. *What was the thing they always say about work relationships?*

I just wasn't sure I could take that risk, now that I realized just how insane my responsibilities were going to become moving forward. The only way I would be able to pay for my sister is if I was offered a permanent job at the agency and my salary increased and I worked full time at the restaurant. I had been hoping to move out of JJ and Bruce's at some stage. I couldn't live there forever.

But Ben was going to be the one deciding who got the job, and the idea of being promoted by him . . . *well*, something about that felt strange. And if Becks found out we'd been together, or worse, were dating, I'm sure she'd have grounds for some kind of sexual discrimination in the workplace case. Not to mention the fact that if everyone found out about us, they'd forever be looking at me wondering why I got the job. Was it because I deserved it, or was it because I'd slept with the boss? Maybe Ben wouldn't hire me at all, for fear that it would look bad if anyone found out? *Shit!*

I took a deep breath. The anxiety crushing down on my chest right now was so intense and I felt like I was about to crumble under it. "Let me take these papers home and read over them, okay?" I took the forms and slipped them into my bag, and it felt instantly heavier.

"Are you sure you don't want me to get a job?" Katie asked.

"Katie, listen, the best thing you can do is get the best marks possible, that's what's going to get you this bursary. Just focus on your studies and let me take care of the rest."

My sister hugged me. It was little things like this that kept me going.

* * *

The financial forms weighed heavily in my bag and on my mind, along with the constant conflicting thoughts about Ben, as I ran around the restaurant feeling more exhausted than I'd felt in a while. I also noticed the extra hundred bucks that "*someone*" had slipped into my wallet that morning. Under normal circumstances I would have marched the money back into the house and back into the wallet from whence it came, but circumstances were not normal right now and I accepted it graciously.

By the end of my shift I had worn myself out with vacillating thoughts about Ben, and because JJ had told ALL the regular patrons about him and his relentless asking me out, every table had a suggestion.

"*Babe, you have to go for it.*"

"*If you don't go out with him I will.*"

"*Don't be a Nancy and just say yes.*"

I walked away shaking my head. It was all just too much for

one person to deal with. Just as I was wrapping up and feeling totally grateful that I was leaving the peanut gallery behind, my phone vibrated in my pocket . . .

Unknown number: How's the thinking going?

Sera: Ben?

Unknown number: WHO ELSE ARE U THINKING OF GOING OUT WITH?!?

I smiled to myself. This was too fun and suddenly all those reasons I had earlier for not going out with Ben, seemed to melt away.

Sera: Actually, there are several other prospects I am currently considering.

Unknown number: WHO?

I paused for a while thinking about a clever retort, but before I could . . .

Unknown number: They can't be as terribly good-looking and funny and charming as me.

Sera: Definitely not as arrogant.

Unknown number: You secretly love it.

Sera: Nope. Hate it.

Unknown Number: Please . . . You love to hate it.

My face broke out into a smile . . . *what did that even mean?*

Sera: So how did you get my number you sick psycho stalker.

Unknown number: One of the many perks of being the boss man and having access to employee's private files.

Sera: And how many other employees are you sexually harassing?

Unknown number: Just you.

God, I wanted to believe that so badly. But at the same time I remembered the conclusions that I'd come up with earlier today. Dating the boss was a very bad idea, leading to potential financial ruin and no Med school for my sister. I took a deep breath, shook my head and tried to snap myself out it.

Sera: I don't know, Ben. I'm not sure it's a good idea.

Unknown number: Wrong answer, Sera.

Sera: Wow. Bossy!

Unknown number: Sera, you have no idea how bossy I can be . . .

Sera: Maybe I'm not as easily pushed around as all the other girls.

Unknown number: I know. And that's why I'm in love with you.

Sera: You shouldn't joke about stuff like that.

Unknown number: Who said I'm joking?

Sera: You're not in love with me. You hardly know me.

Unknown number: I know everything I need to know about you.

Sera: Like what?

There was a pause, a long one, as I watched my phone and saw that he was typing. The tension grew and grew as the typing seemed to go on forever. Finally, when I was just about to explode like a champagne cork out of a bottle, the message came through . . .

Unknown number: I know what it feels like to be inside you. I know what it feels like to hold you. I know what it feels like to eat breakfast with you. What it feels like to stare at you from my desk. I know what it feels like knowing that you're sleeping so close to me.

Holy Shit! I felt like I had just had the wind knocked out of me. I gasped, trying to get air into my lungs. That might actually have just been the most inappropriate, but simultaneously sexiest, thing anyone had ever said about me.

Unknown number: Just give me one date, Sera.

Sera: One?

Unknown number: One is all I need.

I sighed. Every time I thought I had my mind vaguely made up about him, he seemed to change it with his magical charms.

Sera: I'll think about it.

Unknown number: That's still the wrong answer, Sera.

Sera: Sorry. That's the only answer I can give you right now. Besides, give me one good reason why I should go out with you?

There was another long pause as I watched him typing, and then stopping. Typing, stopping. Finally the message came through.

Unknown number: Okay. Enjoy the rest of your night.

I looked at my phone and blinked. That wasn't the response I'd been expecting and I wondered what reasons he'd typed, and then deleted.

22

THE GLOW OF LUSTY-NESS

⌒

I was in full, mundane Sunday morning swing when I passed Ben in the underground parking garage. *Typical!* I was dressed in my Sunday worst, hair piled up under an old cap that read, "Cobra Exhaust pipes," some ridiculous thing our clients had sent us all. They thought it was a stroke of creative genius, though, the way the picture of the exhaust pipe reared up and morphed into a snake. I was carrying a basket of my dirty laundry, undergarments included, and in the other hand I had a black bag full of bottles for recycling.

"Well, hello there." His voice had this ability to stop my world. It was utter madness, but every time I heard it, I felt transported out of myself, de-atomized, scrambled and then reassembled like a sci-fi transporter beam. I turned and found him standing only a few feet away from me, *how had he managed to get so close to me?*

He, on the other hand, was *not* dressed in his Sunday worst. He was sporting some full dapper-suited look that was enough to turn ordinary woman into blithering idiots.

"Ben!" I said.

"Sera. Sera De La Haye." He looked me up and down and smiled and I suddenly became very aware of what I was wearing.

"Laundry Sunday," I said defensively, tugging on my oversized shirt.

"It's a good look for you." He took a step closer, reached out and stuck a finger through the hole in my shirt. (The classy one that I'd gotten free with that box of washing detergent about ten years ago.) His finger grazed my stomach and my skin pebbled in response to it.

"They're not pink, though, but they're just as sexy." His voice dripped with sex and filth and danger.

"Huh?" I followed his eyes down to where they were currently fixated and saw the white cotton panties on top of the laundry pile. I quickly shoved them into my pocket, which only caused his smile to grow.

"You're such a pervert," I said, trying to avert my eyes from that deadly, quicksand smile that you could get stuck in if you didn't have your wits about you.

"So, have you done much thinking overnight?"

I tried to stop my smile, "Contrary to what you might believe, I don't spend all my spare time thinking about you, Ben."

"Really?" he asked. "That little smile on our face seems to suggest otherwise."

"Arrogant!"

"Enamored!"

"Overdressed."

"I could say the same for you." The look in his eyes changed as I felt my entire body shiver under the intense stare of him trying to undress me.

"Like I said, pervert!"

"Perhaps there's more to me than meets the eye. Something you might discover when you go on your first date with me."

"Presumptuous."

"You know, it would be great if we had a conversation that didn't only consist of three-syllable words. But unfortunately not today, I have to go to work."

"On a Sunday?" I asked.

"This calendar thing is becoming a bit of an issue."

"Sorry to hear that."

"We need to present the client with our big, awesome idea soon and we don't have one. And the shoot is scheduled for early next week."

"Not a lot of time."

"There never is in this industry. But I guess that's what keeps it exciting . . . I like challenges." His eyes flicked up and down my body one more time and I tried to ignore their loaded look.

"Why don't you just come up with the idea and save the day? Legend has it that you're supposed to be this creative genius."

"It's not really my job to come up with all the ideas all the time. It's my job to coach others and mentor them to get the best ideas out of them and then refine them. Your last Creative Director didn't really do a good job at that and now my creatives can't seem to come up with any original ideas worth working with. They have potential, but they haven't been challenged or pushed . . ." He paused and ran his hand through his hair. "Sorry, I shouldn't really be speaking to you about stuff like that. It's not appropriate."

"I won't tell anyone you said that."

"I know." He smiled up at me. "And like I said, the calendar shoot is the only piece of work the client actually cares about all year. And he wants to hire this Italian photographer too who is apparently the 'best,'" he gestured air commas, "which just means some very overpaid egotistical 'artist' who thinks the sun shines out of his arse and who thinks he's the most important thing since Picasso."

I laughed out loud at that trying to imagine Ben working with someone who possibly had a bigger ego than he did.

"I honestly think it has nothing to do with the calendar at all, I just think the client likes jetting off to exotic locations and watching a bunch of scantily clad models drape themselves all over his sports cars."

"Mmmm," I mumbled, "sounds like something every guy wants."

Ben took a dangerous step closer. "Some guys prefer their women inside their cars, rather than outside."

"Stop!" I pointed a finger at him. "Why do you do that?" I stepped back. "Why is everything that comes out of your mouth so filthy?"

Ben threw his head back and laughed. "Admit it, you love it."

"I don't!" I retorted.

He shook his head looking amused before walking away to his car. "Yes, you do. And that's why you're falling hopelessly in love with me," he shouted over his shoulder before climbing into his car and driving away.

My mouth fell open in shock and then I quickly yelled after him. "I am not! I am so not! You're wrong!"

"Whatever, Sera." He gave me a wave in the rear view mirror before driving out the garage and out of sight.

* * *

Later that day the second half of the Sunday routine began. Sunday afternoon is the only time that the restaurant is closed and we all go there to do a stocktake, and sometimes JJ likes to practice his new routines in peace. When I arrived they were already there mincing around the place. I stopped and watched them for a while, they looked like they were having a playful debate about where to put the new pot plant. I continued to watch them for a while longer, feeling amused, before stepping in and making the critical decorative decision myself.

"So you have a bit of a smile on your face," Bruce finally said after we'd maneuvered the surprisingly heavy plant into the chosen position.

"It's more than a smile," JJ remarked, "it's the glow of lusty-ness."

"Oh please," I tried to brush it off but I knew that I couldn't fool these two.

"He's gotten under your skin," Bruce said.

JJ tisked loudly. "Under your skin? He's gotten under you."

"So what are you going to do about it?" Bruce asked, opening a bottle of wine and pouring three glasses. Another ritual of ours, Sunday stocktaking and drinking.

JJ took a sip of the wine and then let out a loud breath, as if he was about to announce something. "I've thought about it," he said, "and if you really want to go out with him, I'll forgive your obvious betrayal. Fraternizing with the enemy and all that."

I laughed. "Gee, thanks. So generous of you. But no need to worry, I won't be going out with him."

"You're not even going to entertain the idea of going on a date with him?" Bruce asked.

I shrugged. "I told him I'd think about it."

"Okay, so who's going to film me?" JJ suddenly asked, jumping onto the stage. "It's *Priscilla, Queen of the Desert* night next week and I have to practice my routine."

Bruce took out his phone and went straight to the camera. JJ often filmed his routines so he could watch them later, often inflicting them on us too. "I live to serve you, dear," Bruce said with a smile and pressed record. JJ immediately started belting out the famous Gloria Gaynor song. He followed the first chorus with a very dramatic spin around the stage and an attempt at what I presume was meant to be a pirouette.

I laughed and shook my head. "Like I said, total gay cliché," I teased.

"Oh please, *little miss intern doing her hot boss*."

I immediately cringed at the sound of that, but nodded. "I guess so," I said softly. "Oh God. I'm such a fucking cliché. All I need now is to find out he's some kind of Persian Prince and fall pregnant with his illegitimate baby and then fall in love and get married and become the princess of some far off country called Genovia."

Bruce and JJ laughed out loud. "Have you been reading JJ's romance novels?" Bruce teased.

"What can I say, they're my guilty pleasure," JJ said with a naughty smile.

I shook my head. "No. But every now and then I read the

descriptions on the back. Oh, and P.S., just how many virgin brides are there out there in the world these days?"

"Enough for all those sexy Arab sheiks to claim them as their desert concubines," JJ quipped. We all laughed but JJ quickly stopped us by belting the song out again as loudly as he could. I sat and watched for a while, but half way through the song I got up and gave them all a wave.

"Hey. Where you going?" JJ stopped singing and yelled.

"Home."

"Liar," JJ shouted even louder as I walked to the door, "you're going home to have wild sex with your hot neighbor."

"That's right. And I'm ovulating too so I'll be falling pregnant with his illegitimate baby," I laughed as I exited.

23

INEXPLICABLE ANTICIPATION

⌒

I was almost home when the car suddenly made a loud, ghastly sound. It started swiveling and skidding uncontrollably across the road. I quickly slammed on the brakes in absolute terror and it finally came to a grinding halt.

"Shit!" My heart thumped in my chest and I cursed loudly. I looked around. At least the place I had stopped was illuminated, the road wasn't completely dark, dingy and dangerous. I opened the door tentatively and climbed out.

I immediately assumed it would be some kind of major engine meltdown, complete with flames and dramatic smoke billowing out of the bonnet, but that quickly changed when I saw the state of the front tyre. It was completely flat, and there, sticking out of it, as if it was mocking me, a giant nail.

"Shit!" I cursed again, what were the chances? I stood up and tried to figure out my next move. I didn't have the kind of fancy insurance that you could call when you broke down and they swooped in to rescue you. *Or did I need rescuing at all . . .*

Perhaps the one and only thing my father had given me, was the ability to change a tyre. And only because it had been a necessity. He'd been too drunk to change the tyre himself so had slouched on the side of the road barking commands at me.

I walked to the back of the car and opened the trunk. I had one of those stupid thin tyres that looked like a biscuit. I took it out, as well as all the tools. It was freezing outside and I momentarily thought of phoning the guys for help, but realized very quickly that they probably knew less about changing tyres than I did. The idea of phoning Ben flashed through my mind for a second, but I quickly pushed it out.

* * *

I laid the tyre on the ground next to my car and then tried to locate the jack. But it was nowhere to be found. By this stage my fingers and nose felt like they were about to fall off. And then, just to add insult to injury, a car sped by and through a massive puddle of water and . . .

My face and upper body were covered in freezing cold, filthy puddle water. I wiped my face, trying not to think about what else could be in that water, like rat droppings and drowned earthworm carcasses that had been marinating for days.

I shivered and my teeth began chattering together as the water seeped through my top and coated my skin. It was official, I needed help. I pulled my phone out, dialed JJ and Bruce's numbers, but both just rang. They probably couldn't hear their phones over all the singing, so I left a message. I looked down at my phone, realizing that I didn't really have a choice, unless I wanted to freeze to death on the side of the road, or worse, be whisked away by highway bandits.

I went to my messages, and looked at Ben's number for a few moments, before summoning up the courage to dial it. This was the first time we'd talked on the phone, and despite the cold, my heart started pounding with some kind of weird inexplicable anticipation. I didn't have to wait long, two rings was all it took before he answered.

"Sera!" He sounded so pleased with himself.

"Hey, what are you doing right now?" I asked. "Like, this very second?"

His voice took on a predictable naughty tone. "Whatever you want me to be doing?"

"Okay. And do you have a jack?" I asked, through chattering teeth.

I heard a chuckle on the phone. "Is that what you're calling it these days?"

I let out a frustrated sigh. This was definitely not the time for not-so-subtle sexual innuendos. "Ben, what I need is a *car* jack. And what I really need is for you to please come to the off-ramp of the M1 North and help me change my car tyre, please."

"Shit! Have you broken down?" He sounded worried.

"Yup."

"That's not safe. I'll be there in five minutes. Climb into your car and lock the doors."

"Okay, I will. Uh . . . thanks for doing this." I started climbing back into my car and locked my doors.

"I'd do anything for you, Sera. In case you hadn't noticed by now." He hung up and suddenly I didn't feel as cold, thanks to all the warm flutterings happening inside my body.

It was more like three minutes when I caught sight of the black car tearing around the bend. The car almost skidded to a stop and then he jumped out wearing a full black suit. I almost laughed at the James Bond-ness of this moment.

"Are you okay?" he asked, as I opened my car door and stepped out.

I nodded. "Fine."

He eyed me. "You don't look very fine, your lips are blue. Are you cold?" He reached down and placed his hands on my shoulders. "Shit. You're wet."

"Compliments of a passing car."

"Here." He whisked his jacket off in one very heroic-ish move and passed it to me. "You should probably take off your top and put this on."

"Off?" I looked at him, he wasn't being flirty and playful this time, in fact, he sounded serious.

"Well, you can't keep those wet clothes on in this weather. Take your top off, put this on and sit in the car next to the heater."

"My heater doesn't really work."

"Here," he pulled his car keys out of his pocket and handed them to me, "I'll sort the wheel out, you get warm."

"Okay." I nodded. I was really grateful for his suggestion, because by this stage, I was freezing. I climbed into his car, pressed the fancy start button and turned the heater on full blast. His windows were tinted, something I clearly remembered from the other night, but still I tried to duck down as low as I could when taking off my top. My bra was soaked too, and I unclipped it and slid it off. I wrapped the huge jacket around me and then sat as close to the heater as possible.

The heat immediately started doing the trick, and when I was a little less frozen, I suddenly became aware of the smell. His scent clung to the jacket like a fine mist, and the smell was intoxicating. I looked out the window; Ben had already lifted the car up with the jack and was now putting on the tyre and screwing it in place. Handy both *in* and *out* of the car, I thought involuntarily biting down on my lip as I watched him bending over.

My mind went one way, *fast*. To the deep, dark depths of the filthy gutter. Watching him wielding a spanner was having more of an effect on me than I ever would have imagined—*who knew I loved a man with tools?* Ben seemed completely unaware that I was currently undressing him with my eyes and imagining him shirtless and sanding a floor, or some such thing that required large motorized tools with decidedly phallic-looking qualities.

God, I was terrible. I mentally scolded myself for these seriously wanton thoughts. But I just couldn't help myself when I was around him.

He finally finished putting on the new tyre and then walked back over to the car, climbing in to the passenger seat and started warming his hands by the heating vent.

"It's cold." He rubbed his hands together vigorously.

"Yes, sorry to drag you out in this weather." I suddenly felt bad for asking him to come and rescue me, especially considering he'd been working today and was probably desperate to relax.

But he shook his head and smiled at me. "It's my pleasure."

"When you break down, I promise to come and rescue you," I offered.

His eyes lit up slightly. "Deal. I look forward to being rescued by you then."

"Well, don't go and breakdown on purpose now." I had sudden images of him sabotaging his car just to drag me out at some ungodly hour.

He laughed, "I was actually just wondering if that was possible."

"Ben!" I shook my head and gave his arm a playful slap, but when I did, my hand decided *not* to come away from it and landed up staying there. I looked at it, willing it to behave itself, but it didn't. It gripped his arm a little tighter, and then, to my horror, it started rubbing it. Suddenly, the air and the mood in the car changed. *Shifted*.

It was no longer cold. We were no longer parked on the side of the road, the back seat suddenly looked very inviting and all those silly reasons about why I *shouldn't* let anything happen with this man melted away into oblivion. My hand started traveling up his arm, to his shoulder and then up to his neck. He inhaled sharply and his whole body stiffened when my finger traced the lines of the tattoo that came out from under his collar and ran up his neck, to the back of his ear.

I looked up at him, he was looking down at me with dark, almost black eyes, and there was definitely no hiding what he wanted. The thought made me feel powerful, stirring that inner porn star of mine that had come out a few nights ago.

Don't give in . . . stay strong . . . resist him!

The tiny voices whispered somewhere in the back of my mind,

but the louder voices that were shouting the complete opposite, were inconveniently prevailing. That is, until the sound of my phone ringing squashed them all.

"Shit!" I said, snapping out of the spell I'd just been under. I reached for my phone, JJ's number was flashing across my screen. He was probably worried after my message. And I was right. After assuring him repeatedly that I had not been assaulted, kidnapped or had befallen some terrible roadside fate, I hung up.

The moment between Ben and I had been broken, and suddenly all those rational voices were whispering a little louder again.

"It's not really safe on the side of the road. We should probably get back," I said, and started climbing out the car.

Ben smiled at me, I could see he was disappointed, but trying to hide it. "Cool, I'll follow you home," he said, reaching over to close the door. I was just about to walk back to my car when he called out.

"Sera, I think you're forgetting something . . . *again*."

I turned to find Ben holding my shirt and my bra in his hand. "Unless you're doing it on purpose now?" His devil smile was back.

"I am not!" I quickly said and involuntarily grabbed the jacket I was wearing and pulled it tighter across my chest, suddenly very aware that I was completely naked under it. And clearly so was he, his eyes drifted down to the place that my hands were now clutching and I gripped the material even tighter.

He smiled at me and then raised an eyebrow, "God, you're fucking gorgeous, Sera."

24

A VERY OVERACTIVE
IMAGINATION . . .

*W*e both pulled into the underground parking at the same time. I intended to immediately go upstairs, take a shower and get out of Ben's jacket. I felt like I needed to get away from him. He thought I was gorgeous, and I no longer felt like I was able to resist him, even though I knew I should. And to top all the irresistible sexiness off, he was also genuinely thoughtful and had swooped in like a knight in shining armor to save me from the side of the road. This strange mix of bad boy and nice guy was really doing my brain in, and I needed to put some space between us. But it seemed that the universe had other plans for us. Because as soon as I climbed out of my car, something was thrust into my hands.

"Thank you. Please take these, since you're on your way there too. Hurry, hurry, we're running late." Suddenly I was holding a large box of biscuits. It took me a few seconds to realize what was going on. The caretaker, Raymond, had pulled up next to me and was hurriedly taking bags out of his car.

"Um, I'm not really sure what you want me to do with these?"

I looked over at the strange man. He always wore a polyester tracksuit, no matter what the weather was. He never wore closed shoes either, instead he always wore brown leather sandals, his long grey toenails always on display. He had a full mop of white hair that never looked brushed, a massive Magnum P.I. moustache and always wore a gold chain around his neck. He was at least eighty years old, and according to the stories, had lived in this building his entire life, since the day he was born.

"Body corporate meeting," he suddenly declared loudly and started marching across the parking lot.

Shit. He was right. We all met on the last Sunday of the month, every three months, and that was tonight. I rolled my eyes. As part of my living arrangement with JJ and Bruce, I was the one who went to the usually torturous meetings. The tenants didn't need to go and seldom did, but JJ, being naturally suspicious of people, "*wanted to keep an eye on things.*"

"Okay. Coming," I said begrudgingly, feeling that I would rather be stuck on the side of the road right now, still drenched in cold, earthworm water.

I looked over at Ben who had just climbed out of his car. "I have to go to a body corporate meeting now, so see you . . . ?" I left the question open-ended.

"I'll come with." He walked over to me and took the box of biscuits from my hands.

"You really, *really* don't have to." I shot him a look in which I was trying to convey the following sentiment; *worst, most tedious, deathly boring meetings that this world has ever known.*

But Ben just shrugged, "After you." He gestured for me to continue walking.

Raymond's flat was on the bottom floor, at the end of a very long corridor. The last few meters were always a little tricky to navigate, what with the massive collection of pot plants, garden gnomes and the two big, blue porcelain dogs flanking the doorway.

"Interesting," I heard Ben mumble from behind me.

"Just wait until you get inside," I whispered back to him, stepping into the house. I'd seen the interior many times before, but I always loved watching people's reactions to it when they were seeing it for the first time. Ben stood there with his jaw open.

"It's very . . ." he muttered under his breath, not finishing the thought, which many people did.

"I know," I said. His home was plucked straight from one of those TV episodes about hoarders. There was barely anywhere to stand, let alone sit. Magazines, records and old shoeboxes filled most of the floor and were built into tall towers that looked as if they could fall over at any moment. Then there were the ornaments; every conceivable place was filled with at least six.

"Take a seat," Raymond barked at Ben and I and we both obeyed. The dining room looked like the only room in the house that wasn't full, probably because of these meetings. I sat down in one of the chairs, as Ben sat opposite me, still looking around. Soon some of the regular meeting-goers arrived. Raymond always squeezed twenty-five chairs into his small dining room, but inevitably only six people came. Tonight, thanks to Ben, there were seven.

I was very used to these meetings. Raymond was going to go over all the relevant topics; building insurance, levies, security, apartment rules and regulations and then finally, after what usually amounted to at least an hour, he opened the floor to any concerns and questions. I usually spaced out within the first five minutes, even the sight of Ben across the table from me wasn't enough to keep me present. I had almost completely zoned out, when my phone beeped. Everyone turned and looked at me.

"Sorry." I pulled it out of my pocket and looked down at the screen.

Ben: It's very hard to concentrate knowing that you're not wearing a bra under that jacket of mine.

I snapped my head up and looked over at Ben, he was smiling from ear to ear, and I felt my cheeks flush. I looked back down to the phone and started typing.

Sera: Pervert!

I pressed send and forced myself not to look in his direction, but out of the corner of my eye, I could see him typing on his phone. I quickly put my phone onto silent and waited.

Ben: Look who's talking . . . you were trying to feel me up in the car earlier!

"What?" I only realized I'd said it out loud after a few seconds, when Raymond stopped talking and everyone in the room looked at me again. "Sorry, nothing." I gave them all a smile and went straight back down to my phone.

Sera: I did NO such thing. You're imagining things.

Ben: Nope. I definitely didn't imagine your hand on my arm and your fingers running their way up and down my neck.

I read the message and looked up at him, attempting my best incredulous look, but no doubt failing at it.

Ben: Were you going to kiss me, Sera?

Sera: No!

Ben: Are you sure? Because it kind of looked like you were about to before the phone rang?

My stomach knotted with excitement and I tried to stop the smile that was clearly giving my feelings away. *Why did he always have the ability to drag me into these moments, despite my resolve not to get swept away?* I looked around, no one had noticed what we were doing, and this only added to my now growing excitement.

Sera: Ben, you have a very overactive imagination.

Ben: Oh yes I do. ;) Would you like to know what I'm imagining . . . right now?

Sera: No.

I quickly replied and then looked back up at him. His smile had changed. From flirtatious and playful, to that filthy, dangerous one that made you lose your wits. I crossed my legs tightly and clutched the jacket, in case both suddenly fell open.

Ben: Liar. Of course you do.

I shook my head at him and folded my arms.

Ben: Stop pretending, you're dying to know . . .

The butterflies in my stomach started beating their wings and my heart quickened. I knew that if I continued this conversation, there was a very strong possibility that it might lead to more clothes coming off tonight.

Sera: Okay, fine. Tell me then.

I pressed send and braced myself for what was coming next. No doubt it would be a barrage of wildly inappropriate sexual innuendos, only it wasn't. I sat up, caught off guard by his response when it finally came through.

Ben: I was imagining what sleeping next to you would feel like?

25

A PRISTINE CLEAN SHEEN

I slowly looked up from my phone. Ben had put his phone down on the room table, and was leaning back in his chair looking at me. He smiled, as if he knew he'd gotten me with that message. As if he knew that he had successfully just reeled me in. As if he knew a comment like that, one that was so intimate, was far harder to resist than the ones laced with sex. Our eyes locked and my stomach tightened.

And then, as if Ben had reached across the table with invisible hands and grabbed hold of me, I felt myself being pulled towards him. It was a physical feeling, and it was so incredibly intense. In that moment, every part of my body wanted to be on the other side of that table with him, it was almost too much to bear. I felt my body begin to lean slightly, and saw Ben lean too.

"Okay! I'll now open it up to the floor, does anyone have anything they'd like to add?" Suddenly, Raymond's voice snapped me back to reality. I looked away from Ben, towards the yawning, shaking heads of the other tenants.

"If no one has anything to add, I'd like to raise an issue." Raymond paused for a moment, as if trying to create a moment of gravitas, a dramatic beat before something explosive. "Something very, *very* disturbing has been brought to my attention." His voice lowered and his demeanor changed to something ominous. "And this is not the first time it's happened either. But it has to be the last."

I could see he had people's attention now.

"Someone, possibly in this room even, has been deliberately breaking the rules, over and over again, with potentially catastrophic consequences." His voice took on a sinister quality now and everyone was transfixed.

"And I have the evidence to prove it." He stood up, marched across the room and began digging in a bag. I felt my phone vibrate and looked down.

Ben: What do you think it is?

Sera: ??

Ben: I hope it's something terribly juicy. I'm dying of boredom here.

Sera: Me too! I'd give anything for some action right now.

Raymond returned to his seat, and without another word, put a box down on the table. Everyone leaned in to read it, including myself. I recognized the box immediately, of course. It was mine.

"Someone," he boomed dramatically, "Someone has been using *hand* washing laundry detergent powder in the automatic washing machines."

There was a strange pause in the room, as if people were trying to decide whether this was even a problem. There were a few, however, who were shaking their heads, as if they knew what an issue this was, and how appalled they all were by the discovery.

Oh for heaven's sake. What difference did it make anyway? It's not like my hand washing powder was damaging the machines!

"And for those of you who are wondering why this is such an issue, let me explain." He picked the box up. "Hand washing detergent produces a lot of suds, which in an automatic washing machine prevents your clothes from getting properly clean. So, if you're using this in our washing machine, you are depriving us all of ever having truly clean clothes."

I tried not to roll my eyes at the absolute absurdity of all this. I looked around and could see that his words were having an effect on a few people, who were now looking down at their clothes.

"So, if the user of this illegal powder is in the room, or if there is anyone in this room has any information on the matter, I urge you to come forward."

And then something truly bizarre happened. Ben put his hand up and cleared his throat.

"Hi, I'm Ben White, I've just moved in and I think I might have some useful information about the perpetrator of this crime."

"Mr. White. Firstly, welcome on behalf of everyone here, and please go ahead and share the information."

"Thank you," Ben said, nodding in a grave, serious manner. *What the hell was he up to?*

"This morning I was in the parking lot when I walked past the laundry room." He paused and looked somewhat pained. As if he was about to share something that he really didn't want to. "I hate to say it, but—" he looked up at me and I sat up straight.

No, he wasn't! Surely not?

"I saw who was using the washing powder. And that person is sitting in this very room," he raised his arm and then pointed straight at me. "*Her.*" He said it so loudly that I was sure it was going to echo off the walls.

"What?" I sat up in my seat, utterly shocked that Ben had just ousted me. Everyone turned and looked at me. "I . . . I . . ." I stuttered uncomfortably and then looked over at Ben, I could see he was trying to hide a smile. *The bastard!*

"Sera, is this true?" Raymond turned and asked me.

"Yes, Sera, is this true?" Ben asked too.

"I . . . I . . . I mean, yes. No. I mean, I didn't know there was a difference between hand washing powder and automatic powder."

Ben gasped loudly and his hand came up to his chest, clutching it as if in shock. "You didn't know the difference?" He repeated the words slowly and deliberately. I could see others were starting to buy into this act, and a few were eyeing me with growing disapproval.

"It all makes sense now! No wonder my shirts haven't been gleaming with that pristine clean sheen lately," Ben said.

"Huh?" I looked at him, he was running his hands over his shirt now, as if he was searching it for imperfections. I shook my head. "This is ridiculous. Clothes don't gleam."

"But it says so on the box." Ben suddenly grabbed the box and held it up, reading the words that were printed across it in bright orange. "*Sun & Surf Detergent; For clothes that gleam with a pristine clean sheen.*"

"Oh please!" I laughed and then looked at everyone in the room.

"If it's on the box, it must be true," Ben quickly said.

"Oh really?" I countered, "Because no one in advertising ever lies?"

"Absolutely not." Ben pointed back to the box, "And look here," he read the words off the other side of it, *"As seen on TV."* He paused, scanning the crowd, looking deeply into their eyes, and then he spoke again. "And we all know that if it's on TV, it must be true."

A few heads in the room nodded, but a few were now looking confused.

"By using this detergent, Sera, you are depriving us of our right to clothes that gleam with a pristine clean sheen." He smacked the box back down on the table and folded his arms.

"And what about our right to sleep?" I too looked around the room, "Who heard those terrible noises at two-thirty a.m. the other morning?"

A few people nodded again. "I thought I heard something," one of the older ladies said. "Me too," someone else echoed.

"Well, it was *him.*" It was my turn to point this time. "He probably wasn't thinking about our God-given right to sleep when he was drilling into the wall and moving furniture around, was he?" I turned and looked at Ben, he wasn't even trying to hide his smile now.

"I actually did receive a complaint about noise the other night, but they didn't know where it was specifically coming from," Raymond chirped up.

"Well, I know where it was coming from." I waggled my finger at him. "Ben White!"

"Noise is nothing, Sera De La Haye, but clothes that don't gleam, are everything." He stuck a finger right back at me.

"What? That doesn't even make sense, Ben."

"Fashion is forever, Sera."

I shook my head at him. "What are you even talking about? Besides, why are you so suddenly concerned about clothes anyway, it's not like you go to great lengths to keep them on!" I fired back, knowing full well he'd probably have a good retort for that. And he did.

His eyes moved down to my chest and he bit his lip, "I could say the same for you, Sera!"

"Okay, okay!" Raymond held his hands up in the air. "Let's all calm down here. I think we've clearly touched on some very serious matters here and obviously you two have very serious feelings about them."

"Yes! I have very serious feelings about her." Ben turned and looked and locked eyes with me. "Very serious," he repeated slowly. I swallowed hard and felt the heat rising in my cheeks once more.

"Well, I don't think this is the time or place for it, perhaps you two should meet privately to discuss this further and come to a resolution."

"Great idea," Ben said. "I definitely think Sera and I should meet privately to discuss this matter further." Ben looked at me and winked. I tried to bite back a smile, but couldn't. "In fact, how about Sera and I meet right now in private to clear this all up."

"Uh, I suppose we've almost finished," Raymond said, looking thrown.

"Excellent." Ben shot out of his seat and then looked over at me. "Your place or mine, Sera?"

"Uh . . ." I stood up out of my chair.

"Come, we'll decide on the way." Ben started exiting and I followed him, excusing myself from the meeting.

"I can't believe you did that!" I said when we were out of earshot.

"You were the one that wanted some action." We walked down the long corridor towards the lift.

"Yes, that wasn't really what I was imagining, though."

"It did the trick, didn't it?" Ben nudged me with his shoulder.

"But now everyone thinks I'm some laundry criminal who's ruining their clothes."

We reached the lift and I was about to reach out and press the button, when Ben stepped in front of me, blocking them. "That's true, and the question is, how should we punish you?"

"Punish me?"

"Mmm-hmmm. It's clear you've been a very naughty girl."

I burst out laughing. "Do you honestly think that line is going to work on me?"

Ben smiled, "Not really. But it was kind of fun to say."

I shook my head, pushed him aside and then pressed the button for the top floor. We stood in silence waiting for the lift to open. When it did, I stepped inside, but Ben didn't.

"Aren't you coming?" I asked.

He shook his head and stopped the lift door from closing with his foot. "I have to go back to work. Calendar-shoot crisis."

"But it's nine."

"I know, and I was supposed to be there two hours ago to see what everyone is working on. But I got kind of busy." He smiled at me.

"You bunked work to fix my tyre and then sit in a boring body corporate meeting?" I asked, feeling beyond flattered.

"Something like that." He moved his foot and the doors started closing.

"Bye, Sera," he said, as his face began disappearing behind the steel door.

"Ben," I said, just as the doors closed and the lift started moving.

My phone suddenly vibrated and I looked down at it.

Ben: Did we just have a Mr. Grey, Miss. Steele moment at the lift doors?

Sera: HAHAH! Omg, I think we just did!

I laughed and cringed at the thought of it.

Sera: And OMG, I can't believe you've watched that movie btw!?

Ben: My brother made me watch it with him! Not an experience I would like to repeat, EVER!

Sera: I can imagine.

Ben: BTW, hasn't the new one just opened? Wanna watch it with me?

Sera: NO!

Ben: Yeah. I agree. Besides, whips and chains and blindfolds aren't really my thing.

My stomach dropped to the floor as the lift doors opened. We were back here, once more. And again, I didn't put a stop to it. Instead, I continued.

Sera: Really?

Ben: Mmmm, I prefer not to have any distractions, or anything coming between us.

Sera: Us?

Ben: Hopefully ;) Soon . . .

26

AT FIRST I WAS AFRAID . . .

here was a strange manic energy in the office when I arrived at work on Monday morning. I walked past the boardroom on my way to my desk to discover it was overflowing with yawning, defeated, tired-looking people. Ben was standing in front of everyone talking loudly and passionately. He was waving his arms in the air and still wearing the same clothes from yesterday. He looked like he'd been up all night.

"He's been making teams present ideas to him all night and hates every single one of them," Becks said coming up behind me. "No one has slept." She yawned in my ear.

"Really." I glanced over at Ben and it was the first time I'd seen him looking anything but cool and calm. Dare I say it, but he looked rattled. As I studied him through the glass he caught my eye and gestured for me to come over. A ball of nervous energy bubbled up inside me and I walked over to the boardroom apprehensively. As soon as I was there he popped his head out the door.

"Hey." He looked tired but managed a small smile.

"Hi."

"I have no right to ask you this and if you don't want to do it I'll completely . . ."

"What?" I asked.

He dug in his pocket, pulled out a key and passed it over to me sneakily. "Please could you go to my place and get me some fresh clothes, I have to go to the client this afternoon and I have coffee on this shirt and quite frankly, I think I stink." He whispered.

I took the key between my fingers. "Sure."

"And a toothbrush and toothpaste."

I nodded.

"And deodorant. Some cologne, anything to help me look and feel a bit better." He smiled again and in that moment I think I would have probably done anything he asked me to. The thought worried me. A lot.

I turned to leave but he quickly whispered, "And don't go stealing my underwear." He winked and disappeared back into the boardroom.

I arrived at Ben's apartment about half an hour later and it felt odd letting myself in. It was so relationship-y. I went straight to his bedroom and was surprised to find it looking neat and spotless. For some reason I had it in my head that men, particularly bachelors, were messy beer-can crushing, TV remote hogging slouches that left their smelly socks on the floor. But Ben was none of these things.

I walked over to his cupboard, opened it and gasped. There, row upon row upon row, were suits. The inside of his cupboard looked like one of those suit hire places where grooms go to get themselves kitted out for their weddings. I'd never seen so many suits in one place before, and I'd also never chosen one for anyone either. What was I meant to look for? *Color? Cut? Shape . . . ?*

Instead of that, I tried to imagine him in each one, until I came to a very smart black pinstripe one. I ran my hand over the fabric and imagined his body inside it—*oh God I was turning into a total perv.* I took the suit out, grabbed a black shirt and black tie (I liked him in black), and then paused when I saw his underwear. Was I meant to bring him underwear too?

I reached out and picked one up. *Yup*, I remembered these guys. I remember these ones well! I grabbed some socks and looked around. Next to his bed were two bedside tables and my curiosity started getting the better of me. Suddenly I wanted to throw myself at the drawers, rummage through them and uncover all of Ben's secrets. I bet Ben had many.

I paused. I really shouldn't, *right ?* But I did. I pulled one of the drawers open and looked inside. Nothing. Totally empty. I sighed and closed it feeling disappointed. Ben was still such a mysterious creature to me and a small clue would have gone a long way in helping me unravel that mystery.

I went into his bathroom and smiled. It looked like a women's bathroom. Facial products, colognes and even a blackhead-removing mask sat on a shelf. No wonder he was so fucking good-looking. I grabbed his toothbrush, toothpaste and a roll-on deodorant.

I looked down at the six bottles of cologne and was stumped, so I picked each one up and smelt it until I recognized that familiar scent. The one that had mingled with sex and vodka and sweaty leather that night.

I was just about to put all his things into a bag that I'd pulled out of the bottom of his closet when I saw it . . . unopened gold condom wrapper. Suddenly, the idea that Ben kept emergency condoms in the bottom of a travel bag made me feel a little queasy. What, in case he bumped into a hot airhostess on a plane that he needed to haul into the bathroom and earn his membership to the mile high club? In case he needed to quickly explore some additional creative options with the client while away on a shoot, or in case he bumped into a girl at a nightclub and needed to throw her over the back seat of his car . . . I cringed just thinking about it.

* * *

I didn't want anyone to see me return with his clothes, so I carefully slipped the bag into his office when no one was looking. Everyone was still in the boardroom and I made my way back to my desk.

"Sera." I looked up and Ben gestured for me once more. *Gold wrapper, gold wrapper, gold wrapper.* God, I needed to stop thinking about that. I walked over to the boardroom and he opened the door. "Have a seat." He pointed into the room.

"Um . . . me? But I'm not a . . ."

"Everyone is here. We're all having this conversation together."

I looked around and, yes, everyone was there, not just the creatives. Almost everyone in the company, including the tea lady, was seated around the massive boardroom table. I walked over and sat down.

"I've called you all in here to discuss some changes that I'll be making around the office. I know I've only been here a short time but I can already see that this place is very stuck in it's ways. Comfortable ways."

I raised my eyes and looked around the room.

"I'm going to be pushing you all very hard from now on. We all need to step up our game and start thinking outside the box if we're ever going to make truly exceptional work. Or, we can stay still and make perfectly mediocre work?"

There were some confused nods, which made me think they already thought they were producing exceptional work.

"So with that, is there anyone who thinks they have an idea for this calendar. And I don't want another boring idea that involves glitzy Monte Carlo-like backdrops and clichéd glamorous women standing next to the car looking pleased with themselves and holding expensive handbags. We can do better than that. We can do something far more interesting. Anyone?"

He looked around the room. "Now I have an idea, but I still think we can do better, so if there's anyone in this room who wants to throw something out, free of judgment, then go for it."

I glanced around; people were looking at each other with blank expressions and then looking back at Ben. Suddenly things in the room got very uncomfortable. And just then, at the worst imaginable time ever, my phone beeped loudly.

"Sorry." I rummaged in my jacket pocket, pulled my phone out and saw JJ's message plastered across the screen.

JJ: I need you to tell me what you think of this since you didn't stay to watch the whole thing.

I tried to close the message, but in my panic must have pressed play on the video I just realized he'd sent me.

JJ's voice rang out, singing the Gloria Gaynor tune once more.

"Sorry, sorry." I scrambled to turn it off and in my haste, dropped it to the floor and under the table.

"Shit!" I dropped to my hands and knees and crawled under the table. The bastard device had cruelly made its way to the other side of the table. God this was embarrassing, but it got just worse.

"*Liar*," I heard JJ shout from the phone, "*you're going home to have wild sex with your hot neighbor.*"

"*That's right*," my voice rang out in response and my stomach plummeted. I knew what was coming next, and there was no way I was going to make it to the phone in time to switch it off. "*And I'm ovulating too so I can fall pregnant with his illegitimate baby.*"

Oh. My. God.

27

THE END OF DAYS . . .

I gasped and started to crawl as quickly as I could. I bumped a few knees and crushed some feet as I went but finally managed to grab the phone and switch it off.

I could already hear the murmurs and chuckles coming from the desk above me. No doubt Ben had heard that too. What the hell did he think of me now? Maybe it was actually a blessing in bad, terrible, bad disguise. He'd probably never ask me out again or come within a ten-mile radius of me for fear that I was one of those psycho woman who entrapped men with babies.

Well, nothing to do but face the music. So I crawled across the floor once more and climbed into my seat. I could feel all the eyes on me. I could see all the not-so-subtle smirks being flung in my direction and the one death stare being bored into me by the hectically religious chick from reception who walked around telling people, with great pride, that she didn't believe in sex before marriage and that the end of days was near while handing out pamphlets to her charismatic church.

I felt sick. My stomach churned and then knotted. *What was Ben thinking?* I wanted to look up at him to see the reaction on his face, but just couldn't will my eyes to look away from the tiny crack in the desk they were now fixated on. A silence descended on the room and I wanted to die of embarrassment.

Then I heard Ben's voice. "Does anyone know where that song is from?" he asked. *What the hell was he doing?*

No one replied, even though the answer was so obvious to me. But I wasn't going to say a word.

"Sera, would you mind playing that again."

"What?" My eyes flicked up and met his. I could see he was trying to hide the smile on his face.

"Don't worry . . . just that first bit." A roar of laugher rose up from the room and I couldn't work out what was going on. *Was he deliberately trying to embarrass me?* But with everyone in the office looking at me, I couldn't exactly disobey the boss.

I fumbled with my phone nervously and pressed play. The first few lines of the song blared out again. I quickly pressed pause when the inappropriate conversation about my ovaries that one should only have behind the closed doors of your gynae's rooms, was about to start. I folded my arms and focused all my attention back on that crack and waited.

"Anyone know what that was?" He asked the room again. Silence! "Well, that was an idea! Has no one seen *Priscilla, Queen of the Desert*?" No one moved. "It won awards, it's a famous Broadway show, people! It was made into a movie."

There were a few murmurs now, but no one was actually talking.

"Sera, please can you tell the room about the movie; I take it you've seen it."

"Huh?" My head snapped up again and I looked at Ben.

He sat down. "The room is yours, Sera, please." He gestured at me and my face went bright red. I could feel my cheeks burning.

"Um . . . Okay." I stood up nervously. "It's about these drag queens who trek through the middle of the Australian outback to do a show in a small town called Alice Springs. They buy this massive bus and—"

Ben jumped up now and cut me off, which I was ever so grateful for. "And this is what it looks like." He pressed a button on the computer he'd been fiddling with and the photo of the iconic scene popped onto the screen; the big shiny silver bus, cutting through the barren red desert. One of the drag queens was sitting on top of a giant silver shoe strapped to the top of the bus and a massive piece of silver material billowed out behind them. The room went silent for a moment and I could hear the cogs turning.

"Why is this shot so great?" he asked the room.

No one answered and I don't know what came over me, maybe it was because I had watched the movie so many times, maybe it was because I lived with the walking embodiment of one of the characters from the show, maybe it was because I'd seen the desert decorations being pulled out yesterday, who knows, but I spoke. "Because of the juxtaposition. It's surprising to see those two things together. The harsh, barren desert vs the big shiny bus and billowing material."

"Exactly. This is an image that sticks in your mind because it catches you off guard. And that's what we need," he said. "Now imagine seeing luxury sports cars there instead. Multi million Rand sports cars driving through the desert. The harsh, hot climate. Barren wasteland, dead trees, lifeless. Except for the cars."

A look of acknowledgement started washing over the faces in the room. "It's brilliant," Angie suddenly piped up. "We could shoot in Namibia, they have those really great ghostly looking landscapes and that abandoned town. Very other worldly."

"Great idea. Maybe you can start pulling some visual references of the landscape for me in the meantime, and I'll see you at the shoot too," Ben said clicking his fingers at her. I tried not to roll my eyes, since I knew she was probably planning on christening a ghostly looking landscape or two with him.

"Right, I'll be in my office putting the client presentation together." He started walking out the room. "And, Sera, you'll be coming with me on the shoot later this week too."

He exited and suddenly the whole room was looking at me again. This time the smirks were gone, instead they were replaced with looks of shock, confusion and even some anger.

28

SO . . . YOU WANT TO HAVE A BABY WITH ME?

"*Y*ou know, some people have been working on this account for years and they are pretty pissed that you're going, especially since you don't even work on this account and you are only an intern. It's just one less place for the rest of them." Becks finally spoke after a few hours of tense silence.

She glared at me and I shrugged. I felt bad, there was no good reason for me to go, especially after he'd heard what JJ and I had said and was probably wondering whether I'd managed to make a secret hole in the condom the other night. "I'm sorry, I don't know why he asked me." I looked up at his office and all his blinds were closed. I couldn't take it any longer.

"I'm going to tell him I can't go," I said to Becks. I walked up to his door and knocked.

"Who is it?" the muffled voice behind the door called out.

"It's me, uh, Sera." Awkward. So damn awkward! I was hoping he wouldn't bring up the whole baby thing and we could pretend it had never happened.

A few seconds later the door opened. I stepped inside and he closed and locked it behind me. "I don't want anyone to disturb me, I only had a few hours to pull this whole thing together."

"And have you?"

He smiled and nodded at me. "Thanks to you."

"I didn't do anything."

"Yes you did. You cracked the big idea."

"That was an accident. I really don't deserve to go on this shoot, I mean Becks has been working on this and—"

Ben walked over to the bags I'd brought him. "The deal is that whoever cracks it, goes. And that was you. You saw the thing that no one else could today. In fact, I'm pretty impressed."

I looked down at Ben as he pulled the gold wrapper out the bag and looked at it. "Trying to hint at something?" he chuckled.

"No! It was already in there when I packed the bag."

He shot me a mischievous look, before standing straight up again and unbuttoning his shirt.

"What are you doing?"

"I have to change, I'm going to the client now."

"Yes, but, not here. Not in front . . ." I couldn't speak. He'd unbuttoned his shirt and I could see his chest. His perfect, hard, ripped, *oh-so-very ripped*, tattooed chest. My knees weakened.

"You . . . you . . . can't do this here," I stammered.

"Why, no one can see in."

"I can," I said.

He stopped and grinned at me. "It's not like you haven't seen it before."

"But we're at work."

He ignored me and continued. "Good choice of shirt, by the

way." He smiled at me momentarily, but I was quickly forced to
turn away when he started unbuttoning his belt and pulling his
pants down.

"I can't go away anyway." I tried to sound indignant. "I'm
working at the restaurant every night for a while."

"It's just three days, I'm sure they can do without you."

"Ja, maybe they can. But I can't do without the money." My
candor surprised me.

I heard some footsteps and then I could sense his closeness.
"Can't you pick up some extra shifts when we get back?" he asked.

Truth was, I needed the money right now. It was month end
and I needed to pay school fees for my sister, give her some gro-
cery money, pay the electrical bill, water and rent. So no, I needed
that money now.

"No." I turned around and came face-to-face with him.

"Well, the clients usually give us a very generous per diem for
these kinds of shoots, so if you shared breakfast, lunch and dinner
with me and let me buy you drinks every day, you could save all
that money and I bet it would be more than you could make at
the restaurant."

"Really?" I asked and immediately wanted to kick myself. *Why
was I even considering this?* "I'll only go if you take Becks too and
some other creatives that have worked on this account for years."

He started putting his jacket on now. "I was planning on taking more people anyway. The client loves it when we have a
million people on these shoots. Makes him feel big and important. Sometimes this job is all about stroking egos." With his jacket
now on the look was complete and he looked hot, so damn hot.
He straightened his cuffs and then grabbed the tie. I wanted to

look away, but couldn't. Instead I watched his fingers moving expertly as he did up his tie and tried not to imagine his fingers all over my body again.

"O-o-okay then. I'll think about it," I said and turned as quickly as I could. I unlocked the door and was just about to step out when his words froze me to the spot.

"So . . . you want to have a baby with me?"

My heart thumped in my chest and my stomach dropped. I locked the door again quickly and turned around. "I swear, that was a total joke. It was just JJ being idiotic and telling me what a cliché I was because I'd had sex with my boss and we were joking about it and I said it would be more clichéd if you were a prince and I fell pregnant with your secret illegitimate baby and we fell in love and got married and I became a princess of some imaginary country and all that crap from the romance novels he loves to read."

Ben smiled. "So you want to marry me too now? This is getting more and more interesting by the second."

"No! I didn't say that." My face was suddenly on fire and my forehead felt clammy. "Well, I did say it. But I said it as a joke."

"Don't they say many a true word is spoken in jest?"

"Yes. But don't they also say stuff like the proof is in the pudding and two birds in the bush is like one in the hand or something. Those make no sense."

Ben laughed. "Beauty, brains and a sense of humor. It's a deadly combination." Then Ben's smile was gone and he was suddenly looking at me very earnestly. "Well, I'm sorry to let you know, but marriage and a baby are definitely off the cards—"

"I know! I know." I nodded my head furiously. "Of course! I totally know that!"

"Call me mad, but I usually prefer to do that kind of stuff *after* the women has agreed to go on a date with me first."

"U-u-u- h . . ." My mouth opened to say something, but I had no thoughts. None! I closed my mouth and his eyes drifted down to my lips, stunning me into a silent stupor.

"You are still thinking about it, aren't you?" he took a step closer. My eyes drifted down to his mouth and stayed there. He had the sexiest mouth, especially when it was all over my body.

I gave the tiniest head nod and then followed that up with a little shake. Nod again. Shake. Nod. Shake. It was as if my subconscious was controlling my head and the internal battle it was waging was coming out.

"That's okay, Sera. Take your time," he said as I started inching my way for the door. "But I do expect to see you on the plane when we leave for the shoot though."

I nodded at this and then launched myself at the door handle.

"Max, by the way," Ben called out as I was just about to exit, "I've always fancied a son called Max."

29

DIRTY AND DEVILISH
AND DELICIOUS . . .

I could barely think about anything else that night at work . . . Ben, our imaginary son Max, our upcoming royal nuptials, that sexy black suit he'd worn. But when I saw that same black suit enter the restaurant later that night, a flutter of panic gripped me. I watched from the sidelines as he slid into a seat. His table was in my section, he probably knew that already. I walked over to him as calmly and professionally as I could.

"Hi." I placed the menu down on his table.

"Hi, Sera." He looked up at me. "I'm not here to eat anything, just to have a celebratory drink with you. The client loved your idea."

"It wasn't really my idea," I quickly said.

"Of course it was. So how about two Vodka Cranberries?" He winked at me.

"I'm working, so I can't really drink on the job."

Ben raised an eyebrow and looked around the room. "Please, this hardly seems like the kind of establishment that cares about that shit."

I stifled a smile. He was right. Having a friendly drink here and there with the patrons was almost a prerequisite. I left him and came back with one Vodka Cranberry.

"So you're going to leave me to celebrate alone?" he put on a sad puppy dog look.

I shrugged. "There are other tables, you know." I started walking away but Ben got up and blocked me.

"Seriously, we're leaving to shoot in Namibia on Thursday. It's only for three nights, we'll be back on Sunday. It's going to be amazing, you have to come."

I sighed. "I'll go on one more condition."

"Name it."

"You remain totally, one hundred percent professional at all times. If you keep acting this way, people at work will start thinking that you and I . . . you know?"

"Had fucking incredible sex."

My eyes widened and I cleared my throat. "Something like that."

"Exactly like that," Ben said in a husky sotto tone that made my toes tingle.

"And done," he said.

"Done?"

"I shall be the consummate professional on this trip." He downed his drink, reached into his pants and pulled out his wallet. He grabbed a note, far too much for the one drink, and slapped it down on the table. "I won't try and sneak into your room at night, I will definitely not feel you up secretly under the table or look at you and imagine you naked and think about you at night just before I go to sleep."

"Uh . . . um . . ." I stumbled. "Glad to hear it."

"As long as you promise to do the same." He took a step closer. I tisked loudly. "I don't do stuff like that."

"Oh please. I've seen the way you look at me at work sometimes."

"That's just your over-inflated ego imagining things."

A slow, deadly smile swept across his face. It was dirty and devilish and delicious. "You know, no one has ever spoken to me the way you do."

I shrugged. "What can I say, your charms don't work on me."

He took another step forward until his chest touched mine and his nose was an inch away from my face. I no longer had knees. "We both know that's not true, is it, Sera?" His eyes floated down to my lips and they burned.

"Mmmmm . . ." A nervous moan escaped my strangled throat. "I really have to work now." I backed away but he reached out and stopped me with a hand around my wrist. I looked down at my wrist, his fingers tightened and he pulled me towards him. I gasped when my chest pressed into his once more.

"Good night then, Sera." And then he leaned in and kissed me softly on the cheek. I closed my eyes briefly and drank in his scent. *So damn hot!* If I could bottle it and sell it to other women I would be rich.

"G-g-good night." I finally managed to get the words out as he pulled away from me and walked to the door.

"Wait. You need change," I called after him while scrambling for his change. He waved a hand at me as if to say "no" which I wasn't very happy about. He turned and continued to walk towards the door, but just before exiting he stopped and turned around once more. His eyes met mine and he mouthed something.

I leaned in and tried to make it out. Was it . . . ? It was . . . ? What was he saying . . . ?

"You are totally falling in love with me."

I shook my head at him and mouthed the word "No" as clearly as I could. He gave me one last smile before disappearing out the door.

30

I DON'T NEED TO EAT . . .

I didn't see Ben at all after that night at work, apart from a few walk-bys he'd made in between meetings in preparation for the shoot. I'd wanted to give him his change, from the night he'd bought the drink. I didn't think an $88 tip on a $12 drink was appropriate, and I didn't take charity from people either. But the week passed in such a crazy frenzy of working during the day and then all night too, that I hadn't been able to give it back to him. So when Thursday finally arrived I was exhausted.

I arrived at the airport about an hour and a half early. I'd been so nervous the night before I'd barely slept. I wandered around the airport trying to decide whether to eat breakfast, read a magazine, or shoot myself. I decided on none of those and instead headed into a candy store and grabbed a slab of chocolate. I ripped the paper off and took a big bite and instantly felt better.

"Sera?" I heard Becks call out and turned to see her and Angie walking towards me. Behind them were a few people from production I barely recognized, a copywriter/art director team I knew and someone else I'd never seen before.

I saw more movement to my left and turned. Another person was walking towards me now. Not an ordinary human though. She was the tallest, most gorgeous woman I'd ever seen in my entire life and she was strutting towards me. No doubt this was the model for the shoot. She walked as if she was on a catwalk. Her shiny, shiny, borderline reflective hair billowed out behind her and bounced as her hips jutted from side to side, causing her whole body to sway from left to right with each step. *Who walked like that?* And why had she not dislocated something?

Her little ballerina arms looked somehow separate from the rest of her body and hung like delicate butterfly wings from her perfect shoulders. Her collarbones protruded in that mocking way that screamed, *"No, bitches, I don't need to eat."* I stopped chewing and slipped my chocolate in my bag, she was making me feel like a beached marine animal. Possibly a beached elephant seal.

She was also pouting. Her full lips were slicked with lip-gloss that twinkled in the overhead lights. Who pouted like that? Who pursed their lips together like they were sucking on a lollipop, or worse? Heads turned and people stared—clearly the effect she wanted to elicit. I looked back at Angie and Becks and they both looked positively gutted, the competition had officially arrived and suddenly I imagined Ben ripping open that condom while she licked him like a giant lollipop.

"Hi." I heard another voice and turned once more. It was Ben and he was also walking in my direction. I tried, *oh-so-flippin' hard*, not to let my jaw drop to the floor. He was wearing a casual pair of jeans and a black v neck t-shirt. He looked completely different in that outfit and maybe because it was new, I don't think I had seen him looking better. Judging by the looks on the other's faces, they seemed to agree.

And as if perfectly timed, the three crowds descended on me at the exact same moment. we all looked at each other tossing around those awkward, polite smiles that come from not really knowing each other outside of work. I was trying hard not to let anyone see what I was thinking, i.e. *ripping Ben's shirt from his body with my teeth, rubbing my chocolate all over it and licking it off.* I glanced over at the model. She looked like she was thinking the exact same thing, probably substituting the chocolate part for a low-cal celery smoothie though. Her little eyes twinkled at him, her silky lashes blinked and her pout got bigger . . .

Look at me. I have big, beautiful blowjob lips and I want to put them to good use . . . on you. Crap! *And now I was thinking about him coming on someone's face again.*

The image was so disturbingly hideous that I gasped loudly and then started coughing. I hadn't meant to. And it was so loud that everyone turned and looked at me, including Ben.

"You okay?" Becks asked looking at me curiously.

"Mmmm." I nodded and then patted my chest. "Think I inhaled something . . ." I tapered off. *Inhaled what?* What a stupid thing to say and suddenly I hoped they didn't think I was snorting lines.

"Inhaled what?" Ben asked. He was trying to hide it, but the corners of his mouth twitched into a tiny smile.

"A . . . a . . ." Everyone was looking at me . . . waiting. *Fuck!* "Probably pollen." I was so happy when the thought came to me that I smiled at them all.

"We're in an airport," Ben didn't hide his smile now. "There shouldn't be any pollen in here." He was teasing me. He was trying to rile me up. *The bastard.*

I pointed over at the pot plant behind him feeling pleased with myself, "What's that then?"

"As far as I know, palm trees don't give off pollen." He took a tiny step towards me. The people around us disappeared and I felt myself being pulled into my own private bubble with Ben.

"So you're also a botanist, then?" I teased.

"Only in my spare time." He folded his arms across his chest, causing the neck of his shirt to dip lower, revealing more of that tattoo that I'd found myself thinking so much about lately.

"Fascinating," I said back to him.

"I'm a man of many talents, Sera."

"Really?"

"Yup."

"Good for you."

A movement entered my peripheral vision and made me turn. Becks was leaning towards me with a confused look on her face, and suddenly I became very aware of the people around me again. My Ben bubble popped and when I came out of it, I realized that everyone was looking at us oddly. *Shit!*

Ben must have realized it too, because his demeanor quickly changed. "We don't want to miss our flight, do we? Come." Ben started walking off and everyone followed. I hung back for a moment, trying to gather myself and fight off the plummeting feeling that had just fallen into the pit of my stomach. That moment should *not* have happened. People would start getting suspicious if Ben and I carried on like that. I quickly tried to remind myself of all those really good reasons that I shouldn't date him. I took a deep breath and started walking after the group.

Once at the gates we all pulled out our tickets and then boarded the plane. I found my seat quickly as it was close to the front. I sat down and buckled up as I watched everyone walk past me towards the back of the plane. I glanced down at my ticket again, *was I sitting in the wrong seat?* But my question was quickly answered when Ben slipped in next to me.

31

MISS POUTY LIP

‸

"*O*h wow, you're sitting here too. What a coincidence." It sounded completely untrue.

I gave him a sideways glance. "Really?"

"Ja, I had no idea we would be booked next to each other and everyone else would be seated all the way at the very, very, *very* back of the plane." He shot me a smile and I tried not to reciprocate, but I felt the corners of my mouth twitch in response.

"Hey," I heard someone say and looked up. The model had stopped in the aisle next to Ben's seat.

"Hey, I didn't get a chance to introduce myself," she said in a sweet singsong voice that gave her a slight schoolgirl edge. "Cindy." She extended her hand for Ben to shake. He did. She leaned in closer, closer, closer . . . *too close*. "I'm so excited to be working with you," she cooed. "Your reputation really proceeds you." She smiled. It was the kind of smile that told me she wasn't talking about his professional reputation, but another one entirely. I crossed my legs and folded my arms, which caused her to look up to me briefly. She smiled at me and then started walking again. I sort of wish she'd tripped.

Ben eyed me. "I take it you and Cindy aren't going to become besties in the next few days?"

"I doubt it," I said flatly.

"She's probably a really nice girl if you got to know her," he teased.

"I'm sure she is," I answered sarcastically.

"You're just jealous."

"I am not," I turned and hissed at him. But truthfully, I was. I was so jealous of Miss Pouty-Lip right now and the way her low-cut top had fallen open when she'd leaned over to reveal just the right amount of almost-nipple to Ben.

Ben turned his entire body towards me and leaned forward. "I wouldn't do anything with her, even if she threw herself at me naked." His voice was low and husky.

"Oh, but your reputation proceeds you," I said in a mocking tone, locking eyes with him. And suddenly it was awkward. I could see I'd hit a nerve and he squirmed under my gaze.

"That's in the past," he quickly said. Thank God the airhostess interrupted us at that moment, because the conversation was headed somewhere it really shouldn't be. I bought a Coke and soon felt better when I was washing it down with some Jelly Babies.

"You consume a lot of sugar," Ben suddenly said.

"I know." I popped another Jelly Baby in my mouth and didn't bother to look up.

"You know sugar is bad for you."

"So I've been told. But I need it to keep me awake and functioning."

"That's only because you work too hard."

"No, I don't."

"Really, and how many shifts did you do this week, Sera?"

This time I stopped eating and looked up at him. "Every night this week. That's how many." He said it like a statement of fact. As if he knew exactly how many shifts I'd done that week. He must have sensed my thoughts because he quickly added, "I can hear you coming home late at night. And that's why I'm glad you're coming, you could do with a break and this won't be stressful. You can relax."

"That does sound nice." I suddenly imagined three whole days of total relaxation and I couldn't remember the last time I'd actually relaxed.

"When was the last time you went to bed at a normal time?" he asked.

"What's normal?"

"I don't know, before three in the morning? I mean I know I'm not supposed to sleep, but you *really* don't sleep."

I thought about this for a while and realized that I only really got one normal night a week, Sunday night.

"I worry about you." He looked straight into my eyes.

"This is starting to sound very *not* professional again, Ben. We have a rule about that."

He shook his head. "No, it's called employee wellness. It's also my job to make sure my staff aren't completely overworked, stressed and exhausted. Of which you are all three."

"Don't worry 'bout me. I don't need much sleep to function, from years and years of practice."

"How long have you been working at the restaurant?"

"Since I was fifteen," I said without thinking.

"Seriously? Through school and college and now this job?"

I nodded. "It's been a long time, I guess." I hadn't actually realized that I'd been working there for so long already . . .

Ben was just looking at me now. Staring was more like it and I could see he was thinking about something. His brain was ticking away as he tried to size me up.

"What?" I finally asked when I couldn't take the x-ray stare any longer.

"Nothing. You're an incredible woman, Sera De La Haye."

"Uh . . . thanks. I guess." I wasn't really sure what to say back to him. Compliment him on how incredible he was? "Oh." I suddenly remembered and started digging in my handbag. "I owe you change from the other night." I took out the $88 and pushed it in his direction. He looked at my hand as if he had totally been caught off guard and had no idea what I was talking about.

"The other night," I reminded him. "You paid me with a hundred dollars. The drink only cost twelve dollars. This is your change."

Ben's eyes moved from my hand up to my eyes. "I don't want change."

"Well, I can't accept this." I grabbed his hand and forcefully thrust the money into his palm.

"It's a tip." He smiled at me and tried to push the money back to me.

"I don't accept such large tips." I pushed the money back at him getting irritated at his blatant refusal. "I certainly don't accept charity," I lowered his tray table and put the money down onto it.

Ben looked at the money for a moment or two, confused, and then looked back up at me.

"Sera, you're the last person on earth I would ever consider giving charity to."

"Really?" I was caught off guard by his statement.

"Sure. I don't think I've ever met anyone as self-reliant, strong and independent as you. I mean, you're the girl who was going to change her own tyre on the side of the road at night. You only called for help because you were missing the jack."

"O . . . oh," I faltered. I'd never thought of myself like that before. Self-reliant, *yes,* but strong, *not particularly.*

"It's one of the qualities I like most about you," he said with a smile. Again, I was caught off guard, and it must have shown on my face.

"This shouldn't come as a surprise to you, surely you know by now that despite appearances, I don't only want you sexually. I want much more than that, Sera."

Despite the loud roar of the engines, everything suddenly went very silent between Ben and I. A part of me wanted to open my mouth and say the same thing back to him. But I didn't. I didn't even want to admit it to myself, let alone admit it out loud.

But he was right, this was more than just sexual. *Much more.*

32

ASS-KICKING CHICK . . .

"*S*era? Sera?" I heard Ben say and felt a little pat on my check.

"Huh?" I opened my eyes. *Why was everything at an angle?* I blinked and then became aware that my face pressed into something. Then I noticed the smell. Ben's smell. And then I became *very* aware of the warmth of his neck and, *Oh God*, I must have fallen asleep, and worse, I must have fallen asleep on his shoulder. I quickly whipped my head up and looked at him.

"Sorry, I didn't know I was, sorry, I must have fallen asleep."

"Don't worry." Ben reached up and pushed the hair that had fallen into my face away. "Your little snores are cute."

"No! I didn't." I reached up to touch the itch at the corner of my mouth and realized it was wet. I looked down at Ben's shirt, and there it was, a tiny little wet patch. I had drooled on him. I had drooled, while I snored and slept on his shoulder. I wiped my mouth. "I'm so sorry."

"It's okay, Sera, really." And then he smiled at me. That smile.

Dark, sexy, danger! "A little bit of drool doesn't bother me, I mean, we've shared far more than that before." He winked.

"Eeewww," I laughed. "You just couldn't help yourself there, could you?"

"Nope. You did leave it wide open for me, though."

"Did not." I shook my head at him.

"Oh Sera . . . you know I'm doing this on purpose, don't you?"

"I've kind of gathered that by now. The question is why?"

"Because shameless flirting's all part of the fun, isn't it? Especially when it puts such a smile on your face."

I quickly wiped the smile off my face, "I'll make sure I don't smile again then."

"Try," he said cockily.

"Is that a challenge?" I asked.

"Yes."

"Fine, throw your best one at me. Right now." I folded my arms and looked at him, trying to give him my most serious, unshakeable look.

"Mmmm . . ." He looked me up and down. "It needs to be spontaneous. I'll get you later. When you least expect it."

"I'll be ready," I said.

"I'm sure you will be." He leaned in a little closer and my eyes were drawn to his lips. An overwhelming feeling of wanting to kiss him rose up in me, but this would be the worst place and time for that.

"We better get going." He broke the moment and stood up.

"Of course." I started unbuckling my seat belt but stopped when I saw Ben reach up into the overhead compartment. His shirt lifted up and his jeans pulled down, revealing just enough of his stomach to make mine flip.

"*Shit*," I whispered to myself. This man was harder to resist than chocolate. And that was saying something.

* * *

When we arrived at the National Park in Namibia after a two-hour-long drive in a shuttle, everyone was in high spirits, except me. It felt like I'd just opened some kind of sleep floodgate and every time I blinked it felt like I was going to fall unconscious. I was exhausted, more tired than I'd felt in ages. And of course when I saw the room I was staying in, the tiredness grew. We were staying in the most beautiful rooms perched high up on massive boulders that overlooked the national park below. All the rooms were separate and connected with wooden walkways.

"So meet for drinks on the deck at six and then dinner," Ben had said. It was only three in the afternoon so I had a glorious three hours to bath and catch up on a little sleep. And when I saw the bath . . .

The bath was set up against the window that looked out over the plains of the savanna below. There was a watering hole at the bottom of the rocks and elephants were drinking from the water. The bath was one of those huge round things that was probably more suited for swimming than bathing. I walked past a complimentary bottle of wine on the bed and poured myself a glass while slipping into the bath. The water was warm and the bubbles were so soft that it felt like I melted into the back of it.

I sipped the wine and wondered how long it had been since I had had the time to do something like this.

My phone beeped and I peered over at it on the top of the closed toilet seat.

Ben: What are you doing?

I grabbed a towel, dried my hands and took my phone.

Sera: Bathing.

Ben: Dear God!!!

Sera: What are you doing?

Ben: On a recce with the photographer to look at the places we're shooting at.

Sera: Cool. Have fun.

Ben: Not as much fun as I could be having if I were with you . . .

Ben: How was that?

Sera: Good. But I'm not smiling.

Ben: You're lying.

Sera: Nope.

Ben: I don't believe you.

Sera: Bye, Ben.

Ben: Bye, Sera.

He was right of course, I was smiling. But I wasn't going to tell him that. I finished my glass of wine and climbed out the bath. I walked onto my patio with my towel wrapped around me. It was beautiful and warm here and I still had two hours before I needed to be up there for drinks. I set my alarm clock and lay on the lounger outside and closed my eyes. Only the sounds of nature filled the air. No hooting horns or cars or downstairs neighbors getting into arguments. Just crickets and birds and the distant call of a baboon.

* * *

For the second time that day I was being woken up by the sound of Ben's voice. I vaguely opened my eyes and realized it was now dark and I was still wrapped in my towel and lying outside on the patio lounger.

"Come, let's get you into bed." Suddenly I felt weightless as Ben lifted me up and carried me inside all the way to the bed.

"I need to get ready for dinner," I whispered in a half-asleep way. I was in that strange state where you teeter somewhere between sleep and consciousness and feeling like you're not entirely tuned into reality and the world around you.

"That was hours ago." Ben lowered me to the bed.

"Really?" I clutched my pillow and curled up my legs. "I think I pressed the snooze button." I grabbed another pillow and pulled it towards me, feeling something loosen around me. A cold breeze caught the side of my body and I realized that my towel must have opened.

"This is damp, you can't sleep in it."

And then I realized that it wasn't magically coming off by itself, Ben was pulling it off me and replacing it with the fluffy duvet as he went. He reached over me and pushed some of the scatter cushions away. For a moment his whole body leaned over mine and I'm not really sure what I was thinking, I don't think I was thinking in the state I was currently in, but I rolled onto my back and pulled his face down towards mine.

I laced my fingers through his hair and held his face mere millimeters from mine. My eyes were closed, and I took a deep breath, savoring his smell and closeness and then pulled him in closer and kissed him.

"Fuck, Sera," he whispered against my mouth as I pulled him even more. He had nowhere else to go but climb onto the bed and kneel over me. I continued to kiss him; it was warm and soft and slow. It was the perfect combination of a million different things that had blended together in my strange, dreamlike state. And I didn't want it to ever end.

I finally untangled my lips from the kiss and pulled away ever so slightly, not because I wanted to stop kissing him, but because I wanted to look at him. The room was dark but a small beam of moonlight was rushing through the window, and in this position, the silver light clipped the side of his face, illuminating him just enough to make out the sexy, ghostly curve of his features. I took him all in, God he was beautiful.

"It should be illegal to look like you do," I whispered.

"I could say the same about you."

I shook my head.

"You're so wrong about that," he said emphatically, "trust me."

Even though I wasn't entirely sure I believed him, it still felt good to hear. I pulled his face down again for another kiss. This time it was a short one. I stopped and rolled back over onto my side and pulled the blanket and pillow towards me.

"Goodnight, Ben." I closed my eyes and fell back into a deep sleep with a smile on my face.

33

DREAMY BLUE EYES, BIG THIGHS

~

I sat up in bed the next morning with a fright as the phone next to me rang. I grabbed it and answered in a sleepy voice, "Hello."

It was an automated wakeup call which caused me to shoot up onto my feet. It took me a moment to recall the night before; the bath, the sleeping outside the . . . *Ben!* Ben was definitely part of that recollection and so was kissing him! I had kissed him. Shit! What the hell had I been thinking?

I grabbed some clothes and put them on, rushing out to the reception area where I'd seen the breakfast tables set up the day before. I couldn't believe I'd missed dinner last night, what was everyone going to think of me? I was mortified, I'd have to tell them that I'd slept through it. I raced down the little wooden walkways that connected the rooms and jumped in fright, as a monkey flew past me.

"Shit!"

And then another one shot across the walkway, running

clumsily as it held a candy bar in its hand. Someone must have left their window open, I thought as I stopped and looked to see if any others were coming. But the path was clear and I raced back up the creaky wooden slats to the breakfast area.

When I got to the table everyone was there, including Ben. The model was not, she was probably staying away from solids. I looked around quickly trying to determine where to sit, but all the seats were taken.

"Hey, how do you feel?" Becks turned and asked me.

"Um . . . ?"

"I told them about the plane sickness," Ben jumped in. He stood up and pulled a chair from a nearby table and placed it next to his. It was a tight squeeze.

"Plane sickness?" I asked.

"Like car sickness, but with planes," he replied, gesturing for me to sit.

"Oh, that." I nodded.

"I got it on a long flight once too," the woman in production told me. "It's the change in the pressure, can make you feel queasy."

"Yes, it can," I said sliding into the chair that Ben had arranged for me, the chair that was awkwardly squeezed in and completely too close to him. I made a very deliberate attempt to lean as far away from Ben as possible, even though I was basically sitting on his lap.

I was so busy trying to move away from him, that I hadn't really thought about the impact this would have on the person on the other side of me. I was leaning so far over, that my entire head was practically up against the other guy's chest.

"Sorry." I quickly pulled back as my forehead connected with his chin. The man next to me smiled.

"No problem," he said with a slight twinkle in his devastating blue eyes. I straightened myself up again and wiggled into my chair, bumping the same blue-eyed man with my knee, twice.

"Sorry," I said again, quickly reaching out with my hand to touch his arm in an apologetic manner. I felt his hand come down on mine and our fingers grazed. A tiny little spark shot up my spine.

"It's a bit of a tight squeeze." He let his fingers linger a second too long and then pulled his chair back to give me a little more space.

"Thanks." Oh God this guy was gorgeous too, in the complete opposite way to Ben though. He had a surfer quality to him, tousled shoulder-length blond hair, tanned skin, blue eyes that were the color of the sky. He looked casually unkempt, not in a dirty hobo way, but in that sexy scruffy way. He was wearing a casual t-shirt, I tried not to make it obvious but I quickly glanced down and saw that he was dressed in a casual pair of shorts . . . mmmm, big thighs. *You know what they say about a man with big thighs* . . . As JJ might say.

I quickly flicked my eyes back up to his, but clearly my glance down hadn't gone unnoticed. He smiled at me slowly. It oozed sex and charm and I felt my mouth involuntarily flutter at the corners and my lips curled into a smile. And as for that accent, what was it? Italian? French? I couldn't place it but he could probably tell me I was dying and it would still sound good.

The sound of Ben biting into a slice of toast snapped me out of the blue-eyed moment I was busy having. I looked over at Ben, I'd kissed him last night. Oh crap! And now I was sandwiched between *Kissable Lips* and *Dreamy Blue Eyes Big Thighs*. It was all just a bit too awkward for such an early hour in the morning—or any hour. I jumped up and headed to the table where the buffet was and started pouring myself a big cup of coffee. But just as I'd filled my cup, Ben was next to me making himself a slice of toast.

"So you know you kissed me last night?" he whispered into my ear with a smile in his voice.

"Really?" I feigned shock. "I doubt that."

"No, you definitely did."

"Sorry, have no recollection of it at all."

"I don't believe you."

"I was asleep all night. How could I have kissed you?"

"Nope, you were definitely awake when you kissed me and pulled me onto you in the bed."

"I did not pull you onto me in the bed."

"You were all over me, Sera. I was the one that had to hold you back. Practically fight you off."

"I was not!" I realized I'd said that way too loudly as a few people turned and looked at me—including Blue Eyes. I forced a small chuckle. "I was not aware of that!" I quickly corrected loudly. "How fascinating. Really interesting." I took my coffee and slid away. Ben put another slice of toast on a plate and slithered after me.

"Stop following me," I hissed under my breath. "People will start to notice."

"Only if you admit to kissing me last night."

"Fine! Fine, I kissed you last night. Okay."

"And you pulled me onto you on the bed."

"Yes. Yes. I pulled you onto me on the bed."

"And it was really good," he said.

I swallowed and my face flushed a little. I scooped up some pancakes and popped them onto my plate. "It was good," I mumbled under my breath.

"Sorry, what? I didn't hear you?" Ben jabbed a fork into one of the pancakes on my plate and put it on his.

"It was really good," I said a little louder so he could hear this time and then took a sip of coffee.

"I mean, you basically confessed your undying love to me last night, Sera."

"What?" I half spat my coffee out and then started coughing.

"Too hot to handle?" He gave a tiny chuckle, before striding back off to the table. I quickly glanced behind me and realized that Angie had been watching us. I turned away quickly with a plummeting feeling in my stomach.

34

COLLARBONE ASSAULTER . . .

The shoot that day was hot and relentless. The scenery was amazing, though, and the shots looked great—even if the photographer kept screaming at the model and saying how "*disgusting*" everything looked. The photographer, Giovanni was his name, also happened to be Mr. Blue Eyes from breakfast.

As the story went, he was some kind of famous, savant-esque photographer from Milano who was apparently a bit mad, but the best money could buy. The mad thing everyone could vouch for, because no one watching him work would say he was a sane man. He screamed and cursed and gesticulated wildly. He threw himself on the floor, took photos while doing a headstand and was now topless, his shirt tied around his head like the Rambo of the photography world. I caught Ben's attention a few times and rolled my eyes in solidarity as I could see he was fighting the urge not to scream at the guy himself.

Our first location was on the Soussvlie, a dry, barren desert-like land. I'd never seen such a strange, alien landscape before.

The ground was made up entirely of dry white mud that had cracked in a million different places giving it an uneven surface. The white landscape was punctuated with the remnants of dead trees. They stood out of the ground like lonely black carcasses. In the distance, the bright red sand dunes rose up. And in the middle of it all, a baby-blue sports car that looked so out of place there it was breathtaking.

What also looked really out of place was Cindy, climbing out of the car wearing a short, tight, gold evening dress. Her legs went on for ten miles, and her thimble-like waist attached itself to two of the perkiest, well-proportioned breasts I'd ever seen. I knew this, because she also had no shame when it came to changing in and out of clothes. I tried hard not to gag as she pouted and jutted out her collarbones while climbing out of the car in her eight-inch heels.

"What the hell is this?" Giovanni screamed and everyone came to a dead halt. We all looked around to see what he was screaming about in a kind of panicked state. The best thing to do was to keep this guy happy.

"You!" He pointed at Cindy. "Have you lost your car keys? Have you forgotten how to drive? Or worse, have you forgotten the name your mother gave you when she gave birth to you?" he yelled at her and jaws dropped to the floor.

"Sorry?" Cindy blinked at him like a confused little deer.

"Stop looking so confused. And stop looking like you're dehydrated and stop posing."

"Huh?" Cindy looked extra-confused now.

"Like that." He pointed at his face. "You models are all the same. The same, the same the fucking same! Cheekbones, lips, cheekbones, posing, '*where am I, who am I, am I lost?*'"

Horror washed over everyone's faces as we looked from Giovanni to Cindy and back again. He growled, ripped the shirt off his head and threw it onto the sand.

"I need to meditate." He walked off set in a dramatic huff leaving everyone to stare after him, except the producer, whose job it was to placate the beast. She ran off after him as if someone had lit a firecracker in her pants.

"I guess, everyone take a break," Ben called out, before walking over to a shell-shocked-looking Cindy.

Everyone started dispersing, except me. I stood and watched Ben lay a compassionate hand on Cindy's shoulder. She looked coy and placed her hand over his as he squeezed her shoulder in a commiserative fashion. Or was it a different fashion entirely? A *"meet me in my room later and fuck me"* fashion? I moved away quickly before anyone could see the death stare I could now feel involuntarily shooting from my eyeballs.

The day was sweltering hot, and it wasn't very relaxing. I ducked into the craft tent to get some much-needed shade and a cool drink. I grabbed a cold Coke and just before I'd had a chance to open it, something caught my eye.

"Oh! Sorry, I didn't realize you were, uh . . ." *doing what exactly?* Giovanni was perched in the corner of the tent on a chair, legs crossed, still shirtless and hands posed in some sort of meditative position. He really hadn't been kidding about that.

He looked up at me and smiled. "Peaceful."

I nodded and pretended that I knew the first thing about this spiritual stuff. "Mmm. Good for you."

Giovanni climbed off the chair and his eyes swept over me. "Hot." He said it more like a statement than an actual question.

"Very." I opened the can and raised it to my lips. I must have downed the thing in a few sips.

"Thirsty," he said. He didn't seem like the sharpest tool in the drawer, but he certainly made up for it in looks. Besides, I doubted very much that the women who spent time with him were doing it for the scintillating conversation.

"Sweaty." He stepped towards me and glanced at my neck. And then it happened. Without warning, the man was wielding a block of ice and running it over my collarbones and up and down my neck. The coolness of the ice made my hot skin tingle. But I couldn't move. I was in shock. I couldn't work out if this was the worst, most inappropriate thing that anyone had ever done to me, or if I was actually vaguely turned on by this strange move. *No. This was definitely revolting.*

"Hot," he repeated again, this time adding a little lip bite.

"True. So very true," I said wiggling away from the melting cube and his intense stare. "Well, I feel much better now. Cooler. Thanks." I started exiting the tent and in my haste, almost ran right into Ben's chest. Not awkward. At all.

"Ben! Hello, Ben." I tried to wipe all the water off my neck and collarbones as if it were some kind of scarlet letter that had been branded into me. "Hot. Isn't it?" I smiled at him and quickly ran off. *Was this really happening to me?* Did I really have two men coming on to me? Nothing like this had ever happened before.

We wrapped a few hours after my collarbones had been sexually assaulted with an ice cube and moved on to the second location. It was only a short way away, but the landscape looked completely different. The ground was bright red, as were the massive sand dunes that rose up in all directions. There were no trees this time, just endless red dustiness that stretched out all the way to the horizon. If I'd thought the previous place looked like it was on another planet, this one looked like it would be in another galaxy.

Getting the car into the right place this time had taken more effort as the sand was soft. The art department ran around meticulously cleaning every grain off the car and wiping away the tread marks in the sand. Another outfit was chosen for Cindy, this time it was even smaller and tighter than the previous one.

She really looked like she was putting extra effort into it after the yelling Giovanni had given her. She leaned backwards over the bonnet like she was about to snap her spine in half. She bent and twisted herself like a double-jointed pretzel and pouted and posed her heart out, but still, it wasn't enough.

"Roll in the sand!" Giovanni stopped shooting and pointed at Cindy.

"Sorry, what?" she asked.

"Stop looking so beautiful. It's boring. So pedestrian. Like this." And then he threw himself onto the hot, red sand and rolled. We all watched in jaw-dropping shock as he wiggled his body in the sand and then jumped up covered in the stuff.

"Such a creative genius," I heard Angie mumble and turned. Was she kidding? What was with these people? The guy reminded me of one of those ridiculous artists that spray-painted bananas, hung them on a wall as conceptual art and tried to sell them to people for hundreds of thousands of dollars.

"Genius," she whispered again sounding like she was in awe.

"And so hot," Becks added quickly as they both watched him roll.

I tried to stifle a laugh as Ben looked over at me and gave a tiny headshake. This man was truly ridiculous. Cindy looked at him in total horror as she slowly dropped to her knees in the sand and started rubbing it on herself.

"Okay," Ben jumped in stopping the circus, "Maybe it's time for another break." I glanced over at the client who looked disappointed, as if he was waiting for a half-naked model to roll on the ground like she was mud wrestling.

I walked away and pulled my phone out, this was way, *way* too good not to share with someone who would appreciate it. So I typed a message to JJ.

Sera: This photographer is a total nutcase. He's trying to be all deep and angsty and artsy-fartsy and make the model roll around in the dirty sand so she won't be so "beautiful".

JJ: Oh God. He's one of those.

Sera: According to him beauty is pedestrian.

JJ: Hahah. But is he hot? Those types usually are.

Sera: So hot!

As I was typing a suspicious head-shaped shadow fell over my hands.

"Who's hot?" Ben's voice startled me and I jumped in fright.

"Are you reading my messages now too?" I quickly put my phone behind my back.

"Not intentionally. I was coming to say 'Hi' and just happened to read it by accident."

"Really? I doubt that," I said trying to lock my phone screen behind my back.

"So who's hot?" he asked with that devastating smile that causes your legs to start spreading automatically.

"I wasn't talking about you, by the way. In case your giant ego thought that." There must have been something in my tone that made that sound serious because Ben's smile suddenly faltered and he looked at me curiously.

"Oh. I see." He folded his arms. "So who do you think is so hot that you feel it necessary to message someone about it?"

"Uh . . . um, I . . ." I stumbled over my words as my mouth went dry, and it wasn't from dehydration.

"Wow. It really is someone else." Ben unfolded his arms and put them on his hips in a challenging fashion.

"Excuse me," I said sarcastically, "it's not like I'm not allowed to look at anyone else, I mean, you're basically petting the hot model over there when she's upset and batting her eye lashes."

"Oh. So that's what this is about?" He took a step closer to me and I backed away.

"No. This isn't about anything. It's just, just . . . *hey*, what are you doing anyway? We agreed to keep this professional."

Ben took a big step forward before I had a chance to move away. "Sera, how about we be completely fucking honest with each other, for once." His voice took on a harsh quality and I'd never heard him use that tone before. "Let's stop beating round the bush here and couching everything in unsubtle innuendos and sexting. Sure, it's really fun, but at some stage we need to seriously face the facts."

"Uh . . . what facts?" I asked, a knot of anxiety forming in the pit of my stomach.

"This," he gestured to the space between us, "this couldn't be professional if we tried. It crossed that line a long time ago when you were naked and coming on top of me in my car!"

"What?" My jaw fell open.

"Don't act so surprised and shocked, it's not like we haven't said things like that to each other before. In fact, that's part of the problem. One minute you're telling me you won't go out with me, and the next minute you're kissing me."

I looked around nervously, terrified that someone was going to overhear this conversation. "Stop talking like this!" I hissed angrily. "Not at work."

"Why not at work? We have this kind of conversation just about everywhere else, like body corporate meetings and parking lots and—"

"Stop it!" I cut him off and then walked away as quickly as I could. I marched straight back to the craft tent and walked in to find the collarbone assaulter lying on the ground whispering something to himself. I turned and marched back out to find Ben standing there watching me. I huffed and turned and marched straight into the middle of the set and stopped at the car. I took my glasses off and whipped my forehead as the sweat ran down my face and into my eyes.

God, I must look like hell. I walked up to the car and looked at myself in the rear view mirror. My face was glistening with sweat and my cheeks were flushed red, not from the heat, but rather from what Ben had said to me. I moved my hair out my face, it was sticking to my moist skin and I had to shake my head to free it. Grains of bright red sand stuck to my skin and a dot of black mascara had deposited itself on the skin under my eye, probably due to the sweat. I looked up when I heard a clicking sound, only to find Giovanni taking a photo of me.

Why the hell was he taking photos of me?

35

SHE IS NOT STICK . . .

~

I climbed out of the cool shower that I'd just had back in my room and read a text on my phone.

Ben: Did we just have our first fight?

I stared at the message for a moment or two, deciding what I should say back to him. It *had* felt like a fight, and I'd been feeling terrible since returning from the shoot. The idea that Ben and I were possibly no longer on friendly terms made my stomach twist and churn in the most unsettling way imaginable. I brought my fingers down to the phone and started typing.

Sera: I'm not sure. Did we?

Ben: IDK. But whatever it is, I feel terrible.

Sera: Me too.

Ben: I'm really sorry about what I said to you earlier. You were right, it was wrong, inappropriate and unprofessional. I also shouldn't have been reading your messages. Feel free to hate me, but not for too long.

Sera: I'll try not to.

Sera: Thanks for the apology tho. And I'm sorry I'm giving off mixed signals . . . but I'm confused.

Ben: I wish you weren't.

Sera: Me too.

Ben: Are you coming for drinks and dinner?

Sera: Nah. Need sleep.

Ben: Can I come over? We can chat?

Sera: You need to show your face there tho. You're the boss.

Ben: True.

Sera: See you tomorrow.

Ben: Okay, babe.

Sera: Babe?!?

Sera: Hahah!

Ben: Sweetheart?

Sera: LOL

Ben: Honey?

Sera: I'm rolling my eyes.

Sera: How about just Sera?

Ben: Because you're no longer just Sera to me. You haven't been JUST Sera to me for quite some time now.

Sera: You make it sound like you've known me for ages.

Ben: It feels like I have . . .

Ben: Come on, babe. Just go on a fucking date with me, please?

Sera: I'm still thinking about it.

Ben: You're killing me here. You know that?

Sera: Sorry.

Ben: We've already had our first fight. Had sex, eaten together, gone to bloody body corporate meetings together, work together, travel together and practically live together now too . . . Date???

I was just about to answer him when another message came through.

Ben: Gotta go. Bye. Talk later. X

I sighed and tossed my phone back onto my bed. Maybe I needed to draw up a pros and cons list as to why I should or shouldn't date Ben? I was starting to feel like I wasn't even sure what my reasons for not going out with him were anymore, we were spending so much time together already, what would be different . . . other than the sex and the possibility of love and heartbreak and potential financial ruin from lack of job when stuff fell apart? No big deal!

I needed sleep. We were leaving early the next morning for another location which was half way across the country and the soft bed was calling to me. I climbed in and was just about to close my eyes when a knock on the door interrupted me.

"Room service."

I climbed out the bed feeling irritated by the disturbance. "I didn't order room service," I called out as I walked over to the door and swung it open.

"Are you not Sera De La Haye from room twelve?" he asked.

"Yes, but I didn't order anything."

"Well, someone did." The guy pushed past me wheeling a massive trolley covered in silver cloches.

I walked over to one and opened it. *Immediate salivation*. A perfect fluffy-looking chocolate mousse stared up at me just waiting to be devoured. I opened the next one, chocolate cake. The next one, some chocolate tart thing, and so it went on until I had opened all six and was met with a chocolate feast.

I looked up at the guy. "How much is all this? I mean, I can't pay for it."

He smiled and shook his head, "Compliments of Mr. White."

"Oh. I see." The guy left the room and I tried to hold back a smile, even though no one was there to see it. I grabbed a spoon, plunged it into the mousse and scooped up as much as I could before shoveling it into my face. So not lady like! The dopamine in my brain screamed at me in delight and demanded more immediately. I scooped up a piece of cake next, dunking it into the mousse for the hell of it and because no one was there to see me. The sweetness made my mouth tingle. A beep on my phone stopped me from pouring the mousse onto the tart and adding the cake to it. I looked down at my bed.

Ben: Do you still hate me?

Sera: Moderately.

Ben: Come have a drink with me.

Sera: I don't have drinks with people I moderately hate. ;)

Ben: I'll just have to make you not hate me tomorrow then.

Sera: Good night, Ben.

I put my phone back down and climbed into bed again. This time there was no knocking on the door and I fell asleep easily.

* * *

"You missed some seriously crazy stuff last night," Becks said to me as we all boarded a very tinny-looking propeller plane that seemed way too small for all of us to fit into and more importantly, way too outdated and archaic to be trusted in the sky.

"Oh, what happened?" I climbed in and realized I was right about not being able to fit. Crew were sitting with boxes of gear on their laps and the rest of the gear was lining the tiny aisle. I hoped this thing would be able to take off—especially since I was carrying a few extra pounds from last night's chocolate binge! Ben was sitting in the back with his sunglasses on. Becks and I grabbed the nearest free seats and pulled our suitcases onto our laps.

Becks leaned in. "Well, everyone had way too much to drink. Angie was hitting on Giovanni, hectically. And all he cared about was talking about how creatively stifled he felt and how Cindy was just basically ruining his life. Then Cindy got upset and started saying well maybe the problem lay with his photographs and not her and then he got mad and started freaking out and Ben had to separate them."

"Really?" I tried to get comfortable in the little space I had as well as buckle my belt.

"Yes! And then Ben rushed Cindy off to 'comfort' her, and Angie stepped in to 'comfort' Giovanni . . . if you get what I mean." She winked at me. Of course I got what she meant, that amount of air quotes in one sentence wasn't exactly subtle. I glanced back at Ben and wondered just how much comforting had happened last night.

The plane took off and it was just about the worst, shakiest ride of my life and by the time we landed, everyone was clapping and hugging each other. I'd thought I was about to die at least twice during the flight. Because we were now rushing, we went straight to the next location without checking in to our hotel.

We all piled into SUVs and started making our way through the hot desert. It looked even more remote and barren than yesterday, that is until something came into view. Everyone seemed to gasp at the same time as the old, abandoned mansions that rose up out of the sand dunes came into view. We parked and all climbed out. I realized I was standing in a ghost town, it looked like it had been abandoned a hundred years ago and the desert sands had started swallowing the buildings. The houses were all old, windowless shells. What was left of a railway line ran through the town and an old upturned zinc bathtub lay half buried in the sand.

"It's an old diamond town that was abandoned in the fifties," Becks said to me, clearly she'd done her research.

"It's beautiful," I said, scanning the place, taking it all in.

"Just creepy if you ask me," Becks said and walked off.

"It's going to be perfect for the shoot, though," I said, imagining the cars pulling up to the ghostly remains of the houses. Everything got going pretty quickly after that, and soon the huge trucks were bringing the cars in and Cindy was busy trying on clothing options. The awkwardness in the air was thick, and you could cut it with a knife.

Giovanni hated absolutely everything she was trying on, and Ben was desperately trying to appease him. The producer looked like she had aged ten years overnight and was chewing on a fingernail while trying to assure the client that everything was under control. It was not. God, if this was what shoots were always like, I never wanted to go on one again. But the day was about to get even more horrendous, for me anyway.

"No, no, no!" Only an hour into the shoot and the mad Italian was already yelling again.

The crew stopped and looked once more. This time the morbid fascination was gone and it had been replaced by a kind of irritated weariness.

"I can't work with this anymore." He was pacing up and down like a mad man. "It's too much. I cannot do my job under these conditions."

Talk about a prima donna. Cindy had been left standing there by the car, which was pulling into the driveway of one of the old abandoned houses. Personally I thought the shot looked great, but then again, who the hell was I?

"You see this stick!" Giovanni ripped a dead stick out the sand and held it up, clearly aware that he had a captive audience now. "See it is gnarled and burnt and twisted and broken and beautiful. It is not perfect. It has character, it has life, it has . . ."

And then he turned to me and something fucking awful happened.

"You!" he pointed at me with the stick and the entire crew looked over, including Ben. "You must be in the shoot."

"Huh?" I felt my eyes widen and my mouth fell open. A series of *what*?s rang out from the confused crowd.

"You are like this stick. Don't you see?" He was waving it around now with big arms and I'd lost him. I looked over at Ben who was clearly just as confused as I was. I shook my head.

"See." He ran over to me with the camera and pointed the screen in my face, and there I was. It was the photo he'd taken of me yesterday while I'd been looking in the mirror. Ben rushed over and peered into the camera too, and then more people came until everyone was crowded around me looking at the screen.

"See. Look at the sweat dripping down her face, the make-up that looks like she's just woken up, the dirt on her face, her slightly skew nose."

"Huh?" I lifted my finger to my nose, no one had ever told me that my nose was skew before. God, he was making me sound terrible.

"Imperfect, but beautiful. She is not posing like a model, she just . . . *is*."

"I *is* nothing, guys," I said backing away from the screen in total shock.

"You must be in the shoot. It is the only way I will work, I cannot work with this woman, she is too model. She is not stick."

Jesus Christ. What was with this guy and his stupid stick analogy? "I'm not going to be in a shoot," I quickly said.

"Well, then I don't shoot." He tossed his very expensive camera down on the sand and an assistant shot out of nowhere and grabbed the thing and rushed it off. I scanned the crowd; everyone was looking at me.

"Then you don't shoot," I said, turning and walking away from the total madness. Was he really being serious—it was the most ridiculous thing I'd ever heard.

36

A SILENCE BEFORE THE STORM . . .

~

I rushed over to one of the SUVs, climbed in and closed the door. I peered out the window and watched as a loud, lively debate looked like it had broken out. Everyone seemed to have an opinion, arms flapping, heads being held, fingers pointed and every now and again everyone would stop talking and look over at me in the car.

Then suddenly stillness and silence. *A silence before the storm?* The crowd dispersed slowly, and like Moses and the Red Sea, Ben strode out of the middle of it and started walking towards the car. My stomach plunged. I was getting a very bad feeling about this. Very.

"No! NO! No!" I mouthed through the window, locking the door as Ben got closer. I sat back in the chair and folded my arms defiantly.

"Sera." Ben was trying to open the car door. "Please open the door."

"No." I turned to him, arms still folded tightly over my body. "You people are all mad. I told you I didn't want to come on this shoot."

"Please. Just open the door." He pushed his face all the way up to the window and looked at me with a pair of sad eyes . . . God those eyes were dangerous. They caused sensible women to do very stupid things . . . like unlocking the car door. Ben pulled it open and climbed in. I shuffled away from him quickly.

"So it seems that Giovanni will not do the shoot unless you are his 'stick,'" Ben gestured air commas.

"Mm-hmm," I mumbled. "So?"

"And the thing is, that we *have* to do this shoot and we *have* to finish it now, we can't come back and re-shoot it, we can't get another model and we need to use Giovanni."

I turned and looked at Ben. "So what are you saying? That you want me to be his fucking stick?"

"We *need* you to be his stick. Even the client agrees. And you looked so, so, incredibly beautiful in that shot he took. Everyone thinks so, not just me."

My face flushed red and I touched my hot cheeks. "This has got to be some sort of joke."

"No joke." Ben reached out a hand and placed it on my knee, I flinched at his touch. "You know how you broke down the other night and I came out to help you?"

"Yes." I didn't like where this was going.

"You know how you promised you would come to my rescue when my car broke down?"

"Yes." I really, *really* didn't like where this was going!

"Well, my car just broke down. Big time. Its tyres are flat, there's smoke pouring out of the engine, it's about to fucking explode, and you are the only person in the world who can save me."

I looked up at Ben. He looked desperate. There was no longer anything cool and calm about him. I hung my head and shook it.

"But I'm not a bloody model. I have no idea how to pose and look into the camera and pretend that I am in no way self-conscious about a whole bunch of people staring at me and—"

"That's the point. He doesn't want a model. He wants you. Besides, he's already sent Cindy home in a flood of tears so we basically have no one. It's only a few shots, the rest are just close-ups of the car."

"That sounds so embarrassing. Everyone will be looking at me." I glanced out the window and the entire crew were now standing in a line looking towards the car, as if they were trying to read our lips.

"Please, rescue me!" Ben reached out and took my hand. "And if you don't want to rescue me because you still moderately hate me, do it for the money instead." At that I perked up.

"I get paid?"

"Of course. We have to pay a cancellation fee for Cindy, and then we would have needed to hire another model for the rest of the day, so you'll get those fees."

"Really?" I looked up at Ben thinking about textbooks and groceries and getting a few nights off in the next month. Suddenly that seemed like something that would go a long way in quelling any anxiety I might have. But right now, that money didn't mean as much as keeping a promise I made to Ben, and also, seeing him this upset was breaking my heart.

"Fine. I'll do it," I said sliding towards Ben and the door.

"Thanks." Ben looked me in the eye and I felt his hand gently squeeze my leg, "This means a lot to me. I owe you, big time."

37

TOO MUCH LEANING . . .

An hour later I was dressed in something way too skimpy
for my liking and had had my hair and make-up done. Giovanni
had insisted that the make-up be minimal and the hair look
messy, like *"I'd just made love to someone for a whole day."* I'd tried
not to gag at that.

I walked onto the set trying to look as confident as possibly,
even though I was dying inside. Reactions to the new me seemed
very mixed; Angie was basically death staring me, Becks gave me
the thumbs up, some of the other crew members were looking at
me with confusion (clearly I wasn't their type of stick) but Ben
and Giovanni were staring.

"Let's start immediately. The sun will set soon," Giovanni
yelled and pushed me towards the car.

"Do exactly what you were doing yesterday when you looked
into the mirror," he said.

"Uh . . . okay," I said awkwardly. I had no idea how the hell to
do this, so I just bent down like I had and looked at myself.

"Perfect!" Giovanni yelled and I heard the snapping. "Touch your hair!" he screamed moving closer to me. "Yes. Yes! Bella. Bella." He sounded positively orgasmic now and it was so damn awkward, especially when he came up right behind me. "Now imagine you are about to make love to someone in the car. You want them, you need them, you—"

"Stop!" I heard Ben shout from the sidelines and suddenly he was standing next to us as if he had moved there at the speed of light. "Sorry." He started pushing Giovanni away from me. "I'm not sure it's necessary for her to imagine that, hey?"

I stopped looking in the mirror and stood up straight. Ben placed a hand on Giovanni's shoulder and gave it a kind of manly squeeze and then a hard pat. "Right? No need for that?" And then he turned to me. "Don't worry, you're not making love to anyone in the car," he said very firmly and I wanted to die of embarrassment. He moved off and Giovanni sighed and rolled his eyes.

"Fine. Look into the mirror again then." I bent over and looked into the mirror while Giovanni started clicking again.

"Perfect. Yes! Just like that. Now wipe the side of your mouth, like you've just been kissing someone for hours and you still have their taste on your mouth and your lips are stinging for them."

"Whoa. Stop!" I stood up and saw Ben marching towards us again. He walked right up to Giovanni once more and strategically placed himself between us. "Let's drop her kissing or sleeping with anyone, shall we, buddy?" Ben was smiling but he had a dangerous quality to his voice. And I'd never heard him call anyone buddy before, it was unnerving. I felt so self-conscious right now and my body felt numb with embarrassment. I readjusted my skirt and looked out at the crowd. Becks and Angie were huddled together whispering and a few of the other crew members were smiling. *God, what was everyone thinking?*

Ben gave his "buddy" another pat on the shoulder and then walked away again, shooting Giovanni a dangerous warning glance as he went. Giovanni mumbled something that must have been in Italian and then told me to look in the mirror again. Suddenly I had a whole new respect for models. The poor women. Moved around like mannequins, told what to do over and over and over again.

I looked in the mirror again feeling my face flush. This was the stupidest thing I had ever done in my entire life and I just wanted it to be over now. I felt something around my waist and looked down to see Giovanni's hand wrapping around it.

"Just lean back a little." He pulled my hips and I was forced to lean back, my ass almost colliding with his general crotch area. "Now look into the mirror again."

Fuck! I looked into the mirror once more and could feel the heat coming off Giovanni's body behind me. He was so close to me I could feel his breathe on my neck.

"Stop! For fuck's sake." Ben's voice rang out again and I could see him marching back to us once more. "Why are we even shooting her in the close-ups? We're meant to be shooting the models in the wides. There's no need to be right here." Ben stuck an arm out and started pushing Giovanni back again. This was getting so awkward now and everyone was staring!

"But I want to shoot her in the close-up, with the mirror."

"Well, that's not what the shooting board said."

"I'm changing the shooting board," Giovanni said angrily.

"Well, I'm the Creative Director, and I say you are shooting the models in a wide and the car parts close up." Ben bit his lip, he looked like he was fuming now and not doing a very good job at hiding it. What the hell was everyone thinking? I didn't want to look up. I stood completely still and could feel the death stares that the two men were busy giving each other.

"What's wrong with you?" he asked Ben.

"What's wrong with me is that I don't appreciate you touching my staff like that," Ben hissed back.

"Your staff? Is that what she is?" he said in a mocking tone that made me want to die. I looked up and Ben took a step closer to him.

"Show some fucking respect when talking about Sera, okay?" Ben pointed a finger in his face and Giovanni smiled slyly.

"Fine. Sure." Giovanni started backing away from me.

Ben's arm came up and touched my elbow quickly. "Sorry, but if that guy touches you one more time, I think I'm going to kill him." Ben walked off again and my heart started beating in my throat. I wasn't sure whether to be flattered, or downright frightened by Ben's over-protectiveness. Oh, who was I kidding, of course I was flattered.

"Sera, I want you to open the door of the car like you are about to climb in." Giovanni was far away now and Ben had a self-satisfied smirk on his face.

"Okay." I walked over to the door and opened it. The sun was blazing down on me and I was starting to sweat and this dress was really starting to itch in all the wrong places.

I pulled the door open and stood by it.

"Now put your hand on the roof of the car and lean in like you are looking for something."

"Uh . . . okay." I did what he said, I just wanted this to all be over.

"Lean more," Giovanni shouted and waved an arm in my direction.

I leaned. My dress started creeping up.

"More!" he shouted again as the camera clicked wildly.

I continued to lean. More dress creeping.

"More!" he yelled.

"CUT! Stop." I heard that familiar voice again. "I think she's done enough leaning, don't you think?" Ben walked up to Giovanni and snatched the camera out of his hand.

"Hey. What the hell are you doing?" Giovanni grabbed the camera back.

"Just deleting that last one. A bit too much leaning, if you ask me." He gave Giovanni a pseudo-friendly smile and then waved his arm in the direction of the wardrobe department. "Take her a robe, that's enough."

Ben shouted over at them and they came running towards me with a long white robe. I wrapped it around my tense body and hurried off with them.

"But I'm not finished with her," Giovanni protested.

"Oh yes you are. Trust me. You are so done with her." Ben started walking off the set and Giovanni screamed after him.

"But what am I supposed to do now?"

38

FUCK YOU OR MARRY YOU . . .

I stood in the wardrobe tent shaking. This whole thing had turned into a total nightmare and I was dreading knowing what everyone was thinking. Why had I agreed to something so stupid?

Ben suddenly barged into the tent and gestured for the wardrobe people to get out. They obeyed him immediately. He had the kind of look on his face that would probably stop a charging bull.

"I'm so sorry I talked you into that." He rushed over and placed his hands on the sides of my face. "Jesus, what a prick. I shouldn't have asked you to do that. I'm sorry."

"It's fine," I said.

"But he was putting his hands all over you, I just couldn't fucking take it."

I pulled away from him and walked to the other end of the tent, clutching my robe to me. "Don't worry about it, seriously. No harm done."

"Or course there was harm done," he said, and it sounded like the whole experience had harmed him way more than it had actually harmed me.

"Fuck, do you have any idea what this is doing to me, Sera?" He shook his head and looked over to me.

"I . . . I don't know," I said.

"You're killing me here. I am so fucking crazy jealous right now I want to punch that guy in his pretty Italian face."

"Please, don't," I said quickly. Was he joking? Would he really do that?

"Sera, Sera, Sera." He sounded genuinely exasperated. "You're driving me totally mental right now and I don't know what to do with you, whether I should fuck you, or marry you, or both."

My blood froze. *Fuck me or marry me?* What did that even mean?

"I don't want anyone else to touch you like that again."

I shook my head. "That's not really for you to decide."

"Did you like it when he touched you then?" he asked.

"No. I mean, I don't know. It was so short. I barely felt it. Besides, it was weird and everyone was watching me."

"Even the briefest touch can give you that feeling."

"Feeling?"

"It's the feeling that I've had since I first touched you that night." He took a small step closer to me. "It's all I can think about when I see you and it takes all my self-control not to just walk over to your desk and throw you over it. And if I close my eyes," he closed them momentarily, "I swear I can still feel you and taste you. Your touch is like a drug and all I want is my next hit . . . that's the feeling."

I shook my head, speechless. I felt like I didn't have the actual vocabulary to reply to that. I finally did, though. "No. It wasn't like that."

"So it wasn't like this then?"

Before I knew what was happening, Ben launched himself across the room and started kissing me. It was hungry and desperate and I immediately went along with it. He started walking me backwards and suddenly the back of my knees slammed into the table. It stopped us both and we stared into each other's eyes. His pupils were dilated. His eyes were glazed over with pure lust and hunger and I wanted it. *I wanted him.* I wanted everything, anything, and more. All of it.

"God, I want you, Sera," he whispered into my neck.

"Then have me."

"Fuck, you have no idea how good that sounds." Ben pushed my robe open and ran his hand down the front of my body. He inhaled sharply and I could feel he was hard. He wouldn't have been able to hide it if he tried. He thrust his hips into mine and we both let out a series of ragged, sharp breaths.

A noise outside the tent caused us to both look up. This was so not the right time or place for this.

"Are you decent?" Becks called from outside.

I pushed Ben back, "Uh, um . . . I . . ." I closed the robe and looked at Ben as he tried to adjust the rock hard package that looked like it was going to rip through his jeans at any second.

"Just a minute, Becks, I'm having a quick chat to Sera," Ben cleared his throat and said in the most professional-sounding voice. I stared at him, waiting and watching for his body to return to normal, but when it didn't, he quickly sat down in a chair and crossed his legs.

"You can come in now," he called out.

Becks stuck her head around the door and I hoped my face wasn't as red and flushed as it felt.

"Hey." She looked at me. "You okay? That guy got totally pervvy there."

"Fine," I said quickly.

"I'm glad you stopped it," Becks said looking over at Ben.

"Well, I would have done that for any of my staff. Someone crosses a professional line like that then . . ." Ben's voice trailed off and then he shot up out of his chair—all had returned to normal—and exited.

"Bye. I'll see you guys later."

39

ELEVEN-O'CLOCK GIRL . . .

~~

*W*e'd gotten back to our new hotel a few hours ago already and Becks hadn't left my side. She was currently sitting on my bed babbling about her ex-boyfriend and a whole bunch of stuff I wasn't even vaguely interested in, because all I could think about since leaving the shoot was Ben.

My phone beeped just as she had started telling me about a guy in college that she still had feelings for.

Ben: Is she still there?

Sera: Are you spying on me?

Ben: Yes.

Sera: Well then you know she's still here.

Ben: I can't stop thinking about you . . .

Sera: ;) Me too.

Ben: When the hell is she going to leave?

Sera: Doesn't look like any time soon.

Ben: Come round to my place tomorrow night after you've finished your shift?

Sera: Okay.

Ben: So it's a date?

I tried not to smile.

Sera: Fine. You win. It's a date.

Ben: About fucking time. P.S. You've got me so turned on right now I think I'm going to have to take care of myself.

I half choked slash spat out my wine.

"What?" Becks asked looking curious. "Bad news?"

I shook my head. "Nooo. Just, just . . . you know?"

"Men?" she asked pointedly and then looked me up and down.

I nodded and "uummed" at her, as if we were sharing some girl bonding thing. Something very unfamiliar to me. I'd missed out on the whole *teen girl late night gossip* thing years ago while I was fishing my drunken father up off the floor and working so that the family could eat. Another message pinged on my phone.

Ben: You could always come over later and help me?

This time I tried not to splutter and show the redness that I'm sure had just flushed across my cheeks. I put my phone away and wished that was the case. The last thing I wanted was to be sitting here having small chat.

Sera: I'll see you tomorrow night after work.

Ben: I'll be waiting up for you.

* * *

The next day passed in such an exhausted haze. We all woke up early and headed out to the desert again where we watched Giovanni taking pictures of various car parts. Then we caught that same tin can to the international airport, then flew all the way back to Johannesburg and said our goodbyes at the airport. It was Sunday, so at least we'd all get a bit of rest before work in the morning. I landed up catching a taxi back home, I'd secretly been hoping that Ben could take me, but he had a family thing this afternoon.

When I arrived home I had the house to myself. JJ and Bruce were doing the stocktake and I was only too happy to wiggle out of that one. I was also feeling rather anxious about seeing Ben later, and it would be sooner than he'd expected. He'd forgotten that I didn't have work on a Sunday so he'd be seeing me a whole lot earlier than planned. Not that he would mind. I sat and watched the clock until it finally hit 6 p.m. I hadn't heard or seen him come back, but since it was early evening—technically—his afternoon family thing should be over and I was eager to rush over there and surprise him. I did one last obsessive hair and face check, before rushing out the door to his house.

But the second he came to the door and saw me, I knew something was wrong.

I should have turned away and walked back home, but I didn't.

"Hi."

"Hey." He seemed totally distracted and glanced behind himself nervously, as if someone was in his house. "I thought you were going to work tonight." His tone was strange, I'd never heard his voice like that before, nor had I ever seen the strange, almost unreadable look that played on his face.

"I don't have work tonight." I studied his face in silence and it was very obvious that something was up.

"Ben?" There was a desperation in my voice that I couldn't hide.

He said nothing. An invisible force punched me in the stomach and I knew something was very wrong. My suspicions were confirmed when Ben crept out and closed the door behind him quietly—*What was he hiding?*

"Now is not really the best time," he said. "I've kind of got . . ." He paused and looked guilty as hell. " . . . company."

"Company? Oh." Images of Angie and Cindy and gold condom wrappers flashed through my mind as I looked at him and tried not to show the utter hurt on my face. Meanwhile, my insides turned to mush.

And then I heard it, as clear as day . . .

"Ben." A woman's voice called from inside his flat. My heart started thumping in my chest and suddenly there was a loud buzzing sound in my ears.

"Uh . . . is that, a . . . ?" I tried to talk, but my mouth was so dry that the words weren't coming out.

Suddenly, Ben lowered his head and his shoulders slumped forward. "You should really go now, Sera."

His words hit me like bullets and I took a shaky, unstable step backward.

"I'm sorry," he said, reaching out towards me as if he was trying to apologize—*apologize for what exactly? I'm sorry I fucked you, told you I loved you then flirted with you relentlessly, lead you on and kissed you and pursued you, almost beat a guy up for you and now had been caught with someone else.* I didn't think there was a Hallmark card for that.

I stepped back again, and held up my hands, desperately trying to hold back the tears that were about to come. "No need. It's okay. I totally understand."

He nodded at me and gave a kind of half-hearted smile that looked like it took absolutely no effort whatsoever. I wasn't sure what I was supposed to take from that.

"Come back later," he said—*seriously?* Now he wanted me to come back later after he'd sexed-up-a-storm with six-o'clock girl. Maybe I was eleven-o'clock girl. Perhaps there was a girl for every hour of the day and damn week.

"Maybe not," I said, walking away, feeling more hurt and angry than I knew I should have been feeling. I also felt like a complete idiot for thinking that all the flirting might have meant that he actually wanted me, or wanted *only* me. But now I knew. I couldn't blame him really. It was pretty obvious what kind of guy he was right from the start, from the very moment we met. Ben was a hot, dangerous man-whore who kept emergency condoms in his travel bag and said all the right things to women. It was who he was. I couldn't be angry with him for that—*could I?* And it's not like he'd kept it from me, I knew what kind of man he was the second he'd put his hands up my skirt on that dance floor and then fucked me in his car.

But that didn't stop me from being furious with myself for having let my guard down with him. I hated myself for it. He was dangerous. A mere warning may not be sufficient in his case; perhaps a worldwide broadcast announcement might be enough.

The kind of urgent announcement that interrupts your usual viewing. The kind they might do if the planet was suddenly under attack by an alien species.

And what made him so dangerous . . . was *everything!*

I hated him. And I hated the fact that I would have to see him every day at work too. I was dreading Monday morning, and when it finally came around I had a pit in my stomach.

40

REMAIN VERTICAL AT ALL TIMES . . .

*W*hen I got down to my car that morning I found him leaning against it. *Crap, I forgot about the leaning. I was going to have to tell him that, in my presence, he should remain vertical at all times.*

"You didn't answer your phone last night," he said, still leaning. I wanted to kick his feet out from under him and see him tumble to the dirty floor in that expensive-looking, stupid suit—*I hated his suits now.* I hated those tattoos and those chocolaty eyes, chocolate is bad for you after all.

"Well, I was busy," I said, trying to squeeze past him. But he was blocking my path to the door.

"Listen, about last night—"

I put my hand up. "I don't want to hear. It's okay, no need to explain. Really it's fine."

"Thing is," he continued, still blocking my way, "I think you might have misinterpreted things somewhat."

I edged away from him and walked around the front of my car, but he went around the back and beat me to the door.

I sighed. "I don't think there was any misinterpreting that, Ben. You had another woman in your flat, and you were trying desperately to keep us from seeing each other. Correct?" I asked.

"I did have another woman in there." He paused and suddenly looked guilty as hell. "But it's not what you think . . . It's just . . . Just." He stopped talking and I stood there waiting for more. It didn't come.

"Just who?" I asked. "Who? Who?"

He shook his head, but didn't answer me.

"Great! I'm glad we clarified that. I need to get to work." I started walking away.

"Please believe me. It wasn't like that. I know it doesn't make sense right now, but trust me."

"Trust you?" I scoffed. "Do you know how many times I've heard a man say 'trust me'? And the thing is, the thing I've learnt over the years but somehow forgot with you, or chose to ignore, was that when they do act nice, and they do say 'trust me', that is the time you should do the complete opposite."

Ben gave me a strange look, as if he was trying to imagine who all these men in my life were that had asked me to trust them. And because I didn't want him to ask, I tried to pull myself together.

"Look," I said calming down. "It's not just that, I did a lot of thinking last night and I came back to my original conclusion. I don't date. Ever. And I don't want to be in a relationship of any kind, with anyone. I can't, and I have my reasons for that. And I also cannot do anything to jeopardize my job. You have no idea how much I need it. And sleeping with the boss is not exactly a good career move. So please, can we just forget everything that happened and keep it totally professional? Please . . ." I actually teared up at that.

"Sera—" he said, stepping closer to me.

"Stop," I said. "I'll see you at work." I pushed him out of the way of my car door and climbed in. I sat for a while as I watched him walk to his car. As soon as he got in, I turned the key and yes—*you guessed it*—it didn't start.

"Crap!" I screamed as I hit the steering wheel. All the anger, frustration, hurt and jealousy came bubbling to the surface as I tried again and again and again, but nothing. To make matters worse, Ben climbed out of his car and started walking towards me. I climbed out, humiliated.

"Can I take a look at it?" he asked. "I know a bit about cars."

"No, thanks. I can take it to a mechanic."

"I don't think it's going anywhere. It sounds like the starter motor."

"Aren't you going to be late for work?" I said pointedly. "You don't want to set a bad example for your staff?"

"Come, I'll give you a lift."

"Not a chance, Ben! I am not—" I pointed, "NOT. Ever. Getting back into that car again."

"How will you get to work, then?"

"I'd rather walk."

I huffed and pulled my laptop bag onto my shoulder and started walking, of course that was just about the most childish thing I'd ever done in my entire life—*but hey!*

As soon as I got out of the gate and looked down the street, I realized that I would not be walking to the office, not today, not ever. And Ben's black car was hot on my heels, winding down its window.

"Just get in, Sera." He was sticking his head out the window.

I walked on stubbornly. "No."

"You can't walk to work."

"I can walk anywhere I God damn want to."

"It's ten miles . . . unless you're planning on jogging there?" There was a playful tone in his voice now which I did not appreciate.

"You're right. I can't." I swung around. "It's far too far. But I can always catch a taxi or wake JJ or Bruce up and ask them to take me."

"If you get in the car, I promise we don't have to say a word."

I stopped and looked at him considering it carefully. This was the easiest and most obvious choice or else I would be late for work.

"Not a word?" I asked.

"Not a word."

I climbed in reluctantly and kept my eyes in front of me without looking in his direction once. But he lied, because as soon as he had driven a little way, he started talking.

"Sera, there're some things in my life that are very complicated and messed up and I don't want to share them with you right now, but can't we just try and—"

I cut him off. "Ben. It's not about last night anymore. Last night actually has nothing to do with it." That wasn't really true at all. "There are so many reasons not to do this and they have nothing to do with whoever was in your place last night and whatever state of dress, or undress they were probably in." That last part had come out in the wrong tone and had a kind of angry, jealous edge to it that I really hadn't wanted it to have. "You have your secrets; I have mine. And trust me, if you knew what they were, you'd stay away."

"That's exactly how I feel, too," he suddenly said.

"Well then we have that in common," I said.

"Please, Sera." He reached out for my leg and instead of smacking his hand away, I let him touch it. He squeezed my thigh and I bit my lip. *Why was I letting him do this?*

The car came to a stop and he turned and looked at me. I faced him and our eyes locked. He squeezed my leg and I involuntarily licked my lips.

I was so fucking angry with him, and yet I still wanted him so badly on every physical level possible. We looked at each other and that bubble was back. I felt myself being sucked into it. Further and further and further . . .

The loud honk of a horn behind us made us both jump. The traffic light had turned green and reality came crashing in.

"What the hell are we doing?" I pushed his hand off my knee.

"Sera, there's something so strong between us. An attraction we both can't fight, a connection we can't sever."

I looked down at my feet. Something was under one of them and I lifted it and there it was. Lying on the floor. A woman's hairband. I bent over and picked it up. A long black hair was still attached to it.

"It's been severed, Ben. It's been severed." I tossed the hair band over to him, turned in my seat and looked out the window for the duration of the drive. The conversation had ended, there was nothing he could say right now that would fix this.

It was over.

41

THE MAFIA OR SOMETHING . . .

⁓

*T*he week was awful.

I had to stare across at Ben all day while listening to how every woman in the office wanted to "F" the living daylights out of him, although Vampira was the only one who came straight out and said it.

On top of that, it seemed like all of our clients had gotten together behind our backs and conspired to brief us all in the same week for their massive campaigns. We had print, radio, and TV ads coming out of our ears, and this meant many meetings. Many meetings with Ben. Many meetings where Ben walked around the room—*he never sat in meetings*—being ridiculously brilliant, coming up with one amazing creative idea after another while everyone just sat and gawked in awe.

I hated that. I hated having to sit there taking notes pretending I wasn't hating him, or worse, pining for him.

Ben wasn't helping the situation either. On Tuesday, I caught him looking at me longingly from his office like he was a dog that had been left out in the rain, and, for a moment, I totally forgot myself and stared back. When I realized that the look had actually encouraged him and I saw him get up and start walking towards me, I quickly looked away. It was incredibly awkward when he got to my desk.

"Sera."

"Ben."

Becks was leaning in by this stage. She had been acting strangely that week too. So had Angie, in fact, since coming back from the shoot, everyone had been out of sorts. There was a strange silence for a few moments, which I feared might arouse her suspicious. Ben eventually broke it. "Did you speak to the client about when we can present the radio options?"

"Yes. Yes, I did." I forced myself to look up at him like anyone else would do if their boss were talking to them. "On Friday morning, at ten. I'm sure traffic will put it in your diary," I said and smiled up at him like a good hard-working employee.

"Thanks," he said and started walking away. But then he suddenly turned, "You're very efficient, Sera. I appreciate it immensely. I really value you." I saw Becks look up with wide eyes and I was sure Vampira would fly in at any moment. Unfortunately, Angie too happened to be hanging around. I glanced around and could see the eyes looking at me with confusion.

His eyes flicked around and then he quickly corrected, "And, Becks, you too are highly efficient. Angie, also. Very hard working and all that . . . Um . . . In fact . . ." He looked around, seeming a little strange now. He was using words I'd never heard him use before. "Everyone is doing a superb job. Really impressive stuff. Keep it up." Weird pep talk completed, he gave everyone a two-thumbs up—*which looked odd*—and then disappeared back into his office and closed the door. I watched for a moment and saw him curse himself as he sat down and put his head in his hands.

On Wednesday morning, when I arrived at work, I found a bag of M&Ms in my drawer. They had been opened and the blue ones had been removed. There was a little drawing of a sad face inside.

My heart did a few somersaults as I power walked as fast as I could to the bathroom to splash water on my face and take a moment to regroup. After that I went back to my desk, picked up a file and walked to his office.

"Hi."

"Sera?" He sounded excited. "Come in?"

I shook my head. "Please don't give me chocolates again," I said without making eye contact.

"There's no rule that says I can't give something to my staff."

"There is if it's only *one* staff member. Please, if anyone finds out, they'll assume . . ." I trailed off. "Just please don't. Don't make this any worse than it needs to be. Please."

But the next day when I arrived at work he'd given every single person in the office a chocolate. Desks everywhere were covered. I still got a bag of M&Ms and the blue ones had still been taken out and there was another little note.

X, Y, Z

I allowed myself one short glance over at him. He looked gorgeous, and for a small, stupid second, I stared at him, feeling that overwhelming sense of longing building up inside me again. But the longing was soon kicked aside when the anger came bubbling up again. I'd been vacillating between these two emotions for days now, and it was making me feel physically ill.

But something else was going on in the office too—I could feel it. Women can sense things, and I was getting the distinct impression that both Becks and Angie suspected something. They were doing a lot of talking together, they usually never spoke. They also seemed to be looking at me strangely, unless I was just being paranoid.

But there was no escaping Ben that week. On Thursday morning, I found him fiddling under my car bonnet—*was he ever going to give up?* I'm sure if I looked up the definition of stalker in the dictionary, I may find his smug little face there.

"Um, Ben . . . what are you doing?"

"I was just checking something quickly."

I looked at him and tried not to gawk. He was dressed casually: jeans, a pair of worn Adidas sneakers and an old t-shirt that let me admire all those tattoos which I hadn't seen since that night in the car.

"And what did you discover?" I asked, deliberately prying my eyes from his arms and looking down at my feet.

"It's the starter motor, and it's quite a serious problem. I can't fix it and you're probably going to need to replace the thing."

My heart dropped when I heard those words. I'd suspected it was going to be something big and expensive, but I'd been ignoring it, hoping it might go away. In that moment I forgot how much I was desperately trying to hate Ben. "Crap. You're not serious?" I looked into the bonnet as if I knew what I was looking at—*I didn't*.

"Yup," Ben said, wiping his greasy hands on his shirt.

The absolute terror must have shown on my face, because Ben quickly added, "I know a good mechanic, he owes me a few favors actually. I could phone him and—"

"I don't need your charity, Ben. I'll figure something out."

"It's not charity. I'm really good friends with a mechanic and he seriously owes me a few favors."

I gave Ben the once over. The whole thing sounded dodgy. "You know that makes you sound like you're in the Mafia or something!"

Ben burst out laughing. "I've missed that sharp biting wit." He looked at me with eyes that, if I stared at them for too long, would make me forget every reason for not letting him flip me over my car and then marry me twice on Sunday.

"Thanks for the offer. But I'll be fine." I turned and started walking away.

"Maybe this will help," Ben called after me and I turned. He was holding another envelope in his hand and my mind immediately imagined panties. I gasped.

"No. It's not that." He smiled and walked up to me extending the envelope.

I took it and looked inside. There were more $100 notes in there than I had seen in a long time. "What's this?"

"From the shoot. It's what we owe you."

"Uh . . ." I pulled the notes out of the envelope and something about holding a handful of money that had been given to me by Ben made me feel a little sick. Like I was a cheap whore or someone who could be bought.

"I can't take this." I put the notes back into the envelope and thrust them back to him.

"Sera, this is what you are owed. For a job you did."

"I didn't do the job, though. You stopped the shoot, you're probably not even going to use my pictures. I didn't do anything, Ben."

Ben shook his head looking exasperated. "This is money you worked for. You earned it. It's yours. Besides, it looks like you really need it now anyway."

"I don't need anything from you, Ben," I snapped and started moving off.

"I didn't mean it like that. God, why do you always think that? You have serious money issues by the way."

"What?" I turned and glared at him. "And you have serious boundary issues. Not to mention a whole bunch more which I just don't have time to get into now because I have to get to work."

"Fine!" He crunched the envelope in his hand and shoved it in his pocket. "Don't take it. But let me take you to work."

"I'll borrow JJ's car," I said making my way to the lifts. I pressed the button and folded my arms waiting for the thing to come down. It felt like it was taking ages, which was unfortunate because Ben took it as an open invitation to continue talking to me. He came and stood next to me in silence as I watched the floor buttons lighting up as they made their way down from the top floor.

"What?" I finally turned to him.

"Please don't date anyone else until you decide to give me another chance."

"What?" I almost shouted the word out. "You can't say that to me. Even if I don't want to date anyone else, you still can't say that to me."

The lift finally arrived and the doors opened with a ping.

I looked at Ben once more before climbing in and closing the doors behind me. "Fuck," I cursed loudly and leaned against the wall.

What was wrong with this man? How dare he think I would ever go out with him after all that?

42

TGI WTF . . .

*riday was the day that everything fell apart. And when I say *everything*, I mean my whole world imploded. What do they say, *TGIF?* What crap, it was more like TGI WTF?

I was busy on the phone with a client, trying to explain to them in the most diplomatic way possible that the deadline that they had set for the entire print campaign was unreasonable, and unless they wanted the creatives to work through the night for two days straight, it would be impossible.

I heard the papers on my desk move and then saw a hand pushing them away out of the corner of my eye. I turned and looked up to find none other than the Blue Eyed collarbone assaulter sitting on my desk. I looked around to see if anyone else could see him, and they could. His loud throat-clearing had ensured that everyone sitting near me was now looking at him.

"Uh, Giovanni . . . Hi." I was caught off guard and I immediately looked over at Ben's office to establish whether he was looking in my direction. He was not.

Giovanni smiled down at me and leaned in, making absolutely no attempt to hide anything he was feeling right now. "Your pictures came out as perfection," he whispered.

"Oh. That's nice," I said as casually as possible.

"I've come to bring them to Ben, maybe I could show you them though, maybe over drinks later." He smiled again.

I wanted this guy off my desk as fast as possible so I agreed. "Sure. Sounds good. Now if you'll . . . I have to . . . photocopy something." I jumped up and grabbed some papers off the desk and was just about to move away when Ben came striding out of his office.

Fuck!

"Giovanni, I hope you're not disturbing my staff," he said rather pointedly. I wanted to die.

"No. Not at all, I was just speaking to Sera about something. And I came to give you the photos." He pulled a DVD out and passed it over to Ben.

Ben looked down at the thing with what seemed to be disdain. "Uh, thanks. But you know you could have Dropboxed them to me. No need to come out here and deliver them like . . ." Ben held the DVD up and glared at it, as if he hadn't seen one in ages and was absolutely repulsed by it, "this," he finally said, looking back at Giovanni.

"I'm all about the personal touch," Giovanni said, flicking his eyes back to me. A look that did not go unnoticed.

"I bet you are." Ben's tone was acerbic to say the least and it caused Becks and Angie to start staring.

"Like I said . . . photocopy, photocopy, photocopy," I waved my handful of papers in the air and started moving off as quickly as I could.

"So drinks later, then, Sera?" Giovanni called after me. His words stopped me dead in my tracks. It was as if he was baiting me. Baiting Ben. He wanted to cause drama, he wanted to cause a scene, and he had a captive audience.

"Uh, about that . . ." I turned around again. "I don't think I'll be—"

"Sera's busy tonight." Ben cut me off before I could finish. His tone was downright vicious now, but Giovanni looked like he didn't care. In fact, he seemed to be relishing it all.

"Work related, I'm sure." Giovanni gave a slight snort.

"That's between us, I think." Ben said it snarkily and my heart started thumping in my chest. This was bad. I needed to stop this before it turned into something that would be talked about around that hypothetical water cooler.

"Well, the photocopy machine waits for no one." I turned and hightailed it out of there. But I didn't go to the photocopier, instead I went to the bathroom and shut myself in the nearest cubicle.

"Fuck!" I said to myself as I sat there, the heat and beads of sweat on my face you get from a terribly embarrassing moment prickling my face. "Shit," I hissed at myself again.

I sat in the cubicle for ages, not wanting to move, but knowing that I needed to eventually leave before they sent out a search and rescue party. I flushed the toilet for some level of authenticity and walked out. When I did, Angie and Becks were there.

"Angie. Becks," I said in fright.

"Sera," Becks repeated.

I walked over to the sink and started unnecessarily washing my hands.

"I must say a part of me is slightly impressed." I looked up into the mirror as Angie spoke.

"I'm not sure what you mean," I said.

"I just didn't peg you for the girl that slept her way to the top. I mean I could sense you were ambitious, but in a few weeks . . . Ben and Giovanni. Like I said, impressed."

"What? No. It's not like that at all, I didn't, I haven't, I . . . it wasn't like that . . . it was . . . I . . ." The stupid stutter gave me away immediately and I could see it. My face flamed red and I couldn't swallow.

"So who was better?" Angie moved closer to me with a slyness in her voice. God, women were bitches.

"I didn't . . . I . . ." She flicked her eyes upwards in a sarcastic manner.

"Sera, no point in hiding it. Everyone can see it anyway," Becks said, looking angrier than Angie did.

"Everyone?" I asked, a slight panic in my voice.

"It's so fucking obvious. At the shoot the other day Ben was acting like a jealous fucking boyfriend when Giovanni was touching you, and then when I came into the tent he had some of your lipstick smudged on the side of his face, and then today at the office! Seriously, you could have at least been subtle about the thing."

"Oh," I said flatly.

"And here I thought you were my friend," Becks spat at me.

"Wait, this has nothing to do with us and you and—"

"Oh please, it has everything to do with that, I just didn't think you would stoop that low to get the job. How am I supposed to compete with someone who's slept with the boss?"

"Hey! It's not like that," I protested.

"Then what is it like?" Becks asked. "Because I'm working myself to the bone here and you're just boning our boss, no wonder he asked you to come on the shoot when you aren't even on the account."

"I guess Giovanni was just an added bonus, though," Angie said trying to hide her feelings behind a sly smile. But I could see what she felt. She'd set her sights on Ben, and then on Giovanni and in her eyes, I'd beat her to it.

"Nothing happened with Giovanni and I. And when Ben and I . . . look, I didn't know he was our new boss, otherwise I would never have . . . with him. Ever."

Angie forced a little laugh. Like she was going for an evil-villain laugh. The kind that villains give when they've thwarted the superhero's plans and have him tied to a chair in their secret lair.

"You're good. I almost believe you. But take it from someone that knows how to play this game . . . I know what's going on." Then she eyed me with total disdain, "I just can't figure out why they both chose you, I mean you're so . . . so, Sera." Her contempt for and disdain for me was painted so obviously on her face that I melted in shame under her gaze. Suddenly, I was the trailer-park girl all over again. She had seen that in me, and was now seeing right through me. This was the schoolyard all over again. The girls who'd teased me and made fun of me because of who my father was and where we were now living. In one moment, I was transported back to that all over again. Becks and Angie gave me one last scornful look and then both walked out.

And then I couldn't help it . . . I burst into tears. I rushed back into the toilet cubicle and closed the door behind me. I slumped down on the toilet and let the tears flow. I wondered if I could stay here for the entire day and only slip out once everyone had left work. I looked at my watch, through my blurry eyes I could just make out the numbers . . . 10 a.m. That would be one long wait. So I did the only thing I could. I wiped my tears away, straightened myself up and walked back out there.

I didn't look up at anyone, although I could sense eyeballs on me. I walked as fast and steadily as possibly all the way up to my desk. I grabbed my bag and then started walking for the door of the building. As soon as my feet reached the outside, I ran. The cool air immediately made me feel better. That is, until I saw Ben standing outside having a cigarette. As soon as he saw me, he started walking towards me.

43

IT'S A NO. 5 . . .

～

"*G*et away from me," I hissed at him, looking around to make sure no one could see us.

"Where are you going?"

"Away from here," I said quickly and hurried to my car—OH, I had no car today. JJ had dropped me off. This was just getting worse.

"Sera, please wait."

I swung around. "Ben, you have officially ruined my life."

"That's a bit harsh, don't you think?"

"No. This job was my life, don't you get that? I need it and now it's all ruined and everyone in the office thinks I am a total slut who's trying to sleep my way to the top."

"But that's not true."

"Try telling that to Angie and Becks who just cornered me in the bathroom and accused me of being the office slut, which they will no doubt go and share with everyone in that building."

"What?" Ben stepped closer to me. "Do you want me to talk to them?"

"NO! No. Please. You have done enough." I started walking towards the entrance, but Ben was hot on my heels.

"How are you getting home?" he asked.

"I'll hitch hike if I have to."

"And land up on the news in a ditch tomorrow, I don't think so. I'll take you home."

"Not a chance in hell." I continued to walk all the way up to the security boom. I ducked under it and walked out onto the busy road.

"Please don't. It's not safe standing out on this road."

I swung around and looked at him. "It's safer out here than it is in there," I said pointing at the building that had once felt like a happy sanctuary. A place where I could just be a normal person. Where no one knew my history and I could just be Sera. The playing fields were level and it was a place where, through hard work, I could make my way up because I was good at what I did. Now it was none of those things. And probably never would be.

"Please come back inside, or at least let me take you. If you don't want to drive with me, let me get someone to give you a lift."

I shook my head. "I'll call JJ or Bruce, one of them will be able to fetch me."

Ben stared at me as I pulled my phone out and called. JJ answered immediately.

"Hey. Please can you come and fetch me from work. It's a No. 5," I said. This was our secret code. No. 5 referred to Coco Channel who always wore red lipstick, which in our language, meant code red. We only ever used this under the most dire of circumstances, usually pertaining to my dad when I couldn't speak about it over the phone.

I heard JJ jump. "I'll be there in ten. Stay put." And then he hung up. I looked over at Ben, "He'll be here to fetch me soon."

"Then I'll wait with you."

I shook my head and felt the tears well up in my eyes again. "You are just making this all so much worse by being here with me now. It's only confirming everyone's suspicions." I glanced behind me back towards the building and there, as sure as day, a few faces were at the window looking out at us in curiosity. I turned away from them quickly feeling more ashamed than I had in years. "If you care about me, if you ever really, truly felt anything for me, you will leave me alone and stop making this worse."

I looked up at him and a tear rolled down my cheek. "I do care about you, Sera. More than I've cared—"

I cut him off. "Yeah, yeah, you fucking love me!" I laughed at the absolute absurdity of the statement, I couldn't believe I had almost fallen for that line. "You don't even know me. You know nothing about me. You don't love me, you have no capacity and space for that, I'm afraid you just love yourself too much."

Ben looked at me with absolute sadness in his eyes. "I'll come around later and we can talk about this."

"No, you won't," I snapped. "You will forget I even exist and you will certainly forget I live next door."

I turned my back on him and to my relief, heard his footsteps moving away from me. He was finally gone, and I was finally alone.

* * *

When I got home and had spent sufficient time ranting and raving with JJ and Bruce, I poured myself a cup of coffee, adding a few tots of liquor to it—*because it was that kind of fucking day*—and headed outside to my thinking tree. I had a lot to think about. It seemed that in one day, my worst nightmare had become a horrendous reality. I felt broken, as if I'd been surgically cut up and pieced together incorrectly. Everything felt wrong and out of place.

It was early evening already and when I got there, I found a note on the bench with a flower laid across it. My heart raced. *Had Ben also discovered the one spot in the world where I could be away from him?* Fortunately, I noticed the name "Snow White" written across the envelope. With a big sigh of relief that my hiding place was safe, I quickly tore open the envelope and pulled out the cutest little invitation:

Hear ye! Hear ye! Our fairest princess, Li Hau, hereby cordially invites all the noble ladies and gentlemen of the land to join in celebration of her birthday.

The handwriting looked adult, so I assumed she must have actually followed through and gotten her parents' permission. At the bottom she had written, *Pleez!*

How can you say no to that? Sure, it would probably be a bit awkward going without having met her parents first, and considering that I was eighteen years older than her, but why not? One, it would get my mind off Ben. Two, it would get me out of the house so he couldn't come knocking or tapping, and three, it would give me a chance to finally catch a glimpse of Superdad, which I know JJ would be desperate to do.

* * *

The next morning I went past a dress-up shop and bought a sparkly pink wand that I knew she would love and wrote in the card . . .

So all your magical dreams come true.

My wish for this little princess, more than anything else, was that she could keep on believing in magic for as long as possible. If only magic wands really worked and you could just wish away all the bad. We could all use a bit more magic in our lives.

With all the cars out front, it looked like the entire world had been invited to her party—*mind you, six is a big deal!* I tried not to think about what had happened at my sister's sixth birthday party. How my dad had arrived late, smelling of booze, and had caused such embarrassment when he'd started singing Happy Birthday too vigorously and had knocked over the table with the cake on. Thoughts like these just made me more determined than ever to help my sister and at the same time, made me panic. I needed my job, but at the same time, I wasn't sure I was going to be able to do it much longer. And the advertising world is a small one, no doubt word would have spread about me—I'm sure Angie would have helped that along. And since no one was really prepared to hear my version of the events, I'm sure stories of me would probably gain momentum like the stories I'd heard about Ben.

Yes, this party was exactly the distraction I needed when I walked into a literal zoo. Her parents had obviously pulled out all the stops. There were jumping castles, a petting zoo, pony rides and a woman dressed up like a Princess reading stories and painting faces. It was quite a sight to behold. I felt nervous and awkward walking into a place where I knew no one, other than the birthday girl, but I had to be brave. After all, I had promised JJ that I would sneak some photos of Superdad.

As I got closer and people started coming into focus, someone stood out from the crowd. I noticed her immediately; you couldn't help it. She had to be Miss China. No, that title was not even vaguely adequate. Miss Milky Way was probably more like it. I'd never seen anyone so beautiful before—not even Cindy. She was tall, ridiculously so, like a svelte runway model. She had those long well-toned limbs designed especially for ballerinas. Her hair was dead straight, enviably black and shiny, and her features were perfect. They looked like they'd been airbrushed, smoothed, polished and put back on her face in the most geometrically appealing way possible then finished off with a bit of photoshop. Her features were familiar though. She was clearly Li-Hau's mother. There went JJ's notion of divorced parents. What man would divorce *her*? She walked towards me and even though I was a full-blown straight girl, my breath quickened.

"Hello. Can I help you?" She spoke slowly, with the kind of condescending tone that only someone really beautiful could get away with.

"Hi, sorry. I'm Sera. I met—" But as I was about to finish the sentence, Li-Hau came bounding up to me.

"See. I told you she was real, Mommy!"

"Snow White?" her mother asked.

I gave her a smile. "It would seem so."

Her mother sort of looked me up and down over her perfectly shaped nose—*no doubt wondering how I had been deemed "the fairest of them all."*

"When I wrote out the invitation," she explained, "I honestly thought it was just another imaginary friend." She didn't sound particularly happy about the fact that I was real.

Li-Hau shook her head. "Told you!" Then she took me by the hand and marched me away. "Come. I want you to meet my friends."

As Li-Hau walked me towards the crowd, I spotted Lerato, who gave me a little wave and smile, so I went over to greet her. I was grateful that I knew another adult there at least. While Lerato and I exchanged pleasantries, Li Hau let go of my hand and ran into the crowd.

"Daddy! Snow White is here!" she yelled—*Daddy?* I turned and my entire universe shook—

44

A MAGICAL INVISIBLE WHIP . . .

*I*t was Ben.

But how? But what? But . . . what the fuck was going on?

I froze. My heart felt like it had stopped beating and I was going into full-blown organ failure. My eyes scanned the surroundings, looking for an exit strategy, or a place to hide before he saw me. But when I turned, Miss Milky Way had also started walking in my direction.

I turned and looked back in Ben's direction and when I did, he saw me. The moment that passed between us was more intense than anything that we'd shared so far. He looked from me to Li-Hau's mom and back, and the look that rushed over his face was one of indescribable panic.

Fuck!

Li-Hau's mother started making a faster approach and suddenly Ben was on the move too, straight towards me. They both descended at the exact same time and my heart stopped.

"Hi, I'm Ben," he said, making a point of sticking out his hand in my direction.

My eyes floated down to his hand and I stared at it in total confusion and shock.

"I'm Li-Hau's dad," he persisted. "So you're the Snow White I've heard so much about." He smiled at me, widening his eyes. I could see he was desperately trying to communicate with me. The message was clear.

Play along.

What the hell was I in the middle of?

"I . . . I . . ." I stuttered.

Ben jumped in, talking to Li-Hau's mom now. "So Snow White is real after all." He smiled at her and then turned back to me. "Sorry, I didn't get your name?" He looked freaked out, but was trying to hide it—*and not that well*.

"S . . . Sera," I stuttered.

"Nice to meet you. This is Mei, my daughter's mother."

He emphasized the word daughter as if I hadn't caught on yet.

"I told you, Daddy. She's real," Li-Hau said again.

"Yes you did." He reached down and put his arm around her.

This was Superdad?

I couldn't speak, I could barely breathe. Ben had just pulled me into one of the biggest lies I'd ever been privy too. Clearly he was still with her mother. That was surely the only possible explanation for his behavior and this level of deception. He'd had an affair with me and now he was desperately trying to cover his tracks and I was unknowingly caught up in all of it.

"Well, thanks for coming," he said to me. "Li hasn't stopped talking about you."

He said it like that was some kind of consolation prize. Like that should make me better in some way.

"So, Sera?" her mother spoke again. "How long have you lived at Killarney Gardens?" She was looking directly at me and I was unraveling under her gaze.

"About five, six years now."

"Ben just moved in there," she said, turning to look at Ben.

He nodded. "Yes. It's a nice place."

"It's okay. A little small, if you ask me," Mei said scrunching up her face. *It was her.* She was the woman who'd been at Ben's apartment. She was the woman Ben had been so desperately trying to hide me from. I bit down on my lip to try and stop the tears. This time they weren't tears of sadness, they were tears of anger.

"I suppose the gardens are okay," she conceded. Mei was, without a doubt, the kind of woman that females naturally took an instant dislike to. She had that cool aloofness down to an art form and oozed a sense of superiority out of every one of her pretty, porcelain pores.

"Yes, that's where you met Li, I believe?" Ben suddenly said. "In the garden?"

Mei shot Ben a filthy look. "You let her go to the garden by herself?" She stared daggers at Ben and he looked like his world was about to explode, shatter and collapse into a black hole.

And then Li quickly piped up, "Lerato was right there with me!"

I stared at the little girl in shock. She sounded totally desperate. Something was obviously very wrong. Li looked up at me for

LOVE TO HATE YOU   247

confirmation and my heart tugged when I looked into her pleading eyes.

I nodded, "Yes, I met Lerato there too."

Her mother looked satisfied and I noted that Ben's shoulders
sagged in relief. I'd clearly stepped into the middle of a hornet's
nest, and if I didn't tread carefully, I was going to end up being
stung.

"So, Sera." Mei turned her attention back to me and I wasn't
sure I liked the way she was looking at me. It seemed to make Ben
nervous as well.

"What do you do?"

Ben flashed me a desperate look, and again, I knew what he
wanted from me—*I was never going to forgive him for this*.

"I'm a waitress." At least it wasn't a blatant lie. She looked at
me like I'd just told her I cleaned toilets for a living. I didn't like
this woman at all.

"And you?" I asked, pretending I gave a shit.

"I'm a model."

I nodded. Of course she was a fucking model. Of course Ben
would have had a child with the world's hottest female alive.

"And you?" I turned to Ben, playing the role that had been
forced upon me without my consent.

"Advertising," he said quickly.

"How exciting!" I tried to hide the disgust in my voice, but I
wasn't sure I was doing a good job of it.

"Ben," Mei spoke again, her voice stern and demanding. She was
definitely beautiful, but there was something so ugly about her. "I
really think you should speak to some of the other parents now."

I glanced at Ben. He looked startled again. "Of course. Good idea." He moved away quickly as if she'd just cracked some kind of a magic invisible whip. He didn't look back and walked away as fast as he could.

"I want to show you what my dad got me for my birthday," Li said, taking me by the hand and pulling me in the opposite direction. The last thing I wanted to do right now was look at Superdad's gift. To be honest, I never wanted to be reminded of Ben again.

The next hour was up there with one of the worst of my life. Li was dragging me around, introducing me to her friends, showing me the ponies and making me get my face painted like a butterfly. Looking at her, I felt two things, pity and anger. Clearly he wasn't father of the year after all.

I counted the painful seconds until I could politely excuse myself. I didn't want to disappoint Li, but my skin was crawling, I felt physically nauseous and my brain was about to explode.

Was Ben really with that woman? Maybe they were separated and were trying to work it out? But Ben looked whipped; he was jumping at her commands like a performing monkey—*sign of a guilty conscience?*

Eventually I was able to leave. I said the requisite goodbyes to Li and her mother, who seemed to have warmed up to me slightly. I didn't say goodbye to Ben. He hadn't looked in my direction once the entire time I was there. In fact, he'd done everything possible to stay as far away as he could and I hadn't even seen him for the past ten minutes or so.

When I was finally out of sight of the party, I ran. I ran as fast as my still shaky legs would carry me, but when I got into the street, I found Ben waiting for me.

He approached me quickly. "Sera. It's not what it looks like. I can explain, I promise. I can explain."

I didn't make eye contact and physically pushed him out the way with all the force I could muster. "I don't want to hear it. Just leave me alone."

"But I can't leave you alone." His voice sounded desperate and he grabbed my arm. "It's not what you think."

I finally willed myself to look up at him. I was fuming. "Don't ever talk to me again. Don't ever come near me again." I pulled away forcefully. "And don't you dare touch me again."

"Wait." He moved in front of me. "Please."

"Ben . . ." I put my hands on my hips and glared at him. "You and I together is a disaster. Since we met, since that night, nothing good has come of us. We are so destructive and wrong for each other and all this is the universe telling me loudly and clearly that you are the last man on earth I should ever date, or even be near, for that matter."

"I don't believe that."

"It doesn't matter what you believe. I'm telling you how it is." I shivered as a cold winter breeze went through me. "What happened at work isn't your fault. I brought that upon myself because I should never have let things continue with you. But I did. And now everyone in the office knows what I did, and thinks I'm trying to sleep my way to the top and they also think I did it with Giovanni too. Do you know how mortifying that is? And how it undermines me and all the work I've done there since I arrived?"

"I'm sorry." Ben shook his head.

"No, I'm sorry. I'm sorry I ever met you and landed up in your car that night. But you've got some kind of strange power over me that keeps making me forget myself and act like a mad woman. But it's over now. It has to be. All of it."

He said nothing. Instead we just stood and stared at each other. "Bye, Ben." It felt like my heart was being ripped out of my chest and stomped on by Mei's ten-inch heel.

He dropped his head and ran his hands through his hair. "I'm really sorry. I fucked up, big time."

"Save your apologies for someone who cares." I turned and walked away from him. The second I got into JJ's car I put my head down on the steering wheel. My whole body was shaking from the shock and adrenalin surging through me.

I closed my eyes and the tears just came, smearing the pink face paint everywhere.

45

DEPRESSED, HOMELESS,
PAVEMENT SITTER

~

*B*en came to the restaurant later that night. Needless to say, there was a commotion. I wasn't entirely surprised though—since meeting him I had come to realize that he was about as persistent as a pit-bull on heat.

"Right of admission reserved, bitch," were the words JJ used when stopping Ben at the door.

Waiters turned and looked. Patrons put their knives and forks down. One of the kitchen staff even stuck his head through the door and gawked. Bruce jumped up and pulled JJ away, who by this stage looked like he was going to bitch slap Ben to hell and back.

"Just stay away from Sera now," Bruce said in a much more diplomatic tone. "There's no need for a scene."

"Oh yes there is," JJ said, stepping forward and doing some finger snapping.

"Just let me explain, Sera. Please!" Ben screamed his plea across the restaurant.

"No!" I shouted back.

It was turning into a soap opera. Luckily the clientele at Big John's were used to such histrionics—*and were always interested.* Heads turned from him to me, and everyone looked giddy with excitement, like they had a front-row ticket to the season finale of *The Bachelor.*

"Give me ten minutes," Ben persisted, "and then after that, if you don't want to talk to me again, it's fine." Heads swung around and looked at Ben, then back to me. They were hanging on every word.

"No!" I shouted back again. Some of the patrons and staff looked disappointed by my reply. Clearly they wanted more drama to play out.

"Okay, let me explain it to Bruce then and let him tell you what he thinks."

I looked to Bruce and he shrugged.

"You can explain it to me," JJ said, stepping up again, claws out. Our audience grew extra excited and a few "*ooohhhs*" rose up from them.

Ben looked momentarily panicked, but collected himself, turned to JJ and managed a confident, "Okay."

JJ pranced out the door indignantly and the two of them took up positions on the pavement outside. Everyone in the restaurant looked out the window. Some even got up for a closer look. Bruce came up behind me and slipped his arm around my shoulder. We both watched Ben as he desperately tried to explain his side of the story. JJ didn't look impressed. He tutted and scoffed and switched his hand from hip to hip a few times . . . but then something changed. His face started to relax, so did his posture. He started looking at Ben with a strange look and by the end of it, JJ was hugging Ben and wiping tears from his eyes. Ben too looked like he had a tear—*WTF?*

Bruce and I exchanged looks.

JJ walked away from Ben and came back inside looking like he'd just watched *Steel Magnolias*. The crowd looked like a bunch of hungry lions at feeding time now. "It's good. It's really, really good," he said, wiping a tear away.

"What is?"

"His reason. It's a really good one."

I looked out the window; Ben was sitting on the cold, hard pavement holding his head in his hands. It was freezing outside and he looked like a sad, sorry, pathetic mess. I wasn't sure if he was trying to illicit sympathy by pulling the depressed-pavement-sitter act on me.

"Go and talk to him," JJ said, taking me by the arm and shoving me out the door. I clearly had no choice in the matter. JJ closed the door behind me and locked it when he saw me coming for it. It was freezing outside and I shivered. Ben stood up and looked at me. His eyes looked a little red, as if he'd been crying.

I wasn't sure how to feel about this—*My dad always cried when he was sorry. Standard practice at our house really.*

"I'll never gamble again. I'm sorry." (cry, cry, cry) "I'll never steal again. I'm so sorry." (cry, cry)

Ben started walking towards me slowly. I rubbed my arms as the icy wind blew through me. Ben took his jacket off, and without saying a word, draped it around my shoulders. He did it so quickly I didn't have time to protest, even though the last thing I wanted was an item of clothing that smelled like him anywhere near my body.

We stood in silence for a while before he spoke. "Thanks for agreeing to listen to me."

"Whatever," I said belligerently.

There was another silence as Ben looked like he was readying himself. He took a deep breath and began.

"Mei is my ex-wife," he finally said.

"Ex-wife?!" This wasn't starting out well at all. I didn't know what shocked me more, the fact that he had an ex-wife, or the fact that he was in his early twenties with an ex-wife.

"We've been divorced for four years already. Truth is, we should never have gotten married in the first place."

"So why did you?"

"She was my girlfriend in high school and she fell pregnant when she was eighteen. It was an accident and I thought marrying her was the right thing to do." Ben looked at me. "It wasn't. We weren't compatible, and getting married just made things worse." He paused and ran his hands through his hair again. "We fought constantly, we even fought on our honeymoon. We knew nothing about being married and becoming parents and I was young and dumb, and I was a shitty husband. I . . . I . . ." He paused again and took a deep breath before dropping the bomb, "I wasn't ready to settle down and didn't really take my duties as a husband seriously . . . and I, cheated."

"Really. You're not doing a very good job of redeeming yourself right now," I said, folding my arms across my chest.

"I know. Not my finest moment."

"Finest moment? Well, that's an understatement if I've ever heard one!" I was appalled.

"Okay. It was disgusting. It was wrong, I was stupid. I was twenty years old and I was a dick, bastard . . . is that better?"

I didn't respond. What was one meant to say to that anyway?

"But the things is, I was always a good dad. *A great dad.* I loved Li from the second I found out Mei was pregnant. I was the one who had to convince Mei to keep her, and I think that was part of the problem. She resented me for that, because she wasn't ready to be a mother at eighteen. Who is, I guess?"

"Maybe she resented you because you were a lying cheat," I snapped back and he looked up at me. He looked genuinely hurt. He started pacing up and down the pavement now, looking agitated.

"The whole marriage was a mess and a mistake from day one. But then Li arrived and I held her in my arms for the first time, and I knew she wasn't a mistake . . ." he trailed off and I saw his eyes getting moist.

He stopped pacing and smiled to himself, as if he was recalling a memory. "I was obsessed with her from day one. We were inseparable and I admit it, I gave my daughter much more attention and affection than I ever gave my wife. Another thing she resented, another thing we fought about. Day in and day out. It was draining and we were always at each other's throats and I couldn't take it anymore and that's when I . . ." He paused and looked pained. "It was a one-time mistake and when I told her about it, that's when everything fell apart."

"Sleeping with another woman will do that!"

"I know," he said. A sad, defeated looked washed over him. Like a beaten dog. All that Ben confidence and bravado was gone.

I wasn't used to seeing this side of him and it made me feel very uncomfortable.

"Believe what you like, Sera. I wasn't a great husband, I'm the first to admit that, but I was a great dad . . . I was a *great* dad. Cheating on your wife does not make you a bad dad. *I was a great dad.*"

He kept saying that.

"But Mei couldn't keep those two things separate. I think her ego wouldn't allow it, so, when she filed for divorce she decided to punish me for it. And she knew exactly where it would hurt the most—Li." He started wringing his hands as if the mere memory still haunted him.

"She pulled out every dirty trick in the book, telling the attorney that I was a wild party animal, that I went out with friends and got pissed, that I was a cheating bastard, that I screamed at her in from of Li, that I was irresponsible. Some of the stuff was true, but the rest was blown out of proportion until she made me look like some partying, alcoholic sex addict. By the time she and her lawyer were finished with me, no judge was letting me near Li unsupervised. The irony is that Mei didn't even want to be a full-time mother; Li was living with her grandparents half the time. I should have gotten custody, but she just did all of it to punish me."

Ben stopped. He looked like he was in so much pain that, despite myself, my heart went out to him.

"Then she decided to move back to China with her parents. She got this big modeling job there, and I tried to stop her. I threw every last cent I had at lawyers. I basically bankrupted myself doing it. But she had custody and she could go wherever she wanted. She tried to leave the country without letting me say goodbye to Li, but I found out and went to the airport."

He stopped talking again and turned away from me as if he couldn't bear to look at me. "I reached them just in time, but Mei got her parents to take Li onto the plane. Li was screaming and crying for me, but they wouldn't let me see her. And then Mei told me I would never see her again. I tried to reason with her, '*just let me say goodbye, let me hold my baby and let me kiss her goodbye.*' " His voice was quivering, and I couldn't see his face, but I was pretty sure he was fighting back tears. "I tried to stop her and that's when things went wrong."

He paused again for a long time, kicking a small stone into the road. "I tried to push through the boarding gate, but the security guards stopped me and that's when I lost it. I fought back, and I didn't stop fighting until they had to physically restrain me. I broke one of the guard's ribs."

I gasped at this.

"Of course Mei just used this against me even more and filed a restraining order, even though we weren't even in the same country. She told the lawyers that she was afraid of me, that I was abusive and dangerous and aggressive . . ." He turned around and his eyes sought mine. He seemed to be pleading with me. "I just wanted to see my daughter. I just wanted to hold her and say goodbye."

"Jesus," I said.

"The guard took pity on me, he's a divorced dad too and dropped the assault charges, but the courts made me go to anger management and I've been jumping through hoops ever since trying to prove that I'm not some evil, aggressive person and that

I'm a good father. I got a good job, worked my way to the top, paid my taxes, bought a house, acted like a responsible grown-up and stayed out of fights. I still wasn't allowed to see my own daughter, though. And because of the restraining order I wasn't even allowed a fucking phone call. Not one. Not on her birthday, not on Christmas. I would have given everything for one minute with her. Anything. Everything I do, every day, is for her."

I stood listening to him, but I had no idea how to respond to any of it. It was just so much to take in at once.

"Then she came back to South Africa six months ago and after more lawyers, and more fighting and more courts, the restraining order was finally dropped and I was allowed to see her again. I thought she would have forgotten me, but she hadn't, she . . ." Ben teared up again and I stood there shocked as I watched a small tear travel down his cheek. "She remembered me and when she hugged me, it was as if no time had passed. But it had, I'd missed out on years and years of my daughter's life."

"But you're allowed to see her again?" I asked.

"Yes. It's still supervised, with a court-appointed social worker or her parents or Lerato. Lerato likes me though, and I think she sees how close Li and I are, so she turns a blind eye to us spending time together alone. But that could come back to seriously bite me one day. The other Saturday night when you came over, Mei was there inspecting my new house to decide whether Li would be allowed to have sleep-over visits. My lawyers have been hitting her hard for joint custody, and I think she's starting to get tired of fighting, not to mention seriously financially drained. But I know her. She's looking for one slip-up, anything to use against me. And I know what she's like with other women—" Ben looked up at me and sort of managed a small smile, "—especially women who are more beautiful than her. And especially women that I like. That's why I sent you away on Saturday. Not because something was happening with her. But because I knew that if she saw you and I together for a second, she would see how I felt about you and God only knows what she would have done."

"Why . . . why didn't you tell me any of this before?"

"Because I like you. *More* than fucking like you, Sera."

I shook my head. "That makes no sense. If you liked me, you would have told me the truth."

"The truth? That I have an ex-wife, that I was a bad husband and cheated, that I have a daughter, that I was arrested for beating up a security guard, that I'm in anger management, that I have to check in with a psychologist to make sure I'm fit to see my daughter and that I'm not some aggressive lunatic, that my ex is watching my every move and waiting for me to fuck up in the slightest, that I'm engaged in constant, time-consuming and fucking soul-destroying legal battles."

He started shaking his head. "That makes me sound like the last guy on earth you should date. But I swear, I'm not a bad guy. I just wanted the opportunity to prove that to you before you made a judgment based on my past." He paused and a knot in my stomach started to twist. I'd said that before too, I also omitted tales about my past for fear of judgment.

"I just wanted you to go on one date with me, just one . . . I wanted you to get to know me before I dropped this on you. I know that was wrong and manipulative, and I'm so, so sorry." He shook his head. "My life is so messed up and anyone who gets involved with me is going to have to put up with—"

And then he stopped talking and it looked like something dawned on him. He stood there, deep in thought for what seemed like ages, before he squared off and looked me straight in the eye with an expression I suddenly couldn't read. "You're probably right not to go out with me. I shouldn't have dragged you into this. It was selfish of me . . . but you came along and I wanted to be with you so badly . . . I'm sorry, Sera. I'm bad news. You're too good for me."

He walked up to me and without asking, hugged me. He held onto me so tightly that it was difficult to breathe. I found myself wrapping my arms around him too, and I didn't quite know why. He lowered his lips to my forehead and kissed me. Then he cupped my face and kissed me. The kiss was short, but so full of meaning.

I watched him walk away. I didn't know if I was angry with him, or felt desperately sorry for him. I didn't know if I wanted to hug him and hold him and tell him everything was going to be okay, or I wanted to fuck him, or slap him. He stopped when he got to the car and looked at me. He smiled.

"I'm still totally in love with you though." And then he got into his car and drove off.

46

YOUR MADONNA
IS WAY BETTER . . .

⌒

"*O*kay, so that was intense," JJ said. We'd closed the restaurant and were sitting at one of the tables sipping wine. It was the first time we'd had the opportunity to talk since Ben had dropped all the multiple bombs.

I took a big sip, hoping it might anesthetize my screaming nerves. "I honestly don't know what to think," I said.

JJ took issue with that. "Um . . . what do you mean you don't know what to think? You should know exactly what to think."

"What?"

JJ blinked in disbelief and leaned forward. "Honey, that's a real man right there."

"Huh?" I shook my head. "What the hell are you talking about?"

"Have you ever heard anyone be so brutally honest before?"

"No, but what's that got to do with it?" I was starting to get pissed off.

"Hello, he's not perfect and he can admit it out loud—even if he knows it will paint him in a crappy light. And he accepts responsibility for what he did. He admits his fault. Big respect!" JJ said this while holding his glass in the air momentarily as if he was toasting someone, then took a sip. "I'm not sure I could do that. Could you?" He shot me a very loaded look, and I knew exactly what it meant. I knew I also had secrets that I hadn't shared with Ben. But at least I hadn't pulled him into a very public lie. I was still not as moved by Ben's confession as JJ clearly was.

"How much have you told Ben about your past?" JJ asked. "How many times have you failed to mention it so people don't judge you."

"So what are you saying? That I should forget what happened and go out with him? A self-confessed cheat?"

JJ shook his head. "No. Not at all. You've got to figure that one out yourself, but all I'm saying is that he's the most real human being I've ever met."

Bruce nodded. "It took guts to do what he did."

"I suppose," I said, "but he has an ex-wife and a kid, and he was a bad husband, and he beats people up."

JJ spoke again, "Oh please! But he also got married at nineteen, and to a mad bitch by the sounds of it. Of course he was a shitty husband. What teenage boy wouldn't be? God, I could never have settled down at nineteen. Let alone have a kid and be the kind of father he clearly is."

"So that makes everything okay?"

"No, of course not. But sometimes you have to look at the full picture. Not everything is black and white, Sera. You of all people should know that. Life is full of grey patches."

I put my head down and slumped forward onto the table, letting out a long and loud moan. "Urrrgggghhhh. But he lied to me."

"We've all told lies to protect ourselves," JJ said, throwing the rest of the wine back. "He's also totally mad about you, by the way."

"And that's the other thing I don't get about him. Why? How? He hardly knows me and he claims he's in love. He's obviously mad. And I could never go out with anyone who was a lunatic."

"Love is mental, honey." JJ tipped his glass at Bruce. "Just ask that one how he fell in love with me?" He smiled at his partner affectionately and I turned to look at him.

"I saw him doing a Cher impersonation at a club," Bruce said.

"I do a really good one," JJ piped up quickly.

"You fell in love with him when he was dressed as Cher?" I asked.

Bruce nodded. "On the spot. Love at first sight and I hadn't even spoken to him yet." He turned to JJ now. "Your Madonna is still way better, though."

JJ nodded in agreement. "I know."

I couldn't believe I hadn't ever heard this story before. It had never occurred to me to ask how they met; I just assumed they'd always known each other. "What did you do?" I asked, looking over at Bruce.

"Well, of course I was too shy to speak to him," Bruce said. "I was this nerdy little accounting student hiding my sexuality, and he was this fabulous, loud, performer who was the center of every single room he was in."

"Little did he know how much I loved nerdy little account-ants." JJ smiled over at Bruce.

"So what happened next?" I asked.

"Well," Bruce continued, "I just watched him. I went to all the gay clubs he was preforming at and would sit there and have a few drinks trying to pluck up the courage to speak to him."

"For a whole year!" JJ added loudly while patting Bruce on the arm. "It took him a whole year to finally speak to me."

"And what did you say?" I asked.

Bruce laughed. "I overheard him complaining to someone that he had no idea how to do his taxes, so I offered to help."

I burst out laughing, "After a year, your big pick-up was 'can I help you do your taxes?'"

"It worked, though." JJ leaned over and gave Bruce a kiss on the cheek.

"But you guys were meant to be together," I said.

"And how do you know you and Ben aren't meant to be together?" JJ looked across the table at me.

"What?"

"He seems to think so at least," JJ said topping up our wine.

"He said that?"

JJ nodded. "That guy has it *sooo* bad. And I don't know . . . but I don't think I've ever seen you so messed up over a guy before either."

He was right. I'd never been this messed up over anyone before. What was it about him? From our very first moment together in the car, it was as if something had happened between us that night that made it impossible to be apart. Maybe it had been the way he'd looked at me, as if he knew me? I'd felt so close to him in that moment, for some strange, inexplicable reason.

Love at first sight? I almost missed the whispered phrase as it raced through my head and then disappeared again.

"Aren't you at least relieved that he wasn't screwing someone in his apartment the other night, when he'd asked you to come over?" JJ asked. "At least he wasn't that much of a bastard."

"But he made me lie today." My voice quivered. "I hate lying." *It reminded me of my father.*

"You caught him off guard," JJ offered. "What would you have done in that situation? What if it was him walking in on you, on some crazy run-of-the-mill Saturday night with your dad being dragged off by the police? You would be the first to pretend you didn't know the guy and lie about who he was."

"I . . . uh . . ." I couldn't defend that. It was totally true.

"Let's be honest here, Sera. How many people have you lied to about who your family are, all because *you* don't want to be judged?" JJ wasn't mincing his words, and if anyone else in the world had said something like that to me, I would have been offended. But how could I be offended if he was right. I'd told so many lies about who my parents were and where I was from. I'd even gone as far as telling the girls at my new school, the one I'd tried to make a fresh start at, that my dad was dead when he was actually spending time in jail.

"I'm kind of on JJ's side here, I mean, how long did it take for you to tell Schnitzel about your family and why you were always having to rush off in the middle of the night?"

"His name was Manfred, not Schnitzel!" I looked over at the guys and rolled my eyes. My ex-boyfriend had been German which had automatically landed him with the name "Schnitzel." *"At least it's not Weiner,"* JJ had said when I'd complained about it.

"So what are you guys trying to say here? That I'm also a bad person because I lied about my family?"

"Hey!" Bruce held his hand up. "No one is a bad person here, least of all our Sera. Personally, I think Ben's a nice guy who's made some terrible mistakes that he's genuinely sorry for. We've all made mistakes. I'm not saying you should forgive him and just go out with him but . . ." He shrugged. "Well, I can't tell you what to do. We'll support you in whatever you decide."

I nodded slowly. "And everything at work? How can I go back there when everyone knows and hates me and thinks I'm slutting my way to the top?"

"They don't hate you, they are all just jealous bitches." JJ clicked his fingers.

"But they know. And they think I fucked that photographer too."

"Dolce Delish." JJ suddenly burst out laughing and Bruce quickly followed.

"Schnitzel and Dolce Delish . . . what's with you and these European men?" Bruce and JJ were still laughing.

"I think the real question is what's with you two naming the men in my life after foodstuffs?"

"That is *so* totally untrue. We've been secretly calling Ben the panty smuggler behind your back!" JJ said and the two then roared with even more laughter.

I shook my head with an amused smile and waited for the hyenas to taper off. When they finally did, "Now that you've stopped laughing at my expense, can we get serious again about work." They both nodded and tried to wipe the smiles off their faces. "I just don't think I can go back to work."

"Well, don't then," Bruce offered.

"Great idea. I'll just have to substitute my income by standing on the corner of Oxford Street with all those other girls. JJ, I'll have to borrow some of your whore heels though." I threw the wine back. It was a joke. Sort of. Because if I didn't have that job anymore, then how the hell was I going to make enough money every month? There were only so many burgers and drinks you could serve.

"The guy next door finally sold his shop. And we bought it." Bruce sounded triumphant.

"What?" I gasped. "That's great."

"We were going to tell you tonight and have a bit of a cele," JJ said.

"I can't believe it. That's amazing."

"And there's going to be a shitload to do. We want to set up a coffee shop asap, capitalize on lunch and breakfast," Bruce said excitedly.

"Morroccan inspired. Cushions on the floor, those low tables, intricate mosaic walls, those big brass chandelier lights and crazy strong coffee that will have everyone addicted," JJ continued as if he already had the whole thing planned in his head.

"Sounds amazing," I said.

"We'll even hire one of those hot barristers with a big sexy beard who'll draw all those coffee-loving hipsters in," JJ added with a naughty smile.

I laughed. "Aren't you guys cool."

"And you'll run it and get it all set up," Bruce added.

"What?"

"You know this business inside out and we trust you. Besides, you'll have the world's best bosses who you don't even have to sleep with to get the job."

"Ha ha," I said sarcastically.

"It'll be so much fun," JJ chorused.

I smiled. "It does sound nice." But anything other than going into work on Monday sounded nice. Anything to avoid Ben and all those prying eyes.

I nodded. "When do we get started?" I asked.

47

BAD CAN BE VERY GOOD . . .

It was three in the morning and I was still staring at the ceiling. JJ's words had been playing over and over in my head like a stuck record, and I'd been tossing and turning and getting in and out of bed all night. I even got up and started cleaning my room in a desperate attempt to clear my mind. What *would* I have done had the roles been reversed?

I hadn't told Ben everything about myself either, for the exact same reason he hadn't told me. We were the same in that way— so how could I be angry at him for something I was doing too? But that still didn't stop all the intense emotions I was having right now. It was a mixture of a million different feelings that were hard to piece together and understand. I was confused. About him, about the way I felt about him, about everything . . . that is, except for one thing. I was crystal clear about one thing alone.

I opened my laptop and started writing a formal resignation letter. Once done, I hovered over the send key for a moment, hesitating. But just for a second. I quickly pressed send and watched as the mail disappeared with a whoosh. I was just about to shut my computer when I heard a ping.

It was from Ben. I opened the mail and there were only five words.

"I don't accept your resignation." My blood boiled and my fingers returned to the keys.

"I've already got a new job. I won't be coming in on Monday."

A message flew back almost instantly. "You signed an employment contract that said you would give three months' written notice."

The mail made me furious and I started typing again. "Sue me," I wrote and sent the mail back.

"Maybe I will." Ben's response shot into my inbox.

"Go for it. See if I care." I blasted it off.

"You do care."

"Trust me, I don't. And besides, what right do you have to be angry with me??!!!"

There was a long pause in the messages and I bit down on my nail in anticipation. *Why did I feel this way?* Why did I care so much, and dislike him so intensely all at the same time?

Knock. Knock.

I looked up in panic as I heard the knock on the front door. It was three in the morning, for God's sake. I marched over to the door and opened it quickly knowing exactly who it was.

"What are you doing here?" I hiss-whispered.

"Not accepting your resignation."

"You don't have a choice," I said.

"What job have you got?"

"None of your business." I folded my arms.

"You're one of my best people, I don't want to lose you." The fiery look in his eye and the tone of his voice changed. "You're really good at what you do, Sera. Your internship is nearly over and you're the one who's getting the permanent job. And then you'll be able to start growing a real career, and because you'll be earning more, maybe you won't need to work at the restaurant as much, you could finally get a good night's sleep."

"I'm getting the job?" I asked.

"You're way better than Becks, and you're a harder worker."

I shook my head. "But don't you see, Ben. I could never accept a promotion from you, now that everyone knows. They'll all assume I got it because I fucked you."

"Well, you didn't. You got it because you're good."

"Everyone else won't see it that way."

"Let them think what they like about you."

"No!" I looked up. "That's *your* thing, not giving a fuck about what people think of you. All those mysterious rumors and urban legends about you. That is not me. I don't want to be whispered about and gossiped about."

"I give a fuck about what you think of me. I give a big fuck," Ben quickly said.

I sighed and shook my head. "But that's not the only reason, and you know that. With everything that's happened between us, I can't work for you anymore. You make me crazy. You make me irrational and insane and it's not good. For either of us."

"Insane is good." Ben took a step closer to me.

"No! Insane is very, very bad," I said.

"And bad can be very good too."

"Oh stop it! Just stop it with all your weird contradictory little mysterious statements . . . love to hate you, fuck you or marry you. They are ridiculous. And make no sense whatsoever. You make no sense. We make no sense. And don't say something like making no sense makes sense or some crap like that."

Ben smiled at me, "There's my fiery Sera."

"My? I'm not yours, and besides, a few hours ago you were telling me what bad news you were and how I shouldn't date you."

"That is still totally true. I would kill a guy like me if my daughter brought him home."

"Huh? You see, that makes no sense again." I re-folded my arms as Ben took another presumptuous step forward.

"My life is fucked up and I'm totally imperfect. But I also think that we're perfect for each other." He took another step forward and I knew I had to stop this immediately.

"It's late, Ben. I'm tired. I want to sleep."

"Sure." He nodded slowly. "Can we pick this up in the morning?"

"Pick what up?"

"This conversation, there is still so much I want to say to you."

"You've said enough, Ben. Trust me, you've said enough to last you a hundred lifetimes. Goodnight." I started pushing him out and closing the door, but he blocked me.

"Ben! Please. Let's just call it a night."

He opened his mouth and looked like he was about to give one last big plea, but stopped himself.

"Goodnight, Sera."

48

SNOOPING AND SNEAKING . . .

It was seven in the morning, way too early for a normal person to be up and about on a Sunday, but I was. Mainly because I hadn't slept at all. I'd replayed the conversations we'd had over and over again. The one at the party, the one outside the restaurant and then again at the door.

God, so much can happen in a week and I bundled all my laundry together, wrapped myself up in extra scarfs and put two warm tops on and waddled down to the laundry room. I hated the fact the laundry room was in the basement parking lot, which was as cold as a morgue in winter. And then to top it off, the washing lines were on the roof—they couldn't be further away if they tried.

I walked into the washing room and immediately saw it. A portable CD player. What the hell was it doing here? I walked over to the thing and looked down at it.

"Press Play."

A note written by Ben was stuck to the top of it. I reluctantly reached out and pressed play, nervous of what the hell I was going to hear. Suddenly a cheesy Justin Bieber song filled the room, something about saying sorry and now he was yodeling about her body, or something.

His voice echoed around the room. I cringed and then I skipped to the next song and more music . . .

An eighties power ballad filled the tiny room, like the singer's massive perm probably would if she was standing here. Her gruff voice warbled about more forgiveness and . . .

I quickly skipped and was suddenly confronted with Meatloaf himself, vowing to do all sorts of things for love, except . . .

I stopped the CD and stared down at the player. I didn't really know what to think about this? A CD full of sorry songs wasn't exactly going to make it all better. I pushed the CD player aside and loaded the washing machine. I sat on top of it waiting for the cycle to be over while munching my way through a bar of "sugar free" chocolate and drinking a cup of coffee which had also been conveniently left for me.

Suddenly the sound of a little girl's voice could be heard echoing through the room. I knew exactly who it was.

I climbed off the machine and stuck my head around the corner, just in time to see Ben and Li climbing out of his car. She was giggling and so was he. I stayed there and watched him interact with his daughter. I wanted to watch him, as if inspecting him might give me some of the answers to the questions I had about him. I also wanted to watch him because despite everything that had happened, I just couldn't help myself from being drawn to him.

I studied every little thing about it. The way he held her hand softly as they walked, the way his eyes lit up when he looked down at her, the way her entire face lit up when she looked up at him. Suddenly the machine stopped and a bell started going off. I saw Ben's head lift and look in my direction. He caught my eyes briefly and smiled. I jumped back behind the wall.

Half an hour later I was standing on the freezing cold roof, trying to hang my delicates in the only beam of sunlight penetrating the gloomy winter's day. I had just finished and was almost frozen from the wind when I heard that familiar laugh again. I moved over to the side railing and looked down. Ben and Li were playing in the garden together. He was chasing her around and she was giggling. I sighed. I wanted to turn away and stop watching, but couldn't. In fact, I wanted to see more.

So I took the lift down to the bottom floor again and then tried to creep silently into the garden. There was a small path running against the wall at the back of the rose bushes. If I crept against the wall, I would pop out by the tree and I could see properly. So I put my back to the wall and started sliding across it.

Oh scarf. Oh long, woolen, fluffy scarf that is not conducive to creeping through thorny bushes. I felt it tug as it got caught behind me on some devilish-looking thorns. I turned to undo it and the other side swung out and straight into another bunch of thorns. Both ends of my scarf were now trapped, and every time I leaned over to deal with one side, I pulled the other side even tighter. The more I moved, the worse it got. *Maybe if I bent down and lifted it over my head?* But as I pulled—hard—the one side yanked against the rose bush, snapping the branch and causing the scarf to slap me in the face.

"Fuck!" I quickly ducked in anticipation of the thorny branch plummeting into my eye. Luckily it didn't.

"That's not a very nice word," the little sing-song voice said. My hands were still over my face to protect against the thorns. I pulled them down and there she was, and he too for that matter. Both staring at me.

"My dad says that you should never say that word."

I looked up at Ben and he had an awkward smile on his face.

"Well, your dad is right."

"Dad is right about all things," Li said with an adoring tone in her voice.

"Well, maybe not *all* things," I said gently, "but he is right about that bad word."

"No, I'm right about all things," Ben said teasingly.

"No, I don't think you are." I forced a little laugh. "No one can be right about all things."

"No! My dad is right about everything." Li spoke loudly and sounded wildly protective.

"Hahah, yes, you're probably right," I conceded. I wasn't going to argue with a six-year-old who adored her father more than pink tutus and shiny things.

"So, what brings you to the rose bushes so early on a Sunday morning?" Ben folded his arms and looked at me, his brow furrowing in a curious questioning manner.

"I was going to prune them," I said as fast as possible. It was the first thing that had come to mind—the fact that I was without garden shears was merely an irrelevant detail that hopefully Ben was going to overlook . . . *not likely.*

"I didn't know you were into gardening."

I nodded. "Yup. I love pruning roses."

"Like you love running ten miles in the morning." Ben smiled.

My heart skipped a beat as I watched his whole face change as that naughty, skew smile lit up his eyes once more.

"Ben!" I suddenly declared for no reason whatsoever.

"Sera. Sera De La Haye."

"Mmmm. Ben. Ben White."

"So we meet again," he said.

I looked at him, shook my head slightly in disapproval and shrugged. "It would seem so."

"You know, it's rather apt that you're lurking in the rose bushes, because did you know that your surname comes from the old French word 'haye', meaning 'hedge?'"

"Really?" I was unconvinced.

"I Googled it," he said. "If you don't believe me you can check."

"That's okay, I believe you," I quickly replied.

"By the way, weren't you also down in the laundry room earlier?" he asked.

I nodded. "That was me. Doing the laundry."

"Very diligent of you."

"I try." I folded my arms trying to look casual and not look like a person that had just been busted for snooping and sneaking and general creepy stalker behavior.

"Happen to listen to any good music latterly?"

"Mmmm, not that I can recall," I said quickly. "But thanks for asking."

"Pleasure." He smiled at me and I couldn't help my tiny smile in response.

"And now?" He looked at my scarf.

"I seem to be a bit stuck," I said.

"Why don't you just take the pruning shears and cut that other branch it's hooked on."

"The pruning shears," I repeated.

"You do have some, I presume?" He was gleefully toying with me once more. He knew it and I knew it.

"I wish!" I pursed my lips together and glared at him in a way that implied that if I did, I might be forced to use them on him.

A small chuckle escaped his mouth and I hated how playfully adorable he was right now.

"But seriously, do you need some help?" He gestured to the stuck scarf again.

"No, no. I'm fine."

Now that the one side was free I wiggled out of the scarf easily. I tried to pull it loose from the thorns, but it was stuck, so I abandoned it and slid back out against the wall until I arrived in the garden.

"You're just going to leave that there?"

"It's not going anywhere."

We stood in silence and regarded each other for a moment.

"Li and I were just going to go up and have breakfast, would you like to join us."

"Oh no! No, no, no, thanks." I quickly dismissed the idea. It was insane that he would be asking me such a thing, after everything that had transpired between us.

"But we're having waffles," Ben said, picking Li up so she was at eye level.

"Thanks for the offer, but . . ."

"Please come." Li's little voice rang out.

I looked at her and she looked back at me with those sweet

little eyes. "Sorry, sweetie, I have some things to do so I can't, but maybe next time."

She looked suddenly disappointed and my guilt-o-meter sky-rocketed.

"Please. I'll share mine with you if there aren't enough." Jeez, dagger of guilt through my beating heart. She looked at me with a sad face and slumped shoulders. How the hell was it humanly possible to say no to that? It was not even an option, and Ben knew it, judging by his smile.

"You can't say no to that face," he half mouthed to me.

"Manipulative," I mouthed back.

"Please," she asked again.

"On one condition," I said. "We go out for breakfast. Not up there." I pointed at the apartments. The idea of being in his apartment again was just so intimate and so wrong.

"Deal!" he said looking pleased with himself and raising a gleeful Li up over his head and onto his shoulders.

"Let me just go and change first." I walked ahead.

"You look great." Ben's words stopped me and I turned slowly. I was wearing one of the worst Sunday morning outfits that I had ever managed to rustle up.

"Doubtful." I started walking back towards the building.

"Factual," he shouted after me.

"Hmmph." I wasn't convinced. But as I approached the lift Ben's hand shot out and caught me on the back of my jumper. I turned.

"Come." He pulled me slightly. "You look . . ." His eyes moved up and down my body. "Great." His voice was soft and silky again, like liquid gold and I could feel myself falling for it again, until I became aware of the small person looking down at me.

"You're very pretty," she said. "Not as pretty as my mommy, though. She's the prettiest."

Li was right about that, and in that moment of terrible hair, undress and mess, I didn't really feel like being reminded of how effing gorgeous his ex-wife was. Ben gestured with his head in the direction of the garage.

"Fine," I said. Why should I even care what I was wearing? It's not like I was trying to impress him after all. In fact, maybe the worse I looked, the better.

49

VIRGIN CATHOLIC PRIEST . . .

*sat at the table with Ben in the restaurant that was right around the corner from us. I'd never seen it before though. It was set amongst the most beautiful trees, leading out onto a lawn with a huge kids' play area.

"You know about these kinds of places when you're on the parent circuit," Ben said.

It was such a weird-sounding statement. Ben on the parent circuit! I still hadn't really gotten used to the idea of him being a dad. It still hadn't sunk in. Especially since he looked like the furthest thing from a father. Fathers aren't supposed to be so sexy, and tattooed and they definitely aren't supposed to have sex with people in the back seat of their cars.

Li had run off before the waffles had even been ordered and was currently playing on the trampoline, leaving Ben and I to sit in a strained, awkward silence.

"So you're a father," I finally said, breaking the silence.

"Yes. I'm a dad."

"You know, if you'd asked me forty-eight hours ago what the most unbelievable thing about you could possibly ever be, father would have been at the top of the list. Along with virgin Catholic Priest maybe."

Ben let out a small chuckle.

"I'm being serious." I quickly turned to him.

"I know you are," he said. "Some days it's still hard for me to believe. But I wouldn't change it for the world." Ben turned and looked at me. Our eyes connected and that same, *totally involuntary*, bolt of something shot through me once more. That magnetic thing that was currently making me want to reach out and touch him against all logic.

I sighed loudly and shook my head at the total absurdity of this moment. "What are we doing?" I was feeling exasperated. "What am I doing sitting here with you, *once again*? Why am I with you when I should be angrily avoiding you? Why am I here ordering waffles on a Sunday morning with your adorable daughter bouncing up and down on a trampoline like we are some kind of . . ." I stopped. I didn't want to say family, even if it was exactly what I was thinking. "After everything you've done, everything that's happened . . . I'm meant to dislike you immensely."

"But you don't." Ben's hand inched across the table.

"No! Stop it there, Ben." I pointed at his hand and it stopped its sneaky approach. "I'm being serious, why are we here again, together? Why? It's infuriating."

"I told you, Sera. There's something between us. It was there from the first moment I saw you and it's pulling us together."

"That sounds ridiculous," I mumbled.

"How else do you explain it all then? You working in the same office as me, being my next-door neighbor, the fact we can't keep our hands off each other, that we can't stop thinking about each other and talking and . . ."

"Who says I'm thinking about you?"

He shrugged. "Anyway, we wouldn't be here together if you hadn't been spying on me. Sneaking around in the basement and the roses. You're the reason you're with me. *You* can't keep away." His hand crept again and I flicked it.

"But wait . . ." I pulled my hands into my lap lest I tempt him any further. "But what you did at the party yesterday, it was—"

"Terrible." He cut me off. "And I'm so sorry. I never wanted to hurt you." He looked at me with such sincerity that I believed him.

"Do you think I'm a total asshole?" His voice was soft and filled with emotion. Regret. Hurt.

"Honestly, I don't know what to think about you anymore. I have so many questions."

"Well, ask them."

"You were married?" I said. It was more of a statement than a question.

"I know."

"You cheated on your wife?"

"I know."

"You asked me to date you while keeping your entire life a secret from me?"

"Yes."

"And you beat people up and break their ribs?"

"I know. I know. I sound terrible."

"You do." I shook my head at him.

"And yet here we are," he said.

I nodded and echoed his words. "Yup. Here we are."

"Anything else you want to know, Sera? I promise I'm going to be completely honest with you from now on."

Something bubbled up inside me. A question that I had been wanting to ask so badly, but hadn't had the courage to yet. What the hell. There was no time like the present "You kind of avoided the question last time, so I'll ask it again. Did you really sleep with all the women in your previous office?"

"*Mmm*." He looked cautious for a while. "It's an exaggeration, but yes, I did sort of sleep with a few."

"Sort of? You can't really *sort of* have sex, can you? Unless I'm missing something here? Maybe I didn't learn about this *sort of sex* thing in biology." I leaned in and whispered that, what with all the kids running around.

He ran his hands through his hair. "I definitely used sex as a way of . . ." he looked like he was thinking carefully for the next words, " . . . forgetting. I was in a pretty bad way for a while after Li went, and I wasn't that well behaved."

"Well behaved? That's an interesting choice of words." I felt sick to my stomach thinking about this. I wasn't sure that I wanted this level of candid honesty, even if I'd asked for it.

"And when we . . . that night in the car," I asked, "how long had it been since you—"

Ben suddenly reached across the table and took my hands, but I pulled them away quickly. "I'm not going to lie to you," he said. He looked me in the eye . . . and he looked serious.

Shit, here it comes. He was going to tell me something like he'd had sex with someone the night before, or a few hours before or—"Eight months," he said in a deadpan tone.

"Eight months?"

"Eight months," he repeated, and it still sounded like he was being serious.

"You hadn't had sex in eight months?"

He nodded. "I kind of realized that if I was ever going to get Li back, I needed to start being more responsible, so I started making some changes in my life and eight months ago I stopped sleeping aro—" He cut himself off.

"*Around!*" I finished his sentence. "Sleeping around." I studied his face for any telltale signs of deceit, but there were none.

"You're being serious."

He nodded. "Please don't hate me, Sera. That's all in the past. I'm not like that anymore."

I laughed. "God, I actually wish I could. I wish I could hate you and never want to see you again. It would make this all so much simpler." I snapped my head up and looked at him again. "And don't come with your 'life ain't simple' thing or 'the best things in life are complicated' or—"

"You took the words right out of my mouth." He cut me off with a smile. Our eyes met again and I started to feel the pull once more. The dangerous pull that was so hard to resist. Luckily, loud children's laughter made us both turn. Li was climbing up a tree now and laughing with her new friends. I turned back and looked at Ben, his eyes were glowing.

"She's adorable," I said.

"I'd do anything for her."

I nodded. "I know." You could see he would throw himself in front of a bus for her without a second thought.

"You don't know what love feels like until you have a child." He suddenly looked at me—his look was packed with meaning and subtext and it scared the hell out of me. I shuffled nervously in my seat. "And you? Do you want kids one day?" His meaningful look continued and it was making me very uncomfortable. I fiddled with my hands in my lap.

"Like you said, life isn't simple. And mine is just too complicated," I replied.

"So you won't be falling pregnant with my illegitimate child any time soon?"

"Arg." I hung my head. "Please don't remind me about it ever again. And . . ." I looked back up at him and waggled a finger. "And just for the record, so there is *no* confusion, it wasn't true. It was a joke, just like you wanting a son called Max."

"No. That was true," Ben said.

"Huh?" My voice caught in my throat.

"I want at least two sons and three more daughters."

"You want six kids! Don't you think that's a bit much?"

Ben laughed. "Twelve would be pushing it, six though would be good. Besides . . ." His face changed again. Gone were the playful smiles, and back was that meaningful look. *Damn that look.* "Six seems to be my lucky number."

"How's that?" I asked.

"Well, we met at Club Six and I moved into apartment two zero six." He met my eyes.

"I see." I broke eye contact and looked down at my lap again.

"Sera." Ben's hand came slinking back and this time I let him slide it onto my lap and intertwine his fingers with mine. "I'd really, really like to—"

He looked like he was just about to launch into a whole speech when Li ran up to us and threw herself onto Ben's lap. He let go of my hand and wrapped his arms around her. Just then the waiter arrived with the waffles and they both started eating them. I tried to focus on eating too, but Ben kept looking back up at me. Minutes later Li was gone again and Ben and I were once more alone.

"What I was trying to say earlier," he turned to me the second Li had left, "I would really love to talk to you later, when we don't have so many distractions, there are still some things I want to tell you and . . ."

"Oh God. I don't think I can handle any more surprises, Ben. Not for another lifetime. At least."

"Just come round tonight and let's talk about everything?"

I glanced up to see Li already running up to the table again. I nodded. "Fine. I'll see you later."

50

Once Upon A Time . . .

*H*is door was unlocked—*as usual*—and the passage outside was full of boxes, furniture, tins of paint, brushes and sheets of plastic—*he was obviously playing* Home Improvement *again*. I just hoped he was wearing slightly more than before.

"Ben?" I called as I walked inside.

No one answered. I walked to his room and peered in. I walked back into the lounge and called out again. *Where the hell was he?* Not safe to leave your door open at night like this. I glanced in the direction of his kitchen and his computer was there on the counter. The screen was lit up still, so he must have been on it recently, otherwise the screen saver would have kicked in. Maybe he'd gotten an important email and had to rush off to the office? I walked over to the computer and inhaled sharply when I saw what was filling the screen.

Me. A photo of me from the shoot the other day. I'd almost forgotten about that little embarrassing moment, in amongst all the other ones I was currently having.

"Beautiful, isn't it?" I jumped when I heard Ben's voice.

"Sorry, I didn't mean to snoop on your computer," I said defensively, moving away from it.

"No problem." He smiled and put a can of paint down on the floor. "I just went down to my car to get this." He walked over to the computer and leaned in, looking at the photo. "You really do look beautiful in this." He stood up straight and looked at me. He had smudges of pink paint on his hands and one across his forehead.

"You have some paint on your . . ." I pointed at his forehead.

He ran a hand over it and smiled. "Come see." Without asking, he took me by the hand and led me down the passage and into the second bedroom. I glanced around the room; it had been completely transformed. The walls were a shade of baby pink and looked like the pages of a fairy tale book. Someone had painted castles, princesses and rainbows all over them. The mural wrapped around the entire room, boxes were piled up, and all the furniture had been pushed to one side of the room.

"She'll love it," I said, looking up at the mezzanine level that had been turned into a little girl's dress-up corner.

"I hope so," he said. "Truthfully it's more important that Mei and the social worker like it." He rolled his eyes and gave his head a slight shake, as if exhausted.

"Is she going to like the fact I came to breakfast with you?"

"Li invited you. Besides, we're not even dating, since you still haven't agreed to go on a date with me."

"Well, I did actually. But when I came over you were harboring ex-wives in your apartment and sent me away."

"Yes. That," he said sheepishly.

"So . . ." I folded my arms in a businesslike fashion. "You asked me here to talk. What is it you still have to say?"

Ben smiled, "Talk. Yes. Just give me a moment to get out of my clothes, they're covered in paint and I'm all sweaty." He rushed off to the room at the end of the passage and disappeared. I walked back out to the lounge and sat down, taking the opportunity to glance around. I've always thought you can tell a lot about a person's personality by looking at the environment they live in. On closer examination. There was a lot of pink. The bookshelf was packed with rows of books for Li and on a nearby shelf stood a picture of her and Ben that melted my heart a little. I got up and walked over to it. He was wearing hospital scrubs and holding her in his arms; she was clearly a newborn despite the wild crazy mop of black hair she already had. The look on Ben's face as he gazed at her was indescribable. Another photo showed a shirtless, tattooed Ben cradling a naked, sleeping, pudgy Li in his arms. And then a photo album caught my eye. It was labeled, "The story of us." I opened it and immediately recognized Ben's distinctive handwriting.

Once upon a time there was a man who didn't know what real love was, until the day he met the most beautiful Princess in the entire world—There was another picture of Li and Ben in hospital scrubs, but this time he was looking directly into the camera. His smile was massive and it lit up his eyes. He looked a lot younger than he did now, but equally gorgeous—*dammit.*

I slammed the book closed quickly, feeling a stab of something deep inside. I was so touched by the love he had for this little girl that it forced me to wonder what it would have felt like to be so cherished. A tear left my eye and rolled down my cheek.

"Hey, are you okay?"

I turned and Ben was standing right behind me.

I shook my head. "Not really," I finally managed to mutter.

Ben reached out and wiped the tear across my cheek with his thumb. His touch felt good.

"I really am sorry, Sera. I never meant to hurt you." His other hand came up and touched the other side of my face.

"I know," I whispered.

"Is it too much to ask you to forgive me?" His other hand cradled the side of my face and he stepped closer, holding my face between his hands. "Or do I need to beg and grovel?" A tiny smile darted across his face.

"How would you do that?"

"Like this." Suddenly Ben started slipping down. He got closer and closer to the floor until he was on his knees and then suddenly he reached down into his pocket and started pulling something out. I gasped in absolute shock!

"What the hell?" I reached down and started pulling him up again. "Are you going to . . . uh, were you going to . . . you were, uh, *propose*?"

Ben burst out laughing and laid his hand on my shoulders. "No. But if you want me to . . . ?"

"No! God, no!" I pulled away quickly feeling like a total idiot. But Ben was so weird and unpredictable that I wouldn't have put some totally inappropriate proposal past him.

"You sure? This *is* the second time you've brought it up." He laughed.

"What's in your hand?" I asked and pointed at the hand that had reached into his pocket moments ago.

He opened it and held it out.

"You think you can bribe me with chocolate?" I asked, taking it from his hand.

"It worked last time." He said and then without warning, playfully pulled me towards him again, wrapping his arms around me and locking me into a hug.

I closed my eyes, not wanting to look him in the eye right now. *God, I felt like an idiot!*

"Open your eyes, Sera."

I shook my head and closed them even tighter. "Mmm-uuhh." And then I felt his lips coming down onto mine. They were soft and gentle and I was reminded of the way he'd kissed me in the car that night. No one had ever kissed me like this before—*except him*. I began to forget myself. Forget everything that had happened between us. And when his hands moved to my lower back, my mind went completely blank. Then he pulled me closer and started walking me backwards towards his . . . *Bedroom?*

51

KISSING DAZE . . .

*H*alfway down the passage to his room, Ben stopped walking and had me pinned against the wall, kissing me. We tried to walk and kiss at the same time, which didn't really work, so we were forced to make another kissing pit stop—*this time I was doing the pinning.* After a few more steps, he managed to get my top off, which caused another delay, as it seemed to call for more kissing. These kisses were concentrated in a more southerly direction. I'd never been in such a full-blown kissing daze. Ten minutes prior to that moment I hadn't even realized such a state could even exist.

I wasn't even sure we were going to make it to the bedroom, because with only a few feet to go, Ben held me up against the wall and I wrapped my legs around him to pull him nearer.

After some serious kissing, we finally arrived and tumbled onto Ben's bed, but the second we did, Ben stopped kissing me.

"What?" I asked, breathless.

"You really are something, Sera," he said, running his hand over my naked stomach.

"Something?" I lifted my hand to his hair—*I'd wanted to play with it for so long*. I brushed it back and it stood up like a Mohawk, causing a small chuckle to escape my mouth.

"What have you done to me?" He lifted his hand to his hair to investigate.

I smoothed it down again and it flopped into his face, causing another small chuckle.

"You're terribly cute," he said, circling my belly button with his fingers, which made me giggle.

"Ticklish." I pushed his hand away.

"Really?" His eyes lit up with one of his now famous devilish looks. "And this?"

He lowered his mouth to my stomach and started kissing it. Kissing it all the way up to where my bra started and then down to where my pants started. I wriggled, but not because it was ticklish.

"No," I said. The word was breathy.

"And this?" he moved his mouth over my bra and up to my neck.

"No."

"And if I did this?" he asked, taking my bra strap between his teeth and pulling it down over my shoulder.

I shivered as the one side of my bra came off and he traced his mouth over my bare breast.

"*No.*"

"Good," he said, undoing my bra rather stealthily and tossing it aside.

But instead of continuing, he just lay there and stared at me for a moment. "We should do this properly, the good ol' fashioned way," he said, gently stroking his fingertips over my naked chest.

"And what . . . um, what way . . . is that?" I was barely able to form words, let alone sentences at this point.

"Well, we still haven't been on that date." He smiled, planting a kiss between my breasts. "Go out with me? Let's start from the very beginning again. A clean slate."

"And Mei? I thought you said she hated other women? That it might jeopardize things with Li."

Ben smiled, it looked like it wasn't for my benefit. "I'm very confident I'm going to get joint custody. Probably in the next week actually. The court-appointed social worker has recommended joint custody, and I also think Mei is tired of fighting. Not to mention broke. Once I legally have joint custody, there is nothing she can do to me."

"A completely clean slate?" I asked.

"Sparkling clean." He leaned in looking excited. "We put everything behind us, and start over."

"Okay," I finally whispered.

"Tomorrow night then?" he asked, and teased me with some more small kisses.

"Mmmm-hmmm," I said—*that was all I could manage at that stage.*

"Good," he said, coming up to my lips again. "By the way, I'm not going to sleep with you tonight, Sera . . ."

I nodded, waiting for him to say more.

". . . I'm going to wait until you're madly in love with me." He smiled that naughty smile and I burst out laughing.

"So confident."

"Yup. And when you are, I'm going to make love to you all fucking night."

I gasped. My heart raced and my breath got stuck in my throat. He lowered himself over me again, his lips brushing mine as he whispered, "I'm counting the seconds." He kissed me again and I opened my mouth to feel his tongue inside me. We stayed there kissing for ages, before he stopped and pulled me off the bed.

"So what say we paint a little girl's bedroom bright pink?"

"Sure." I nodded and reached for my top, but he pulled it away from me.

"No. Keep it off." His eyes were staring straight at my breasts.

"I'm not painting topless."

"I'll take mine off too." He whipped his shirt off and my eyes drifted over his naked chest. God, he was hot. And it felt like forever since I'd seen him this undressed.

"Okay." I nodded, feeling quite hypnotized by him at that moment. He was obviously working his black magic again, because who on earth would agree to paint a bedroom topless?

Me. That's who.

52

MARIAH CAREY
WOULD BE ENVIOUS . . .

"*You* didn't have sex?"

"We didn't have sex," I repeated.

"You didn't have *sex* ?"

"We didn't have sex."

"You *didn't* have sex?" JJ was repeating the line like a broken record, emphasizing different words each time as if that might change my answer somehow.

"Jesus, JJ. Get over it. For the tenth time, we didn't have sex." I smacked him on the arm playfully. He was still wide-eyed with shock.

"So you painted a room topless, and you didn't have sex?"

"Exactly," I said innocently.

JJ eyed me suspiciously, "I hope you're not keeping secrets from me."

I laughed. "Oh please. I couldn't keep a secret from you if I tried."

It was already 5 p.m. by the time I'd been able to relate last night's events to them. I'd woken up at 1 p.m., my body obviously knew that this was the first day of my entire adult life that I found myself unemployed, and it was making the most of it. I'd then had a leisurely coffee downstairs by the tree, and now I was flipping through décor magazines with JJ while we came up with ideas for the coffee shop.

"So what do you think of this?" JJ asked, holding up the magazine.

"I'm not so sure a Mercedes Sports Car would look good in the middle of the restaurant," I said, looking at the magazine.

"No. Not for the restaurant. For me?"

"You?"

"I think I would look good driving it around," he said, looking at the shiny silver thing.

"You have a perfectly good Audi already," I said, going back to the décor magazines.

"Well, I was thinking that maybe you could have it and I would get a new car."

"Me? No. You can't give me your car."

"Why? You need a car, and it's time for my midlife crisis."

I shook my head. "I could never accept that. Ever."

JJ put the magazine down on the floor and looked at me with something that resembled anger—he'd never looked at me like that before.

"What?" I asked, feeling worried.

"Sera, why won't you let anyone help you?" he asked, sounding frustrated.

"Help is a few bucks for petrol, not a car. And I do let you guys help me, in fact," I hung my head, "I think I let you help me way too much and I really need to start paying rent around here."

"Stop it!" JJ held up his hand. "That's ridiculous. You're our family. We're not going to charge you rent."

"JJ, I can't accept a car from you!" I said firmly and looked back down at the magazines. "You guys have been far too generous over the years and I have no idea how I will ever be able to pay that back."

"Jesus!" I heard JJ snap angrily and looked up, "You really—"

A loud beeping on my phone cut him off. It was a message from Ben.

Sera, I will pick you up at exactly 6:45 pm. Dress <u>very</u> formal. XX

"Shit." I read the message out loud and looked over at JJ. The "dress very formal" line had me spinning. Luckily I lived with a drag queen who came with a closet that even Mariah Carey would be envious of.

JJ shook his head, seeming a little angry that our previous conversation was over. He then looked down at his watch, "Well, there's no time to waste, I guess." He stood up and marched me through to his bedroom. He sat cross- legged on the bed while I rummaged through the closet. I passed the blue sequin dress— *the dress that had started this whole crazy thing.*

"That!" JJ said, pointing at a long gold and black dress. It was strapless, tight and really, really formal.

"Isn't it a bit OTT?" I said, turning it around to discover that it didn't have anything mildly resembling a back.

"There's no such thing as too over the top." JJ took it from me and held it up against my body. "Yes, this will do very well. Mr. Sex Bomb won't know what hit him." JJ lowered the gown and peered at me. "You really didn't have sex?" he asked again. Then he winked playfully at me. "Okay, let's get you into this. But she's tight, so we may have to grease you up."

An hour and a half later I was ready. JJ had insisted on doing my hair and make-up again, and this time he was much more subtle. My hair was simply blow-dried and straightened. My eyes were very subtly bronzed to match the dress. Then he added some eyeliner, bronzer on my cheeks and some red lipstick. "Every girl should own a great red lipstick," he said—*JJ said this every time he put on lipstick. He was also fond of quoting Coco Chanel, who had once very dramatically said, "A woman without a fragrance is a woman without a future."*

After my *Pretty Woman* reveal to Bruce we waited in the lounge for the knock. My nerves were completely on edge. By the time I heard the knock on the door, my heart was positively trying to escape my chest—*quite a painful feeling when my chest was squeezed so damn tightly into that dress*. I opened the door only to have my breath violently ripped away from me.

Ben was wearing a tuxedo and looked amazing. Although the blood flow to my lower body had been cut off, I was glad I was wearing the dress, because clearly we were headed somewhere very formal.

"You look incredible," Ben said, eyeing me with a look that made me feel like I wasn't wearing a damn thing.

"I was thinking the exact same thing," I said, sounding a bit coy.

"You should," he said with a teasing smile. "You really do." He winked at me and walked into the room to address JJ and Bruce.

"I'll have her home at midnight on the dot," he said, giving them a small wave.

He was teasing, but the whole thing did feel like prom night. JJ and Bruce were clinging onto each other like proud papas. It was amusing, somewhat touching and mildly disturbing all at the same time, since I knew my "dads" were secretly rooting for me to have sex with him.

"You can keep her for as long as you like," JJ said with a naughty smile—*definitely not something a dad would say.*

Bruce was not so liberal. "Just treat her like gold," he said, "Or I'll kill you." He flashed Ben a warning smile.

Ben turned and looked at me, making me melt. "Don't worry," he said. "I will." Then he offered me his arm, smiled at Bruce and led me out.

As we opened the door, I heard a last teasing, "Our baby is growing up," before we went into the hall.

"I just want to get something from next door quickly," Ben said, leading me towards his place.

"Sure," I said.

Ben took out his key, unlocked the door and led me inside. When I looked up, I was overcome with dizzy excitement, and I heard a loud gasp escape my throat.

53

À LA MASTERCHEF . . .

*I*t's strange how all your senses seem completely interrelated, as if you can't experience anything through one alone. One seems to ignite the other, which ignites another, making the experience a full-body one. The first thing for me was sight . . .

Ben's apartment was dark, but the entire place was drenched in .the warm, flickering golden glow from a million candles. Candles on tables. Candles clustered on the floor. Candles on bookshelves and windowsills and outlining a path from the door to the dining-room table. Together, they gave off a subtle warmth, which I could feel throughout my entire body. Then there was smell . . .

Something rich and sweet that made my mouth water, like cookies fresh from the oven. A nostalgic smell.

All of my senses were awake and alert, so when Ben placed his hand on my bare lower back, I winced, not from pain or surprise, but from pleasure. Everything felt more heightened suddenly.

He led me to the dining-room table, set with three sets of cutlery, different plates and bowls, flowers and colored napkins. He

pulled out my chair for me, and as I sat down he placed an envelope on my plate with a smile.

I opened it and pulled out a handwritten note.

Menu
Starters: Freshly baked, hot Lindt chocolate brownies with
pecan nuts and cream.

Main: Salted caramel chocolate tart served with homemade
Snickers ice cream.

Dessert: White chocolate mousse served with candied
strawberries.

My face almost cracked from the smile that spread across it.

"Your kind of menu?" he asked with a playful tone in his voice.

"Wow!" I looked towards the kitchen and inhaled the smell
coming from it. "You really can cook desserts."

"Li and I do it together. If you think you have a sweet tooth . . ."
He drifted off slightly and then changed the subject quickly,
purposefully.

"Can I get you a drink?" he offered, sounding and looking like
a waiter now. He had assumed a very stiff pose, with one arm
crossed over his stomach and the other by his side.

"What do you have?" I asked.

He indicated for me to turn the menu over. I did.

Drinks: Water. With ice.

"I sort of forgot to buy drinks," he said and shrugged playfully.

"Water is perfect." And it was. It was so perfect that Ben would
serve iced water with a three-course dessert-only meal. It was just
so Ben. So totally, strangely, marvelously, perfectly weird.

"The ice might not be frozen yet," he said as he walked off in the direction of the kitchen. "In fact, I lie, I have no ice."

Even more perfect.

I watched him as he fiddled around in his kitchen like an expert, à la *MasterChef.* I hadn't expected a date like this at all. Not in my wildest dreams would I have pictured this. I was sure he was going to take me out, but this was far, far better.

"Here we go." He came up to the table and placed the first course in front of me. He grabbed one of the napkins and laid it in my lap—*a little too seductively.* He didn't hide the fact that, in spreading the napkin, he was focusing far too much on my upper thighs.

"Sorry, couldn't resist." He looked up at me and gave my lap one last, very long, slow stroke. He walked round the table and sat opposite me. He didn't have a plate in front of him.

"Not eating?" I asked, but before he answered, he pulled my bowl into the middle of the table and grabbed a fork.

"Sharing is caring," he said and scooped up a mouthful. I followed his lead, and when I finally popped a bite into my mouth, I was met by the most warm, gooey chocolaty experience ever.

"*Mmm*, oh my God. Where did you learn to bake like this?" I asked. But as soon as I did, his mood changed a little.

"I baked a lot when Li left. It soothed me. In my anger management group, they suggested we find a hobby. So I baked."

I had been hoping that this topic wouldn't come up tonight. I didn't mean to be selfish, but this was our first date, and the first attempt at any kind of an "us." Our lives were both so complicated, but just for tonight, I wanted to forget all that. I wanted to pretend it didn't exist. Fortunately, Ben was way ahead of me.

"But I don't want to talk about stuff like that tonight," he said with a reassuring smile. "Clean slate!" he quickly added.

"What do you want to talk about then?" I said and popped in another warm mouthful of chocolate.

Ben flashed me a naughty look. "How amazing you look in that dress. It should be illegal to dress like that, you know."

I blushed. Ben had a way of making me feel like the most beautiful woman alive, something I'd never felt before.

"Why do you look like you don't quite believe me?" he asked.

"I suppose a part of me doesn't."

"You're beautiful, Sera," he said, gazing at me disarmingly. "Everyone can look good covered in make-up," he said, "but not everyone can look as good as you do in glasses and a ponytail. Not to mention cute and sexy all at the same time."

"That's not what I looked like the first time you met me," I said with a slight laugh.

"True." He looked like he was considering this for a moment. "But I'm also fond of the pay-by-the-hour look."

"What?" I gasped and burst out laughing.

My laugh tapered off and our eyes met with a jolt. I've never received an electric shock, but this was pretty damn close.

"So, are you in love with me yet?" Ben asked with a devilish smirk smeared across his face.

I blinked at him. "Uh, no."

"Well, if you're not now, you will be after the next course." He got up again and walked back to the kitchen.

54

COOL-UNCOOL-I-AM-SO-COOL

"*O*h God," I moaned loudly. "I don't think I can breathe." I was pulling at my dress, trying to make some space between it and my skin. The three dessert courses, which I'd polished off—*I had practically licked the bowl*—were taking their toll, especially on the already too-tight dress. Ben smiled as I lowered myself onto the couch with great difficulty and the grace of a large walrus.

"No, I'm being serious," I urged. "I don't think I can breathe." I grabbed at my ribs, which felt like they were being crushed. "Unzip me, please." I tried to roll over, it was very ungraceful. "I swear I'm going to faint, or something."

Ben jumped up and went to work on the back of my dress. I sighed loudly as he unzipped me and I could suddenly breathe again. My stomach also finally had the space it needed to pop out.

"So Victorian of you, Sera," Ben said as he dragged his fingertips over my exposed back. "Soon I'll be getting out the smelling salts when you have a fit of the vapors." He lowered his lips to the back of my neck and kissed me, moving across my shoulders.

"Or not." His voice dripped with sex. "Maybe I won't resuscitate you and I'll just have my way with you instead." His kisses moved back to my neck and then started creeping down my spine.

"That's disgustingly pervy," I whispered.

"I can be *very* pervy, Sera. Just wait and see." He had a smile in his voice, but it almost sounded like a threat—*a threat I hoped he would carry out.* "So you know I totally lied when I said I was going to have you home by twelve."

"Really?"

"I thought we could go out, have a few drinks, hit the dance floor. You know, a trip down memory lane."

I did like a good dance, and images of that first time Ben and I danced together flooded my mind. "Why not!" I said. "As long as I can change out of this dress." I got up, holding the dress up so it wouldn't fall down.

"Will you wear that blue sequined thing again?"

"Absolutely not," I said. Then I smiled at him and walked out.

* * *

An hour later we were deposited at the bar area of one of Jo'burg's trendiest clubs—*in that non-cool-non-trendy sense.* It was a place crawling with creatives from the film, advertising and art industries. To be honest, places like this always left me feeling uneasy, a less-than outsider. People walked around in clothes that cost more than my entire wardrobe, clothes that ironically were designed to look old and second-hand as if the wearer didn't care what they wore (only, they all cared very deeply)—*Why buy new clothes that look that old?*

Ben had lined up some shots of Tequila across the countertop—
I hated Tequila.

"Well." Ben held up a shot. "To us, on our first date." I smiled
at him, as he threw one down and bit into the obligatory lemon—
*a custom which makes the whole hideous experience . . . well . . .
even more hideous than it needs to be.* I scrunched up my face as I
threw one back, grabbing a glass of water to try and wash it down
without gagging—*did I mention I hate Tequila?* Ben laughed at
me and pushed another one my way.

"Are you trying to get me drunk?" I asked, noting the bad-boy
look plastered across his face.

"Of course. And then I plan on taking total advantage of you."

"Maybe I'll be the one taking advantage, Ben." I said it in the
sultriest voice I could muster before I threw back yet another shot.
"Aren't you having another one?" I said and pointed at the last
one on the counter top.

Ben shook his head. "I'm transporting precious cargo tonight."

"Fine then." I took the last one and threw it down as well. The
warmth and the buzz was instant, and it gave me the courage to
take Ben by the hand and lead him onto the dance floor.

The cool crowd was already there swaying to some obscure
electronic music, but after some laughter and our own version of
swaying about, our bodies finally began to move in time to the
strangely rhythmic music. I quickly learnt though that going out
with Ben equated to going out with a celebrity. Every few minutes we were interrupted by über-cool people popping by to say
"Hi," including a large handful of rather attractive women. The
kind that simply walked up to him and planted kisses on his
mouth, or hugged him for a little too long, or let their hand linger

on his shoulder. One even tucked a stray piece of his hair behind his ear.

Every time it happened, Ben looked my way sheepishly, trying to shrug them off. There was really only one way to deal with this. I pushed my way past one of them—*the one batting her eyelashes and flipping her trollopy hair as she talked*—and I pulled Ben towards me, and into the most inappropriate kiss that cool club had ever seen. The kiss continued until our bodies began to get into the rhythm again, swaying together as we kissed deeply and passionately, not caring who was watching. I felt Ben's hands come around to my lower back and he pulled me in even tighter, slipping one of his legs between mine, pushing them apart so his knee rubbed against me.

Perhaps we lost ourselves a little too much because the people and the background melted away into a distant muffled blur. Our kiss intensified, growing hungrier and more desperate by the second. He pushed his hips into me and I could feel that he was rock hard. I lost myself even more as I rubbed into him.

One of his hands left my lower back and traveled slowly up to my waist, but it didn't stop there. It traveled a little further up my side, and with his fingers splayed working their way up to my rib cage, he very quickly, and deliberately, moved his thumb around to my front and grazed my breast through my dress. I gasped, stopped kissing him and looked into his eyes only to find pure, unadulterated lust etched into them.

Keeping eye contact, I slipped my hand between us and ran it over the front of his pants, watching with delight as he bit his lips in response before taking me by the nape of the neck and kissing me once more. We moved to the music, our hips rocking against each other; the tension building and building, until it felt like too much to contain in this place.

I broke away and took Ben by the hand, marching him out of the club past several girls giving me some looks. A few of them turned to each other and whispered. But I didn't care. He was mine and I was going to make sure they all knew. I'd probably regret this in the morning—Tequila courage often comes with morning-after regrets—*did I mention I like Tequila?*

Minutes later, we were in the car, and Ben was speeding off to "find a quiet spot." We were like two teenagers out of their minds with hormone-induced madness. I slipped my hand into Ben's jeans while he drove and continued to touch him. I could see he was desperately trying to focus on the road as his breath quickened and he gripped the steering wheel tightly, his knuckles turning white.

"Sera . . ." His tone was whispery and urgent. "You're going to have to stop doing that."

"Why?" I continued. I was loving the way he looked right now, almost out of control—*in my control.*

Ben grabbed my hand and pulled it away. "Fuck. Stop. You're going to make me come." He took my hand in his, kissed it and ran it across his cheek. Then he took a deep breath and looked at me again.

"So come," I said, trying to pull my hand away and put it right back where it had been.

Ben shook his head. "No. Not like this."

"Then how?" I asked, the alcohol and dopamine was surging through my veins in a way that was turning me on more than I'd ever been in my life.

"The right way." He took my hand and kissed it again. *What the hell was the right way?*

"I'm starved. What say we book ourselves into a ludicrously overpriced hotel and order everything on the room-service menu?" Ben asked, changing the subject.

"Um." I felt the color drain from my cheeks and a knot twist in my stomach. This, right here, was one of the many reasons I never socialized with people from work. Ben might have the money to book an expensive hotel room whenever he wanted to—I did not. I would never be able to contribute financially if this was the kind of thing he had in mind.

"On me!" he clarified quickly. "This is my date." He slipped a hand around the nape of my neck in a comforting way, as if he'd somehow read my mind. But, even though he was offering, I still hated not being able to pay my way, or at least contribute as an equal.

"Hey!" Ben clicked his fingers in front of my face. "Stop thinking." He ran his hand over my forehead and playfully straightened my scrunched up brow with his fingers. "Or you'll need Botox soon."

"Okay." I half smiled and nodded at him, even though I still didn't feel good about it.

Then his fingers slipped down the side of my face and he took me by the chin and tilted my head towards him. He took his eye off the road for a second and looked me in the eye. "You're far too young and beautiful to worry about stuff like that."

"How do you know what I'm worrying about?" I asked.

A strange look passed across his face, but as quickly as it had appeared, it disappeared, and he shrugged. "My powers of telepathy," he said flippantly and the subject was dropped.

55

BUMP INTO A BACKSTREET BOY . . .

In the dictionary, under the word *spontaneous*, there should simply be a picture of Ben, although I doubt anyone would ever look up any other word in the dictionary if that really were the case.

From a three-course dessert meal dressed in formal wear, to dancing at a club, to an impromptu hotel check-in, Ben was full of surprises. There was no one else quite like him.

And he wasn't joking about ordering everything on the menu either. As soon as we got to the room, he picked up the phone, dialed reception and started ordering everything he could, including several bottles of champagne. The room was amazing: a huge bed, massive TV, huge bathroom, massive bath—*everything there was big*.

As soon as Ben put the phone down he walked over to me and kissed me again. I don't think I could ever get used to the feeling of him kissing me.

"Start running a bath," he said, slapping me on the bum as he pulled away and started fiddling with the TV. I walked over to the bath, it was situated on the other side of the bedroom in a very open plan bathroom. One could sit in the bath and watch TV and talk to the person in bed if you wanted. The bath was also huge. It was big enough for two, which was clearly the point. I poured in the sweet-smelling bubble bath and added a spot of fragrant bath oil, then sat on the rim running my hand in and out while I watched Ben flip back and forth through the stations until he found the music channels.

"Um . . . We have the soothing sounds of Kenny G, the groovy sounds of Motown, the killer riffs of hardcore rock, some bump and grind Hip-Hop, and some pop stuff." He cringed. "Let's give the pop a miss, I'm not a fan of barely pubescent boys singing and dancing."

"Me too." I moaned, "Bruce and JJ are obsessed with One Direction though. It's a bit pervy old-man if you ask me."

Ben turned. "It must be a gay thing," he said. "My brother worships Gaga and secretly hopes to bump into a Backstreet Boy in a back alley."

I laughed loudly.

Ben flipped channels again. "Oooh, what's this?" The sounds of a babbling brook, birds chirping and wind chimes filled the room.

"You're not serious?" It was the kind of stuff they played when you went for a massage, or the kind of stuff a stoned hippie might listen to while contemplating matters of deep, esoteric importance."

"Why not?" he said, moving towards me. "It serves my purpose." He was wearing his dirty bedroom look again and sat right next to me.

"What purpose is that?"

"To get you to relax some more and then shamelessly seduce you."

I shook my head. "I'm already relaxed," I said, as the sound of a wave crashing into a wind chime filled the air.

"I know. It suits you." Ben started walking over to me with a look in his eye that could not be misinterpreted, but a knock on the door interrupted the moment. Room service had arrived. I sat on the lip of the bath as I watched him clear the little dining table, pick it up and carry it towards the bath. He then grabbed some glasses, dimmed the lights and opened the champagne.

"Ever had a midnight feast in a bath?" he asked, popping the champagne and pouring me a glass.

I took it, smiling at him and shaking my head.

"Well, it's very simple. Just take off all your clothes and climb into the bath." His eyes moved over my body slowly. "I'll be right behind you."

56

I Googled You

So . . ." Ben said once we'd settled into the bath together and had adequately stuffed ourselves with food and drunk more alcohol. We were facing each other, our outstretched legs intertwined. I'd just had the pleasure of watching him undress, again. It was definitely not something I could ever get tired of. His entire back and torso were covered in intricate tattoos that ran all the way up his neck. One arm was completely covered too, all the way down to his hand, even some of his fingers. Looking at him like that, you could dismiss him as nothing more than a total bad boy, but he wasn't. He was so much more than that.

"Do you realize I know nothing about you, Sera?" he said, lifting my legs out of the bath and resting my feet up on his shoulders. The move caught me off guard.

"What do you mean?" It was hard to concentrate when he started rubbing his hands up and down my legs.

"I mean just that. I know nothing about you."

I smiled. "I thought you told me once that you knew everything you needed to know about me."

"I did. But that was then, and this is now. And now I want to know everything."

I shrugged. "There's nothing that interesting, to be honest." That was a blatant lie.

Ben looked at me flatly. "I don't believe that for a second," he said. "Because you once told me that your life was very complicated and that you also had secrets." He leaned in. "So what are your secrets, Sera?"

I shrugged again, becoming very uncomfortable with where this conversation was headed, but also knowing full well that it was probably time to tell him.

"How about I tell you what I know about you, and you fill in the blanks?" he offered.

I nodded.

"Okay, so I know you live next door with JJ and Bruce who are super protective over you, way more protective than just friends. But they're also not your dads, so I'm guessing there's an interesting story there. I also know you work at a restaurant at night and on weekends to supplement your income, because you need money for something. You never talk about your family, so my guess is that there's another story there too, not a particularly good one either, I'm guessing."

"Well, that was straight to the point." I pulled my legs off his shoulders and brought them up to my chest, clutching them and getting into a sitting position. Suddenly I felt more naked than I really was.

"Sera . . ." He sat up and moved towards me, wrapping his

arms around my knees and placing his chin on them. Then he looked up at me. "There's nothing you could tell me that would make me think, or feel, anything less for you."

I knew this conversation was inevitable, but I still didn't feel ready for it, even though I knew that Ben had shared everything with me.

"Your life can't be more fucked up than mine," he said and smiled at me as if it was meant to reassure me—*I wasn't reassured*.

"I . . . I . . ." I tried to start, but the words seemed to get caught in my throat.

Ben sat up further and moved even closer. "Okay. I have a confession, I already think I know what some of it is."

"What is it?" I asked.

"Well, I Googled you and an article about your father came up . . ." His voice tapered off. It sounded like a question rather than a statement. I knew immediately which article he was referring to. The delightful one about my fraudster father being arrested for ripping off his company—*my family's proud heritage*—leading to our very public eviction that gave the entire neighborhood something to watch that Sunday—*I'd half expected people to grab lawn chairs and make popcorn*. My shouting, crying mother, my drunken father, my terrified sister watching her room being packed away— and me, trying to calm everyone down and be the sixteen-year-old adult that I should never have had to be—*should I tell him all that?*

Should I tell him about life in the trailer park? My dad's gambling and the prostitutes, and all the money he owed and all the jail sentences he'd served for petty theft. Tell him about my mother's complete pathetic devotion, depression, anxiety, co- and pill dependence? Is that what I was meant to tell him? Was

I meant to tell him that my sole purpose in life was to give my sister a better future, a responsibility I would have for years to come?

I was lost in thought and barely noticed that Ben had been watching me.

He moved closer. "Why are you so afraid of telling me?" he asked. He was so close to me now that it left me nowhere to go unless I could miraculously melt my way into the water. "Can I tell you what I think?" Ben said. Then he jumped out of the bath with a splash and, before I could react, I felt him get in behind me. He slid me forward a little and then pulled my body back so I was leaning against his chest. Then he wrapped his arms around me and I let my head fall all the way back against him—*it felt good*.

"I think that our pasts and our circumstances shape us and make us who we are. Especially the bad parts. Having Li taken away actually made me become a better father to her now that she's back in my life. The bad parts are building blocks. And from where I'm standing, you're just about the best person I've ever met, so whatever happened, I think you turned out pretty well. Perfect, really."

I tilted my head up to look at him. His lips came down and grazed my forehead. "Whatever you tell me, Sera, won't change the fact that I'm still totally in love with you."

I laughed again. "No, you're not."

I felt two strong hands come up under my arms and then suddenly I was being turned around in the bath. We were face-to-face now, our naked bodies pressing into each other as the warm water lapped against our skin. And then he smiled at me.

"No, actually, I am. I'm in love with you, Sera."

Suddenly I was dizzy. He'd said this so many times before, but until now, they had all sounded like they'd been said in jest. This time it didn't sound like that.

"You're being serious?" I could barely talk.

"Yes." He leaned in and whispered against my mouth.

"I . . . I . . ." I stuttered, unsure of what I should say back to him. Besides the obvious three words that were appropriate in a situation like this and that were sitting on the tip of my tongue, wanting to come out. Even though I'd barely acknowledged them to myself yet.

"It's okay. You don't have to say it back to me. In fact, you don't have to tell me anything you don't want to right now."

"I don't?"

"No. You'll tell me all about your life tomorrow night while we lie in bed together naked after I've made love to you because you've finally confessed your undying love to me."

I burst out laughing again. "God, you say the most ridiculous things sometimes."

"They aren't ridiculous if they're true."

I shook my head and rolled my eyes at him.

"By this time tomorrow night, you're going to be totally in love with me, Sera."

"And how do you know that?"

Ben's hands roamed down my naked back and he cupped my bum. He pulled me firmly towards him and the water around us rippled. I let out a breathy moan as he slid one of his legs between mine. If he was trying not to have sex with me tonight, this wasn't exactly the right thing to be doing.

"Trust me. I just know these things."

57

BEN 4 SERA 4 EVA

~

*I*t felt like we stayed in the bath kissing for hours. I couldn't remember the last time I'd kissed someone for so long. And when we weren't kissing, we were staring into each other's eyes and smiling like idiots.

By the time we'd climbed out of the bath, my lips were red and stinging from the endless friction. Ben wrapped me up in a towel and then took me by the hand and took me to the bed.

It suddenly dawned on me that this was our first sleepover together. It was strange how our relationship had played out in reverse: sex on the first night to not having sex during our first official sleepover. But with Ben I couldn't imagine the relationship playing out any other way. He constantly surprised me. "Which side of the bed do you sleep on?" he asked.

"Um . . ." I hesitated as I tried to remember. "I think that side." I pointed to the left, but before I could move to climb in, Ben took me by the shoulders and marched me to the other side of the bed.

He pulled the blanket down and maneuvered me in. He then jumped over me and climbed into "my" side.

"Why did you do that?"

Ben moved closer. "Because," he said slowly, loosening the towel and letting it fall to the floor. His hand reached inside and ran over my stomach. "I don't want this to be like sleeping in bed with any other guy."

I pushed his hand away quickly. "That's kind of rich coming from you." I'd intended it to come out playfully, but there had definitely been a slight sting in my voice.

"Okay, let's just pretend we're both innocent virgins doing everything for the first time and—"

I burst out laughing. "Not likely."

"Why? It's not such a leap, everything I do with you feels like a first." The look in his eyes transformed the moment again.

I sighed out loud. "Did you enroll in a course where they taught you what women want to hear? I mean . . . *are you for real*?"

"You'll just have to find out tomorrow night." His contagious smile had me smiling again.

"What the hell have you got planned for tomorrow night?" I asked, giggling slightly as I wrapped my arms around him. Suddenly, without warning, Ben rolled me over so I was sitting on top of him.

"I already told you what's happening tomorrow night," he said with that familiar confidence.

"That I'm going to confess my undying love to you?" My tone was slightly mocking.

Ben nodded, looking dead serious. "Exactly!"

"You're crazy, you know that?" I laughed, putting my hands on his chest and then running them over the lines of one of his tattoos. We both watched as my fingers traced the dark lines up and down his torso, his arms and neck. He let out a sigh as goosebumps broke out across his skin.

"There's a gap here," I said when I came to a place that hadn't been covered. He tilted his head up and looked down.

"Oh, that's where I'm getting our names tattooed. Ben 4 Sera 4 eva!" He followed the sentence with one of those iceberg-melting smiles.

"Like I said . . . *crazy!*"

He wrapped he arms around me. "You think I'm joking?" he asked.

I stopped and thought about it for a second. Did I think Ben was capable of tattooing something like that on his chest? *Well*, if there was one person on earth who might do something that ridiculous, it probably would be Ben. "I'm not actually sure," I confessed.

Ben pulled me down and laughed. "Oh Sera, Sera, Sera . . . you'll just have to wait and see, won't you?"

58

A SMALL HUMAN GIRL CHILD

W̶e woke up completely tangled in each other's arms and legs. Even our fingers were intertwined.

"Morning," Ben said when I finally opened my eyes. He was propped up on his elbow, looking at me intently.

"Have you been watching me?"

He smiled and looked up at the clock on the wall. "Only for half an hour."

"You've been staring at me for half an hour?" I turned to face him, keeping my hand over my mouth, for fear of morning breath.

"Did you discover anything interesting?" I asked.

He shrugged. "Nothing I didn't already know."

"Like what?"

"Just how beautiful you are."

I bumped him playfully with my arm. I still wasn't used to the constant flow of his compliments. "Thanks."

"Time to get up. We have a big day ahead of us."

"What big day? We didn't plan anything today, did we?" But

then I remembered the so-called strange, mysterious night that Ben kept alluding too.

"I'm taking Li to the zoo today. She's currently obsessed with polar bears and I promised I would take her to see one." Ben climbed out of bed and searched the floor for his clothes. "I'd love you to come."

"Uh . . . isn't it a work day?"

"It's Youth Day today. Public holiday."

I nodded. I'd totally forgotten about that.

"So let's be kids and eat cotton candy at the zoo and spend the whole day together having a great time."

"I don't know, Ben. It feels weird."

"What about it is weird?"

"How should we act in front of her, now that we're . . . ?"

"Dating?" Ben sighed and placed a hand on my shoulder. "For now. Just friends," he said, moving his hand up to my cheek and smiling, "but as soon as you confess your undying love for me, and I sign those joint custody papers, I'll stand on the rooftop and shout it to the world with a loudhailer." He nudged me and I nodded.

We'd spent the previous evening deliberately not talking about all the complicated issues, and I'd almost forgotten they even existed. Until now.

"I really want you to get to know Li. She's a massive part of my life, and I want you to be a part of my life, too. A big part."

"You're so confident about this . . . about us." I gestured at the space between us. "We've only known each other for a few weeks and you seem so sure. How?"

"I'll tell you tonight."

I sighed loudly and shook my head. "What the hell is so special about tonight, Ben?"

Ben just winked at me playfully. "I told you already—"

I cut him off. "Yeah, yeah, I'm going to confess my undying love to you, yada, yada, yada . . ."

Ben's playful smiled faded. Suddenly he looked serious.

"What?" I sat up quickly, concerned by the rapid shift in his demeanor.

"Sera." His voice sounded strange, and I wasn't sure I liked it. "When I didn't tell you about Li and Mei, it was manipulative. I was trying to get you to go out with me under false pretenses. I didn't let you decide for yourself whether you wanted to. This time, I'm not going to do that." He tucked a loose tendril of hair behind my ear and continued, "Spend a whole day with Li and I, and then see how you feel about me after that because I'm a package deal . . ."

He paused.

"You gave me one date, now give me one more day and experience the other side of my life. If you feel like it's all too much, you can tell me tonight. But after today, you'll have the full picture to make your decision."

I nodded. "Fine. But I can't go to the zoo dressed like this."

* * *

Ben dropped me at home and went to fetch Li. I walked into my bedroom and peeled off the clothes from last night and climbed into a bath. I was more nervous about spending a day with Ben and Li than I had been for our date the night before. It still hadn't dawned on me entirely. Perhaps it was because I was still in so much shock, but Ben had a daughter—*an actual living, breathing female human being. A small human girl child.*

Ben was a package deal. Dating Ben meant inheriting a small person—*a very cute one, mind you.* But it also meant inheriting an ex-wife. Mei would always be in his life, whether I liked her or not, she would always be Li's mother.

I started playing the movie in my head . . . *the big one.* If Ben and I ever got married, I would become a stepmother. JJ and Bruce would kind of inherit a step-grandchild—*oh God, they would be beside themselves with hysterical excitement. Just imagine the costumes.* This wasn't just getting into a relationship with a guy I liked. And I did like him . . . maybe more than like. This was big.

"You missed your curfew last night!" I heard JJ call from outside the bathroom door.

"Sorry, Dad!" I joked.

"It's too late for sorries, young lady. You're grounded. No cell phone, no TV, no boys . . ." I heard JJ roar with laughter. "God, I've always wanted to say that! Thanks."

"Pleasure," I shouted through the door.

"Soooooooooo?" He dragged out the 'o' for added effect, and I knew exactly what he was asking about.

"No. We didn't have sex," I said, standing up and wrapping a towel around me.

"God, you have a filthy mind, that's not what I wanted to know about."

"Really?" I opened the door and eyed him suspiciously. "Then what do you want to know?"

JJ waltzed around my room for a while, I guess trying to drum up some dramatic theatrical beat before he dropped the question. Then he sat on my bed and crossed his legs. "Are you totally, madly in love with the guy yet?"

An instant bolt of heat rushed through me and scorched my cheeks. "Uh . . ." I reached up and touched them, no doubt they were as red as JJ's lipstick. "Why does everyone keep asking me that?"

I grabbed a hand towel, flipped my head down and fastened it around my wet hair, trying to hide my schoolgirl flush.

"Who keeps asking that?"

"You and Ben. Ben keeps asking me if I'm in love with him yet. In fact, he thinks I am going to 'confess my undying love to him tonight.'" I stuck my hands in the air and started gesturing wild air quotes. "I mean, have you ever? Have you ever heard of anything more presumptious, and egotistical and weird, I mean, who says stuff like that and it's also totally ridiculous and—"

"So you *are* going to confess your undying love to him then?" JJ interrupted me and before I could think about it, the words came out.

"Probably." I nodded and a massive smile swept across my face. "Yup. I'm in love with him. I'm in love with the weirdest man I've ever met!" I put my hands on my hips and shook my head while JJ laughed. "Am I mad? After everything he's done, and the lies and the child and cheating and and and . . .'"

JJ shot up and smiled at me mysteriously as he sashayed to my door and exited.

"What?" I shouted after him, "Aren't you going to say anything?"

I stuck my head out the door and watched him swish down the passage—he never walked. "Seriously, the one time I actually need advice you aren't going to dispense it?"

"You don't need any advice. You already know exactly what to do, it's written all over your face! It's been written all over your face since that night in the car with him."

"Really?" I reached up and touched my cheeks and smiled to myself. He was right. I did know what I wanted to do. I knew what I wanted, more than anything. And that was Ben. Ben and all the complications he came with.

I was totally in love with him. It had taken me by surprise and sneaked up on me when I wasn't looking for it, but it had happened and I couldn't wait to tell him.

* * *

I couldn't remember the last time I'd been to the zoo, certainly never with anyone as enthusiastic as Li. She ran ahead of us, skipping with excitement. She squealed and jumped as she watched the elephants getting fed and made funny faces at the playful monkeys swinging from the branches. She did a *Happy Feet* dance when she saw the penguins and when we finally got to the polar bears, she educated me about the nature of their fur.

"It's not really white. It just *'reflectionerates'* its *'arroundings'*," she instructed—*Who knew?* Pretty impressive for a six-year-old, but I understood where it came from as each sentence was qualified with, "*my daddy told me that*."

Ben nodded at me with a tiny smile. "True story that. It's

amazing how perfectly adaptable polar bears are," he said, suddenly sounding like a cute science nerd.

The whole day felt so *right*. Something about the three of us just clicked, as if we'd known each other for ages. We all just fit.

As I watched Ben walking in front of me with Li bouncing happily on his shoulders, another realization dawned on me: this was what I'd always wanted. A sense of family. Togetherness. I wiped away a tiny tear as I watched father and daughter laughing together. They were eating cotton candy and a sticky piece had gotten stuck to Ben's nose and Li giggled hysterically as she pulled it off. It was a true Hallmark moment. They were officially the front cover of a bestselling Father's Day card. A cute video that would no doubt beat all the fluffy kittens playing with balls of string to go viral.

And when Li declared that I was her best friend, I secretly wiped away another tear. Everything about the day was making me feel so emotional. I looked up, and found Ben smiling at us. He was smiling at me, as if he'd known me his entire life and I was part of his world already.

59

HOMELESS DEPRESSED CHIHUAHUAS

⌐

*W*hile Ben dropped Li off, I went home to the guys. It was so predictable. The second I walked in, I was met by two sets of curious eyes.

"And did you tell him?" JJ said, the first to jump in.

"Not yet," I said. "I'm telling him tonight."

"Tonight, hey?" JJ said with a smirk before handing me a coffee. "Feel free to accidentally *not* use protection and fall pregnant with a little Ben baby!" JJ added while wickedly smiling at Bruce. To my surprise, Bruce smiled back conspiratorially.

I choked on the coffee. "What?!?! Are you mad?"

JJ shook his head. "What can I say, I'm hungry for a grandchild."

But JJ's comment didn't strike me as funny. "Have you both forgotten I practically have a child to support already?" I asked. "My sister. God, I wouldn't be able to afford a baby. Not now. Not ever. You guys will just have to get a puppy."

JJ put his hand on his hip and suddenly looked angry again, like he had yesterday. *What was going on?*

"You know," he said, "Bruce and I have being trying to do this subtly over the years. But subtle doesn't seem to work with you, Sera." He turned to Bruce. "I think it's time to have the talk with her. Don't you think?"

Bruce nodded. "It's about seven years overdue already," he said. Suddenly, I felt very nervous.

"What's going on, guys?" I'd never heard them talk like this and it put me on edge.

"You are the worst, and I mean the worst," he shouted the words out, "at accepting any kind of help from anyone. Do you know that?"

Bruce nodded. "The worst."

"It's actually irritating. You walk around incapable of buying decent clothes and paying for the things you want, or for your sister's education, when we walk around with so much money and no one to give it to."

JJ's tone caught me off guard. He genuinely sounded angry.

"You never accept our help. Like the car offer?" JJ asked before leaning in closer. I glanced to my left and Bruce was doing the same.

"Um . . . I, I . . ." I stuttered.

Bruce spoke up, "You seem to think it's some kind of charity hand out. When it's not. We don't want to help you out of charity, Sera. We want to help you because we care. You're part of our family. That's what family does for each other. They help out when times get tough."

I scoffed loudly. "That's not what my family does."

JJ slapped his hand down on the arm of the chair very loudly. "Stop it! Stop being such a suffering martyr, Sera."

I did a double-take at his words. "What?"

"Right now. Right in front of you, you have the means to dig yourself out of a hole. How much is your sister's med school? Twenty thousand rand? Forty thousand rand? That's nothing for us. For heaven's sake, let us help you. I for one don't want to watch you walking around the house depressed and stressed about money. It's becoming so boring."

"What?" It was all I could manage. I was downright offended.

Bruce got up and moved over to the couch next to me. "I think what JJ is trying to say, is that you don't have to carry all these burdens alone."

"Exactly," JJ added. "Especially not when you're going to get the money one day anyway."

I looked from Bruce to JJ confused. "What do you mean?"

Bruce placed a hand on my shoulder. "Who do you think the beneficiary in our will is?"

"Who?" I asked.

"One day when we're both six feet under, you're going to get everything," Bruce added.

The stab of emotions I felt with that single sentence completely overwhelmed me. I looked at both of them dumbfounded.

JJ tutted loudly. "Well, who the hell else are we going to give it to? We don't have kids. If not you, we'd donate it to charity . . . drag queens in distress, or homeless depressed Chihuahuas or something."

I managed a slight smile through the tears that were starting to well up. Still . . . "I could never accept that," I said.

JJ stood up and gestured at me angrily. "See?! There you go again with your 'woe is me' attitude." He started imitating me.

"I'm Sera, and I'm not good enough to accept something like that."

Bruce held up his hand. "JJ. Just calm down."

"No," JJ said and stamped his foot. "It kills me. I mean, your wardrobe, for heaven's sake. You won't even let me take you shopping! And you take on way, way too much. You work too hard, you look after your sister, your mother . . . who's looking after you?"

"I look after myself," I said quickly.

JJ shook his head. "Let us help. You do so much for us and you won't let us do anything for you." It looked like JJ had a tear in his eye and my stomach suddenly twisted into knots.

I was in total shock. This conversation had thrown me completely. JJ stormed off to the kitchen and banged a coffee cup around. Bruce got up, too, but then turned and looked at me.

"I know JJ is being a bit harsh," he said, "but this is something we've been talking about for years, and it's just frustrating you won't accept our help, especially when we see you suffering in silence. Think about it, Sera. You don't have to carry on living like this."

And with that, he walked away, leaving me reeling in shock. *Had I just had my first fight with the guys?*

60

I LOVE YOU, OKAY. WHATEVER.

◡

JJ was right about one thing, accepting help had always been hard for me—*especially financial help*. It always made me feel inferior. To accept money meant that I would have to accept who I really was. And that would mean having to accept what people had once called me at school, "poor trailer trash."

I'd been so determined to prove everyone wrong, to prove that I could rise above my situation, no matter how bad it was. But this had come at a terrible cost for me: A hand-to-mouth existence, debt up to my eyeballs, no savings and nothing to call my own.

It was also hard for me to accept that Bruce and JJ wanted to do this for me because they considered me family. My idea of family was so twisted. Families destroy, they don't help. They break things, they don't fix them. They are cruel and hurtful and do more harm than good. I was determined to break that cycle with my sister. But, more than that, I felt that I needed to do it on my own, to prove to the world and especially to my father, that he hadn't broken me.

Going to Ben's place now felt like the last thing on earth I wanted to do. Knowing Ben, he would know something was up the second I walked through the door—*which, of course, he did.*

"What's wrong?" he asked after we got into his apartment. He'd come back with a bag full of chocolates, which I'd started digging into the second he handed it to me. I barely tasted anything as I unwrapped two bars at once, taking bites out of both at the same time.

"Have the chocolates done something to offend you?" Ben said with a slight smile. I shook my head.

"I think I just had a fight with JJ and Bruce." *Mars Bar smashed. Kit-Kat gone. Next?*

"Really?" He sounded surprised. So was I. I was more than surprised. I was downright floored.

"First fight we've ever had," I said and stopped eating. I felt sick—*too much, too fast.*

"What was it about?" he asked, leaning in and wiping a smudge of chocolate off my face.

I scoffed and rolled my eyes. "They said I don't accept any help from them, financially." What had JJ said that had caused that stab in my stomach? "That I feel like I'm not good enough, or deserve their help. That I take on too much."

"They're right."

"What?"

"You do take on too much. I've seen how you work."

"Work?" Suddenly I felt attacked.

"You work every night at the restaurant and I've seen what you do at work. You often do other people's work and are often the first to arrive and last to leave." Ben slid into the seat next to me.

"Don't get me wrong. It's an admirable quality. But it's too much. And it's not just work that you don't accept help with."

"What?" I asked.

"That day you came to work upset, and I asked you what was wrong, you didn't want to talk about it. Maybe I could've helped? Even if it was just to listen while you ranted?"

Now I was more convinced than ever that Ben had chatted to the guys. I didn't like this, and I certainly didn't need it from Ben too. But he continued . . .

"Sometimes you walk around with a dark cloud looming over your head. If you just let people in . . ." Ben said, trying to reach over and take my hand. I pulled it away quickly.

"Jesus. Did you and the guys have some kind of secret meeting? Did you all agree to give me shit about this at the same time? I came here thinking that we were going to have a perfect, romantic, amazing night together after the day we had, which was awesome, by the way. I certainly wasn't expecting this. Now I just feel angry and all I want to do is shout when actually what I wanted to do was tell you that I love you and—"

I stopped myself—*I said it*—I hadn't meant to say it like that. I'd had such different expectations for this moment and now it had come out clumped together in an angry rant.

"Could you repeat that last part?" Ben asked with a smile that practically lit up his whole face. "I'm not sure I heard it."

I blushed at the thought of repeating myself. "I said I love you, okay. Whatever." I shrugged, as if that would somehow make the statement seem more casual—*it wasn't. It was definitely one of the most "un-casual" things I'd ever said.*

Ben leaned towards me with that dangerous twinkle in his eye. "Okay? Whatever?" he asked.

"No. Not whatever. Okay?" I chuckled at the absolute lameness of that sentence and tried again. "I've fallen in love with you, Ben. I'm in love with you." I felt so vulnerable saying those words out loud.

Ben didn't say a word; instead, he stood up and took me by the hand, pulled me to my feet and marched me down the corridor towards his bedroom.

61

GANGNAM STYLE

Okay, we'd had sex before, so why the hell was this so damn nerve wracking?

I'll tell you why.

It was because of that damn glint in those dreamy chocolate-brown eyes of his. That confident swagger he had and that assertive way he took me by the hand and marched me down the passage without hesitation. Without even looking back at me. Like I was his. It was in the way he got me into his bedroom, immediately took his top off, and tossed it to the other end of the room. His "devil may care" attitude was so ridiculously sexy—*especially now.* It was in the way he pointed for me to sit on his bed as he strode across the room, bent over and turned on the heater—*how did he make turning on normal household appliances so damn crazy hot?*

But then, it changed. Ben walked over to the bed, sat down next to me and everything changed. Suddenly things between us started feeling awkward.

"God," he said as he ran his hands through his hair, "it's stupid, but I don't think I've ever been so nervous about anything in my entire life."

I blushed. "Me too."

"I feel like a teenage girl losing her virginity."

I managed a small laugh. "It would be truly bizarre if you knew what that felt like."

"Okay," Ben said, jumping off the bed again, "let's start over." Then he exited the room and closed the door behind him. I looked at the door wondering what the hell he was about to do. Suddenly he burst through it and strode towards me. I burst out laughing because the action seemed so comical. Then he slid up next to me . . .

"Is this seat taken?" Those were the first words he'd spoken to me that night at the club. He said them in that same sexy, husky tone that had immediately caused me to go wobbly—*it was having a similar effect on me right now*. I played along.

"Depends who's asking," I said, turning to him. His face lit up when he realized what I was doing.

"The name's Ben," he said, then took my hand and kissed the back of it, maintaining intense eye contact. My hand tingled. "And you're Sera," he said. And then suddenly, as if a light bulb had been flicked on, I remembered something important about our first night together.

He'd known my name.

"How do you know my name, Ben?" I asked, still playing along in a sultry sexy voice.

Ben leaned in.

"I have a confession to make."

"Mmm?"

"I've been watching you, Sera."

He said it in a way I wasn't sure was a joke. Was this role-play or—*no, surely not?*

"Watching me?"

"For about three months."

"What do you mean?"

"Well, the first time I saw you was when my brother was performing." He gave a tiny smile as he looked like he was remembering, "You were with JJ and Bruce and the three of you didn't stop laughing the whole night. I think you guys were actually meant to be 'in disguise.'" He gestured inverted commas with a smile. "But who wears oversized shades in a nightclub, right? You guys stuck out like sore thumbs." He laughed at the memory. "And I thought, I'd really like to get to know that girl. The girl with the amazing smile and contagious laughter that had me captivated all night."

Okay. Pause. Were we still role-playing here? Had I told him about the night we'd gone out to spy on his brother? I wasn't sure.

"Tell me more," I prodded.

Ben moved in closer, bringing his lips all the way up to mine. He didn't kiss me, though; instead, he gently and very softly moved them over mine.

"Then, two weeks later, I saw you at another party. Seems we're both on the same gay club circuit." He shot me a knowing look and I smiled back at him. "You looked so damn sexy that night, and I wanted to speak to you so badly, but I was too nervous. So I just sat in the corner and watched you." He smiled his devastating smile at me. "God, you looked so confident and happy, and did I mention sexy? Fuck, you looked beautiful that night."

I bit my lip a little trying to remember the night he was refer-ring to. "Do you remember what I was wearing?"

"Perfectly. That tight, black pencil skirt that drives me mad and your little corporate white-collar shirt that makes you look like a schoolteacher. And then JJ pulled your shirt out and tied it in that knot in your waist."

"I remember that." JJ hated it when I went out in my work clothes.

"And then he pulled out your ponytail, ruffled your hair and in that exact moment all my school-boy/librarian fantasies came true. I tried to come over and talk to you but . . . so I basically went to bed fantasizing about what it would be like to be with you and kicking myself for not having spoken to you."

My heart started beating faster and faster as it was quickly becoming clear that he was no longer role-playing. This was real.

"Why didn't I see you?"

"I told you, I sat in the back . . . and then I asked someone who you were. And of course everyone knows JJ and Bruce. That's how I knew your name."

Ben kissed me. "Sera," he said, then pulled away and looked me in the eyes before going in for another small kiss. "Sera," he said again, then went in for a deeper kiss. A long, deep kiss. God, he tasted so good, I wanted to eat him.

"Did you see me again?" I asked, reeling from the kiss he'd just given me.

He nodded. "Seems you and the guys like to go dancing." His hand crept onto my thigh and he kissed me behind my ear. "It was the most ridiculous dancing I'd ever seen."

An image flashed through my mind and I knew which night

he was referring to. "We were doing our Gangnam Style impersonation," I said, but the words came out breathy. Ben had slipped
his hand in between my thighs and pushed them open.

"You looked so happy, but then . . ." He stopped half way
through the sentence and I knew why. I remembered what had
happened next.

"You took out your phone and your whole face changed. Suddenly you looked like the saddest girl in the entire world and I
wanted to know why. And I wanted to run across the room and
hold you. In that moment, it felt like you were showing me this
other side of yourself, this vulnerable, private side. A side that you
didn't show people, that you keep safely tucked away, like me. But
I'd seen it. And I felt like I knew you. I can't explain it any other
way, but from that moment I just knew I wanted you."

My breath caught in my throat. That was just one of the many
nights that my sister had phoned me. I didn't remember the spe-
cifics, but it was something to the effect of dad, gambling, money,
stealing, maybe even a hooker.

"That night I decided that, if I saw you again, I was going to
talk to you, and ask you out."

"Wow." It was true, everything he'd said. And finally it
explained the way he'd looked at me in the car that night, as if
he'd known me. It also explained why he'd been so persistent, so
early on. Ben had been watching me from the dark shadows of
the nightclub. He'd been fantasizing about me. It was just about
the fucking sexiest thing that anyone had ever said to me in my
entire life—*slightly pervy . . . very sexy.*

I pushed Ben down on the bed and climbed on top of him,
suddenly driven by overwhelming lust. The idea that I'd been

watched and fantasized about made me feel so sexy and uninhibited. I pulled my top off over my head and threw it across the room next to Ben's shirt. My bra soon followed.

"Ben," I said as I leaned down, our naked chests pressing into each other, "Are you going to keep your promise now?"

"And what promise would that be?"

I kissed his neck and breathed into his ear, "That you're going to make love to me all fucking night."

62

THE CUNNING HAND OF FATE . . .

Ben smiled at me. Languid. Slow. Sexy, and all for me. "I always keep my promises," he said. "But not like this."

In one quick, fluid movement, Ben rolled me over onto my back and slid his body over mine. He felt hard against me. And heavy. I felt crushed under his weight and I liked it.

"Oh Sera, Sera," he said, staring into my eyes.

"Yes?"

"Nothing. I just like saying your name." And with that, he kissed me. His facial hair was rough, his lips were velvety, his mouth warm and sweet tasting and his tongue soft. The textures and feelings all combined and mingled into something amazing and unforgettable.

It's one thing to have sex with someone. But it's another thing entirely to be doing it with someone you've fallen desperately in love with.

Our clothes were off and there was a chill in the air. I shivered. Ben quickly pulled the covers over our heads and we were enveloped in warm darkness. The heat under the thick duvet suddenly made everything seem so much more intense and heightened.

Ben kissed me again, but this time, his mouth traveled down my neck and over my breasts. It felt good. And when his warm tongue brushed my nipple, I inhaled sharply. The air inside the duvet was getting hotter now. It was almost too thick to breathe.

"Mmm. You taste like chocolate," Ben whispered.

"Really?" I giggled slightly as his tongue came out and he licked me, as if he was really tasting me.

"Seriously. You actually taste like it."

I giggled and pulled his head up for another kiss.

"How's it even possible that you taste that good?" he continued.

I put my hand over his mouth. "Stop talking and just kiss me."

"Yes, ma'am." Ben came in for another kiss and I opened my legs, letting his body slide between them, wrapping a leg around him to make sure he couldn't escape—*he was mine now.* The kiss soon took over our whole bodies and Ben ground his hips into me. My own hips lifted, swayed and thrust up to meet him. Over and over again. We kissed, while our bodies rocked together. Faster. Harder. More breathless. Until Ben finally pulled away, gasping for air.

"Sera, Sera, Sera . . ."

"Ben, Ben, Ben . . ." I whispered back, playing along.

"You're so fucking tasty I could eat you," he said.

I winced when I felt a little bite on my neck. And then one on my shoulder. Then my neck again.

But then I felt him move lower. "I wonder what you taste like here," he said before I felt a tiny nibble on my stomach. His soft kisses and warm wet tongue moved further down. He kissed my hip bone, my inner thigh and then . . .

I gasped.

"Ben." His name came out fast and desperate as I felt the first tingle throughout my entire body. Every nerve—from head to toe—felt like it was on fire. The waves of sensation rushed through me like an incoming tide. Building, growing more violent, and more intense. I closed my eyes and threw back my head. It was all I could do as I was overcome with pleasure.

My breath grew faster and faster and my need for fresh air increased. It felt like there was no oxygen left under the covers. I gasped for oxygen and, not getting enough, I grabbed at the duvet and yanked it down. And as I took in that first breath of cool air, I came.

It was the most intense thing I'd ever experienced. I felt like I couldn't contain all the sensations in my body. It burst out of me and filled the whole room as I writhed and moaned loudly.

And then, just as the sensation was tapering off, I felt Ben inside me. His mouth immediately came up to mine. He kissed me hard and moaned against my mouth as he moved inside me.

No coherent thoughts formed. My brain just switched off.

Our bodies developed a rhythm. As if we were both moving in slow motion. With each stroke, each thrust, each touch of our lips, our breathing and our bodies moved more and more in perfect unison. We were no longer separate people. We were one.

As our breathing and bodies went faster and harder, only one thought penetrated the thick haze—*I don't want this to end*. Before the thought could grab hold, it left me as pure pleasure took over once more.

Our bodies moved faster still.

"Sera, I love you . . ." Ben whispered, the words getting stuck in his throat as his body started to tense and his grip on my fingers intensified. I felt my muscles tensing too and I wrapped my legs tighter around him, even tighter.

"I love you too," I said.

The moment was so intimate. Ben let go of my hands suddenly and then grabbed my face, looked into my eyes and came. I watched, transfixed, as his eyes seemed to cloud over for a few moments, before returning to normal. When it was over, we didn't move. We stayed like that, our noses touching, our breath rushing in and out of each other's mouths and still staring into each other's eyes.

When our breaths had finally slowed enough, Ben finally spoke.

"Sera," he said, "you do know what this means, don't you?" He wiped some sticky strands of hair off my face.

I looked up at him and shook my head.

"You're mine now. Officially. You belong to me until the day we're both old and ugly and wrinkly and using walkers." He smiled.

"That sounds slightly creepy," I said, smiling up at him.

"I can be a bit of a creepy guy."

"Well, you did stalk me," I said, running my fingers through his wet hair.

"Hey, I didn't stalk you. I wanted to talk to you all those times, I really did. But every time I tried I just . . ." He shrugged, looking coy, then rolled us both over so that he was on his back and I was sitting on top of him. "I was shy. I chickened out," he finally said.

"I can't imagine you being shy for one second."

"What can I say? You have that effect on me, Sera."

My stomach filled with butterflies at the thought of him sitting shyly in the corner trying to pluck up the courage to talk to me.

"I have another confession to make, Sera."

"Mmmmm?" I asked slightly wearily.

"Once I knew your name, I went looking for you on Facebook."

"Really?"

He nodded again, looking sheepish. "I thought about sending you a friend request. But I didn't."

I smiled down at him. "Well, I would have turned it down anyway. I don't accept friend requests from strangers. Especially creepy ones."

He shook his head at me. "Not creepy. Just in love. From the first moment I saw you laughing, I had to know you."

I felt the smile on my face getting bigger. "So moving into this building, the job . . . that was a total coincidence?"

Ben chuckled, "That, my dear Sera, was the cunning hand of fate just confirming what I already knew."

"And what did you know, Ben?"

"That we were meant to be together. That somehow, after that night in the car, I would find you again."

I felt my face go warm from the rush of emotions that swept through me.

"So I kept my promise. Are you going to keep yours?" he asked, taking my hands in his.

"What promise?"

"I still don't know you. Not really." He lifted one of my hands to his mouth and planted a soft kiss on the tip of one of my fingers.

"The whole truth," he said in a soft coaxing voice.

"Okay. But can we have pancakes and coffee first?"

Ben smiled up at me and nodded. He eased me off him and climbed out of bed, returning with two large, warm fluffy robes from his closet. "I stole these from the hotel, in case you recognize them."

"What?" My mouth fell open. "You didn't?"

"I wanted to commemorate the beginning of our relationship."

"Relationship?" I asked teasingly.

Ben wrapped the warm robe around me. "I told you. You're mine now."

He took me by the hand, and marched me out the door to the kitchen. "Sera White. Has a good ring to it, don't you think?" He turned and flashed me a wicked smile and my heart literally stopped in my chest.

63

TEAM BEN AND SERA

~~

I think the pancakes, and seriously strong coffee, helped with the disclosure because, within a matter of minutes, I was telling him everything. Stuff I hadn't told anyone other than JJ and Bruce. And it felt good, like opening the floodgates on a dam that had been stocked to capacity for years. The words flowed out of me and I felt myself getting lighter and lighter with each admission.

Ben sat opposite me looking serious while I babbled. I told him about how my father was the loser dad of the century. How he gambled our life away and screwed hookers. How he'd landed up in jail more times than I could count. How my mother was constantly and morbidly depressed and wallowed in her self-pity all day long. How I was the sole breadwinner who needed to feed, clothe and educate my sister. How broke I was. How much debt I was in. I even quipped that if my car didn't miraculously fix itself, I would have to get a job as a pole dancer to raise enough money for a new one.

I told him that I barely earned enough to live on, and if it wasn't for my rent-free accommodation and the fact JJ and Bruce bought all the groceries (something I felt bad about), I would probably be back in the trailer park. I went on and on for almost an hour and when I was finished, Ben just looked at me with an expression I couldn't decipher. It made me nervous.

"What?" I asked brusquely, feeling suddenly very defensive.

Ben shook his head. "Nothing. It's just . . . Sad. That's all."

"Sad?"

"Yes. You deserve so much more."

Something about that statement suddenly pissed me off. Was he looking at me like I was a charity case all of a sudden?

"What?" Ben asked, reaching over and taking my hand.

I shrugged, feeling suddenly tearful. "I don't want you to think of me as some sad, pathetic charity—"

He cut me off. "I don't. I would never."

He looked sincere and I believed him. But there was something else in his look I couldn't quite interpret.

"What are you thinking?" I asked.

"I was wondering if there was anything I could do to help?"

Now it was my turn to cut him off. "No. Absolutely not," I said. "I can handle it. I've been handling it for most of my life. I'm fine." I averted my gaze and fiddled with the last pancake on my plate.

Ben looked at me quizzically. "Why won't you accept any help? Your car, for example; I told you, a mechanic owes me a favor."

"No." I stabbed the pancake hard—*the sudden move even surprised me.*

"Why? I don't understand."

The fucking tears felt like they were coming again. "Because, I . . . I . . ." I reached up and wiped my eyes before a tear escaped. "I don't want him to win. If I can't do it on my own, then he's won. It proves that he's beaten me. Broken me. I won't let him do that. I can't."

Ben nodded solemnly as he thought about what I'd said. "I totally understand that. But, what if people around you want to help? Not because they think you can't do it, but because they care? That's not showing weakness. Actually, that's you proving to him that you can move on and create a life with people that love and care about you. Isn't that a kind of win in itself?"

This was the second time I'd heard this sentiment echoed in the last twenty-four hours. The horrible feelings flooded in again as I remembered the fight I'd just had with JJ and Bruce. "That's kind of what JJ and Bruce said, too."

"Well, if three people are telling you that . . ."

I dropped my fork. "I don't know," I said, shaking my head, feeling very confused. "I don't know—"

Suddenly, as if by some kind of sick, divine joke, my phone rang. I immediately glanced up at the clock on the kitchen wall, and, when I saw that it was nearly 3 a.m., my stomach dropped. Only my sister phoned me at this hour. And when she did, it was for one reason only. I jumped up and rushed for my bag immediately.

"Are you okay?" I asked, as soon as I picked up. I glanced up and saw Ben had moved closer to me. He looked worried.

My sister sounded desperate. "It's Dad. He's here. He's drunk and he's causing a scene. The landlord said they're going to call the cops and kick us all out if he doesn't leave."

A scene. That was a euphemism. I knew what "a scene" was. There would be yelling, swearing, throwing of things, maybe even some hitting. "I'm coming there now." I hung up and ran to the bedroom to change into my clothes.

Ben followed behind me and started changing too.

"What are you doing?" I asked.

"I'm coming with you."

"No, you're not."

"Why not?" he seemed genuinely confused.

"Um . . . because this is *my* family. It has nothing to do with you."

"We're in a relationship now, Sera." He tried to move closer to me and I instinctively took a step back.

"So?"

"So?" He sounded angry. "Couples help each other. We're a team. Team Ben and Sera." He ended that with a small smile.

I imagined his words splashed across the front of another Hallmark card, but I was still unmoved. It was one thing telling him about my family, but it was another thing altogether for him to witness their chaos and destruction first hand. But Ben persisted.

"Besides," he said firmly, "I'm not letting you go driving around in the middle of the night alone. It's not safe."

He had a point. "Fine," I said. "But you're waiting in the car."

64

TRUST ME

〜

*B*y the time we got there, the situation was already explosive. I couldn't see them at first, but I could hear them screaming at each other. We parked the car and I immediately saw Ben's hand reach for the door handle.

"Stay in the car, Ben. Please." I couldn't hide the desperation in my voice.

Ben simply nodded, reached over and took my hand. "You know where I am if you need me." I nodded at him and climbed out the car.

My sister ran up to me immediately. "Dad rocked up about an hour ago," she said. "He's begging Mom for money. She doesn't have any, so he's screaming at her and the landlord—"

At the mention of his name, the angry landlord walked up to us, fuming. "If you don't get that man off this property in five minutes, I'm calling the cops." I glanced over at his house, which was only a few meters away from the cottage my mom and sister stayed in, and saw his wife and kids peering through the windows.

They looked frightened. I didn't blame them. My dad wasn't the kind of guy you wanted coming onto your property at three in the morning. Especially when he was drunk and wanting money.

"I'm so sorry. I promise I'll sort it out."

"This is the fourth time this has happened!" His face was now red with rage.

"I know. It won't happen again, I swear. I'll get rid of him."

The landlord shook his head and looked down at me with something resembling pity. "I like you and your sister," he said, "and you always pay the rent on time, but I'm sorry. I can't have you living on the property anymore. I have a family. Kids." He looked over at his window. "They don't need to see this."

I nodded. I didn't blame him for feeling this way. "I understand. Again, I'm sorry."

Katie looked at me with sheer panic and, as always, I was overcome with a desperate need to make her feel better. "It's okay," I said. "I'll make a plan. Start packing your things and I'll deal with Mom and Dad."

We walked towards the cottage, and as I got closer I could see two figures silhouetted against the curtains. They were swinging their arms around wildly, and I heard words pouring out of their mouths that no two people should ever say to each other.

The second I got inside, my dad pounced. "Sera. Sera." He reeked of alcohol. His shirt was creased and stained with coffee, and he was barefoot and bleeding, as if he'd walked through a thorn bush.

"I've figured it out. I know how to beat the system. It's all in this formula I've worked out. I swear. It's a sure thing. We'll be rich. I swear." His voice quivered, high pitched and desperate.

Do you know how many times I'd heard this story before? He always had a way to beat the system. Some "get rich quick" scheme always brewing in his head.

"I just need a couple of thousand," he went on. "That's all. In the morning we'll have a thousand times that. This time it's going to work. Trust me."

"Trust me." Another line I'd heard over and over again.

"Dad. I don't have any money."

"Don't fucking lie to me, Sera." He stuck his finger out and pointed at me. He was shaking, no doubt from the alcohol.

"Sera . . ." My mother jumped in now. "Just give your father the money. Just give it to him."

I looked at my mother. Her face was tear-stained. Her hair was matted and unbrushed. She was pale, pasty and flabby looking. She looked like she hadn't gone outside, exercised or seen the sun in years—*which was true*. She was a broken shadow of the woman she once was, the vibrant woman who had gone swimming with me as a child. Who'd played hide and seek with me. There was nothing left of that woman anymore. Every trace of her was gone now, and it was all thanks to my father. He was a cancer.

I looked from my sad mess of a mother to my father. He had a wild look about him tonight—*more so than usual*. "Dad. I don't have any money." I said it as calmly as possible.

"You're lying again." He was screaming now and waggling his finger just inches from my face. I could smell cigarette smoke and cheap perfume. "What's this then?" he asked as he moved to the kitchen table and started picking up the brand new big heavy textbooks and reading the prices.

"Two hundred. One hundred and fifty. One hundred and

twenty-five . . . I'm guessing you bought these for your sister?" He was waving the big, hardcover biology textbook around now. "So how did you buy her these?"

Without warning, he jumped towards me and pulled my bag off my shoulder. In a moment of pure terror, I managed to push him and he went stumbling backwards like the sorry drunk he was.

And then it happened. *Again. The inevitable.*

"Don't push your father like that," my mother shouted at me, rushing to his side.

After all these years, my mother was still choosing him over us.

I looked at my parents and suddenly all the anger that I usually felt for them evaporated. Instead, I calmly watched my mother pandering to my abusive, drunk father and all I felt was pity. They were sick. They needed help. But they were also poisonous and I couldn't keep letting them ruin my life—*my sister's either.* This had to end—*tonight.* I needed to change things once and for all.

"Katie. Go get your things. We're leaving."

My mother looked at me with a strange look. "Sera? You don't mean that."

"Mom. I'm taking Katie with me. Not you. As far as I'm concerned, the landlord can call the cops on both of you. It's time you sorted yourself out." I couldn't believe I'd just said that. But it was time to end this cycle now. Before it was too late.

My sister made a move for her bedroom and then I felt the pain. I wasn't sure what it was at first, but when I heard the loud thud and looked down, I saw the textbook drop to the floor. My face felt hot and wet all of a sudden. I lifted my hand to it, and my fingers came away red.

It all happened so fast after that. Ben was there. He was screaming at my father. I could hear the words, but it was as if I no longer understood English. I had no idea what he was saying. My head was throbbing too hard to make sense of anything. Katie ran towards me and I felt wobbly, so she sat me down.

My dad and Ben were shouting at each other, and my mother moved herself in between them, until my dad pushed her away. She too fell to the floor, hard, and started crying. My father then pushed Ben and, when Ben hit him, he crashed to the floor. The last thing I saw was Ben grabbing a handful of bank notes and throwing them in my father's face and then coming towards me.

Then everything went black . . .

65

SHAPES AND OUTLINES
OF THE WORLD

When I woke up, my eyes hurt and they felt sticky, like someone had poured glue into them. I finally managed to open them ever so slightly after a few painful blinks. Through the small gap between my lashes, the shapes and outlines of the world around me came into soft, blurry focus. Everything looked very white. Too white. I blinked a few times until my eyes finally adjusted.

I tried to sit up, but my head protested with a loud, angry thump. I grabbed it and took a deep breath, willing the excruciating pain away. When the hard thumping finally subsided to a dull grind and my eyes fully adjusted to my surroundings, I noticed where I was: A big, white, bright hospital room—*a private one with a lounge and a spare bed*. I looked around the room feeling confused. I had no recollection of how I'd gotten there, or what had happened. And there was no one there to explain it to me.

But then it slowly came back to me. My dad. My sister. The fight. The textbook. I reached up and touched my forehead, feeling the rough stitches protruding. The second my fingers came into contact with them, I felt an unbearable, sharp pain that made me instantly nauseous. I closed my eyes again, shutting out all the other stimuli so I could concentrate exclusively on quelling the rising nausea and pushing away the pain rippling through my head and radiating down my neck.

With my eyes closed, more flashes of memory appeared: My mother lying on the floor after my father pushed her. My sister. And *Ben*. Ben hit my father. I suddenly felt a jolt of panic. Where was my sister? Was she okay? Ben? What had happened after I'd passed out?

I turned as I heard the door open. JJ and Ben walked in carrying coffees. They noticed that I was awake and both rushed over to my bedside looking relieved.

"Oh thank God," JJ said, taking my hand and kissing it. "I was so worried you were going to die."

"Die? What happened to me?" I screeched. I immediately wished I hadn't, because screeching pushed me over the pain threshold once again.

Ben jumped in quickly. "JJ doesn't mean die, *die*. You're fine, just a minor concussion." He sat down on the other side of the bed and took my hand, kissing it and holding it against his cheek. "You're okay. Everything is going to be okay." His voice was so soothing that I almost believed him. But I knew full well everything was not okay—*not by a long shot*.

And then JJ burst into tears, loud wailing tears. "I kept thinking that if you died, you would die angry with me after the fight we had—"

"JJ, I'm not dying," I cut him off quickly.

"Are you still angry with me?" he asked, looking genuinely worried. "Please say you're not angry with me, or I don't know what I'll do!"

I shook my head. "I was at first. But I'm not anymore."

He sighed. "Thank God!"

"Where's Katie?" I asked.

"She's upstairs with your mother." Ben was stroking my hand and looking at me. He looked tired, like he had been up all night—*he probably had*.

"What's upstairs?"

"Psychiatric ward."

"What? How did she end up there?" There was clearly a lot I didn't know about last night.

"After your father hit you—" Ben started to explain.

"Bastard!" JJ quickly cut in. "If I had been there I swear I would have taken him down. Like last time."

I smiled slightly and Ben spoke again, "We thought your mother was having a heart attack, so we called the ambulance and you were both rushed here. But when the doctors saw her, they confirmed it was a panic attack."

"Her wrist and ankle are also broken from the fall," JJ said. "Bruce and I spoke to the psychiatrist and he gave us the name of a place where she can get help."

"Help for what?"

"Depression, anxiety, toxic codependency, pills . . . take your pick, Sera."

JJ was right. I'd been hoping she would get help for that kind of stuff for years.

I sighed and shook my head. "She won't agree to go. I know her."

JJ squeezed my hand. "She has. Bruce and I had a long talk with her and she's going in next week after she's discharged from hospital. I think the panic attack—she thought she was dying—and your father hitting you has her finally seeing the light. Last night was a bit of a wake-up call, for everyone."

"Where is this place? How much does it co—"

JJ cut me off quickly. "It's taken care of. Don't start. I don't want to fight with you again."

"And this room—" I looked around—*a hospital room like this cost a fortune, and I didn't have medical aid.*

This time Ben squeezed my hand. "Sorted," he said and kissed my open palm.

"My father?" I asked, my voice quivering—*my father who had thrown a textbook at my head.* Despite the pain in my head, my heart felt worse somehow. It was broken. Even though he didn't act like it, he was still my father.

"Bruce is booking the dickhead into rehab as we speak," JJ replied.

"What?" I sat up straight and grabbed my head when it thumped again. That couldn't be right.

"Easy," Ben said then helped me back down and adjusted the pillow behind me. "Don't make any sudden moves."

"How?" I finally asked when the loud throbbing in my head had calmed down. "Are you forcing him in?"

"No, actually," Ben said. "He fell to pieces after you passed out. Didn't you hear him?"

I shook my head. I hadn't heard a thing.

"He was the one that called the ambulance," Ben explained. "He even rode in the back with you. Of course I accompanied him, but he wouldn't leave your side. He was crying and apologizing over and over again. He didn't stop."

"He always apologizes." I teared up and grabbed my stomach as if it were in pain—*it was. An invisible knife was stabbing me.* I closed my eyes and thought I could hear him promising, over and over again, that he would get help. I thought I remembered him holding my hand. Telling me he loved me. That he was sorry. That he wanted to be a better father.

JJ leaned in and put his hand on my shoulder. "He offered to turn himself over to the police, he was so distraught. Bruce arranged for him to go into rehab instead. We thought you would want it that way."

I nodded and closed my eyes.

"Even though he's a total asshole who I still hate, he does love you," JJ added. "In some very fucked-up and strange way."

There was so much to take in. In one night, everything had come to a loud angry head. The chaos that was my life had exploded, leaving behind a huge ugly mess. A mess that had splattered all over Ben. I wondered what he thought of me now. Would he really still want to date me—especially with a small daughter—if this was what my life was like? I didn't know if I could be so accepting.

"Sera," Ben whispered in my ear as he leaned in. "It's all going to be okay." He kissed me softly on the side of my face. "I'm here for you. We all are. It's time you saw that."

I felt a soft hand on my leg and heard the legs of a chair scrape across the floor. "I'm going to give you two love birds some time," JJ said before leaning in and kissing my forehead.

I lay in silence for a while, listening to the sound of Ben breathing next to me. "I'm sorry," I finally said.

"What are you sorry for?"

"Everything. How you've been dragged into this mess and—"

"Stop it. I told you, I want to be a part of your life. Even the bad bits."

I managed a small smile.

"I've wanted to be a part of your life since the first time I saw you," he added. "I love you."

I closed my eyes when they started welling up with tears. "I love you too."

With my eyes still closed, I felt him stroke my hand. "Sera White, hey?" he said.

I opened them again and looked at him, a smile plastered across his face.

"Whatever!" I quipped.

"We'll see. We'll see," he said, coming up and softly kissing my forehead.

EPILOGUE

I sat on the lounger by the pool and looked out over the beautiful blue sea. I had that stuffed feeling from completely over-indulging over Christmas, but I'd also never felt more content in my entire life. So much has changed in a year and a half.

I've been doing a lot of hair braiding, finger painting and have been reading a lot of fairy tales lately—*Li's favorite is Cinderella, of course.*

Bruce and JJ decided to retire and move to their holiday home in laid-back Cape Town a few months ago—*JJ even decided to stop coloring his hair and embrace his grey.* There were many tears, and long goodbye hugs, and dramatic soap-opera moments as if they were flying off to Timbuktu never to be seen again. (Cape Town is a short three-hour flight away.)

Ben and I are still "stuck" in the extended honeymoon phase of our relationship. I have a suspicion that it's not going to wear off anytime soon. He tells me he wakes up every morning feeling like he won the Lotto—*he always did know how to charm the pants off a girl.*

Katie, too, is loving her well-deserved break from all the family chaos before she heads off to Med school, thanks to the JJ and Bruce scholarship fund. They insisted because, as JJ pointed out, they are both on the wrong side of sixty and will no doubt be needing medical care as they age gracefully—*and dramatically.*

But no one is having more fun than Li—*who of course is completely stealing the show!*

JJ decided that his little holiday project was to put on a show with Li, complete with outfits, solo numbers, choreography and the whole bang shoot! My favorite moment has to be when he dressed her as Marilyn, singing Happy Christmas—instead of birthday—to us all.

Bruce and JJ had left their apartment in Jo'burg to me. At first Ben thought he could DIY the merger of our two apartments by bashing a hole through the wall—*they make it look so easy on the TV shows, don't they?* In the end, we contracted a team of professional builders and now we have one, *huge* apartment.

Li has her own room—*now painted "Frosted Tulip", not pink.* She's been spending more and more time with us now that Ben officially has joint custody. Even Mei isn't a major issue any more. She got over herself a bit when she realized the convenience of having so many other people willing to invest in her daughter's life—*a convenience she is not afraid to abuse—we don't mind though.*

And Katie's room is right across the hall from Li's. Often, in the middle of the night, Ben and I hear the pitter patter of Li's little feet as she sneaks into her "big sister's" bed. Likewise, Katie sees Li as the little sister she never had. We've made a monthly date to go to the zoo as a family, and Katie loves teaching Li some new fun fact about a different animal each time.

I've never been happier. I've even been opening up to people and have my first official friend, other than the guys. Becks got the job at the agency and one day appeared at the coffee shop and from that day forward, we've been inseparable.

I mean, what more could a girl ask for? The man of my dreams, my sister, a friend to confide in for the first time ever, and our adorable little Li, all under one roof. I'll admit that it was a bit strange falling into the whole 'soccer mom' routine, complete with the big mommy car and the school runs. Katie left the school she was at for a fresh new start, and now that Li is in Year 1, they both go to the same place. Every other day Ben drops them off and the strange looks he gets at the school as people try to figure out how everyone is related . . . is priceless.

I've taken over the restaurant and launched the coffee shop next door. It's been crazy. One of the biggest, strangest changes of all is that Ben's brother now regularly performs at Big John's . . . have you ever! When he and JJ met for the first time it was awkward for about ten minutes before he confessed to being absolutely star struck with JJ and in complete awe of him—*oh how the tides do change when JJ's ego is stroked.*

Mom has moved into a secondary care house after completing a stay at a treatment center. She pops in for regular visits at the coffee shop and it's really nice to keep in touch with her and see how far she's come since the divorce. Yes, the divorce. She finally did it. She's still got a long way to go until she regains her former self, but she's okay.

As far as Dad's concerned . . . I'm still not entirely sure how I feel. Just before we left for Cape Town for the holidays, I got a letter from him, a heartfelt invitation to attend his one-year birthday at Gamblers Anonymous. He says he needs to make amends. Ben offered to come with me and hold my hand, but I decided not to go. I still need more time.

In moments like this one, I realize how happy I am. Sitting by the pool with all the important people in my life around me. Katie and Li are swimming and JJ and Bruce are in the kitchen making cocktails. And Ben . . . he's next to me. *Take a snapshot please and post it on a Hallmark card.*

When I look at everyone, I realize that I finally have the family I've always longed for—my very own, unique, crazy and amazing blended family with two 'sort of' dads, a man I love, a little girl and a big little sister.

I look over at Ben and smile, completely content. He smiles back, reaches out and takes my hand. Something catches my eye. Something looks out of place and it takes me a few minutes to grasp, as I look from one wrist to the other, he's made an addition to his tattoo collection. I notice the word 'ME?' on his left wrist first, and, of course, it makes no sense, until I look back at the other wrist . . . 'MARRY'.

MARRY ME?

ACKNOWLEDGMENTS

The biggest acknowledgment and thanks really does need to go to my husband.

I said that this story was a bit about my husband and I. Truthfully, a few of the events in this story, and a couple of lines too, were inspired by actual events that took place between the two of us. (NO, not the car thing! I'm far too un-bendy for such shenanigans!)

I fell in love with my husband in less than 30 seconds. True story! We were put into a team together for a game of '30 Seconds' and he was terrible at it. I'd never met anyone so bad at the game in my life, but by the time the sand ran out, for some inexplicable, strange reason, I can say with 100% certainty, that I was in love with him. What was so downright bizarre about this whole thing, was that I had known of him for about two years already, and for that entire time, had disliked him immensely! I thought he was arrogant and odd (not in a good way). When I told friends of my sudden love for him, they all replied with a "*but I thought you hated him!*". No one really believed me, or thought it was real. I told him three weeks later how I felt, even though I barely knew him. As it turned out, though, he'd been in love with me for the past two years – hence his strange oddness around me. Still, most of our friends questioned these so-called feelings we had for each other, and I don't think anyone thought it would work out, or last.

But I knew it would work the day that I moved house. I called a rental agent and told him what I wanted; a two bedroom apartment in Killarney. He told me he had one, it was available immediately and offered to show it to me that afternoon! So I went to see it. And out of all the many, many, *many* apartment buildings in the suburb of Killarney, all the many, many, *many* apartments, and out of the 5,200 people who lived in the suburb at the time (according to a census) the apartment he showed me happened to be – by some crazy stroke of fate – next-door to his! Not two doors down, not in the same building, or on the same street . . . but quite literally next-door! We both took this as a sign, and decided to move in with each other right away. I think we had been in a relationship for only a month at this stage, but we did it anyway. Because we knew it was real.

And now, nine years later, one child, three weddings (one elopement in Las Vegas, one celebration for friends and family, and one meeting with a lawyer to sign papers and make it legal) we're still together. And if it wasn't for this personal story, I don't think I would have ever written this book; he's also in advertising, only wears black, wears sunglasses inside, and yes, I did land up working for him! (But I'll still vehemently deny anything ever happening in a car!) So thanks husband, Gareth, for coming into my life and making it more interesting. I guess some thanks must also go to Jeff, the estate agent who unknowingly sealed the fate of the relationship.

Now on some practical notes. I'd like to thank Jessica Smit, who I've thanked in all my books, because she is the one who always gives them a first edit, like she did for this book too.

I'd like to thank Tamlin, who's been there since the Killarney days, and who looks after my son as if he was her own, which gives me the time to write!

I'd like to thank my bff Owen, and his bae Lance, they are constant comic inspiration for my books, and have been my proud supporters from day one.

Last, but not least, my editor Kate and everyone at Headline Eternal for believing in me and publishing my books, and my agent Erica.

Thanks for reading this book of mine! I wish you all many strange, inexplicable, fateful love happenings and relationships that work – despite all the odds!

TALKING ROMANCE
WITH JO WATSON

Your guilty pleasure?

Mmmm, tricky. I'm not sure we should feel guilty about anything we like, but I did once tell people that I LOVE watching Dr. Phil, I watch every single episode and they replied to me, "Oh, is that your guilty pleasure?" I also love watching Dr. Pimple Popper . . . soooo satisfying!

Your childhood crush?

Right, shall I embarrass myself here and say I thought McGyver was quite hot when I was young. Even worse, I actually thought his hairstyle was cool.

Best date – fictional or real?

Definitely Ben and Sera's first date in *Love To Hate You*. It was perfect in all its imperfection, but I won't give it away. But I loved writing it.

The most attractive quality or feature in a hero?

Humor. I am such a total sucker for humor! I would take humor over anything else, including looks! Making me laughing is way better than a six pack – any day of the week.

The hottest accent?

I don't find the French accent sexy, at all. There, I said it. I don't swoon for French accents. I'm not sure I find any particular accent very sexy, I can tell you though that my Siri speaks in an Australian accent, which for some reason, I find rather soothing. Maybe a man with a Russian accent, something Eastern European and mysterious sounding though?

Bad boys or clean-cut heroes?

Something in between! I certainly find a clean-cut guy a bit too boring for my tastes, but I also don't like cocky, arrogant Alphas. Those are a massive turn off for me. Honestly, if I had to meet some of the heroes I've read in books in real life, I'd probably land up punching them! I like a person who is real. Just themselves, nothing else.

Most romantic gesture?

I keep saying this is all my interviews, and I know it's hard to believe, but I am not a very romantic person in real life. Neither is my husband. We're useless when it comes to romance and remembering things like our anniversary. We did elope to Las Vegas and get married – it was a Star Trek themed wedding with a man dressed up as Spock presiding over it (Yes, we're lame like that!) I guess that was rather romantic. It was certainly funny, and you know how I like funny! We laughed the entire way through our vows.

Turn the page to read an
excerpt from

Burning
Moon

Available now from Headline Eternal!

PROLOGUE

I'm sorry, I can't.

I'm sorry, I can't.

I'm sorry, I can't.

No matter how long I stared at the scribbled note, the meaning stayed the same. I held it up hoping, praying that the sunlight would illuminate the other words that had been written in magic invisible ink.

But nothing appeared.

Just those four tiny little words . . . and yet they had the power to bring my whole world crashing down around me in an instant. Splintering and exploding into a million little pieces.

I finally managed to pry my eyes from the note and found myself staring into the terrified faces of my stepsister and two best friends. They were looking at me as if I was about to have a celebrity meltdown, shave my head, and then poke someone's eye out with an umbrella. They looked very concerned. Like I was a ticking time bomb waiting to explode.

And they were right.

I was.

Tick. Tick.

I was teetering on the brink of insanity. I could feel it trying to suck me in like an all-consuming black hole. The tug was almost too hard to fight.

Did I even want to fight it?

But what would happen if I let go? I knew I was in shock right now, drenched in a sort of numb, detached feeling. But I could feel the other hostile emotions bubbling their way to the surface and fighting to take control.

I blinked. My eyes were stinging.

I tried to open my mouth and speak.

It was dry and nothing came out.

I looked at my best friends Jane and Val, my rocks, the two people I could always rely on for help . . . But they said nothing. Not a word. Just terror plastered across their faces.

I shifted my gaze to my stepsister Stormy-Rain. Unlike her name, she was a ray of tie-dye-wearing sunshine. She had the ability to turn even the most terrible situation into a positive. *Again . . . nothing.* Just stupefied horror plastered across her now-ashen face.

I looked down at my shaking hands; they were crunching the corners of the note. My heart felt like it was going to break through the safe confines of my rib cage, taking my stomach and lungs with it.

Rage combined with shock and gut-wrenching sorrow, and I snapped. It overwhelmed me, rising up from the most primitive part of my soul where logic, rules, and intellect wielded no power. This was a place of red, raw, uninhibited emotion.

And so I screamed at the top of my lungs until my voice went hoarse and my throat was raspy.

"Get me out of this dress. Get me out of it. Get it off!"

My desperate fingers frantically ripped at my wedding dress, a dress that had taken my two friends ten minutes to get me into, thanks to the intricate crisscross ribbons of the bodice. But I was trapped.

Jane and Val sprang into action, simultaneously grabbing at the stubborn ribbons, but it was taking too long. The air around me became too thick to breathe, and I felt like I was drowning.

"I can't breathe. I can't breathe. It's too tight."

Val made a move for the knife that had arrived earlier with the room service, and, without hesitation, she sliced through the intricate satin ribbons. The sound of the serrated knife eviscerating them was like fingernails down a blackboard; it made my skin crawl. But I could feel the bodice getting looser and looser, until it finally slipped down my aching body and pooled lifelessly on the floor.

I was finally free.

And then the tears came. Hot, wet tears streaming down my cheeks and streaking my flushed skin with angry black mascara lines. The tears turned to sobbing.

I looked at my dress, reduced to a pathetic puddle of ribbons, satin, and beads at my feet. But I still felt trapped. *My hair!* The perfect updo, held together with delicate pearl clips. Suddenly, it felt like every strand of hair was tightening around my head, like a boa constrictor going in for the kill. My fingers ripped, desperately trying to free it from its pearly captives.

I wanted to get the pearl clips removed. Gone. Off. Out. I wanted to rub every single trace of the wedding away.

I pulled out my earrings and grabbed the nearest tissue, rubbing my red lipstick off until my lips hurt. It smeared across my face like an ugly rash.

If someone were standing outside the window looking in, they would have pegged me for a crazy person. And I wouldn't have blamed them. Because somewhere in the back of my now-estranged rational brain, I knew I looked like a lunatic escaped from a mental asylum in desperate need of a straitjacket and drastic electroshock therapy. But how the hell else should I be . . .

Because he . . .

Michael Edwards—fiancé of one year, perfect boyfriend of two—had left me, Lilly Swanson, just ten minutes before I was scheduled to walk down the aisle. The bottle of perfume that he'd wanted me to wear today, insisted I wear, because "it was his favorite," mocked me from the dressing table. So I picked it up and threw it against the wall, watching it shatter into a million pieces, just like my life. I was hit by the sweet smell of jasmine and felt sick to my stomach.

What was I going to tell the five hundred guests who were sitting in the church waiting for me? Some had even flown here to South Africa all the way from Australia.

"Hi, everyone. Thanks for coming. Guess what? SURPRISE! No wedding!"

A wedding that my father had spent a small fortune on.

A wedding that was going to be perfect.

Perfect, dammit. Perfect!

I'd made sure of that. I had painstakingly handled every single tiny detail. It had taken months and months of meticulous planning to create this day, and now what?

Things went very blurry all of a sudden. I vaguely remember my brother James bursting into the room, screaming insults and then vowing to kill him. He even punched the best man when he claimed to have no knowledge of Michael's whereabouts. My rational, logical father tried to find a legitimate motive for Michael's behavior, insisting we speak to him before jumping to any rash conclusions. Hundreds of phone calls followed: Where was he? Who had seen him? Where did he go?

At some stage the guests were told, and the rumor mill went into full swing . . .

He'd had an affair.

He'd eloped with someone else.

He was a criminal on the run.

He was gay.

He'd been beamed up by aliens and was being experimented on. (Hopefully it was painful.)

People threw around bad words like *bastard, asshole,* and *liar.* They also threw around words like *shame, sorry,* and *pity.* They wondered whether they should take their wedding gifts back or leave them. What was the correct protocol in a situation like this?

While the world around me was going mad, I felt a strange calm descend. Nothing seemed real anymore, and I began to feel like a voyeur looking at my life from a distance. I didn't care that I was sitting on the floor in my bra and panties. I didn't care that my mascara and lipstick were so smudged I looked like Batman's Joker. I just didn't care.

Some minutes later my other brother Adam, the doctor, burst in and insisted I drink a Coke and swallow the little white pill he was forcing down my throat. It would calm me, he said.

Shortly after that, my overly dramatic, theater-actress mother rushed in to give the performance of her life.

"Why, why, why?" She placed her hand across her heart.

"What is this, a madness most discreet? A stench most foul?" She held her head and cried out, "Whyyy?!"

"For heaven's sake, Ida, this isn't some Shakespearean bloody play." I could hear the anger in my father's voice. Even after eighteen years of divorce, they still couldn't be civil to each other.

"Lest I remind you that all the world is a stage," my mother shouted back, the deep timbre in her voice quivering for added dramatic tension as she tilted her head upward and clenched her jaw.

"There you go again with your crap! Clearly you still haven't learned to separate fantasy from reality!"

"Well, I managed to do that with our marriage!"

Adam jumped between them. "Stop it. This isn't the time!"

And then all pandemonium broke out.

The priest came around to offer some kind of spiritual guidance but exited quickly, and very red-faced, when he saw my state of undress. Some inquisitive relatives stuck their heads through the door, painted with sad, sorry puppy-dog looks, but they, too, left when they saw me spread-eagled on the floor.

An enormous ruckus ensued when the photographer burst in and started taking photos of me—no one had told him. The ruckus became a total freak show when my favorite cousin, Annie, who had designed my dress for free as a wedding gift, saw the state of her "best creation" lying crumpled and torn on the floor. She looked like she was about to cry.

Then the room went very blurry and the noises around me combined into one strange drone.

I closed my eyes and everything went black.

WARNING: Being jilted at the altar in front of 500 wedding guests can lead to irrational behaviour, such as going on your honeymoon to Thailand alone. Recovery will lead to partying the night away at Burning Moon festival – and falling in love with the person you least expect . . .

Don't miss *Burning Moon,* the first book in the Destination Love series.

Available now from

HEADLINE
ETERNAL

Newly single.

Holiday of a lifetime.

Bumping into 'the ex'.

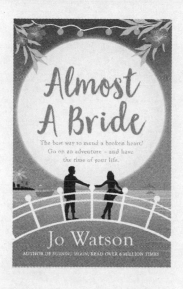

For more laugh-out-loud, swoon-worthy hijinks,
check out *Almost A Bride*, the second book
in the Destination Love series.

Available now from

When you go to Greece to meet your family but end up snogging your smokin' hot tour guide. #sorrynotsorry

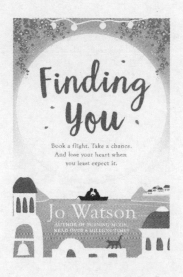

Get ready for a rollercoaster of a rom-com on the beaches of Santorini with the third Destination Love book, *Finding You.*

Available now from

HEADLINE
ETERNAL

FIND YOUR HEART'S DESIRE...

VISIT OUR WEBSITE: www.headlineeternal.com
FIND US ON FACEBOOK: facebook.com/eternalromance
CONNECT WITH US ON TWITTER: @eternal_books
FOLLOW US ON INSTAGRAM: @headlineeternal
EMAIL US: eternalromance@headline.co.uk